DAWN'S EARLY LIGHT

**PIP BALLANTINE
& TEE MORRIS**

ACE BOOKS, NEW YORK

THE BERKLEY PUBLISHING GROUP
Published by the Penguin Group
Penguin Group (USA) LLC
375 Hudson Street, New York, New York 10014

USA • Canada • UK • Ireland • Australia • New Zealand • India • South Africa • China

penguin.com

A Penguin Random House Company

DAWN'S EARLY LIGHT

An Ace Book / published by arrangement with the authors

Ace Books are published by The Berkley Publishing Group.
ACE and the "A" design are trademarks of Penguin Group (USA) LLC.

For information, address: The Berkley Publishing Group,
a division of Penguin Group (USA) LLC,
375 Hudson Street, New York, New York 10014.

ISBN: 978-0-425-26731-8

PUBLISHING HISTORY
Ace mass-market edition / April 2014

PRINTED IN THE UNITED STATES OF AMERICA

10 9 8 7 6 5 4 3 2

Cover art by Dominick Finelle.
Cover design by Lesley Worrell.
Interior text design by Kelly Lipovich.

For Jack Mangan, the Iron Man of Podcasting

*Thanks for having us saddle up and head out west
for a ride across Night's Plutonian Shore.*

ACKNOWLEDGEMENTS

Once more we set out on another bold adventure, and once more we have plenty of kind folk to thank for helping us.

Boundless thanks to Danielle Stockley of Ace, who showed enormous faith in us and the Ministry; and to our agent, Laurie McLean, who is, as always, our favourite agent of OSM.

Thanks as well to the many authors who have made the time and brought their talents to the Parsec-winning *Tales from the Archives* podcast and to the Ministry Protocol anthology. Because of you, our horizons are broadened and our eyes opened even wider to the joys of steampunk. We are proud to have each and every one of you within the ranks of the Ministry roster.

The fine folk of Detroit, Michigan, who welcomed us to their city, showed us the passion that will not die, and gave us so many reasons to include their city in this novel. We sincerely hope the Paris of the West will rise as a phoenix and return for us all to enjoy in the future.

Jessica of Ties That Bynde Designs, Inc., for educating us on a gentleman and his intimate apparel. Oh, how real life can provide such inspiration!

Finally, thank you to the steampunk community all over the globe, who have welcomed us in and inspired us with their creativity and kindness. We hope you enjoy this journey across America with Eliza and Wellington.

ONE

❧

In Which Agents Books and Braun Take in Some Exercise Whilst on Their Transatlantic Cruise

Truly there was nothing more delightful to Eliza D. Braun than a jolly good foot chase; whether it was across London's rooftops in the morning, an afternoon tearing through the streets of Paris, or slipping in and out of the darkest shadows of a night in Cairo. The way muscle and sinew worked in concert with one another, and the exhilaration of a fresh quarry just within reach was a breathtaking, beautiful reminder that she was truly alive.

At least that was what Eliza had told Wellington Thornhill Books, Esquire, at their first dinner together aboard the transatlantic airship *Apollo's Chariot*.

Wellington had the breath knocked out of him as he skidded across the metal gangway. He scrambled for purchase but it was ultimately futile, and he slipped free of the deck. Just in time, the archivist managed to catch hold of the scaffolding, its metallic chill driving through his skin. His grip tightened on the internal skeleton of the behemoth rumbling around him, which was the only thing currently keeping both his dignity and his life intact. Ahead, he caught a glimpse of Eliza continuing the pursuit that had started at her cabin, her skirt hitched up immodestly around her knees.

It had been fortunate that they had returned at the very moment the intruder had slipped out of Eliza's stateroom. The thief was certainly fleet of foot; and had led them a merry chase through the hallways, and now into the belly of the airship. Now they were at least four full stories above the main cabin, and climbing higher into the hull. Wellington could do nothing but admire how Eliza was keeping pace with the intruder.

"Must make sure to ask her who her cobbler is," he muttered before pulling himself back onto the walkway. Wellington was in his third day as *active* field agent, and already he found himself inappropriately attired for a proper foot chase. It remained a mystery what Doctor Sound had been thinking in reinstating Eliza to her position in the Ministry, and promoting him to a similar station.

Wellington had sudden insight as to why, when up ahead he saw Eliza pull out a Remington-Elliot from where it had nestled against her thigh. He was to provide some kind of model for levelheadedness.

The archivist deliberately slid right into her, knocking them both over in an undignified sprawl of arms and legs.

"Bloody hell, Wellington," Eliza yelled, struggling to disentangle herself, "what are you doing?"

"While I realise you are caught up in the rapture of the chase, might I remind you," he began, motioning around him, "we're thousands of feet over this rather large body of water called the Atlantic Ocean. I would rather you not rupture the envelope that is holding us aloft."

Eliza stared proverbial bullets at him while tucking away her gun. "Are you suggesting I would miss?"

Wellington decided to choose silence rather than further argument. Instead, they both looked up to see their target climbing higher into the ship, with a haversack bouncing against his back.

"You would think whatever he is carrying would slow him down a tad," he observed.

"Amazing what a little pursuit can do for a thief. It's

probably full of loot from the other passengers." Eliza motioned to a nearby stairwell. "Head him off. I didn't see any weapons on him and he's not taken a shot, so maybe we can flank him."

"Understood," the archivist replied.

"Be careful, Welly," she said with a grin, before spinning about and bounding up the stairs two at a time, "I still have uses for you."

Just what those could be quite boggled his mind. She had quite the effect on him, that was for certain. Wellington shook his head, and then ascended the opposing stairwell, the metal underfoot clanging and echoing dreadfully as he ascended.

What could this thief be thinking, running upwards through the envelope of *Apollo's Chariot*? If he were wanting a quick escape, procuring one of the standard *aeroflyers* transatlantic airships now employed as deterrents against pirates would have been the logical option . . .

. . . unless he was a saboteur, as well. If any of the bladders here were to fail due to puncture, it was unlikely a rescue could happen before the gondola and all passengers and crew therein would sink into the chilly waters churning far below.

Yet such a dastardly plan would spell doom for the thief as well. Exactly what was this chap's game?

Wellington's ponderings about dire outcomes came to an abrupt stop when something hit the metal gangplanks hard above his head. He gathered immediately that Eliza must have caught up with the thief, and was doing her best to slow him down or teach him the error of his ways.

The archivist kept climbing, finally reaching a junction for all the maintenance stairwells. Despite being this high up in the *Chariot*'s envelope, he was still warm.

Then again, he was engaged in a rigorous foot chase, so . . .

The thief bounded up from the opposite stairwell and made it halfway across the platform before he noticed Wellington. He stumbled to a stop and spun back to where he had come from, only to find his escape blocked by Eliza.

"Mate," she said with a soft chuckle, "I'm sure as a cracksman, you can pick your marks carefully; but you really made a bad—"

Her jibe was cut short as he pulled a gun and fired. Eliza was lifted off her feet and Wellington felt the impact of her landing through the soles of his shoes. The archivist bolted for Eliza's side as the thief continued upwards.

"I thought you said he was unarmed?" Wellington barked as he ran by her, his eyes scanning along the envelope's wall.

"I said . . . I didn't see anything on him," she wheezed. "Doesn't mean he's unarmed. Your concern, by the way? Most touching."

"While I know you are quite safe in your Ministry-issue bulletproof corset, we can't say the same for the *Chariot*'s hull, now can we?" he snapped back.

The assailant's footsteps were pounding away from them, and Wellington let out a soft sigh of relief; it did not appear as though the thief wanted a stand-up fight.

"Can you run?" he asked, looking up in the rigging.

"That I can manage," she assured him. "Don't think for a moment I'm going to let him just slip back into the ship. I wish to have a word or two with him."

She yanked Wellington by his lapels along one of the adjoining gangplanks. Just ahead he could see the thief, his lead on them a substantial one.

However, that lead would not last for long. Wellington could also see ahead of him the curve of the *Chariot*'s inner hull. This gangplank was nothing more than a dead end.

When they were within twenty feet of him, the thief came to a stop, and then—curiously enough—pulled out a pocket watch.

Eliza drew her three-barrelled pistol, this time without any interference from her partner. Wellington caught a glimpse of the look on her face and felt sorry for the thief when she caught up with him. "Got somewhere to be, mate?" she asked, her voice projecting with all the skill of a Shakespearian actress.

The thief closed the watch's cover, its *snap* echoing around them. His narrow face bore an unsettling smile. "As a matter of fact, yes, I do."

"Hate to disappoint you, but I think you're missing that next appointment of yours."

Despite Eliza's bravura, Wellington had a sinking feeling in the pit of his stomach.

"Really? Is that before or after"—the thief's arm jerked forwards and a small box, apparently tucked high in his sleeve, landed in his hand—"you let this ship fall from the skies?"

Eliza's brow furrowed as she took a step back.

Wellington noticed the haversack that had so prominently bounced on the thief's back was now absent. He looked around them, five stories underneath stretching into the belly of this airship. Their man must have dropped his pack over the side of the gangplank, letting it fall to a lower landing or worse, in between one of the ship's massive bladders.

The thief's thumb toyed with the switch, the sole decoration of the palm-sized box, as his other hand reached into his jacket pocket. Keeping his eyes on them both, he produced some brass contraption that fitted snugly in his palm, its dull surface covered with what appeared to be metal talons. Wellington did not get a better look at the device before their cracksman reached above his head and pushed the invention into the *Chariot*'s skin. The device immediately whirled downwards, cutting a fine slit in the side of the vessel.

"I'm sure you have a bit more heroic banter to share," he said, his smile widening, "but I must be off."

His thumb flipped the switch just before tossing the box into the air. Wellington lurched forwards on instinct; and like he was a fielder at Lord's, he caught the device in two cupped hands.

Eliza looked between them both, just before grabbing Wellington and dragging him back the way they came. "Come on! He had the backpack when he shot me."

Wellington tried not to think of the controller in his hand. He knew he was probably not going to like the answer when he asked her, "If I were to return the switch to the 'off' position, that would be horrible, wouldn't it?"

"Advanced bombs have a specific means of disarming, either with a sequence or a removal of the leads between detonator and explosives," she said over her shoulder. "Simply turning it off could trigger fail-safes that would detonate the bomb right away."

"Yes, that would be horrible," Wellington agreed. "Quite horrible."

"There!" Eliza cried, pointing to a weather-worn backpack

lying idly along the side of the gangway. The closer they drew to it, the louder the ticking grew. "I think we found his present."

Tick. Tock. Tick. Tock . . .

"The outside pocket is bulging," Wellington spoke, his voice dry. "The one closest to you."

Eliza swallowed hard, reached inside it, and then froze. The ticking grew even louder when the brass box slipped away from the bag. She flipped the latch away and peered inside.

Tick. Tock. Tick. Tock . . .

"Well?" Wellington asked, his voice cracking slightly. "What kind of bomb is it?"

Eliza inclined her head before stating calmly, "The kind you use to boil eggs with."

He blinked. "What?"

Eliza took Wellington's hand and moved his thumb forwards. The ticking stopped as did the timer inside the brass box.

Growling like a mad woman, she leapt to her feet, bounding back to where they had left their thief. Wellington took off after her, and both stopped upon catching a glimpse of the thief's leg before it disappeared into the abyss outside. He had to be a madman.

Wellington and Eliza pulled apart the tear to feel a hard blast of cold air. Once his eyes adjusted, Wellington could see the thief surrendering with no fight to a fall that Icarus would have known all too well. Beneath him was the endless blue-grey expanse of the Atlantic.

This would have been his final resting place had the massive ornithopter not swooped in from underneath the *Chariot* and circled around to snatch him up. The wings beat hard several times before the craft angled upwards and caught what Wellington could only surmise was a strong current. They watched the vehicle soar higher and farther into the sky until a cloud bank devoured it completely.

Eliza gave a great sigh of annoyance and released her grip on the canvas.

"Well doesn't that just get your dander up?" she said, leading him back to the haversack. She even kicked it around for a moment or two, until it expelled the rest of its contents—watches, rings, necklaces, a jeweler's loupe, and a pincushion decorated with an assortment of needles.

"I want a whiskey," Eliza muttered.

He bent down and shovelled the valuables back into the haversack. "Well now, let us not lose perspective: we did disturb a robber on an airship full of wealthy people. He escaped, yes, but without his catch. I would call that a win."

She looked him up and down, her lips pursed. "Wellington, consider your own words just now. He leads us all the way up here, pulls a fancy escape, and he leaves his haul behind?" Eliza shook her head, staring back down the gangway.

"But, Eliza, we still managed to thwart—"

"Wellington," she snapped. "Don't look at the facts as if you are in the Archives. You are in the field now, en route to America. The details you note and keep in mind mean the difference between travelling back first class or in a pine box. Something tells me that we are missing something"—her foot idly kicked the pincushion—"and that in my experience always comes back to bite you in the bum." She heard the soft tearing of fabric and gave a little grumble. "Come on, the Ministry owes me a drink, and we should really inform the crew about this rather large hole they need to repair."

The archivist knew better than to argue with her. Besides, he had his own uncomfortable feeling she was right.

INTERLUDE

❧

In Which Doctor Sound Is Called
Away and Has Not Even Time
for a Spot of Tea

Getting a summons to appear before Her Majesty the Queen was something that Doctor Basil Sound had not been expecting. Not today. Not even this week. In fact, when the message had arrived through the pneumatic delivery system and Miss Shillingworth presented it to him in his office, the Director of the Ministry of Peculiar Occurrences had quite lost his appetite. He'd pushed away the ham sandwich he'd just been ready to devour, and read the note with growing trepidation.

Despite the stack of papers on his desk, and a full afternoon of meetings scheduled with his agents, he'd risen quickly from his work, told Shillingworth to cancel all of his appointments, and caught a hansom cab to Buckingham Palace.

His mind was whirring as he went, his thoughts not even scattered by the rumbling of the occasional motorcars. Perhaps signs of technological progress like that would have held his attention, but unannounced summonses such as this rarely, if ever, meant good news. Though he always maintained as jovial an exterior as possible when dealing with his Ministry staff, that always melted away the closer he drew to the heart of the British Empire. Once he had an ally in the Crown; but according to the clockwork model in his office and calculations from the Restricted Area, the Queen's favours were nearing an end.

Sound adjusted his gloves and watched out the window as his hansom approached the broad façade of Buckingham, its smooth white edifice with the new east wing presenting a strong, indeed stern, face to the great, unwashed masses. It conveyed all of the majesty of the Empire, but none of its humanity. *A commentary,* he mused as they rolled up to the gates, *on the state of Britannia.*

Reluctantly surrendering his place in the cab, he stepped down, and presented the message to the Royal Guard on duty. He in turn fed the message to the tiny *cryptoregister* that sat in his station. The device gobbled up the paper, and in the process read the almost invisible series of indentations on the paper itself. If it did not match the code for that day, or indeed had none at all, things could get intimate between Doctor Sound and the fixed bayonet on the end of the Guard's rifle.

Sound passed through a warren of passages and entry halls, and through additional screening processes where his likeness was examined in every detail. With each additional layer of security—far many more in place than on his last visit—the whisper of suspicion in his head grew louder.

The Queen had only just recently returned to Buckingham Palace, having spent more than thirty years in various states of seclusion at Osborne House, on the Isle of Wight, or at Windsor Castle. Many said her return was too late to salvage the public's perception of her. Sound could not decisively conclude if that opinion were true, but she was without question not the woman she had been before the death of her husband in '61. In her early years Victoria had been quite the wonder— a veritable force of nature, determined to lead her country to greatness. It was one of the great sorrows of Director Sound's life that he had not been able to save her from a life of widowhood.

Such melancholy and fruitless thoughts were diverted however, when Manning, the Queen's manservant, finally opened the door to the Marble Hall, and walked smartly over to Sound. That their meeting was taking place in the more intimate surroundings of these less formal apartments, the director chose to take as a good sign.

He got to his feet, dusted off his trousers, and followed Manning into the Centre Room. It was not a simple room by any standards, but remarkably intimate by royal ones. It was painted a deep red that reminded Sound immediately of blood—another change from the last time he'd visited. Every light fitting, piece of furniture, and the whole ceiling was covered in gilt. It looked rather like a bordello he had found an unfortunate need to visit in Marseille. It was a fraction off-putting to be visiting one's aging monarch in such a setting.

So, the director was momentarily distracted when he found the veiled Queen seated at a modest desk close to a lit hearth, and at her right hand . . .

"Ah, Basil, old man, looking fit and confident, as always," spoke the Duke of Sussex, Peter Lawson. "I was just talking about you."

Doctor Sound tightened his jaw for a moment, but then forced himself to relax. "Favourably, I hope."

Lord Sussex merely smiled in reply. "I am just heading out on holiday to Europe with my family, but before parting I needed a moment of Her Majesty's time." Sussex turned back to Victoria and bowed low. "Thank you for that most precious commodity. I now depart with a light heart."

"Your loyalty in this matter is appreciated," the woman in black spoke gently. "Please give my regards to your lovely wife."

He straightened to his full height and made to leave, but paused on reaching the director. "Your agents, Sound, do live dangerously, don't they?"

"We serve at the behest of Her Majesty," he replied.

"But of course you do."

Sound gave a slow nod to him. "Bon voyage, m'lord."

"Merci," Sussex returned.

The door closed behind him, but the director found no comfort whatsoever with the departure of Lord Sussex. In fact, Sound felt as if the heaviness of the room were threatening to suffocate him.

"Thank you for coming." Her Majesty Victoria, by the

Grace of God, of the United Kingdom of Great Britain and
Ireland Queen, Defender of the Faith, Empress of India, finally
spoke, her voice muffled but as strong as it had ever been in
her youth.

Though what expression went along with it Doctor Sound
could not tell. A heavy black veil obscured her face, and her
body, swathed in voluminous yards of dark fabric, didn't move
as she addressed him. Her hands wrapped in black velvet
gloves rested still on the desk in front of her. The fact that this
woman had started her reign as a bright-eyed, energetic young
woman was impossible to imagine.

He cleared his throat. "Your Majesty knows that she can call
on me night or day and I will come. You and I have shared so
much that I owe you more than I would any other sovereign."

"It is lucky then," Victoria went on, "that you do not have
any other sovereign than I." He could not ignore the sharp
edge in her voice, and he wondered if he had somehow given
her the wrong impression that he wanted another one? He felt
immediately that he'd got off on the wrong foot.

He shifted his stance and averted his eyes lest she think he
was staring. Without any visible clues to her mood this was
going to be an awkward interview.

The Queen leaned towards him, her veil swinging but remaining in place. "I will keep this short, Doctor Sound. I need you to
do something about Bertie."

He blinked. The *last* thing he expected from Victoria was
what had just come out of her mouth. The Queen knew full well
that he and the Prince of Wales shared a close relationship—just
as had once existed between Sound's predecessor and Prince
Albert, Edward's father.

She had always resented her eldest son for reasons that baf-
fled Sound, and that meant she'd left Bertie to his own devices.
In such circumstances he could easily have become a dilettante,
flush with the excesses that his position would have allowed
him, but Sound had been careful to guide the young prince
away from such a life, and towards passions that his father once
pursued. Science. Physics. Engineering. The director was very
glad to have succeeded, and the prince had become a staunch
supporter of the Ministry—something that often worked against
them when it came time for his mother to be involved.

Doctor Sound sighed, and only just managed to avoid pressing his fingers to the bridge of his nose. Victoria knew that expression of his far too well. Instead, he straightened. "And what would Your Majesty suggest I do, exactly?"

The Queen clasped her gloved hands together before her. "I wish my son to leave our shores for a little time. He has become entirely too concerned about our health and general well-being, and has stopped taking an interest in his own pastimes."

"I see," the director replied evenly. "That doesn't sound like Bertie at all."

"Indeed not," the Queen said, her voice firm and resolute. "I took it upon myself to enquire on what might improve his demeanour." She turned away from Doctor Sound to the desk and read from what appeared to be a series of notes written in her own hand, "The Americans are hosting a clankerton symposium in San Francisco. Quite the gathering of inventive minds. Rumour has it that they've even managed to winkle old McTighe out of the Highlands for it."

She extended the paper to him, and Sound raised an eyebrow at the gesture. The slip in her hand never faltered or waivered as it remained stretched out towards him.

"Knowing of the bond between you and Bertie, I charge you with overseeing the particulars of this trip. Perhaps a few weeks among those of his curious ilk will lighten his mood. Even though I never can, or shall, look at him without a shudder, he is still my son and heir."

It was not the first time Sound had heard his monarch's dismissal of her child in such a heartless manner, but it still distressed him that she held him accountable in the incident that had killed her husband. Bertie had been working with his father in his laboratory when the experiment suffered a catastrophic failure. Bertie had not been able to save his father, but no sane person would ever have blamed him for that. However, the Queen had been driven quite mad by the loss of her beloved husband, and rather than blame God, or fate, or just blind chance, she had fixated on Bertie as the one responsible.

As he was musing on that, he abruptly realised that the pause had stretched out into a rather long and uncomfortable one. Her Majesty had been the last to speak, so convention demanded he have some kind of answer.

"Indeed," he muttered through his moustache, "but Bertie will make an excellent monarch when it is finally time for—"

"Basil!" her voice cracked from beyond the veil, jerking him out of his reckless talk. "I am not in the ground yet, and my son needs to be made aware of that, and not constantly poking and prodding at me."

Her tone verged on hysterical, and the director felt a chill rush across his skin. At one time Sound had been apprised of the Queen's health on a weekly basis, but in the previous year she had got rid of the venerable Doctor Benson and replaced him with what Bertie described to him as "a young Turk of a general practitioner." Perhaps this was the prince's concern.

Sound decided that the best way to deal with this powder-keg situation was to back up slowly and come at it another way. "I was merely pointing out his melancholy could be borne from a deep-seated concern. It is that compassion, no doubt inherited from you, that will make him an excellent monarch."

No reaction, no response. Damnable veils.

He sketched a little bow and kept his voice as low and deferential as possible. "I will do all I can to assure his safety when abroad, Your Majesty."

The gloved hands resting on the desk clenched. "He's waiting for you in the Bow Room. I suggest you talk to him immediately. Good day, Doctor Sound."

He was just backing away when Victoria spoke again, seemingly unable to resist another jab. "I sincerely hope that you are a better judge of character with Bertie than with your Australian."

"Ma'am?" Sound enquired, hoping to sound as clueless as possible.

"Agent Bruce Campbell," the Queen went on, her voice light but somehow packed with venom. "I understand he was one of your brightest stars—you even made him deputy director—but I read the report this morning that you had to sever his employment with the Ministry. It seemed his negligence led to the death of a Miss Ihita Pujari, another agent of yours. If you were not a covert branch of my government, it would be quite the scandal."

For a long moment the only sound in the room was the relentless ticking of the clocks. That Her Majesty knew about

Campbell's fall within the Ministry impressed him particularly as he had omitted it in his report to Sussex. His suspicions of Campbell's loyalties and Sussex's reach were no longer as such.

"Yes, I suppose it could have been, but unfortunately Agent Campbell's dismissal was the only appropriate disciplinary action. I could no longer trust him to act for the well-being of the Ministry. Most unfortunate, but not the first time such tragedies occur, as I am sure you are well aware, Your Majesty."

"I stay apprised of all activities within my Ministries, Doctor Sound, but I am pleased to hear you are in control of your agents. Several of them have come very close to earning the same fate as the Australian." Her veil swayed—the only indication that she was annoyed.

Sound gave a polite nod in reply, silently relishing in his assurance concerning Books' and Braun's goodwill mission to America. It would possibly stop them from drawing the attention of the Queen—unless it was already too late.

"Your Majesty can rest assured, I have all my agents on newly shortened leashes."

The silence descended again. Sound's mind was racing over what story he would spin if the monarch should ask for further details. Luckily, she did not press.

"Then go, do the same for my son!"

The director nodded and left the splendid room with an icy pit in his stomach. He turned in time to see the doors shut, but he stood there a moment getting his bearings, not entirely sure what had just happened. Certain people and events, he knew without question, were fixed in time. They were reliable as rock, and even a person such as himself came to depend on them. His gaze still boring into the door that had shut before him, Sound felt as though someone had removed the Rock of Gibraltar from under him.

The person whom he had just spoken to had been a complete stranger.

TWO

❧

In Which Our Agents of Derring-Do
Arrive in the Americas

The airship captain gave Eliza a warm smile, a smile that remained confident even in light of her rejections while on their transatlantic journey.

"Miss Braun"—and when Captain Raymond spoke her name, Eliza did wonder for a moment that her knees did not give way—"when you cross the Atlantic again I hope you will choose *Apollo's Chariot*. We would love to have you."

The double entendre was blatant, but she managed to ignore it. It was true, the captain's voice alone could keep a teakettle piping hot, and he possessed a chiselled jaw and eyes as brilliant as the sky they just sailed across.

Despite her reputation, her head was not for turning.

"Thank you," she replied with the sort of manners a lady of polite society would have been proud of. "This has been a lovely voyage."

Eliza smiled at Captain Raymond, but once down the gangplank it was replaced by a twisted frown of frustration. Her hands clenched on her purple travelling dress. She had been put quite out of her usual good humour, and it was all one person's fault. Wellington Books was being entirely too obtuse, a trait Eliza attributed to his gender.

Her first thoughts on touching down in America should have been about the case that awaited them, but instead they lingered far too long on the archivist and that damnable kiss he had planted on her in the Archives. The tumult of feelings it had awakened was confusing; and as her way demanded, she wanted them sorted out. Yet, it seemed Wellington had wiped away any memory of the encounter. It was as if it had never happened.

Eliza tugged on her gloves and stood in the sun, looking up and down the quay. Wellington was nowhere to be seen. Typical.

On their journey, she had at first imagined that Wellington Thornhill Books had no inkling of how to proceed. That could explain the quick luncheons, the brief dinners, and his insistence that they sleep in separate cabins.

On the second night they were in the air, after trying unsuccessfully to get to sleep, Eliza decided as primary agent to take control of the situation. Dressing in a nightgown that was far from scandalous, but still suggestive enough to make her accessible, she knocked on the door adjoining their cabins.

When no reply came, she picked the lock.

His room had been empty. At *two o'clock in the bloody morning*, his room had been empty. Once again the mystery of Wellington Books confounded her.

And yet, the memory of that kiss would not go away.

With a sigh, Eliza stared once more up and down the quayside, only dimly hearing the hubbub around her.

On occasion, she had passed through the United States when returning from South Pacific or Asian assignments; but this would be her first assigned case in the country. The harbour town of Norfolk, Virginia, appeared no different than any other she had known in her travels around the world, but it was the collection of accents that caught her attention. She recalled the background information provided by the Ministry: since the end of America's Civil War over thirty years ago, Norfolk had transformed itself into a significant international port. It in fact rivalled New York and Boston in the number of people passing through. The Chesapeake Bay, seen from a porthole in the airship, was both vast and lovely. Thanks to her heritage as a woman of New Zealand, Eliza always had a particular affinity for seaside towns.

The taste of sea salt momentarily distracted her, but the bald fact remained that while porters continued to pass by, there was still no sign of luggage or Wellington Books anywhere.

It was the sudden honking and the cries of ladies behind her that made her spin around. Her eyes went wide in surprise. The horseless vehicle emitted a soft, almost melodic *chitty-chitty-chitty-chitty* rhythm from its undercarriage as it slowly pulled up next to the gangway. It was the length of a landau, but minus the elevated perch where a driver would have sat. The body was lower to the ground and ran on what sounded like and appeared—on account of the thick wisps seeping from the undercarriage—to be internally generated steam power; and Eliza begrudgingly admitted to herself the motorcar sported a rather smart, stylish look with its black, red, and brass detailing, polished to a blinding sheen. She could see her luggage sitting behind the driver in its long and luxurious velvet seat.

Wellington waved cheerily as he brought the car to a halt right next to where she stood.

"Good Lord, where have you been hiding this monster?" she said, adjusting the brim of her hat so as to better examine the unexpected transport.

"In my home," he said brightly, lifting his driving goggles and resting them against the cap covering his head. "This was my big project following the analytical engine."

"And you brought it with you to the Americas?"

His eyes followed the lines of red trim within the metal and wood with obvious pride. "I finished working on it while on the trip. Granted, there are a few modifi—"

"You mean," Eliza began, a muscle twitching in her jaw as she pieced together what had been occupying all his time, "you've been spending the past five nights and days working on this contraption?"

"Well, of course I have. How else should I have been preoccupying myself?" he asked.

Innocence was an endearing quality—at least in young children. In a grown man, it was infuriating.

Eliza only just restrained herself from giving him a bloody good thump. "Yes. What else? An educated mind could only fathom the possibilities."

"Besides, this was for our mission," he continued, "and I wanted to have it ready for extensive and rigorous field—"

Eliza shot her hand up, immediately silencing him. "Welly, please . . . just stop." Wellington's brow furrowed, a look she was growing accustomed to when he lacked a clue, particularly when it came to her. "I think we should just get to our contact. So," she said, walking around to the passenger door, "let's be off."

She opened the door and froze. Waiting for her in the seat next to Wellington was a leather cap identical to his, with two exceptions. Instead of being of weather-beaten brown leather, this cap was a bright white with pink lace around its edges. Second, on the top of the cap's crown was a large pink bow, matching the tint given to the riding goggles that came with it.

Her eyes looked up from the cap to Wellington in absolute horror. He looked quite pleased with himself.

"Surprise," he said cheerfully.

It simply would not be born. Eliza dropped the atrocity without comment onto Wellington's lap, snatched the goggles and riding cap off his head, put them on herself, and situated herself in the passenger seat.

Without protest or contradiction, he took a deep breath, donned the ridiculous cap and goggles, looked over his shoulder to make sure the way was clear, and wrung his hands on the steering wheel.

"I say," he said on releasing the hand brake, "things do look quite . . . pink . . . through these goggles." He cleared his throat and asked Eliza, "Do you think you—"

"Not if the fate of the Empire hung in the balance," she seethed. "Drive."

With a roar of gears and pistons, the great beast lurched forwards and soon they were off, the cadence of the car's engine providing an oddly comforting backdrop in their drive along the docks.

Wellington had certainly given his horseless carriage many little amenities. The seats were comfortable and the ride itself, even with the uneven parts of the road, was as smooth as their time on *Apollo's Chariot*. Wood panelling enclosed the dashboard, and every stylish detail was in evidence, down to the various dials and gauges changing with every ping and pop from the motor.

"Is it a safe assumption to make," Eliza called over the chugging engine, "that Axelrod and Blackwell have not even heard a whisper about this fine carriage of yours?"

"Please, do not evoke their names," he grumbled. "I'm trying not to think of my analytical engine left to their whims and devices back in the Archives. But yes, I kept this project very much off the books. This is a personal endeavour that I want to offer to the Ministry once properly engaged and executed on a genuine mission."

"Welly," Eliza said with a laugh, "it's just a motorcar. A clever variation on horseless carriages. Hardly groundbreaking."

He glanced briefly at her. "Even something as simple as your corset needs proper field-testing." Wellington's eyes dipped down to the two gauges flanking the steering wheel. "Right now for example, I'm curious as to how far a full boiler will take us."

The car chugged along, and Eliza tried not to crack a smile in reaction to the looks they drew from those they passed. She wondered how many were in response to the car itself, and how many were to Wellington's fabulous headgear.

In the silence Eliza contemplated how Doctor Sound had made clear his intent to keep close tabs on them, having his hand forced by circumstances she and Wellington created in Case #18960128UKEA. Their results could not be denied, but the Duke of Sussex was putting pressure on Sound in turn. Regardless of the plot they uncovered, they had been working outside Ministry parameters, compelling the director to lend them as "goodwill advisors" to the American agency, the Office of the Supernatural and Metaphysical. This was hardly the first time Eliza had been shipped off somewhere until the heat of the moment blew away, but back then, she only had herself to worry about.

Their automobile chugged and rumbled to a stop outside a small pub called the Artifice Club. As the engine settled reluctantly into silence, Wellington ripped off both cap and goggles, and smoothed his hair into some semblance of tidiness. Now Eliza could make out the sounds of boats in the harbour and the usual din of an establishment such as this one.

"This is where we are to meet our contacts?" Eliza asked, looking up and down the street. Anyone waiting for them could not fail to have noticed their entrance.

There was very little around the pub, save for other small establishments that catered to sailing vessels, schooners, and fishermen. The area was more dedicated to nautical professions than aeronautical ones. Eliza could see no noticeable hazards, apart from the tavern itself. The way they were dressed, their motorcar, and their manner of speech would all attract attention. It was a conundrum that did not bode well for smooth operations in the field.

"According to the file," Wellington said, with a shrug.

"Any idea who we are looking for?" Eliza asked, shifting in her seat.

"She said she would introduce herself in an appropriate fashion."

Eliza's brow furrowed. "Come again?"

"Security greeting, of course," Wellington replied brushing his beard.

She swallowed back a groan; she hated the formal greetings between agencies. "Lovely, we get to speak in code, do we?"

"Proper procedure, Miss Braun," Wellington chided. Then he reached into his coat pocket. "And that reminds me . . ."

A ten-pound note appeared out of his wallet, and she recalled the bet he'd made that they would never be on assignment in America.

"Oh, that is not necessary, Welly . . ."

"A wager is a wager." And he extended the ten pounds to her again.

Eliza snatched the note from his hand gleefully, debating whether she would be investing in a stunning new outfit from Paris, or a new long-range sniper rifle.

She clambered down from the automobile, before her companion could offer a hand, and preceded Wellington into the tavern. The Artifice Club was an eclectic mix of patrons, ranging from true salt of the earth types to wide-eyed youngsters enjoying the late afternoon entertainment. One gent made eye contact with her, gave a slight nod in greeting, and then returned to his ale.

In her survey of the pub, Eliza paused to watch the artist performing on the modest stage. The spectacled man was of considerable carriage, wearing a fine boater and impressive cravat, and behind him sat an even more impressive collection of beer, single malt scotch, and bourbon. Apparently, all for him. In front of him were three gramophones playing "Daisy Bell," "Daddy Wouldn't Buy Me a Bow Wow," and "Ta-ra-ra Boom-de-ay," all at the same time. Perhaps in the hands of a novice, this could have easily become an unforgiving onslaught of noise, but this gent possessed an intimate understanding of the three songs. Through a series of keys and cranks, the artist was altering tempo, and starting and stopping one or two of the music hall songs while the third continued, in effect creating one complete song.

And it was quite the toe tapper coming from the stage.

Wellington leaned in. "Exactly how is he doing that?"

"He's mixing. Apparently, it's all the rage here in the Americas."

He nodded, tipping his head askance as he watched the man work the gramophones. "And he's wearing a lab coat because . . . ?"

Eliza shrugged. "Everyone needs a signature style, I suppose."

As they walked farther in, she noticed a slight girl seated at a table at the rear of the pub. It was not just her purple petticoats and stripes that made her stand out, but also her tidiness, etiquette, and carriage. Eliza hated stripes—though they were all the fashion. Their contact also had a pair of sun spectacles balanced on the tip of her nose. Eliza could only surmise that was her notion of blending in.

"I think we found our contact," Eliza whispered to Wellington.

She made to walk to the table when the archivist caught her arm. "We are supposed to meet at the bar," he hissed.

He wasn't serious. Was he?

It's like dealing with a child, Eliza thought, but she knew she had to pick and choose her battles. She forced a tight grin as she followed Wellington to the bar. He leaned against its weathered wood and motioned for the publican. The barkeep appeared, and his brow knotted as he looked the new arrivals over.

Eliza realised that they stood out nearly as much as the woman in purple.

"Sir, a whiskey, if you please," Wellington ordered in a tone far too loud and purposeful.

"Welly," Eliza whispered tersely, "perhaps you should just order a beer? Same effect." She cast a wary glance at the woman who was trying, but failing, to blend in with her surroundings. So far she had pushed her sun spectacles up to the bridge of her nose, smoothed out her skirts, and then looked at the two of them, placing a hand upon her chest, as if noticing them for the first time.

Bloody hell, Eliza thought, burying her face in her hand. *It's Amateur Night at the Alhambra.*

Through his clenched teeth, he replied, "All part of protocol. Just play along." The shot glass was placed in front of him, which immediately went up in the air as Wellington toasted those assembled. "God save the Queen," he proclaimed, "and God bless America."

The amber dram disappeared from its glass, and Eliza crossed her arms in front of her as Wellington struggled for air. His free hand caught the bar as the other gripped the shot glass tightly. *How,* she marvelled, *could this man have been such a master of deception during their time with the Phoenix Society and yet here be about as convincing as a street urchin running for a seat in Parliament?*

"Not quite the quality you're used to?" Eliza asked sweetly.

Wellington coughed in reply. At least he was still breathing—and standing.

The waif had now gathered up enough courage and was standing before them. She looked between Eliza and Wellington quickly and then leaned forwards. "At midnight, the lion roars."

Oh for God's sake. Eliza found herself frozen in disgust.

"But at dawn," her partner wheezed, his voice creeping back to its normal baritone, "the eagle's cry will be heard."

"Subtle," Eliza stated wryly.

She thrust out a gloved hand, shaking theirs in an enthusiastic greeting. "Felicity Lovelace. Welcome to the United States of America. Would you care for something to drink?"

"Another whiskey, Wellington?" Eliza asked with a sly grin.

"I think not," he answered quickly. "Perhaps something less . . ."

"Potent?"

"Volatile."

"I've read your particulars, Miss Braun," Felicity returned quickly, and then spoke in what sounded like a baited breath. "A white wine for the gentleman, a beer for the lady, and I'll have another . . ." She paused. "Well, I'll have another."

"Right then," the barkeep said, looking at the three of them. "Wine, beer." And his eyes twinkled a bit as he said, "And a Coca-Cola."

Eliza and Wellington looked at Felicity askance. "It helps calm my nerves," she said with a shrug, her speech getting a little faster the more she spoke.

Calm her nerves? Then it dawned on her when the beer reached her hands. *Ye gods, you must be joking.* "This is your first assignment, isn't it?"

"No, actually, this is my tenth," the American returned, but the tremble in her posture hardly reassured Eliza. When the woman's bubbling tonic arrived, she took a long sip from it before adding, "I'm not necessarily *in the field* is all. I'm usually working on logistics, but this time the director agreed to let me accompany my partner."

"I see." Eliza smiled, nodding slowly. "Doctor Sound did say we were working with our counterparts. You're the archivist then?"

"Librarian," Felicity corrected.

"There's a difference," Wellington contributed, "if you'd care—"

Eliza's eyebrows raised slightly, and he stopped mid-sentence. He was learning. "So," the New Zealander continued sweetly, "why exactly have you reached out to the British Empire for help, Miss Lovelace?"

"Please, call me Felicity—everyone does."

Eliza raised her beer at her. "Eliza." She motioned to Wellington. "Welly."

"Wellington," he muttered, taking a sip of his wine. "This joint operation is hardly a new venture. If memory serves, your agents have worked alongside ours before, yes?"

"Before my time, and in light of that mission, there was some opposition in reaching out to you for help."

Eliza crooked an eyebrow. "Some?"

"All right," Felicity said, her fingers tapping rapidly against her glass, "there was a good amount of opposition, but I knew you had something we lack." She looked at them for a moment, and then said bluntly, "Experience. OSM is still a relatively new department."

Eliza darted a quick look at Wellington. It looked like admitting that was hard, but there it was. America was a country still on the mend, yet this was a proud nation preferring to handle its own affairs alone.

"What's the game then?" Eliza asked.

Their counterpart went for her coat pocket, but froze at the sound of the tavern door being flung open.

Under a wide-brimmed Stetson, a man who was in desperate need of a shave surveyed the Artifice Club. His gaze was cold, hard, and sized up everyone in the pub in an instant. He was broad shouldered and trim, the kind of build that would have given Campbell a moment's pause before engaging in fisticuffs. This newcomer almost faded into the intermittent shadows, dressed in dark colours of denim and leather. When he turned to where they sat, his mouth bent into a wry grin. It made his face shift from stern to quite handsome. He pushed back the brim of his hat and gave Felicity a nod.

"Thank goodness we're working covertly," Felicity said, shaking her head ruefully. "Otherwise, he would stand out."

Eliza got to her feet, feeling an equal smile form on her face. "I don't think a man like that could possibly do anything but stand out." She felt, rather than saw, Wellington stiffen at her side.

She took her time walking around the table, closing the distance between them in long, slow strides. Eliza stopped just as the hem of her dress brushed the newcomer's soiled, worn pants, and looked up at him. He hooked his thumbs in his belt, took in Eliza from head to toe, and nodded while his lips widened to show a smile that threatened to catch her breath and claim it for his own. Clearly, this cowboy liked what he saw.

Good for him, she thought.

That was when Eliza's right hook sent him sprawling to the floor.

THREE

❧

In Which First Impressions Are
Proven to Be Everlasting

"Been a while, hasn't it, mate?"

She could hear Wellington and Felicity scrambling out of their chairs, but her eyes remained fixed to the man on the floor. True, there had been a time when having this ruggedly handsome man at her feet would have been quite satisfactory, in an entirely different situation.

"Do we know each other," the man said with a slight laugh while rubbing his jaw, "or is this how you all in jolly ol' England say 'Howdy'?"

"Ninety-three. San Francisco," she hissed leaning over him.

His brow furrowed momentarily, but then his eyes sparkled. He managed a throaty laugh.

"The Rum Runner," he said. "I remember now—that was a good time."

"My partner and I were nearly killed in that brawl!" Eliza was abruptly aware that her hands were once more balled into tight fists. She could feel the urge to clock him again swell. "And for the life of us, we couldn't figure out why you set those thugs on us."

"I needed an exit, and you two seemed like you could handle yourselves." He looked her over as if she were a prize side of beef hanging in a butcher's window. "You're still looking like a nice filly ready to ride."

"I was in hospital—an *American* hospital—for a week." She shook her head. "Bloody chamber of horrors, that was!"

"Good Lord, Eliza!" Wellington looked between the fallen American and her. "Are you looking to start another war between the Empire and the United States?"

"We whipped your ass once before," the American grumbled, now sitting up. "We can do it again."

"Says the man on the floor following one punch," Eliza bit back.

"I would prefer there be no more arse-whipping, if you please." Wellington actually stood between them, and reminded her, "We are here as a professional courtesy."

"You're here because our boss wanted to put on a dog-and-pony show for those Capitol Hill types," the American cowboy retorted.

"Oh for Pete's sake, Bill," Felicity chimed in, her sharp tone making all three of them start, "would you please shut up."

"She hit me first!" Bill protested like a child caught at playground hijinks.

"You probably had it coming," Felicity replied with a tilt of her head. Bill went to protest but the librarian held up a single finger. Apparently, that was enough to keep him quiet. "Mr. Books, Miss Braun, this is my partner, William Wheatley."

Eliza blinked. "William Wheatley? *Wild Bill* Wheatley? Is your *partner*?"

He tipped his hat to her. "Nice to know my name gets around even in Her Majesty's Empire."

"Can I hit him again, Welly?"

"No!" Wellington snapped. "For goodness' sake, what can you possibly have against Wheatley here?"

It was going to be embarrassing to bring up, but she was forced to now. Eliza glared at the grinning American. "Wellington, I cannot begin to run down some of the diplomatic disasters this wanker has left behind for my previous partner, Harry, and I to clean up. Ontario. The Bahamas. Newfoundland.

We could always tell when 'Wild Bill' had been in town. I mean, what kind of secret agent runs into an objective and chooses to blow it to kingdom come when leaving? Hardly *secret* operations."

"Yes," Wellington said evenly. "Hardly."

Eliza held a gaze with her partner for a moment before returning it to the still-smiling cowboy. "But Harry and I officially 'met' Bill here when returning from an assignment in Hong Kong. We found ourselves making a stop in San Francisco for a few hours, so we popped into the pub closest to the aeroport for a celebratory drink."

"And that would be the Rum Runner?" Wellington asked.

"Before we finished the first round," she continued, "a group of ruffians surrounded our table *and it is all this git's fault.*"

"Yeah, not one of my best days with the Office," William began. "My cover had been blown . . ."

"Really?" Eliza interjected. "First time in the field with your 'big boy' guns, then?"

Bill's eyes darkened. "Look, that contact of mine had been a reliable one . . ."

"Except for that one time," Felicity sang softly.

"I was outbid. Found myself in a bad situation. Those varmints knew I had a meeting at the Rum Runner. So once the fire got hot under the skillet I looked for people that could pass for associates."

Eliza was having none of his smooth talk. "So you chose the British gent, immaculate haircut, stylish bowler, and with his fair lady on one arm."

"Exactly."

Eliza remained flummoxed by his complete lack of logic. "I *am* going to hit him again!" she declared.

The American threw his hands up. "I'm just going to stay down here then til you get over that!"

"Eliza!" Wellington implored.

"Honestly, your other tell was the dress you were wearing." Bill ruffled his dark hair. "Now I've known me a fine lady or three, but none that wore skirts with folds like yours. The way the fabric was layered didn't look right."

"The way the fabric was layered?" Wellington asked, blinking incredulously.

Bill rested his arms on his knees and looked up to Wellington. "Partner, if'n you want to charm the ladies, it doesn't hurt to know a thing or two about the latest fashion and what the phillies are wearin'."

Eliza pursed her lips. "So you knew I had access to a pair of garter pistols? Really, you expect me to believe that?"

"You didn't look like no dockside whore, so I took an educated guess." He then looked around at everyone from where he sat. "So, can I get up now?"

"Of course," Wellington said, reaching down to him.

The man bent down to pick up his hat, keeping his own intent stare on Eliza as he dusted it off.

"Partnered with 'Wild Bill' Wheatley." She sniffed, returning his gaze. "Thank God my corset's been reinforced."

"Sounds like you got a problem with the American way of doing things," Bill snapped. "I do what I do, and get results. I'm thorough."

"Is that what you call it? Thorough?" Eliza began, planting her hands on her hips, knowing full well she was perilously close to looking like a fishwife.

"I hate to interrupt this—I believe you would call it in the Americas—Mexican standoff, but if I recall, Miss Lovelace was about to brief us on why we have been called here." Wellington gave a nod to Bill. "Mr. Pot." He then turned to Eliza. "Miss Kettle. Follow me, if you please?"

"Your partner there," the American spoke right by her ear, "he's not quite right, is he?"

Eliza answered, but kept her eyes on Wellington. "In many ways, but he grows on you."

"Nice punch there, Braun," the American mumbled.

"Thank you," she said, dropping him a little curtsey. "I have been working on it since San Francisco."

He shot her a rueful glance and then swept a quite passable bow. "Then shall we join our partners, before they get restless?"

"Yes, let's." She led the way to the table, where they both took seats with far less tension than on their initial meeting. The barkeep had already refreshed their drinks and even included a freshly pulled beer for Bill. Felicity was casting her eyes wildly from bartender to patron as her fingers nervously tapped a large envelope.

"Felicity, come on now, these boys don't really care about our business. Unless we got leads to a fishing spot or a sunken ironclad, we are just having drinks and looking at a map of the beach." Bill took up the beer and winked. "I know this place."

"As well as you knew that contact in San Francisco?" Felicity asked, her eyebrow arching slightly. Bill paused just as his beer was about to reach his lips, but she merely shrugged. "It's worth asking."

"Just educate them, darlin'," he replied, before taking a long sip, "'cause that is what you do."

Felicity pursed her lips for a moment before opening the envelope. She spread out a map of the United States' eastern seaboard before them, and tapped upon the state directly underneath Virginia. "Just south of us is a small strip of land connected to North Carolina that is comprised of several townships—Currituck, Nags Head, Kitty Hawk, Hatteras, Ocracoke, and so on. Collectively, this area is referred to as the Outer Banks."

"And if memory serves, this area," Wellington said, running his fingers along a stretch of ocean off the North Carolina coast, "carries the charming moniker of Graveyard of the Atlantic. Well over five hundred wrecks within these waters, yes?"

She looked up from the map in surprise. "You know about the Outer Banks?"

"I know that rather treacherous currents and particularly shallow sandbars have given this stretch of the Atlantic a rather dubious reputation." Wellington tilted his head. "I also carefully read your rather thorough case summary."

"You thought it was thorough?" Felicity asked, her cheeks reddening the longer she considered Wellington. "I did spend quite a bit of time on it." Clearing her throat, she produced from an envelope a section of transparent cellulose with a variety of markings on it. A continuous line matched the jagged coastline of Virginia, North Carolina, and South Carolina. The overlay now displayed a variety of small boat-shaped marks dotting the area Wellington had indicated as the Graveyard of the Atlantic. "These are known shipwrecks of the past twenty years. Green signifies wrecks from 1875 to 1890. The yellow are markers from '90 to '95." Felicity overlaid another piece of film over the first. "This is the activity grabbing our attention."

These red marks were hardly the same number as the green and blue. What did intrigue Eliza was this concentration of shipwrecks seemed focused along three inland markers.

"Miss Lovelace, are these markers," Wellington said, following them along the coast with a single finger, "Cape Henry, Currituck, and Bodie Island?"

"Yes, all these lighthouses have recently passed inspection so we know they are in full working order."

"So how many years of shipwrecks are we looking at here, Felicity?" Eliza asked, passing a hand over the collection of red markers. "The past year? Past two years?"

"Not shipwrecks. Disappearances." Felicity swallowed. "Just in the past *month*."

"It gets worse," Bill replied. "Look closer at the markers."

Eliza and Wellington leaned in and noticed that of the twenty markers, five of them were marked as circles, not boats.

"Airships," Felicity spoke, her tone grim. "That began happening two weeks ago."

Wellington's fingertips traced the line of red markers. "You're saying these vessels have all disappeared?"

"If'n these ships did wreck, nothing—I mean nothing—ever made it to shore." All eyes turned to Bill. "No corpses. No wreckage. It's as if the Atlantic just opened up and swallowed 'em whole."

"Have you taken a closer look down there?" Eliza offered.

"With what?" Bill scoffed. "One of them fancy submarine things?"

Wellington's brow furrowed. "You mean, your organisation does not have access to one?"

Felicity and Bill cast a glance at each other.

"I'm just gonna sit here and drink my beer," he grumbled.

"There are plenty of warning indicators along our coast, and the reputation of the Graveyard is secondhand knowledge to ship captains," Felicity assured them both. "But why airships are disappearing we cannot make heads or tails of."

Eliza followed the line of recent calamities, her index and

pinkie finger measuring the distance between the two of them. "This looks to be about an area of roughly seventy miles. From this area of Virginia stretching to"—Eliza leaned in and read—"Kill Devil Hills. What a charming name!"

"While waiting for you two, Felicity and I have been watching the area like hawks on the hunt. So far, nothin' but boats and ships comin' in and out like clockwork. No missed schedules."

Felicity gave a nod as she folded up the map and placed it along with her overlays back into their envelope. "Bill's plan was to start here and follow the trail of disappearances."

"Just a moment," Eliza spoke up, her brow furrowing, "this seems like a simple matter of investigation. You're calling on us for experience? What sort of experience do you need?"

"Told you we didn't need 'em," Bill said, finishing off what little remained of his beer.

"Well, yes, this is a matter of investigation, but my own concern is that we lack experience concerning *æthergate* travel. That technology from Atlantis that you all commandeered from a nefarious organisation called the House of Usher could be behind these disappearances." Even in light of Wellington's reaction, Felicity shrugged. "Then there is the matter of the Janus Affair."

Eliza cocked her head to one side. "The what?"

"That is how we refer to your most recent case," Felicity said with a perky smile. "The Janus Affair."

"A bit melodramatic, don't you think?" Wellington said with a groan. "Typical Americans."

"Look, I know we're all good friends now," Bill said, giving Eliza a wink just before continuing. "That don't mean we trust you all blindly. We're both in the business of keeping tabs on each other. Best to keep an eye on and an ear out for what your good friends are up to, right?"

"I would agree," Wellington said, his colour seeming to return as he fixed his eyes on Felicity, "but I would imagine your own experience—was it, six years ago? Yes, I do believe it was six—with the Dudleytown Experiment would have prepped you for this most admirably."

Eliza felt a surge of pride in her partner. The Dudleytown

incident had been big news, even in the Ministry, and quite the mess for OSM. Wellington mentioning it was a nice way to take down their American counterparts a peg or two.

Wellington had apparently decided two pegs wasn't enough. "But perhaps lacking any comprehension of transdimensional technology matters little to your office, but it did cost your government, what, an insignificant Connecticut hamlet, yes?"

Bill leaned forwards, his eyes seeming to be on fire. "You watch yourself, Johnny Shakespeare. Dudleytown was *my* case."

"Why not see if we can fold space and time with the peculiar rock composition of the area? So what if it drives a few people mad?"

Bill was abruptly on his feet. "How about you and I go outside and discuss the laws of science, just the two of us."

"I sincerely hope we're just getting all the posturing out of the way early," Felicity chimed in, "so that we could make some progress before another sea or air vessel disappears?"

Wellington turned to the librarian and gave her a delightful smile. "Yes," he said, raising his glass of wine, "but I would prefer to pick the next meeting place, as this wine is hardly what I would call . . ." He paused, considering the glass, and then said, ". . . wine."

Bill grunted and slowly lowered himself back into his chair.

"Let's get back to the reason we reached out to the Ministry of Peculiar Occurrences." Felicity looked around at them all, as if with her smile she'd mend everything. "Apart from Bill's Dudleytown experience, we know very little of the mechanics behind transdimensional teleportation."

Eliza caught Wellington's glance, but she spread her hands wide; she had no idea how much to share with them. "Right then—what is our next move?"

"We have accommodations waiting for us at Swan's Retreat. It's an exclusive hunt club in Currituck County, North Carolina. We'll be posing as an American couple," Felicity said, motioning to herself and Bill, "showing friends from England the local duck-hunting grounds."

"You know how to shoot at all, pard'ner?" Bill asked.

"Yes," Eliza said with a smirk, "he does." Wellington tugged at his collar, his gaze not meeting hers. "But something tells me he will probably not partake of the game North Carolina offers."

Bill nodded as if he'd expected it. "That's too bad." He turned to Eliza. "What about you, Lizzie? You know your way around a gun?"

Eliza crooked an eyebrow at the smirk on Bill's face, but managed to control the desire to wipe it off violently. "Looks like you've already made up your mind about that," she replied sweetly.

"Your firearms expertise is irrelevant, Eliza," Felicity said dismissively. "Women are allowed at the hunt clubs as guests of their spouses, but not allowed to shoot, ride, or partake of—"

"We will just have to state the obvious at Swan's Retreat," Eliza interjected. "I'm not from around these parts."

"Oh, I think we're going to have a grand ol' time in Carolina," Bill said, giving a satisfied sigh.

"Well then," Wellington said. "Let us gather your belongings. Our chariot is outside."

"Got everything I need on my horse so I'll just meet you all there." Bill motioned to Felicity. "My partner, on the other hand . . ."

"It's just a few things," she protested.

"Like the kitchen sink," he retorted, counting off on his fingers, "the bedroom vanity, the ballroom chandelier . . ." He paused. "Am I missing anything?"

Eliza looked between Felicity and Wellington. And Welly had dared to call her and Wild Bill "pot" and "kettle"?

"A glimpse of things to come, Mr. Books," Eliza whispered pointedly to her partner. "I would wager you'll be requesting a recall to London before the week is out."

INTERLUDE

❧

Wherein the House of Usher Calls
upon Divine Providence

Van's words echoed around her church, even as she closed the door behind her parishioners.

"Life is short and we do not have too much time to gladden the hearts of those who travel the way with us. So be swift to love; make haste to be kind. Swifter still to forgive," she had said to her flock only seconds ago. *"And may the blessing of the one who made us, who loves us and who walks the way with us still; the one, holy and undivided Trinity be with us this day and remain with us always. Amen."*

As she leant against the doors, she wondered if anyone had heard those deeply meant words. She kept repeating them in the hope that someone would. If just one took her words to heart, to practise the Gospel she imparted, that would make everything worthwhile.

This was, as she called it, the chance for everyone to get a better look at the one and only female missionary daring to start a church in this area of Virginia. It was one thing to be a servant of God, but women were *not* supposed to be preaching in churches. At least, that was the general consensus.

However, Van had never been one to follow the general

consensus. She'd heard it all when she was in the seminary. The South was too humid. The congregations would be backwards in their line of thinking. The folk earning a living there were tough and preferred the fire and brimstone sermons over the gentle hand of a woman.

Those things might have well been true. Virginia—particularly in the summer—was not for the faint of heart.

When the last person funnelled out, she was alone in the modest but inviting church. *Lord,* she prayed silently, her grip tightening on the Bible, *grant me the strength to carry on and continue your work, and bless our little town with peace and understanding. Amen.*

Van took a deep breath and opened her eyes once more. The peace of the Lord was with her. She felt it inside, much like the ember that would soon give life to a bonfire. Wrapped in faith, she left the church for the office just across the lawn.

Her eyes immediately fell on Everett, the head pastor of their church for coming on two years now, outlasting any of the other men that came out here to run things by a year. He was counting the money from the offering plate, his face stern as he jotted down a few notes in a small ledger.

That expression of his told her the piano would remain out of tune for some time yet.

"How was the service this morning?" His deep baritone voice echoed, even though he was speaking at a conversational volume. To Everett, gravitas came naturally, which was a real asset when giving sermons.

"The same." She took her seat at the smaller desk. "The same faces as always."

He nodded, touching the pencil to his tongue before continuing with his ledger keeping. They both wished attendance had improved, but in fact it had dropped off once the novelty of a female priest had worn off. Van settled into her desk to work on her next sermon when the sudden *clank* from the pneumatic messaging tube made her freeze. Despite her travels back and forth across the country, Van still could not get used to the fact that even out here in the breathtaking majesty of God's great Shenandoah Valley, their church was connected to a pneumatic messaging system.

She opened the canister and pulled out the single slip of

parchment within it. *Noon*, the message read, followed by a simple stamp of a raven.

Her eyebrow arched sharply and then her eyes went to the sole clock in the shared office. Eight minutes before twelve o'clock. They obviously knew when she would be walking out of service to the minute.

She tore up the tiny note into several pieces and threw it into the little potbelly furnace. Thoughtfully, her fingers strayed up to the cross she always wore around her neck. This tiny symbol of her faith was adorned with a single gear where the two arms of the cross met. It had been a gift from a clankerton who'd been smitten with her when she was just about to enter her training. He had given up on her by the time she'd emerged from it. The cross reminded Van of the frailty of humanity, and the strength of faith.

So then, why did she feel such hesitation whenever she accepted an assignment? Was she still not doing the work of the Lord, after all? Sometimes, you had to be the shepherd to the lambs. Sometimes, you had to be healer to the sick.

As her thumb turned the gear, she also understood sometimes you had to be the sword of God.

The bottom arm of the cross extended to its full length with a quick *click*. Swiftly she slipped the chain of the cross over her head, inserted it in the keyhole on the top surface of her desk, and gave it a single turn. Before her feet, a small trapdoor popped upwards, and slowly a wooden staircase unfurled, extending underneath their office.

Van made the mistake of glancing at Everett before descending into the dark; his expression said that he was most definitely not pleased. He returned his disapproving gaze to the remaining paperwork for the morning's offerings, completely ignoring what his fellow cleric was up to.

She reached for the lantern hanging at the bottom of the steps, struck a match, and then turned up the light once the flame caught. The sconce's glow pushed aside the shadows to reveal a small analytical engine, her pride and joy, sitting in the corner of the room.

Perhaps it was an indulgence, but she was guaranteed a small amount of privacy and confidentiality when using it. The money should have gone to the church, but this device was in a sense keeping the church together. It was her personal line of communication with those who called upon her for specific talents.

When noon struck, the green light on the panel before Van switched to red. She threw a few connectors forwards, awakening the amber display in front of her. It squeaked lightly when she adjusted it to a more comfortable reading position. Yes, along with the piano, her analytical engine was also in need of some maintenance.

```
TARGET IS FAST APPROACHING NORTH CAROLINA.
APPREHENDING OF TARGET ALIVE—TOP PRIORITY.
ELIMINATE ANY OPPOSITION.
RESPOND IF AVAILABLE.
-HOU
```

Van tapped her lips as she thought about the shadowy organisation. It had been at least six or seven years since the House of Usher had been active in America. What could it mean that they now wanted a hunt and retrieval from her? Whoever this mark was, the House wanted him or her badly, considering the terms of the bounty.

The term "Eliminate any opposition" would be her judgement call—and solely hers—in the field. She had made a pledge to herself that in these assignments, her sword would only take a life if her own was threatened. She was not an assassin. She was a tracker and a retrieval specialist.

Accepting this commission would see to the many needs of their church. The piano would finally be tuned, and the roof fully repaired in time for next winter. There could even be some money in the coffer for a garden. Meals for the poor.

Her fingers had already begun typing before her eyes returned to the screen.

```
ASSIGNMENT ACCEPTED.
PLEASE FORWARD AVAILABLE IMAGE OF TARGET.
WILL LEAVE IMMEDIATELY FOR N.C. ON DELIVERY.
```

Van's thoughts scattered when the signal returned to red. She flipped the switch underneath, and the display began to assemble itself, line by line. In an hour's time she would have the face of her latest assignment. Even the telegraph could not offer that.

As the image assembled itself, she would have plenty of time to pack for an unexpected journey south. Van connected two more leads, and flipped a switch that would provide a printed copy of her screen once the image finished its travel through the æther. She turned towards the wall to the left of the machine and gave a section of its moulding a gentle push. The top half of the wall slid away, revealing several rifles and handguns. After a moment's consideration, she took down the quad-barrelled Winchester-Henry-Armstrong 1892, and felt the weight in her hands. Stopping power and distance were guaranteed, provided the target's weight was not an issue.

Van propped the '92 up against the wall and looked over the handgun options in front of her. Her fingers ran along the edges of a wide, rosewood case. She tapped the sides of the box, wondering if these would be needed.

Apprehending of target alive is the top priority, she recalled from the message. *Eliminate any opposition.* The House of Usher wanted this target with no expense spared. The order was brief, but told her so much. There was no suspicion of opposition. It would happen. Without question.

Van pulled the box free of the wall case and flipped open its brass latches. The pair of .38 Smith & Wesson revolvers within duly reflected the lantern light. She had not picked up either pistol yet, but the wooden grip under her brushing fingertips felt warm, as if expecting her touch.

Closing the lid to the case and then hefting the rifle free from the wall, Van ascended the staircase, her speech to Everett already prepared. Two weeks. She'd only be away two weeks. Three weeks, at the most. For that amount of time, she would be able to do so much good for the church and their little town. Even her stoic partner would see that. The reappearance of the House of Usher could provide a welcomed windfall, and a gift from above.

Van had to keep the faith that was why the House of Usher had returned to America. She didn't dare contemplate the other possibility.

FOUR

In Which Our Dashing Archivist and
Elegant Librarian Come to an
Arrangement, Much to the Dismay
of Our Colonial Pepperpot

Their arrival at the Outer Banks, Wellington Books decided, was quite the triumph.

For one thing, that rather brash American, Wheatley, was nowhere in sight. He had to be behind them by a few good hours at the very least.

Second, the couples either on the veranda or walking the grounds of Swan's Retreat enjoying the light, salt-kissed air and bracing breezes of North Carolina barely noticed Wellington's motorcar as it approached. Some engineers designed motorcars merely as retro-fitted horse carriages, creating in the process noisy, vapour-spewing monsters. However, Wellington had been paying close attention to the works of Karl Benz in Germany. Much like Benz's aerocraft, Wellington's motorcar was a streamlined, self-contained transport, able to vent any excess steam from a series of pipes through a single exhaust at the rear of the vehicle. The end result was a body less square and more rectangular, the wheels nearly half the diameter of a typical carriage. He had also taken several designs of combustion engines from Benz, Diesel, and Everett; and then incorporated several "Fox Corrugateds" to increase both heat transfer and overall strength. Through a series of struts, chassis, and insulators, Wellington invented a solution to the noise his mechanical marvel would have produced, the end result a delightfully soft medley of chugs, pops, and pings that barely drowned out the sounds of the local fauna.

At least until the boiler's pressure release values would reach critical and expel any excess gases. Birds took flight when the engine's quick, concussive *bang-bang* shattered the solitude of the resort. The first two times it happened on their trip between Norfolk and the Outer Banks, Eliza's *pounamu* pistols appeared seemingly from thin air. By the time it happened on the causeway to Swan's Retreat, Eliza merely pinched the bridge of her nose, apparently not happy with the announcement of their approach.

"Subtle, Welly," she grumbled.

"I would agree," he replied smugly. "As subtle as it can be." Whatever was her problem now?

"I don't see why, having made this motorcar of yours practically whisper silent," she said, shooting veritable daggers from her eyes, "you haven't been able to silence the two pops that sound more like gunshots. You have made us all the talk of the resort—and we've only just pulled up. Truly, this thing is—"

"Absolutely delightful!" squealed Felicity. "And it was such a comfortable ride compared to your average stagecoach." Felicity's eyes were dancing with delight as her hands gently ran along the motorcar's cushions. The backseat, where the librarian sat, resembled a chez lounge built into the rounded back of the car. The plush, red velvet couch folded upon itself, completely hidden from view until needed.

Wellington glanced pointedly at Eliza, and then craned his neck to say over his shoulder, "As you are the first to try the tumble seat, thank you for saying!"

Eliza opened her door, muttering just loud enough for Wellington to hear. "Two peas in a pod . . ."

While Felicity did not catch what she said, she did look at Eliza askance when she slammed the motorcar door shut. She blinked, then looked back to Wellington. "I'm sorry? The tumble seat?" Felicity looked around her. "Why is this called the 'tumble' seat?"

He opened his mouth as if to speak, but paused. Eliza was carrying her own luggage, capturing the attention of many on the porch. "Well, it's a bit difficult to explain presently." He watched her ascend a few more steps before going back to the luggage in the trailer. He recognised his portable analytical and his own suitcase. There were eight others stacked neatly in the wagon.

"I beg your pardon, Age—" And he caught himself. He was a field agent, and out in the field he had to maintain secrecy. "Er, Miss Lovelace, but exactly what is all this?"

"I was not certain what resources we would have out in the—" Then it was Agent Lovelace's turn to pause. She cleared her throat and continued, her voice far louder than necessary. "I mean, I was not sure what reading material I would have while on vacation. While I may seem like a simple woman to you, my studies do matter."

"No reason for the theatrics, Lovelace," a voice whispered from behind her, causing the librarian to jump slightly. Eliza glared at her. "If you want to blend in, just act naturally. You can act naturally, can't you? Or *is* this natural for you?"

Felicity blushed. "I suppose I am a bit nervous, Miss Braun. Considering circumstances."

"See? That wasn't hard, was it?"

Wellington glanced away from the two ladies and looked over the suitcases again. Across these suitcases, Felicity Lovelace had packed a small library. A part of him appreciated, and even admired, her for doing so. The practical part of him looked at her with abject terror. Books were heavy to begin with. Packed in suitcases? They would be a labour of Herculean standards to move.

And Felicity was so . . . tiny.

"I suppose we should call for a porter." He cleared his throat. "Preferably one of an automated, mechanical nature."

"What's the problem, Johnny Shakespeare," called a voice from the top of the steps. "Can't handle a few suitcases?"

Impossibly, "Wild Bill" Wheatley stood at the top of the steps. Wellington determined not to ask how he'd managed that feat.

"Glad to see you all made it here," Bill said, motioning along the length of Wellington's motorcar. "So that contraption of yours held together?"

"It performed beyond expectation," Wellington said proudly.

"So I heard," he quipped with a smirk. "I thought we were under attack or somethin' . . ."

Wellington pressed his lips together lest something uncouth escape him. "Allow me to offer a hand with Miss Lovelace's luggage." He examined the suitcases, and selected the two closest to him. Yes, they were heavy, but nothing he could not manage. He then motioned to Bill with one of her suitcases. "The sooner you assist your companion here with her bags, the sooner you can all regale us with how you beat us here from Norfolk."

The cowboy guffawed. "First beer's on you, pard'ner."

Wellington managed to get Felicity's bags up to the top of the stairs, where he remained to enjoy the sight of the OSM agent nearly topple from the weight of the one bag in his grasp. Wheatley blinked as he contemplated the solitary bag that nearly brought him to the ground. He glanced back over to Felicity, now unfurling a pink lace parasol as she took in the Carolina landscape, shook his head in disgust, and heaved the bag again. His face was quite ruddy by the time he reached the step where he had earlier postured for Wellington's benefit.

"Still wish to forgo the Portoporter, Mr. Wheatley?" Wellington called.

"No," he grunted through gnashed teeth. "I'm—fine. Just—'cause—we're—" The suitcase landed on the step above Bill with a thud so heavy Wellington felt it at the top of the landing through the soles of his shoes. "—comin' to the Swan's—don't—mean . . ." Bill huffed as he looked up to where Wellington stood, looked back to the car, then back up to Wellington, Felicity's two suitcases flanking him. He took a deep breath, heaved, and resumed his slow ascent. "Don't mean—we can't—fend—for ourselves."

Wellington grinned, and he straightened his own vest and descended the stairs, giving Bill a nod as he passed. "A true frontiersman spirit. Well done!"

He had returned to the lodge's lobby with his own bags just as Bill reached the top of the landing with his first bag.

Wellington's grin was now a brilliant smile as he watched from the corner of his eye the American groan as he stood, turned, and slowly descended towards Felicity's remaining suitcases.

"Aren't you a lucky sod?" Eliza quipped, joining him in the foyer. "Lovelace packs bricks in her suitcases, and you choose the two that just happen to hold her clothes and sundries?"

Wellington fixed his eyes on her, and then couldn't help but wink. "Luck, Miss Braun, has nothing to do with it. I watched both the Portoporter and that rented cart hitched to us. Easy to deduce which ones were ladened with the heavy burden of knowledge."

Another shudder came from the landing. Bill's face was now a deep scarlet.

"Much like our American adventurer is at present."

After another fifteen minutes or so, Bill finally set down the last of Felicity's packed library with a thud. He was breathing as if he had just played several sets at Wimbledon.

"God save the Union! A fine specimen you are," Wellington said, motioning with his walking stick at Bill's shoulders. "Atlas himself would be impressed at the weight you carry."

Then he turned to survey their new accommodations. Swan's Retreat was, even by Wellington's standards, quite impressive, far from the wilderness hunting lodge he had envisioned. If he had not known the outside was on the Outer Banks of the Carolinas, Wellington would have thought himself on the deck of a White Star cruise liner. However, rather than the drone of air motors around him or the sound of a sea vessel's whistle, he was instead surrounded by the casual conversation of men in hunting jackets and ladies gossiping with one another.

He and Eliza had just made eye contact with the concierge when Eliza suddenly stood between him and the desk, threw her arms around his neck, and squealed, making many a head turn.

"Oh, Reginald!" She beamed and gave him a rather fervent kiss that nearly toppled him over. "You have made me the happiest newlywed in all of the Empire!"

"Er, um . . . think nothing of it," Wellington stammered, feeling the heat rise under his skin. He was drawing a blank.

Ye gods, what were their cover names? "Nothing at all . . .
Esther." Eliza's smile widened. He got it right. Feeling every
neck muscle tighten as he craned around her face to peck her
on the cheek, he added, "I thought you would enjoy the fresh
sea air here in the Carolinas."

With a delightful little giggle, Eliza crinkled her nose, and
then continued to the front desk, leaving him there quite befuddled.

Wellington smoothed out his cravat and cast a nervous
glance over to Agent Lovelace who was eyeing him curiously.
She darted her eyes to Eliza, then back to Wellington, asking
him silently, *The vapours?*

His nod of reassurance, he knew, was anything but.

When he joined Eliza at the desk, she nuzzled in closer to
him, fluttering at him her sapphire blue eyes as if she had caught
a handful of dirt in them. There was no reason or rationale in
this odd game she had chosen to play at this very public moment;
but like all of her antics, he was sure there was going to be an
uncomfortable point to it.

"Welcome to Swan's Retreat," the concierge recited his
greeting.

"Thank you, kind sir," Wellington replied brightly. "Reginald and Esther McPhearson."

The man at the desk's expression remained stoic as he
replied, "As I surmised." With a light snort, he looked down at
his ledger and found their names. "We have you staying with us
for six days, five nights." He glanced back up at the two of
them, and Eliza giggled again. "How fortunate we are for that."

Wellington was now feeling a different kind of heat rise, but
his anger was immediately quashed by Eliza's reply. "Oh, such
manners here, Reginald. I did hear that the southern states of
the Americas excelled at hospitality." She patted the concierge's hand and nodded. "I think your establishment here will
suit us down to the ground."

"We do hope so," the attendant spoke evenly, though Wellington could clearly hear the undercurrent of loathing in his
voice. Particularly when he added, "If you desire to anything,
just—"

"Ask?" Eliza blurted. "I can assure you we will, provided

Reginald and I do not awaken and find ourselves mute." She then burst into a cackle. "But how ridiculous of a notion, don't you think?"

Wellington felt dizzy. *You are* still *upset about that?* He'd fooled her into silence on that mission, so perhaps it was only fair.

"You are booked in Room Ten." He slid a single key across the blotter towards Wellington. "I will instruct the bellman to see to your luggage."

"Thank you," Wellington managed, wincing slightly at Eliza's sudden squeeze of his bicep. They were ten paces away from the desk before he asked his partner through a forced smile, "I do believe I apologised for what happened at the Phoenix Society. Several times."

"Just hedging my bets, Welly," she began through her own tight smile. "Simply making my presence—and my voice—known to all at the outset."

"Did you wish to include all of North *and* South Carolina in your proclamation as well?"

She gave a slight chuckle. "Oh, Wellington, you know how I indulge in excess."

He went to retort, but paused in mid-step. He then pulled gently on Eliza's arm, and guided her towards an easel. The announcement written there lightened his mood considerably. Perhaps his first official field assignment would yield a promising diversion or two:

We are proud to bring you
Edison's Electrical Extravaganza
SATURDAY!
The Amazing
THOMAS EDISON
and his discussion of
ELECTRICITY
IN THE HOME!
EIGHT O'CLOCK
Reception to follow event

"Reginald?"

Yanked back to reality, Wellington turned to look at Eliza,

who was casting her gaze between him and the poster. He hated how transparent he was when around her.

"But it's our honeymoon," she proclaimed, then adding, rather louder than necessary, *"Dear."*

Yes, no mistaking it. That was a warning.

"I understand that, Esther, but this is Thomas Alva Edison," he returned. *Please, Eliza,* he pleaded internally, *please understand.* "Appearing here! In the Outer Banks of North Carolina! During our stay here at the Retreat! What are the chances?"

"But there is—*so—much*—for us to do while we are here," Eliza said, her character remaining intact but glimmers of annoyance flashing in her eyes. "Our time in the Carolinas will simply blink by."

"We have five nights in the Carolinas, my sweet," immediately tumbled off his tongue. It frightened him a bit how calling her "my sweet" came to him so easily. Not that he minded. "And yes, I promised to show you all the sights of this quaint beach resort, but you know"—and she did know—"how much I enjoy the sciences. This is just for one night. When else would such an opportunity like this present itself? Not only to hear the proficient inventor speak but to actually meet him in person?" he asked, motioning to the reception announcement.

Eliza's mouth twisted into a grimace. "Really, Reginald, I fail to see what is so fascinating about a man carrying a death wish. He is tampering with forces of nature, believing he can control the elements and bring them into fine establishments such as this?" She clicked her tongue. "No thank you."

He was not going to give up on this so easily. "But, Esther, *darling*, this is a once-in-a"—and his voice dropped to almost a whisper as he muttered—"bloody"—then shot back to full volume on—"lifetime chance to meet one of the greatest scientific innovators of our time." He was begging. He really didn't care. "Please?"

"Well, I certainly have no intention of attending with you, Reginald," Eliza answered.

A throat cleared behind them. "I would love to attend."

Both Wellington and Eliza turned slowly. Felicity's face lit up with a friendly smile as they made eye contact.

"My own husband"—here she gave a wide sweep of her arm

to indicate Bill standing nearby—"does not really have a mind for the sciences. Would you mind, sir, serving as my chaperone?" She took a deep breath before going on. "Seeing as we are two newly wed couples vacationing together in North Carolina that would not be improper."

Out of his peripheral vision, Wellington caught Eliza rolling her eyes. Heartbreaking as it would be to miss out on such an amazing opportunity, she was absolutely right: duty and charge must come first.

Wellington was therefore surprised to hear himself say, "I would be delighted. I'm certain my wife would not mind."

Eliza flinched at his side. Wellington gave her a pat on her hand, but refused to look at her directly. He knew what would be waiting for him if he did.

Felicity grinned and bounced on the balls of her feet. "Your kindness knows no bounds."

"Yes," Eliza seethed, "you could say his generosity steals all sense from him at times."

A shrill whistle cut through the din, its piercing note causing a few of the women to let out a chorus of little shrieks. They all spun about to see Bill removing two fingers out of his mouth as he leaned casually against the front desk.

"Felicity," he called across the silent lobby to her, "you okay with a queen in your room, or are you wantin' a king?"

"A king if it is available, Bill," she replied, giving him a forced smile.

When she turned back to Wellington and Eliza, her smile was a hint tighter than it should have been. "We're checked in under our real names. That's what happens when I let the field agent with the penchant for firearms make the hotel arrangements." She sighed. "Pity. I was hoping to travel incognito my first time in the field."

"Shall we take a look at our accommodations?" Wellington asked.

"Yes, let's," Eliza said, gently pulling him closer to her. "We have a lot to discuss, dearest."

Those were the last words Wellington heard from Eliza as they found their way to Room Ten. Despite the chill, the staff had opened the room's windows so the sea-scented air greeted their senses, along with the crashing of the nearby surf.

"So," Wellington muttered as his eyes took it all in, "this is how the field agents live?"

While not as spacious as Eliza's apartments back in London, the suite here at Swan's Retreat was most well appointed. The Atlantic breeze casually toyed with the sheer draperies hanging from high above a receiving parlour. Wellington's eyes continued from where they stood into the main bedroom off to his left. His eyes also noted a second bedroom, perhaps for children or other relatives, to the right. Between both rooms, a door led outside to a small deck where one might watch a sunrise or simply enjoy moonlight on the ocean's surface.

All this luxury sprawling before and around him became inconsequential as Eliza's anger abruptly shattered its serenity.

"Really, Wellington? *Really?!*"

"Esther, *darling*," Wellington stammered as he looked about the room wildly, "do lower your voice!"

"Oh, stuff it, Welly. I suspect at Swan's Retreat they don't wire the suites with recording devices nor do they spy on their guests. You probably have to pay extra for that." Eliza paused, pursing her lips together as her hands came to rest on her hips. Her fingertips wiggled against the fabric and creases of her skirts. She was not mad, Wellington realised. She was livid. "So before our luggage arrives, let's just get this out! I don't know who I want to shoot first—you or that annoying Lovelace woman!"

"Now, have a care. Felicity is quite charming, in her own, rather unique, way."

Eliza's eyebrow arched slightly. That tiny gesture never failed to terrify Wellington.

He adjusted his necktie. "It is harmless. I see no danger in two patrons of science and technology partaking in a lecture, colleague to colleague."

She nodded, her eyes narrowing on Wellington. "Colleague to colleague? Is that what you call it?"

Eliza was making no sense whatsoever. "Whatever are you on about?"

Her head jerked away, and her tone became very cold. "Never mind. You think I am being foolish."

"That is not what I said," Wellington insisted. "I am merely trying to understand why you are taking such umbrage. I did not ask you to attend, as I am well aware you are about as interested in the works of Thomas Edison as you are in those of Verdi."

"Might I remind you, Welly, that we are on a mission? That means sightseeing and local entertainment is considered a distrac—" Eliza's words caught in her throat. She was now looking him over head to toe. "Just a moment, we are on a mission."

"Yes," Wellington agreed. "And you are stating the obvious because—"

"Because I am looking at your suit, Welly, and I can tell you are not armed."

Bugger. She noticed.

"I am armed," Wellington insisted.

Her brow knotted. "With what? A Derringer '81? We need something with a bit more stopping—it's not the Derringer, is it?"

"Not . . . exactly."

Eliza screwed her eyes shut. He could see muscles twitching in her jaw. "Please, Welly," she began, "*please* tell me it's not one of Axelrod and Blackwell's experimentals."

Wellington felt his throat go dry. "She calls it the Nipper."

"The Nipper?!" Eliza screamed. "This is your first field mission and you are armed with an experimental called the Nipper? *What were you thinking?!*"

"I was thinking"—and Wellington couldn't stop himself from saying it—"baby steps. Yes, I am skilled with sidearms—"

"You're a bloody marksman of most lethal abilities, you are!"

Perhaps it was the trip. Perhaps it was the presence of that bombast Wheatley, but now Wellington could feel his own dander start to get up. "I am not going to discuss this with you any further! You can have the master bedroom. I am a man of simple means, as you know, and I will manage just fine in the guest bedroom."

"The guest bedroom?" Eliza folded her arms in front of her chest.

"Yes. I think that would be best. Besides, as you have said, we are on a mission, so the fewer distractions the better, yes?" When her shoulders fell, Wellington's exhaustion took the place of his anger. This was growing tiresome, and just a bit silly. "So what have I cocked up this time, Eliza?"

Eliza went to open her mouth, immediately closed it with a snap, then whirling about, picked up her skirts, stormed into the master bedroom, and slammed the door behind her.

The archivist-now-field-agent stood there, staring at the door, waiting for it to open again. However, the door didn't budge. Wellington couldn't be sure, but he thought he heard a muffled, aggravated scream over the omnipresent sound of the waves of the Atlantic.

"Hysteria," he muttered to himself as he picked up his suitcase. "Has to be."

INTERLUDE

❦

In Which the Sands of Kitty Hawk
Shift in Dangerous Directions

Dunes shift. Coastlines, under the elements, change. The sky is full of fleeting moods. So too the usually pretty face of Sophia del Morte, which was currently marred by a frown. She now stood on the sandbank, looking out to sea, her dark eyes underneath an equally dark hat scanning the horizon with eagle-like determination. This looked like the right place.

From the inside of her corset she withdrew the detailed map of the Outer Banks that the Maestro had given her. These details included coordinates, something Sophia trusted. If she were off her mark by the smallest distance, things could go disastrously wrong. That he should place his own fate so securely in her hands made even this seasoned assassin quiver with delight.

She had travelled by an exceedingly fast charter vessel, the *Mercury*. It was hardly comfortable compared to the Maestro's massive airship, the *Titan*, but she had required speed above all. He had been most emphatic about where to be and at what time. Even with the swiftness of her charter, she'd arrived in Newport News, Virginia, only to immediately run from aeroport to train depot, catching the one train that could take her to some poor excuse of a town in North Carolina, then grabbing a coach—again, chartered by the Maestro—that whisked her to the edge of the eastern seaboard overnight. She was exhausted but still focused.

An airship as huge as *Titan* would draw notice everywhere it went, no matter if the port was a major terminal or one barely used. Here, on this lonely strand of beach, there was no need to worry about being observed. Sophia could not wait for the reunion.

She flipped open the rear cover of her timepiece, revealing its compass face. According to the Maestro's coordinates, Sophia needed to move a little farther west. She hitched the haversack up a bit tighter against her back, hefted the Lee-Metford-Tesla Mark IV higher on her shoulder, and followed the agreed-upon bearing. She was thankful for the choice of garments, her trousers and stout boots making easy work of the treacherous footing. She half ran, half slipped down through the sand and low grasses, her nostrils full of the smell of salt, which she always equated with the smell of fish—dead fish, in particular. Then there was the sudden grinding of grit in her mouth. Even though she had her black jacket buckled against it, kept her head lowered and her mouth shut, she just knew that in the evening she would need a thorough bath to get the sand out of every nook and cranny.

Many people loved the beach, and Sophia del Morte was most assuredly *not* among them. Her profession had taken her to many unpleasant places before, and this barren wasteland of waves, wind, and dunes was merely another. She understood the Maestro's reasons for choosing this site, but why couldn't his ideal location have been within reasonable distance of a pleasant hotel or perhaps a vineyard? Sophia sighed, turned, and spat out more sand that had worked its way into her mouth, and resolved to forebear it, and most certainly not whisper any complaint. She had only made that mistake once.

The compass in her hand chimed. She pushed her dark lenses up the bridge of her nose and looked around her, a slow smile spreading across her face. Yes, this barren stretch would be ideal. Her smile faded however when her eyes followed the coastline to where she would make ready the Maestro's arrival.

She was not alone.

Two men in their rolled up shirtsleeves were working fever-ishly on some sort of contraption. It was a round cigar-shaped object about as tall as Sophia herself, and held in a cradle made of iron. She was curious by nature; and perhaps if she'd been on any other case she would have endeavoured to find out what they were up to, but the fact was they were stymying her plans.

This would not be born.

So engrossed in their work were these two gents that they never noticed Sophia's approach, even though she was making no particular effort to be quiet. Standing only a few feet behind them, she tilted her head as she considered their invention in more detail. Strapped to the outside of the cylinder were a number of wires and tubes that, Sophia hazarded, contained various fluids, gases, or both. Not a large amount, but they were held in some sort of array that would mix them together. From the base, a small amount of steam was slowly seeping free, only to vanish into the Carolina breeze.

Or perhaps it wasn't steam at all, because it looked thicker and heavier than the surrounding air. In fact, the dense mist seemed to *fall* from the apparatus. Now, Sophia was com-pletely mesmerised by the device.

One of the men, the one with less hair, had some small hatch open. "Do you think the thrust calculations are closer this time?" he asked while fiddling around with the inven-tion's inner workings.

The other, the possessor of a fairly decent handlebar moustache, after passing him various tools, returned his own attention to various pressure gauges along the contraption's hull. "They better be. We don't have enough fuel to try again until next month," he replied, and then gave a guffaw. "Unless we get a few more repair jobs from the Detweilers."

The balding one returned the chuckle. "The Dangerous Detweilers of Dayton. Their mishaps alone could fund *three* launches."

True to form of socially inept *schlockworkers*, neither of them were going to notice her anytime soon—a situation Sophia was not accustomed to. There was simply nothing for it, but to state the obvious. "A very interesting-looking contraption," she said with what she had been told was her most disarming smile.

The men spun around as if she had already stuck a knife in their backs. She must have made quite an appearance because their mouths literally dropped open. Now, she held their undivided attention. Perhaps they were not used to a woman carrying a rifle, or perhaps they just had very ugly women in this part of the world. She would not have been surprised. The number of American men on the Continent seemed to indicate to her that their women were not worth staying home for.

"Our apologies, ma'am," the moustached one began, "we didn't notice you."

"And that's saying something," the balding one added, his smile unexpectedly alluring.

Charming as the bald one was, she opened her pocket watch and was reminded of what little time she had remaining. It had to be now. Sophia waved her hand at the device. "Intriguing as your experiment here is, gentlemen, you must give this area of shore to me. Now."

The two men wiped their hands on their pants and straightened, seeming to work together as one machine. Their once separate demeanours—the balding one being a touch flirtatious, the moustached man actually blushing ever so slightly—slipped away before her eyes, replaced with hard, stern looks.

How precious.

"I'm sorry, ma'am," the balding one said, "but I believe we were here *first*. If you were looking for some peace and quiet, Kitty Hawk offers plenty of spots to choose from other than this one."

"But *this* is the spot I desire," Sophia replied, her fingers splaying slowly around the shoulder strap of her Lee-Metford-Tesla.

Sophia could almost hear their outrage warring with their good manners. Then, after standing in this awkward silence, the balding one spoke again. "Look, you're just going to have to wait. We have a launch to tend to, barring any catastrophic failures."

Flicking into sight like a serpent's tongue, a concealed blade sliced through the tight space between the men. A loud *clang* ran through the air, immediately followed by the angry hiss of half a dozen slashed lines coiled around the device. The men leapt back, yelping in horror as various fluids, many of them either catching fire on contact with one another or creating more of the heavier-than-air mist, spewed in every direction.

"You mean, like that?" Sophia asked. When she brought up her throwing arm a second time, another blade appeared, catching the sun as she slowly turned it in her hand.

They looked upon her anew in that moment, as if she had only just appeared. Their eyes bore into her with the same intensity they had devoted to their now-bleeding experiment, and the silence, once feeling awkward, had now turned ominous, marred only by the occasional fizz or crackle from the damaged machine. Sophia used this moment to look for vulnerabilities she could exploit. She'd rather not waste precious time, but you could never tell with men. Sometimes intellect would surrender to masculine pride, driving the male of the species to foolish acts.

These men however seemed to be exceptional.

The bald one used his hands, now encased by heavy gloves, to tip one end of the device's cradle up. The moustached gentleman immediately ran to its falling tip and caught the device before it hit the ground. "Come on, Orville," he snapped, the leaking cylinder now suspended between them like a bleeding soldier suspended on a stretcher. "Wind's too strong for an accurate altitude test, anyway. Let's get back to camp, and leave this *lady* to her thoughts. And herself!"

Sophia allowed the man his slight. It was evident their flight of fancy had been toiled over for some time, only to be ruined in seconds by her. If these "Dangerous Detweilers of Dayton" were as profitable as the men had insinuated, perhaps they could return with a repaired model. She waited until both men had disappeared over a sand dune before unslinging the rifle and haversack. The long, heavy string of contacts she withdrew resembled a necklace of diamonds, cut emerald style, their flat silver surface smooth and slick under Sophia's fingers as she adjusted them into a wide circle perhaps ten feet in diameter. She paused in her arrangement of this array only to check the time. It would be close, but she would be ready.

The last item from her pack introduced to this apparatus was the flickering power source snatched from the Culpepper airship just before its fatal descent over Essex. The device would have passed for a deck prism as the power source was secured on a flat circular base and surrounded by triangular planes. On closer inspection, though, it was not reflecting light, so much as creating it.

The Culpepper twins had been quite clever in the power source's development, but they were nowhere near the true application of their *electroporter*.

Sophia went to the centre of the circle created by the leads and secured the power source on its stand. Once connected to the array, the prism began to hum, growing louder and brighter as it did. Even after she cleared the circle, she continued to step back. The noise—more of a vibration from the array that she felt in her very skull—turned Sophia's steps into a graceful backwards jig. Her hands pressed against her ears but could not cease the thrumming in her head. Instead of collapsing into a ball, she screamed against the assault, determined to watch the sky and see this incredible creation of science do its work.

The thunderclap drowned her scream out as the circle of silver threw brilliant whips of immense energy upwards into the sky, scattering crying seagulls in all directions. A few of the more curious beach birds found themselves trapped by these tendrils, falling dead from the sky once released. She knew this power intimately, having seen and experienced it while the machine had been under the control of the Culpeppers.

Now this control of light, space, and time belonged to the Maestro—just as had always been his plan.

Sophia threw her hand over her eyes as the light grew too bright for her to bear. She was no longer screaming as the thrumming vibrations had now transformed into a rumble, a rumble that split the air suddenly with an almighty crash.

When Sophia finally tasted the salt air and returned to reasonable thought, she found herself on her back, pushed into the dunes from the amplified electroporter's concussive force. She now looked into the sky at the wonder hovering above her.

Though she knew this would have been, provided the device was a success, the sight of the *Titan* overhead made her breath catch. Its droning propeller rose above the sound of the waves pounding on the sandbanks; and while the envelope itself was storm cloud grey, sunlight managed to catch the hanging gun positions. All in all, the Maestro's yacht was a thickset, pugnacious-looking airship, prepared to deal the world a bruising.

Sophia smiled as the *Titan* turned to port and then lowered to disembarkation level. Her heart began to race as she saw the hatch in the belly of the airship slide open.

A ladder unfurled and, on the lower rungs striking the ground, a tall form climbed down it double-time. It was Pearson, the valet. As he dropped to the sand, Sophia felt a little niggle of disappointment. No smile greeted her from the valet's stern, drawn face; no sign at all that she had even done a passable job.

Still, it was not Pearson's goodwill she desired. She waited impatiently as he guided the massive airship lower until, with a single swipe of Pearson's hand, the *Titan*'s multiple anchors dropped, burying themselves deep into the Carolina sand. From where the rope ladder had dropped, a gangplank extended as the leviathan of the air continued its slow, controlled descent.

She strode past Pearson with a word, and they entered the airship's belly. As they went deeper into the gondola it got warmer and warmer, returning to a more comfortable temperature once beyond the engine room. A handful of guards, dressed in steel grey uniforms bearing, just above their right breast, the insignia of the *Titan*, acknowledged Sophia with a little bow. Beneath her notice or concern, she did not return the salute but fixated on the path ahead.

Pearson opened a final bulkhead door and ushered her in. It was dark. The Maestro always preferred shadow, but then so did she.

"Signora del Morte," his voice wheezed, accompanied by occasional bursts of steam escaping from his breathing apparatus. "You have done excellent work this day."

Compliments from him were few and far between, and Sophia took what he offered with both hands. It was like rain on a parched garden. "Thank you," she whispered. "I am honoured to serve as herald to your arrival in the Americas."

"An office you fulfilled admirably," he wheezed. "This final test of the electroporter, I would safely say"—and he motioned with his metallic encased hand—"was a rousing success. We are now able to proceed to the next stage: recruiting our latest candidate to come work for me, once he leaves his current position, that is." She heard the machine move, a subtle creak and rattle of gears. "And, of course, your next task."

Sophia felt a bitterness form in her mouth. "I will not be here to work alongside you?"

"You, my dear Angel of Death, shall use the electroporter to journey to San Francisco."

Her mouth immediately dried up as the horrific image of Chandi Culpepper emerging from the prototype came to mind. There was the flash of unnaturally bright light, then the scream accompanied by the malformed and distorted madwoman . . .

"Is there a problem?" the Maestro asked.

"No, Maestro," she lied.

His good hand reached from the shadows with a leather folio. "Your orders."

"And what will you do here?" she asked as she took the attaché from him.

A few seconds had passed before Sophia realised what had made the Maestro mute. She knew the question had been a mistake even before he spoke. "This is your business because—?"

She searched for an answer, but all Sophia could be certain of was the sweat breaking out on her skin. She opened her mouth. No words came. At first. "I . . . I simply wish to understand my service to you, Maestro. To make certain my objectives are clear."

"Understand my service"—and he motioned to the billfold she tightly grasped in her hands—"by understanding your orders."

"Yes, Maestro," she said without blinking or hesitation, her face completely devoid of any emotion.

"Come closer, Signora," the Maestro wheezed suddenly, a pair of malevolent crimson eyes glowing softly from the shadows.

She felt the folio's leather dig underneath her nails, her memory of when she was last within the Maestro's reach—and consequentially, in his grasp—still very vivid.

The brass-and-leather fingers reached for her, slowly and languidly. "If there are any problems here in the Carolinas . . ." The Maestro's voice was accompanied by assorted hisses and creaks, as if bellows within his suit were working hard. But why? Was he trying to keep his own emotions under control as well? ". . . I will call for you." Those final words were punctuated with his fingertips brushing her cheek ever so gently.

Sophia was having a hard time breathing, particularly when feeling his cold, metallic caress. Fear and desire mixed together in the pit of her stomach. "Of course, Maestro."

His fingers stopped their forward progress just underneath her chin where they lingered for an instant longer, the red points of light seeming to flare brighter now that she was close.

"Arm yourself, my Angel of Death," the Maestro whispered to her. "This foreign soil is not without its protectors."

Sophia nodded. "Yes, the House of Usher have dealt with OSM before. I can take care of anyone they have in their employment."

"Of that, I have no doubt."

Sophia motioned to the folio in her hands. "I am certain it is in here, Maestro, but will I be able to recognise my target in San Francisco?"

The laugh that came echoed within the metal suit, making it seem as if more than one man was amused by the question she was posing. It was terrifying and wonderful all at the same time.

When the answer came it made her smile as well. "His name is Albert. As he is heir to the throne of England, he will be difficult to miss."

FIVE

❦

In Which Miss Braun Begins to Enjoy American Hospitality

"**I**n America, we call this scoping the territory." Bill grinned at Eliza and slid her a shot of a clear liquid across the table where they were seated. She glanced around the tiny bar and pressed her lips together, even as she wrapped her fingers around his offering. Apparently, they were the only ones taking this case seriously.

As a frown formed on her brow, she decided that part of her anger was related to the mounting suspicion that the other two, apparently cross-referencing previous Ministry investigations against open OSM cases, had the better end of the deal. This establishment smelt of fish, sea salt, and unwashed men, and was not the first place she would have picked as a night out on the town with a handsome foreign agent.

Not that she was going to tell Bill she thought he was handsome. She couldn't imagine how arrogant he would get if she let that one slip.

Quagmire's—the territory they were currently scoping— was a little building on the sand, with windows easily rattled by the whistling wind and a handful of bleak-looking locals enjoying a limited choice of spirits. A far cry from Swan's Retreat.

Eliza picked up the glass and drained its contents in one motion. Whatever she had just knocked back down her gullet burned her throat and—she was most certain—the inside of her stomach, but she made sure not to let any hint of that cross her face. "Smooth," she uttered, wiping her mouth with the back of her hand, "but I really don't think the locals are quite used to women sharing their drinking space."

Bill seemed, for the first time, to take notice of the attention they were drawing: the dirty looks of the inhabitants. "Well, I do believe that is because they have never seen such a beautiful woman in all their lives."

Eliza raised both her eyebrows and sighed. They had dressed down for this little bit of infiltration; but the resident population of the Outer Banks was so small, they would have drawn notice no matter what they wore. Apart from the rich little country resort, the rest of these giant sandbanks' inhabitants were better described as "salt of the earth." *Or perhaps, of the earth and sea,* Eliza mused.

Her thumb brushed against her Ministry-issued signet ring and, ignoring the odd tingle the tracking device imparted, she lowered her voice as she leaned closer to her companion. "This lot don't look like they have seen many women. Full stop."

Bill let his gaze roam over their fellow drinkers and then nodded slowly as he refilled her tiny glass. "You have a point there, but think on them as toys in your experienced hands. We need information on the area, and these boys have what we need."

Eliza looked him up and down, and replied tartly, "I'm not exactly sure how you do it here, but I am not about to sit on all of these blokes' laps for information when we don't even know exactly what it is we need to ask . . ."

The American's laugh, for a moment, managed to drown out the roar of the wind. "What do you take me for, Miss Braun? I might not be no gentleman from England and all, but I'm not about to ask a lady to pass herself around like that!" He kicked back his own shot and then slapped a fistful of dollars on the table. "No, I believe in doing things the old-fashioned way."

It took only an hour to change everyone's perspective in

the room. It was amazing the change that could be wrought with the application of cash. By the time Bill's money was gone, they had made themselves a colourful collection of new friends in North Carolina. Eliza paced herself with sips of the rotgut Quagmire's palmed off as liquor, only wetting her lips.

Bill on the other hand was letting nothing go to waste.

With his bowie knife slicing through the air, Bill performed wild tricks ranging from juggling tosses to the always-popular parlour game of knife's tip skipped between the spaces of his splayed hand. It was a miracle, on seeing Bill's antics, that he still possessed all his fingers. After winning yet another round of this harrowing stunt of accuracy, Bill threw his knife at his own feet and broke into a dance to a tune the old man in the corner was belting out on his tin whistle. It was a jaunty little ditty, and Bill's feet certainly flew.

A smile was forming on her mouth. Despite his brashness, arrogance, and the former incident in San Francisco, she was starting to see how Bill operated. He was a man's man, and had so few pretensions that normal working folk didn't feel as if he was talking down to them.

It reminded her of how she operated.

Bill ended his show with a flourish as the locals exploded in adulation. He stumbled through the flurry of back slaps and shoulder punches to flop in the seat before her. "They might be dirt farmers," he said, wiping the sweat off his face with his sleeve, "but these folk sure can drink."

"And that is the sum and total of what we've learned?" Eliza tilted her head and fixed him with a relatively sober gaze.

"Not quite," Bill said with a grin. "I've been pepperin' the talk with questions about anything that just wasn't right. I kept hearin' the same thing: talk to Merle. Accordin' to the lore, he's seen things." He took a swig of his beer.

Eliza looked at her partner, and shrugged. "Merle is . . . ?"

He pointed to an older man huddled in the corner, nursing a glass of whiskey, avoiding everyone's gaze. Eliza noticed immediately that there was something strange about the man's legs. With a little more observation she discerned a prosthetic, just visible through long tears in the fabric. The fixtures she could only just see did not look well cared for, pitted and scarred by a life at sea. Much like the man it was strapped to.

Bill leaned over. "Veteran," he muttered. "Surprised the old codger has lived this long."

"He's a man, Bill. Not some horse that should be put down on account of a crippling wound."

He took another swig of his beer. "Take a good look at ol' Merle, and tell me that what he's got is something resembling a life."

War was something this child of the even deeper south—namely the Pacific Ocean—had never experienced. Peering into the eyes of this old man, however, she could only guess at the horrors he had seen. Wellington sometimes wore that look in unguarded moments.

Eliza waved over the bartender, such as he was, and bought the bottle from him. "Leave this to me," she muttered to Bill, and strode over to the corner.

He had the look of a beaten, but still very angry dog. The pity Eliza felt welling inside her vanished when Merle locked eyes with her as she approached. His hand slid down his good leg. The snarl growing on his face, and her own instincts, warned her of some kind of pistol there. Her own hands were full, but she could drop the glasses and bottle in a moment to pit her speed of youth against his advanced years and experience.

Not tonight, she thought as she cast a warm smile his way.

After a moment, his hand slid back into view, his eyes, grey as the ocean, still fixed with hers. A smile twitched in the corner of his mouth as he raked her form up and down. "What do you want, girl?"

His gaze shifted abruptly from her to the glasses and bottle she set in front of him. The hardness softened slightly on seeing how very full the bottle was.

"I hear you're Merle," she said, taking a seat next to him. He was busy staring at the whiskey still sloshing inside the bottle. "I also hear you know what goes on around here."

Merle reached for the bottle, but just then his gaze travelled past her. Immediately he seemed to deflate. Eliza turned in that direction to see a knot of men muttering among themselves, their callous nods and gestures towards their corner making her skin prickle. She breathed easier when Bill appeared, offering another round which they graciously accepted. Just before they turned away from view, Bill looked over to Eliza and winked at her.

"Is that true?" Eliza asked, turning back to Merle.

"Maybe," he grumbled in reply, his eyes boring into the worn table under his hands.

"How long have you called the Outer Banks your home?"

"Since before you entered this world, girl, I can tell you that."

Eliza nodded, filling one of the small glasses. She looked Merle over. Whatever was in this tiny glass could have been what Axelrod and Blackwell used to clean their contraptions. It certainly couldn't hurt this old-timer.

"That means you've seen a lot," she said, sliding the drink closer to him. "Maybe even some things you shouldn't've."

He snorted, picked up his drink, and raised it to his lips. "You think anyone here believes a crazy old man? Believes in Blackbeard's Curse? Even with what I've seen . . ."

A curse? Perhaps as credible as hauntings, but sometimes a lead could spring from wives' tales and superstitions. "Maybe it's because you're talking to the wrong people."

His gaze hardened again. "What's that s'posed to mean?"

"It means, Merle, that these men haven't seen what you've seen, have they? They're too young to have fought in the war. Some people can't believe in anything spectacular because they have small minds, small lives." Merle downed the drink quickly, the glass knocking softly against the table. She poured him another shot. "They don't like to imagine anything exists beyond their own little world, but you . . . well, you know better."

The lines around Merle's face deepened as he frowned up at her, searching her face for some sign that she was stringing him along. Eliza held his gaze unflinchingly.

Merle tilted his head and nodded as if acknowledging that. "Like how you were only on your second shot before coming over here? How many has that beau of yours had? Seven?"

Eliza's mouth bent into a grin. "Nine."

"Nine?" The old man gave a rough bark she could only assume was a laugh. His fingers wandered over to the glass and tightened on the shot, once finding it. "Guess all this shit bourbon here is finally taking a toll on me."

Eliza poured herself a glass, just in case. "You mentioned a curse."

He leaned forwards over the table and gestured her in closer. "It's real, you know? Blackbeard's airship, *Devil's Shadow*, went down here. He was en route to Ocracoke, but had to stop at Corolla for a quick refuel. There was a ship moored offshore. He thought it was *Queen Anne's Revenge*, but it wasn't." He exchanged his now-empty glass for Eliza's. "Not sure who it was that done it, but Blackbeard's airship fell from the sky that night. A ball of flame that lit the Currituck Banks for miles."

While akin to a fantastic yarn to chill children in front of a hearth's fire, Merle's story actually had merit. Early airships in the nineteenth century were truly experimental, usually a long gondola with several balloons suspended overhead. Pirate vessels were particularly dangerous as the easiest lighter-than-air gas to purchase through underground channels was hydrogren, hence why airships were not so common in the Golden Age of Piracy.

"Are you sure this wasn't the Fire Ship of New Bern you were seeing?" Eliza asked.

A bushy eyebrow crooked at that query. "I may be a damn drunk, girl, but I know the difference between where I live and Ocracoke. Next time, know your geography as well as your local lore."

Eliza often talked with folks who had seen and heard things that would earn them anything from a dubious reputation to confinement in an asylum. He carried with him the look of a haunted man; but in that bold statement, he displayed a cold sobriety.

"So Blackbeard crashed off Currituck then?" she pressed.

"Folks all swear it's the Graveyard of the Atlantic?" Merle hissed. "What's happening is more than just shallow shoals."

Eliza swallowed and glanced back over her shoulder. Bill and his new friends were still working through a pair of bottles; but if he were trying to keep a pace with these gents, he might be losing feeling in his legs at any moment.

She turned back to Merle, fixing her eyes with his, as if it were only them in Quagmire's tonight. "Go on. Tell me what you saw."

He tugged on her arm and bent towards her ear. "A sword of flame, come rising from hell itself, blasting ships from the sky and cuttin' vessels in half. Saw it with my own eyes the other night. I had just come home when Blackbeard's sword plucked an airship out of the sky. I thought it was just the drink . . . then I saw the bodies wash up. It was as if Sherman had come back . . ." His voice trailed off as tears spilled from his eyes.

Eliza reached out and took Merle's open hand. He had not asked to be a witness, but there was a real chance he was drinking harder than before to erase recent memories. He had seen enough death for one lifetime.

A quick blink, and his face twisted into a chiselled grimace. "Next morning, the corpses were gone, but like all the other ghosts of the Carolinas, they'll be back."

She refilled his glass and nodded. "Where did you see this?"

"Off Corolla, near the lighthouse," he grumbled.

With a heavy sigh, she slid the bottle within his reach. She eyed the god-awful bourbon for a moment, hoping he would have no recollection of their talk, or much of anything else for that matter. "Keep an eye out for Blackbeard. We need alert folk like you around here."

The old man nodded excitedly, and downed the shot glass in his grasp. Turning on her heel, she strode back to Bill and the collected locals. One glance into Bill's glassy eyes and she knew that this evening was just going to get longer.

"We need to go," she whispered to Bill.

The men around him whooped and whistled. "Gonna get something sweet tonight, Billy boy!" one of the sailors blurted.

Perhaps the melancholy of the old soldier had sucked the evening's amusement from her. Because Eliza could not stop herself from rounding on the offending sailor. "Why don't you just shut your flapping gums, mate!"

Laughter coupled with feigned shock at her retort filled her ears. The sailor stepped up to Eliza, his jocularity turning sinister in an instant. "You gonna shut them for me, missy?" he snarled. "I can think of *one* way to occupy my mouth with you."

Bloody Americans. They really didn't know a warning when it bit them in the arse. "Now how can you follow through with that," she began, "when you have a split lip?"

He leaned in closer. His breath stank. "What split lip?"

Bill, the collected sailors, and the assorted deckhands never saw Eliza's palm heel strike, but they did see the sailor's head snap back, his mouth and chin covered in his own blood.

"That one," she spat.

The men surrounding them were no longer smiling. Bill burst into a hearty chuckle as he gave Eliza a playful rap against her corset while the circle of sailors slowly closed the space around them. "Now settle down, Lizzie. We're just havin' a laugh. No harm. Right, boys?"

"Your little missy, Bill, needs to learn her place," another sailor spoke, his eyes fixed on Eliza.

"Mate," she seethed, "if you even tried—"

The man exploded, sending his glass hard to the floor. *"Am I talking to you, whore?"*

Now the silence was thick, pressing against Eliza's sides, threatening to squeeze her last breath out of her. Every eye was on them.

Bill hooked his thumbs in his belt buckle, shaking his head ruefully. "I was about to do that, Enoch," he said, "but you had to go on and be rude." He looked over at Eliza and she gave a little gasp. The glassy eyes were now quite clear, quite focused. "How about you apologise?"

"How 'bout you go to hell?" he snapped, stepping free of his group. His stance was hardly steady. Must have been trying to match Bill shot for shot.

"Just apologise to Little Lizzie and everything'll be back to the way it was," Bill urged, taking off his hat.

Eliza's gaze jumped from Enoch, back to Bill. Did this horse's ass call her "Little Lizzie" just now?

"Why? She somethin' special?" he growled back. "This trollop got a special way of sucking—"

Bill's head launched forwards and the crunch of Enoch's nose was clearly heard, providing those in Quagmire's their only warning before he flipped a nearby table, sending glasses and bottles flying everywhere. A single shot glass slapped into the OSM agent's grasp, and he threw it at a dockhand reaching for a pistol, knocking the man off balance. Bill then leapt on a lone chair left behind by the toppled table, and jumped into the throng of men with whom he'd been sharing convivial drinks. His battle cry—Eliza had heard it called a "Rebel Yell"—served as a ceremonial cannon, signalling the beginning of tonight's entertainment.

A few of Enoch's friends closed on Bill in quick order, but there were others around that were either siding with Bill in defending "Little Lizzie's" honour or simply itching for a good brawl. By the time Bill was free, thanks to a few gallant strangers, Enoch was back on his feet, towering over the OSM agent. Bill hooked the tip of his boot under a bottle at his feet, and kicked. The glass slapped into his hand, which he in turn slapped across Enoch's face. If this had been a comedy troupe at a music hall, the bottle would have shattered for comic effect. As this was a tavern somewhere on the American East Coast, the thick glass remained intact. The dockhand's jaw wobbled inside the man's skull as rivulets of blood shot out of the man's mouth.

The blow *should* have landed the man out cold, but Enoch spat free a tooth and then brought a beefy fist round to Bill. Enoch's uppercut lifted him off his feet and sent him back to a chair that collapsed under him with a loud snap. Eliza winced a fraction, hoping what she had heard had been the chair and not Bill's back.

Bill certainly wasn't stopping to check. He bounded to his feet, grabbed up the closest empty chair—most were empty as the brawl now held everyone's immediate attention—and swept it in a wide arc, knocking the four men charging at him back a pace or two.

Ministry orders dictated, as this was a goodwill operation, that Eliza should have jumped into the growing chaos and helped her fellow agent out, but their first meeting in San Francisco gave her a moment's pause. That, and she was quite enjoying watching from outside the event how Agent Bill Wheatley handled himself. The man was quite a machine.

Her enjoyment was interrupted by massive arms wrapping around her from behind. Whatever kind of clumsy attack it was, it was over as her boot heel drove down hard into the attacker's foot, earning her a whiskey-accented scream into her left ear. She then turned and slammed her fist into the man's nose. Brief as the skirmish had been, it attracted the attention of a table full of dockhands. One of them, a man with slicked-back blond hair, drew a bowie knife similar to Bill's from his jacket.

Now, officially, she was no longer *watching* the fray but following orders.

Eliza loved a good bowie as much as the next woman, but the knifeman was just waiting to join the evening's diversion a little too enthusiastically. She took a step back, and felt her own foot brush against an empty bottle. Considering Bill's fancy footwork, Eliza hooked her toe under the bottle, kicked it up into her hand, and threw it at the man, all in one swift sequence. This time, the glass did shatter against the man's head, and he dropped the knife with a yelp—which turned into a scream when Eliza took three quick steps and side-kicked him backwards into his friends.

The thunderclap froze everyone in place. Eliza turned to see Merle crack open the blunderbuss-style shotgun, ejecting its spent shell that rolled across the tavern floor to disappear in the dingy shadows.

"The girl was kind enough to buy me a drink," he announced as he slipped in a replacement shell. "Now I'm a drunk war veteran with a loaded blunderbuss. That makes me dangerous."

"You got two shells, old man," a sailor mocked.

"Keep talkin' and I'll just have one," he warned. "Consider this a southern gentleman's thank-you, miss. Now I think you and the beau ought to leave."

A night out with a colleague, a bar brawl, and a lead. The night with Bill had not been a complete loss.

"Well, this has been delightful," Eliza said brightly against the quiet. She turned back around. "Bill," she called, "you done?"

Bill's left cheek was a dark red, leaning with every moment to purple. The sailor behind him bent down, picked up Bill's Stetson, and shoved it into his shoulder, crushing the hat's crown.

"Jus' a minute," he slurred, forming his crumpled Stetson back into shape. Once his hat was resting as he thought it should, Bill thrust his elbow behind him, sending the sailor to the ground. "Okay, I'm done."

She jerked her head towards the exit. By the time they were back out in the night, music had resumed, conversation was returning, and Bill's demeanour had gone from aggravated to extremely satisfied. Outside a blast of ice-cold wind hit them in the face, but after the humid dark of the public house, this was quite refreshing. Eliza led the way back up the sandbank, and towards the road they had walked down earlier in the evening.

"You Americans are making me homesick, you know that?" With a look back at Quagmire's, she turned back to where Bill's horse waited patiently. "Well, come on, Bill, we've got a morning ahead of us tomorrow."

"Hold on," Bill said, trailing behind her. "The old man was really on to something?"

"I know that look. Merle may sound crazy, but he saw something. Tomorrow morning, we do what we do best."

He motioned with his thumb back to the pub. "I thought *that* was what we do best."

The clouds slipped away from the moon with timing that Bill could not have worked better if he had placed an order for it. The smile she caught from him, even with the swollen jaw, was both charming and wicked. She stretched. "That, my heavily bruised counterpart, was merely a prelude."

"I look forward to the opening act," Bill said, his voice low and husky.

Eliza could not help herself as she laughed into the night. "You know, Bill, I am starting to like you . . ."

He tilted his head up and laughed, matching her stride for stride. "All part of my wicked plan."

SIX

❧

Wherein the Atlantic Surrenders a Secret

"And exactly how much alcohol had this supposed lead of yours enjoyed last evening?" Wellington asked, engaging the motorcar's hand brake.

Eliza tilted her head, considering. "He was on his third, maybe fourth, shot . . . from my bottle . . ."

"Hardly seems reliable," Felicity offered from the tumble seat.

Wellington watched carefully as Eliza shut her eyes and took a long quiet breath. Meticulously, she placed the goggles around her neck, which he knew did not bode well. They both turned to Felicity, who was wearing the pink driving cap Wellington had donated to keep her curls in check. She looked silly, but quite endearing.

"Were you there last night, Miss Lovelace?" Eliza asked, her voice steady.

"No," the librarian replied.

"Then I suggest you refrain from the assessment of the investigation before you hear all the facts." Eliza turned back, with her eyes narrowed in a dangerous fashion. "Both of you."

"Felicity has a point," he dared. Even as her ice blue eyes bore into him, Wellington continued. "The man is a war veteran, and I have no doubt he suffers a great deal with what he's seen in the battlefield."

"You weren't there, Welly," Eliza stated.

"No, Eliza, I wasn't," and then he paused, wringing a hand lightly on his steering wheel, "on that particular battlefield." He was pleased to see her gaze soften slightly. "What I'm saying is that battlefield trauma can affect one's perception of the world. Introduce a liberal amount of alcohol into said perception—"

The rhythmic hoofbeats of Wheatley's horse interrupted his thoughts, and soon enough the chestnut mare appeared alongside the motorcar.

Wellington shook his head at the state of the American. While Bill was slightly better presented than he had been the previous night, he still looked as if he had been on the wrong side of an argument with a cricket bat.

Deciding not to comment, Wellington reached out, opened his door, and offered a hand to Felicity. As he assisted her down, he looked back to Eliza.

"As I was saying, add libation to someone as unstable as this Merle, and you—"

"Actually, it's Major Brantfield," Bill slurred.

"Merlin Brantfield?" Felicity asked, her hand going to her chest.

Eliza turned towards the librarian, her eyebrow crooking slightly. "You know Merle?"

"CSA Major Merlin Brantfield is known on both sides as the Magician from Manassas," Felicity said. "He was promoted to the rank of major shortly after the second battle there. It was thought he'd be the next General Jackson or Lee."

"That shell of a man . . ." Eliza blinked. "So what happened to him?"

Felicity became sombre, casting a quick glance to Bill, who was also slightly ashen. "Sherman's Carolina Campaign."

Wellington understood then. He had studied the controversial "scorched earth" strategy of Union Major General William Sherman. Somehow, this man with whom Eliza shared drinks had survived it all. That must have left deep scars indeed.

"Very well," the archivist said, tugging the lapels of his coat. "I believe then that just past these dunes is the beach?"

"Yep," Bill said, slapping saddlebags over his shoulder. "And somewhere out there is a wreckage, or evidence of such."

"Bill," Eliza said, "Merle told me the bodies were gone by morning."

"And if Merle isn't seeing things, those corpses didn't just get up and excuse themselves. If they did"—Bill paused, taking stock of his pistols and how many bullets he had—"we got bigger problems than disappearing ships."

"Let's go about it then," Wellington replied.

Once clear of the dune, the four agents stood with the open expanse of the Atlantic stretching off to the east, the deep violet of night slowly receding. Even with the promise of a dreary day, their view was stunning as the sea crashed against the shore, the tendrils of its foam stretching deep up the sand.

"So," Wellington said, placing his hands on his hips. "Which way?"

"Just give us a minute, Johnny Shakespeare," Bill insisted as he removed the bags from his shoulder.

At first, Wellington thought the objects Bill removed were large books—about the size of the registers one would find in a town hall. The American passed one to Felicity while he took the other. From their spines, the agents extended antennae, then unclasped the cover to reveal a collection of gauges and buttons rather than text. Bill spun a small hand wheel a quarter turn then hefted the book in front of him, while Felicity mirrored his actions.

"Airship and sailing vessels all carry onboard small wireless beacons. During normal travel they serve as handy ways to keep track of a ship's bearings," Bill said, checking the gauges as he began walking along shore in the direction of their resort. Felicity was walking in the exact opposite direction. "In case of a catastrophe, there should be enough water in the boiler to keep the beacon active for four days."

"So if what Merle saw was real," Eliza concluded, "then there should be a signal."

"Unless," Felicity said over her shoulder, "the boiler suffered a breach. It is hard to—" Her words cut short as she looked up from the gauges. "Bill!"

Her partner closed his own book and shoved the device into Wellington's arms as he passed. Wellington glanced over at the Americans before daring to open the book. Dials and needles stared back at him, all unmoving until he turned in the direction of Felicity and Bill. He only managed a few steps until one of the lights at the top flickered with the tiniest of sparks. He turned the hand crank to the left and the casing grew warmer in his touch. That was when the needle in the gauge marked "Signal Strength" bounced lightly.

"Oh, this is ingenious," Wellington whispered as the needle moved again, then once more, clearly in some semblance of rhythm.

"How strong?" Bill asked.

"Faint from here, but we're definitely getting a signal," Felicity replied. "Maybe a mile in this direction?"

"Right then, back to the motorcar?" Wellington offered, closing the tracking device.

"Afraid not," Bill said, casting his glance down shore. "The mechanics of your fancy ride will gum up the works of our trackers. We are gonna have to hoof it."

Bill took the tracker out of Wellington's arms, much to the archivist's dismay. He would have liked more time with this OSM innovation. While their own ETS worked on a private network of wireless transmissions, this device apparently was able to tap into all manner of æthercommunications and focus on a specific signal. He wondered how it was doing that . . .

His question, it seemed, would go unanswered as Bill took the devices and slipped them back into the saddlebags.

"After you and Bill returned last night from Quagmire's," Felicity spoke up, "I took the liberty of accessing recent traffic, both air and sea, so if this ship that Major Brantfield claims was taken down exists, we should be able to see if it is listed as late or missing."

"Had any vessels disappeared before our arrival in Norfolk?" Eliza asked.

"Two," Felicity said, "the *Cherie* and the *Alexandria*. Both airships."

Wellington turned to look out to sea. "It's possible then, if Brantfield saw either ship that night, the wreckage out there awaits us?"

"Possible." Felicity shrugged. "But considering the lead . . ."

"Better get walkin'," he said, then tossed his duster to Eliza.

"Just in case it gets a bit too chilly. Carolina winds tend to fool you into thinking you'll be fine, right before they start bitin' to the bone."

Wellington straightened up at Eliza's grin as she slipped on the long coat. He did not care for that particular look on her.

In silence, the four continued down the shore, the sky above now decorated with bands of clouds slowly forming a featureless sheet of steel grey. The temperature sank lower and lower with each step. *Eliza was probably particularly cosy in Bill's jacket,* Wellington found himself thinking.

He frowned. Why could she not see right through the American? She was usually much more savvy than this. The wind pushed back a few locks of her hair, and Wellington couldn't help a slight smile. Something about being by the ocean made her even more beautiful.

Thinking on that made him almost run into her when she stopped suddenly. Wellington's gaze followed where she was looking.

"Miss Braun, I stand corrected," he said as they all took in the dramatic wreckage in the distance.

Fluttering in the breeze was the remains of a half-inflated balloon. There were mizzenmasts and yardarms, snapped as if they were kindling meant for a fire. Scorch marks pitted and marred the hull of the long gondola that would have hung underneath the envelope. Wellington looked around them, and sure enough what appeared at first to be merely driftwood half-buried in the sand was actually a body. He soon enough found more.

"Why haven't the authorities been here?" he said sternly.

"We're in a pretty remote area," Bill said, apparently taking count of how many bodies had washed onshore, "and this didn't happen two nights ago."

"When do you think?" Eliza asked

"Last night." Bill dropped to one knee for a closer look at the nearest dead body. "After Lizzie and I were at Quagmire's."

"That certain, are you?" Wellington asked, looking around at the wreckage.

No reply came. He turned to Bill, who was now holding his Stetson over his heart, looking up at Eliza. "Yeah. I am."

The three of them drew closer, and Eliza gave a quick gasp of recognition. "Enoch?"

The man was massive, his jaw quite swollen and nose slightly crooked as if struck with something hard. From their early morning's repast, he did recall Eliza regaling him with stories of a rather large man who Bill had attempted to fend off with a bottle of alcohol.

As they drew closer to the derelict, Wellington surveyed the area to see if they were alone, but no ships, air or otherwise, hovered over the choppy waters. The dunes reached higher than he liked, towering over them by at least two stories. He paused, tapping his fingers against his hips as he surveyed the terrain.

"Something amiss, Welly?" Eliza asked, motioning to his less-than-elegant stance. "Ready for trouble?"

"Just . . . just . . ." he stammered, suddenly feeling the stress of her regard," . . . getting a lay of the land is all."

To his surprise, she nodded in approval. "I don't like the dunes either. There's just too much opportunity to pin someone down from there." She playfully rapped him on the arm. "Excellent instincts."

Suddenly, the cold seemed less bothersome. He smiled back at her. "Shall we get a closer look at your lead?"

"Oh," she said, slipping her arm into his, "a walk along the beach to the site of a shipwreck. You really know the way to a girl's heart, don't you?"

They drew closer to the major damage that must have brought down the vessel. Much of the hull had been blasted away, one hole in the keel and a larger breach where an engine and propeller array would have been. Wellington gave a gentle pat of her arm before slipping away to get a closer look at the smaller damage point.

Felicity, returning from the bow, gestured along the hull as she said, "She's christened as the *Delilah*. There's no record of this ship either coming or going in the past week."

"Really?" Eliza asked. "Not even for a moonlight cruise?"

"I would have seen it," she stated. "The beacon we heard could be a standard distress signal. Even the illegal ones carry those."

"A ship not registered in any logs, incoming or outgoing." Bill followed the ship from stern to bow. "Smugglers?"

"That stands to reason," Eliza concurred. She turned back to Felicity. "Maybe you can run down any previous history this ship has with the local law?" Felicity nodded, produced a pad from inside her coat and quickly jotted down a note. "Bill, when you and Felicity looked at the recent disappearances, did you notice if any of them were unregistered like the *Delilah* here?"

"No, but I guess Felicity has something else to add to that list once we get back to the Retreat. Don't ya?"

Felicity glanced up from her pad. "It wouldn't kill you to make an aether transmission, or maybe crack open a ledger now and then."

Bill rolled his eyes. "Darlin', that is exactly what your job is—cracking open them books."

His partner shook her pretty head. "If this particular vessel is a pirate ship, that would explain the lack of action from local and state government," Felicity said. "But this still does not explain what Major Brantfield claims to have seen."

Wellington continued to stare at the hole in *Delilah*'s keel. "But Brantfield saw something. We're staring at what we've never had until now—evidence." There was something about the keel damage that he was missing. "Still no closer as to why it's happening."

"Could dimensional travel cause damage like this, Agent Braun?" Felicity asked.

"In my experiences utilising æthergate travel, if something like this happened as a result, it has never been reported." Eliza came from around the remains of the stern. "But we have seen plenty of damage done when something similar to æthergate science goes horribly wrong."

Wellington smiled wryly. "In that case you call the Janus Affair, a reverse of polarity caused catastrophic failure. Failure far worse than what we're seeing here."

"Æthergate science is still a science," Bill offered. "This could just be a bad day at the lab."

"But there are two problems to this deduction," Wellington said. "If pirates are making their ships disappear completely, never to be seen again, these must be the best-equipped but thick-as-clotted-cream pirates."

Felicity crinkled her nose as she looked up from her memo pad. "How so?"

"If a pirate is burying their treasure, presumably they will want to be able to get it back. Why hide something forever?"

"Fair enough point, Johnny Shakespeare," Bill said, "so what's the second problem?"

"Not all the disappearances have been unregistered ships, have they?"

Felicity clicked her tongue. "He's got a point, Bill."

"I know," Bill grumbled. "I know."

Regardless of the overcast morning, Wellington felt quite warm, as if the sun were shining directly on him, just for him.

But then the chill of the day returned. "Since we're all kickin' around ideas, how about this: pirates aren't making their own ships disappear, but can you think of a better way to pillage a ship? Just take the whole damn thing."

Git, Wellington seethed. "Quite a good deduction." He waited as Bill walked around to the opposite side of the wreckage before continuing. "So let's expand on this theory—the disappearances are pirates, plucking ships from the sea and sky. The *Delilah*, an unregistered airship . . ." He pointed in the direction from where Eliza appeared. "Now there's a notion."

"What?" Eliza asked.

"Extrapolate, Miss Braun. What if dimensional forces are indeed at play and the *Delilah* blew their engines trying to combat it?"

"I think I see where you are going with this." Eliza walked down to Felicity and pointed to her legal pad. "We will need to contact Ministry headquarters and have them pull Case #18940912SWFA. It involves a device called the Frankenstein Array."

"All right," she began, writing feverishly. "And what does it do?"

"The array theoretically collects and regulates electric surges created during thunderstorms."

Felicity paused in her note taking. "Theoretically?"

Eliza nodded. "The design implies it can do that, but if

your calculations are off, even in the slightest, you don't have a power collector so much as you have an amplifier."

"If memory serves," Wellington said, "the laboratory where you found the Frankenstein Array is located where the hamlet of Lugano is."

"Was." Eliza raised her hand at Wellington, keeping him silent. "It wasn't me. The House of Usher had started a sequence with it when a thunderstorm happened in the valley. I think they wanted to vaporise Geneva."

Felicity shrugged. "The last I heard, Geneva was still standing."

"Remember that part I said about calculations being off?" Eliza asked. "The north wing of Frankenstein's stronghold was vaporised . . . along with Lugano."

"The problem with the Frankenstein Array," Wellington interjected, "is that you need incredibly bad weather to use it. Why would anyone dare such conditions?"

"If they were mad enough and knew the potential of something like the Frankenstein Array, they might. We never concluded if the schematics were destroyed in that blast. Usher could have sold them through underground circles." Eliza walked over to the hole Wellington had earlier been studying intently and shouted, "Bill?" From the other end of the wreckage, the silhouette of the American agent appeared. "Think you can make it to the wheelhouse?"

"The gondola's listing pretty hard," his voice echoed through the hull, "but I think I can, yeah."

"See if there's anything you can find up there that can give us a clue as to their heading or destination, and weather reports. If they were using a Frankenstein Array, then they're waiting for storm fronts to come rolling in."

Wellington's eyes darted between the hole in the keel and the spot where they had just seen Bill pop up. "Just a moment," he muttered, standing where Eliza had called out to Bill.

"What is it?" his partner asked, her brow furrowing.

"In Major Brantfield's account, how did he describe the catastrophe again?"

"A sword of fire, I think he said."

He looked back at the damage to the keel, and Wellington silently chided himself for not noticing it sooner.

Eliza looked at the hole. "What am I missing?"

"The hull," Felicity said with a gasp. "Observe its decided curvature."

Wellington had seen the keel damage as merely part of the engine room's, but now when he looked again, he noticed large chunks of its metallic hull were bent inward, as if something had punched through the gondola.

"The engine didn't fail on account of a power overload, nor did it fail during dimensional travel. This," Wellington said, tracing the metal's bend with his finger, "was the entry wound, and that," he said, pointing to the hole where an engine had once been, "is the exit wound. This ship was run through by something hot enough to melt metal on contact." Wellington stepped back to examine the damage from a new perspective. "A sword from hell itself, he had said?"

Gunshots, in a sudden burst, tore away at the metal scraps at the ship's entry wound. Wellington grabbed the screaming Felicity as Eliza drew her pistols and started firing back in quick succession, providing cover for the moment.

"Fall back!" Eliza screamed as she reloaded her pistols. "Fall back behind the stern when I start shooting." She snapped her second pistol shut, then took a long slow breath. Wellington admired the way calm washed over her face. "Now!"

With Eliza unloading her pistols in the direction of the hostile gunfire, Wellington and Felicity crouched low to the ground and scrambled for the *Delilah*'s stern. Bullets kicked up sand and rock around Eliza, continuing to shuffle back until her pistols were spent. She then turned and bolted for the wreckage, small explosions, usually associated with explosive shells, following in her wake.

"Five gents, armed with what sounds like Rickies," Eliza said, collapsing by Wellington and Felicity. She started fishing out bullets from her belt as she talked. "That's the good news."

"And the bad?" Wellington asked.

"They have the high ground." Her words stopped as holes suddenly appeared in the hull. "From where I saw movement, they're on that dune you were eyeing up." She finished loading the pistol in her grasp, twirled it in her hand, and offered it to Wellington, handle first. "Something tells me, this time, you won't throw it back at me."

He took the weapon, still warm from Eliza's touch. Exquisitely balanced. The *hei hei* design against the ivory was still quite appropriate for Eliza, only lovelier up close. He glanced up. "But I have the Nipper . . ."

She actually rolled her eyes. "I am sure that thing is cute, but in this situation I think my gun is more appropriate."

She had a point.

Then Eliza D. Braun grinned. "Shall we dance?"

Wellington gave a slight nod. "I'll lead."

Leaning out from cover, he caught a glimpse of a shooter high on the dune. He took a shot but merely sent the man's hat into the air. How he hated the crowns of American hats. They were so ridiculously tall!

From his side, Eliza fired, but her aim was more level to the ground. He looked in the direction of the shot just in time to see one man fall while the other ran for cover. Wellington's eyes immediately darted back to his original target. A small section of the dune was slowly rising up. It was just enough of a target to take his shot. This time, from the glimpse of spray reaching into the air, Wellington knew he hadn't missed. Two more shooters popped up from the top of the dune just before Wellington slipped back behind cover.

"One on the ground, one *in* the ground," Eliza said over the rapping of bullets against the hull. "One target down on the dunes, two still remaining."

The archivist dared to get a peek from their hiding place, but chunks of the *Delilah* raining down on him forced him back. "There are more up there. At least seven remain." Wellington watched a man topside attempt to sprint for a flanking position. Wellington's shot was a step faster. "Correction. Six. How many rounds left, Eliza?"

"Five in the belt, and then we're done. Now where the hell is Bill?"

Felicity, who was cowering on the ground, offered no suggestions.

Wellington decided to concentrate on staying alive rather than worrying about the erstwhile agent, but that was when all thought was momentarily obliterated.

The dune looming overhead exploded; sand, dirt, and high grass flying in all directions. Eliza bolted out of their hiding place and drew a bead on the other man she had seen advancing on them. He staggered back, his brow knotted as if he were trying to understand what happened to his compatriots on the dune; then he dropped hard to his knees before surrendering to the ground. Another shell launched from the deck, tearing away at a small ridge of sand. The shot was enough to bring down the rest of the dune on top of what sounded like a trio taking cover behind wreckage and flotsam.

"Found the ship's armoury!" Bill's voice called from the top deck of the *Delilah*.

Wellington looked over to his side to find Felicity in a tight ball next to the hull, her fingers in her ears. He tapped her gently on the shoulder and she gave a start.

"I think we're safe," he offered.

She pulled her hands away. The poor thing was shaking like a leaf. He offered her a spot of help in standing, but suddenly Felicity was wrapping her arms around him. Wellington could now feel her trembling all over, feel her body pressing into his own form with each deep breath.

"Easy there, Miss Lovelace," Wellington said, his hand searching for the right way to console the terrified woman.

"I am reminded why I prefer the library work over fieldwork," she said with a gasp. She was looking up into Wellington's eyes, her own gaze soft, vulnerable, and yet quite alluring. "The quiet."

"Yes, well, umm . . ." He tried patting her back a little harder, but her embrace on him tightened. "All's well that end's well?"

"You were amazing, Mr. Books," she said, her eyes wider, her smile warm and alluring.

"Yes," a voice came from behind him, "a wonder on the battlefield, aren't you?"

He craned his neck to look over to Eliza. Why did she look so upset? She didn't have a traumatised librarian clinging onto her like ivy. Wellington gave Felicity two more quick pats on the back before wrenching free of her.

He stumbled over to where Eliza was removing a satchel from one of the would-be assassins. "Rather lucky, don't you think?"

Eliza opened the bag, rummaging through it. "Luck has

nothing to do with it," she said, looking up at him. "Welly, why would assassins—all of them carrying satchels—come for us at a shipwreck and break into an open shootout?"

Wellington paused, then saw the reasoning there. "They were just as surprised as we were."

"Bring me that other man's bag," Eliza said, returning to the one in her hands. "I have another idea."

As she began pulling out an assortment of items, Wellington went to the second dead man and relieved him of his pack. Inside he found an assortment of heavy glass bottles.

Eliza took a whiff of one of the bottles she had set out before her and recoiled. Shaking her head, she peered into Wellington's bag. "Just what I thought."

"What?"

"These are accelerants. I would have no doubt the men topside are carrying liquids that are volatile in nature. Maybe even high strength acids."

Wellington looked back at the other man and then up at the dune where the sniper had been. Only five of them, but with the right tools, they would make easy work of this site. "Cleaners?"

"No bodies? No wreckage? It would make sense to have them waiting on a word, in case of something like this." She returned her attention to the corpse, and then sat back on her haunches. "Well now," Eliza said, lifting up the dead man's hand and inspecting his ring, "looks like this case just got a touch more interesting."

The shooter, much like his friends, was not a man of means nor privilege. They all wore the trappings of labourers; whether that labour was on the docks or farming fields, it was difficult to conclude. Harder to conclude still was how this man and the other nearby came to wear such fine silver rings, each displaying the same sigil carved in a cut of obsidian. Wellington felt himself shudder slightly at the sight of the raven.

He looked up to the dune still smouldering from Bill's attack. He then turned back to Eliza. "If the House of Usher are involved—"

"One step ahead of you." Eliza relieved Wellington of her pistol before calling out, "Bill! We got to get a move on!"

Both Bill and Felicity appeared from the stern. Bill was

carrying what looked like a pair of small cannons. "Got you a little something to remember me by, Lizzie. Where to now?" he said with a sparkling grin.

"We've identified these boys. They're with the House of Usher."

"Really?" Felicity's hand went to her chest. "Do we need to call the home office for reinforcements?"

"Absolutely not," Eliza said. "We still don't know how they are doing this. We need to find Merle again."

The librarian glanced at her own notes, then back over at the wreckage. "To see if there's anything else he can remember?"

"That"—and then Eliza glanced down to the two dead Usher agents—"and see if he's still alive."

SEVEN

❧

In Which Heroes Are Rediscovered

When Eliza walked into Quagmire's, there was very little sign of their previous night's brawl, save for the absence of tables and chairs. The bartender must have recognised her, considering how quickly he reached for what she could only assume was a shotgun, concealed underneath the bar. The sound of Bill's own rifle hammer being pulled back and locking into a firing position, however, froze the man where he stood.

"Where does Major Brantfield live?" Eliza asked, her eyes boring into the bartender's.

"What makes you think, missy," he seethed, "that I know where a drunk like Mer—"

Eliza grabbed the man by the collar of his shirt and yanked. His face slammed hard into its smooth, worn wood with a crunch.

"Where does Major Brantfield live?" she asked again in exactly the same tone.

"All right," he yelped clasping one hand to his nose. "Let me put this another way . . . fuc—"

Her fingers found his shirt collar, and once again the bartender's face connected with the bar.

"Next time," she said, her voice never faltering, "I won't be so polite."

She heard Bill chuckle as the burly barkeep, struggling to breathe, muttered the whereabouts of Major Merlin Brantfield.

"Thank you," she said sweetly, jerked her head at Bill, and stormed out of Quagmire's.

Wellington had already disengaged the hand brake before Eliza was settled in the passenger seat. They rumbled away from the saloon in a cloud of white steam, Bill on horseback only a few paces behind.

"Went well then, did it?" Wellington asked in a calm tone.

Eliza shot him a look, and pointed to a side track. "Down there." She wasn't about to get into an argument with him about her methods. Bill was in many ways more in tune with her than the archivist.

They passed through low scrub, and bounced along the sand for a few minutes until they saw a shack that looked to be held together by willpower alone. Beyond the dilapidated dwelling, the powerful, grey waves of the Atlantic continued to pound and dig at the wide, sandy shore. She couldn't imagine a more desolate spot, and she had seen a few.

Eliza checked both pistols, glanced at the portable cannon Bill had so sweetly presented her at the *Delilah*, and then reconsidered as she calmly replenished her belt with spare bullets. Throughout she did not look in Wellington's direction. "What have we got, Bill?"

"We each have those shell-lobbers. I got the Peacemakers," Bill said, dismounting his ride, "and I also got this." He slipped free of its holster an impressive rifle. Running along the top of the barrel was a coil, connecting with the microgenerator just above what she could only assume was the receiver. It resembled a Winchester model, but there was no lever action. "Say hello to American ingenuity—the Winchester-Edison 96X. It's a prototype."

"How many shots?"

"Six sixteen-gauge shells." He then motioned with his head to the small coil running above the barrel. "The coil gets out a burst somewhere in the range of two hundred kilovolts to five thousand megavolts."

"Five thousand *mega*volts?!" Wellington exclaimed. "That's a range between stun and incineration!"

Bill shrugged. "Told you it was a prototype."

Eliza smiled slightly, but turned the conversation in the direction she wanted. "And you, Wellington, I take it you still have the Nipper?" She hated that damn thing, but at least he was armed.

He checked his left pocket, then went to his right, and fished out the tiny, bulbous weapon. Bill let out a snort and flipped the safety off the 96X, coaxing a tiny hum that grew higher in pitch with each second.

"Fair enough." Eliza gave a nod. "Stay sharp, everyone."

"Are you sure about the crest?" asked Felicity suddenly.

"You can say, without equivocation, that Usher and I have a past," Wellington returned, his eyes darting between Eliza and Felicity. "I would know that raven's crest at a glance."

"I've never met any of their agents before. This is fantastic!"

"Come again?" Eliza asked.

"This means a *second* correlation is being established between OSM and the Ministry. We already have such an instance, although that mission—Operation: Plutonian Shore—was not a sanctioned partnership such as our present one. It involved an agent of yours, a Mr. Bruce Campbell, if memory serves . . ."

Eliza stared at her, stunned into silence. Was Felicity's head rushing over a cross-reference? She looked over to Bill, who shook his head and shrugged.

Felicity continued to drone, "The Ministry was seeking a bizarre artefact—"

"Agent Lovelace," Eliza bit, her patience for the woman slipping faster than the final grains of sand in an hourglass, "I don't know if you have taken account of the current situation, but what we are about to do demands stealth." She closed in on her, and Felicity leaned back as Eliza drew close enough to smell the touch of perfume on her. "Therefore, with all due respect, shut it!"

Felicity's eyes widened, and she nodded. She bit her bottom lip and then whispered, "My apologies. It's just . . ." And the strange excitement returned to her eyes. "This is a cross-reference in the making. *This is so exciting!*"

Eliza narrowed her gaze on her, contemplated stuffing her into the boot of Wellington's motorcar, but instead made the mental note that librarians were on par with archivists as odd ducks that could work her last nerve to its breaking point.

"We go in quiet, we go in ready," Eliza said.

"Stay close, Felicity," Wellington whispered to her, "and stay low."

Yes, Felicity, Eliza seethed, *you do that.*

She motioned for Bill to flank their position while the three of them crept up to the front porch. With the exception of the ocean, there was no sound, not even the creaking of a rocking chair that sat motionless against the few warped floorboards. Her eyes looked over the sides of the shack. She noted a few bullet holes in the window, but it was impossible to tell if said bullet holes were from earlier today or the previous decade.

Bill peered from around the opposite end of the house, his 96X up and ready, but only for a moment. It slowly came down as he tried to make sense of something he was looking at. Eliza glanced back at Wellington and Felicity before she stepped out into the open.

"Merle?" she dared to call. "Merle, it's Eliza. The girl from the pub."

Another step, and then Eliza saw what was holding Bill's undivided attention.

The dead man was still gripping the Smith & Wesson Schofield but from the splatter of blood on his hand and wrist, he had tried to stop a wound before pulling the trigger, and there was a good chance he didn't manage to do that. Eliza pointed both her pistols forwards as she stepped up to the porch.

"Merle, you okay?"

The response she heard from inside was nothing more than a low gurgle.

"He's alive!" she shouted, holstering her weapons.

Merle was sitting up against the far wall of the shack; a shotgun and two pistols, both more appropriate for history books than battle, were scattered across his lap. He looked exhausted, but Merle's eyes widened with relief and perhaps hope on seeing Eliza. She tried to count the number of holes they had put in him, but there were just too many. A couple in his stomach, she knew that for certain. One in his left shoulder. His right knee was completely mangled.

"Oh dear God, Merle," Eliza said, not sure where it was safe to touch him.

He winced as he pointed with his unscathed arm. "Out," he whispered, the pain in his breath cutting Eliza deep. "Out."

"You want to be outside, on the porch?" she asked. She could tell in his eyes that he hadn't been drinking. He was terrified.

"Out!" he wheezed, pointing again for the doorway.

"Bill!" she called, grabbing underneath his good arm.

Bill slipped in; but on working his arm underneath Merle's injured arm, the old man lurched, letting out a gurgled groan.

"The man's bleeding internally," Wellington said, slipping behind Merle to give Eliza additional support. "Hold his arm steady, and watch the knee."

The three of them hefted Merle and carried him low on the ground. This was when Eliza saw not only the dead man in the doorway but two more opposite Merle. Three against one, and the "Magician of Manassas" had bested them with antiquated firearms. She could see as they carried him that he was in agony, but when he felt the open air in his hair, his features softened.

"Let me take a look at him," Wellington said, removing his coat and bending down.

Merle slapped Wellington's hands away from his shirt and slowly shook his head.

"Major," Bill said quietly, "you got to let us help you."

"I've seen this before in Africa," Wellington said sombrely. "He doesn't want us to."

Merle stared at Wellington knowingly, perhaps recognising another soldier. He then looked over to Eliza and smiled. "Knew—" he whispered, "you'd—come."

"I bet you say that to all the girls." Despite all the horrors she'd seen, her throat tightened. She took his hand. "Merlin, you were right. We found another ship. Something happened to her."

He nodded. "*Delilah*. Know its sound." His eyes rolled in his head, but Merle blinked, took in a painfully deep breath, and snapped his eyes on Eliza. "Curri—tuck. Light. Something—not right."

"Did you see it again? Last night?"

"Saw—something," he wheezed.

"Sir," Wellington spoke softly, "we will look into it. You have our word."

Merle's hand clenched on Eliza's. "Know—you—will."

From behind her, she heard Felicity say, "I couldn't find anything on these men in the way of identification. Except for these." Eliza looked over her shoulder to see Felicity pass on to Bill a silver ring she recognised at a distance.

"Usher boys," Bill said.

Something brushed against Eliza's ankle. She looked back to Merle, now looking down at his good hand. "Heard this name—after—you left."

Eliza looked in his hand. A small piece of paper with a name: Clayton Mercersion.

"Smuggler," he whispered.

"We need to find out who this is," Eliza said, passing the name to Felicity.

"Certainly," she replied.

"Merle, thank you."

Eliza went to take Merle's other hand but she paused. Apparently underneath the slip of paper, there had been a medal. Now in plain sight, it was warm to the touch. How long had he been holding on to that?

"Southern Cross of Honour," Bill said, his voice tight. "Awarded for valour."

"Stay," Merle managed to gasp out.

She took the old man's hand and smiled. "Okay, Merle. Okay."

Wellington and Bill, in tune for that particular moment, both doffed their hats and held them by their sides while Felicity took a seat on the dilapidated stair connected to the porch, her head bowing as she did so. Eliza took Merle's hands, the Southern Cross pressing into their palms, and settled in next to him.

"You're not alone," she whispered to him. "You did what was right, and you're not alone. Rest now."

In silence, they watched the eternal machinations of the

earth, a simple splendour of nature, as the waves rolled and churned against the Carolina shore. Regardless of his time lost in drink and loneliness, today Major Merlin Brantfield would die with honour, and with respect.

EIGHT

❦

In Which an American and God's
Own Are Blinded by the Light

The horse clipped and clopped its way down the beach, the glow from Thomas Edison's gaudy display of light casting their shadow ahead of them. Seeing that monstrosity on the beach in the daylight was an eyesore, but seeing it lit up at night was nothing more than technological posturing. It also cast a strange glare that made stargazing difficult. Once free of it, however, she could then enjoy the Outer Banks nightscape.

Eliza looked down at the horse and suddenly asked, "What's your horse's name?"

"Athena," he said, urging their mount forwards.

"An appreciation for the classics," Eliza said with a chuckle. "You're a man of hidden interests, Bill."

"Don't be lettin' your mind wander now," Bill chided. "Maybe our partners are enjoying a night off, but we are still in the field. Tonight, it's a lot of hard sweat, boredom, and watching your back, since the crew would stick you in the kidneys for a share of loot."

"Last night it was a saloon brawl. Tonight, we're smuggling contraband with outlaws and cutthroats." Eliza cocked her head. "Are you trying to sweep me off my feet or something?"

They both chuckled as Athena continued to trot deeper into the darkness. Now free of Edison's silly display, the night sky opened up before them.

"It's damn beautiful out here," Bill murmured, pressing closer to her. "Mind you, the company helps."

She'd heard that tone of voice from a variety of men on a variety of continents. Out of the corner of her eye, she observed Bill as covertly as she could, and wondered what Wellington would have said had he been with them instead of with Felicity at Edison's lecture.

Yes, Wellington.

Eliza pressed her lips into a hard line. The archivist who had kissed her so thoroughly in the middle of his own shelves, still stubbornly refused to talk to her about what had happened. What's more she was sure that he was actively avoiding being alone with her for that very reason. Wellington Books was many things, but he was most certainly a man of conviction. He had told her in the Archives that he did not want to put her at risk simply by loving her.

No, wait—he never said love. He said he *cared* about her a great deal, and that was hardly the same as being *in love* with someone. Could the kiss have been nothing more than an impulse on his part?

Merely thinking about all this was draining away her good mood, but still she began to plot ways to get Wellington alone and force out of his mouth what was going on in his head. Perhaps he was in the adjoining guest room, but there was not a lock built yet that she couldn't pick. She contemplated with a grim smile the archivist waking up with her atop him, pinning him to the bed, and demanding some explanation of his behaviour. He wouldn't be able to wriggle his way out of that one.

If only she'd brought some of Blackwell's truth serum from the chemistry clankertons. The side effects were supposedly minor.

"Eliza." Bill interrupted her train of thought most effectively by pulling her even closer. Athena had come to a halt.

She spoke over her shoulder, finding herself nuzzled quite comfortably in the crook of Bill's neck. "What's your game, Bill?"

"Look," he urged, pointing forwards, "just ahead."

Against the expanse of stars, gigantic shadows bobbed back and forth along the beach. Men could be heard clambering between the cut-out suspended in the night's sky and the shore. Bill eased her down to the sand, slipped off Athena, and pushed her in the direction of the resort.

"No need to fret," he said. "She knows where to go. And so do we."

They had not walked for more than a few minutes before torches became visible. The calls between ship and shore were discernable now. Eliza felt her blood rush. New Zealand was an island nation, and she knew smugglers when she saw them.

"This place is still a den of pirates." Bill chuckled. "Just like in Blackbeard's day."

Eliza rapped her knuckles against his chest. "So what's the plan?"

Dusting the sand off his clothes he stood up. "Follow my lead." He held out his hand to her. She kept her eyes on him. "Now come on, Lizzie, have a little faith in your Wild Bill."

After a moment's further hesitation, Eliza let him lead her towards the torches and shadows.

They could just make out the pale canvas of the dinghy's balloon when a torch appeared from the dunes. One of the men advancing on them was armed with a rifle. It was too dark for Eliza to tell which one; but in the present setting, any rifle pointing in your direction was a bad rifle. "Who the hell are you?"

It was a reasonable question. The rest of the people loading the boat froze, their gazes on the agents as intent as foxes. Eliza crossed her arms, appearing to shiver in reaction to the cold, warming her hands inside her jacket. Under the lapels, her fingers gripped each of her pistols, just in case they decided to be more like wolves.

Bill threw his hands up in the air and gave a friendly chortle. His broad Texas accent was gone, suddenly transformed into the southern drawl of the Carolinas as he said, "Clayton Mercersion sent us here. Said there was work to be had."

The rifle lowered, but Eliza still kept a hold on her pistols. The rifle was still too high for her liking. "Clayton sent you?"

"Yessir. Told us to hitch our horse by Swan's Retreat then

start walking. Said we'd find you here." When Bill turned to Eliza, his face and posture were softer. He looked meek. "Me 'n' my girl here, we're good workers, never stop. Ain't that right, Mary?"

Eliza stepped up, tightening her grip on herself. She felt herself hunch, and let her eyes hop back and forth along the shoreline. "Yessir," she muttered.

That was all she dared. She *desperately* needed to work on a southern American accent.

The smuggler's face was still concealed in the darkness, but he was taking measure of the two of them. It seemed possible to actually hear the cogs turning in his head.

"So Clayton sent you?" the leader's voice trailed off. "And what's Jack's thinkin' about this, I got to wonder?"

Bill turned to Eliza, and shook his head in such a way only she saw it. She looked down, but refused to let go of her pistols.

"Well, seeing as Jack is still in jail, I don't know. I jus' talked to Clay over at Quagmire's and—"

"Goddammit," he swore, dropping the rifle to his side. Eliza's grasp on her own pistols eased as the smuggler spat and said to the crewman closest to him, "I'm tellin' you, one day Clayton's going to be recruiting a greenhorn outta that pisspot and it'll be the law! You watch!" He shook his head. "Well, climb on in."

"Yes, indeed, sir, yessir," Bill said. "I'm Joshua, and this is my gal, Mary. Clayton said you really needed the help, and I'll be honest, mister, we really need the coin."

"Clayton's got a soft spot for every sob story in these parts," the smuggler grumbled.

They climbed into the small airship alongside three other men and the cargo. A moment later, they were away from the surf and in the air, slipping upwards into the night. The men around her were as silent as rocks, remaining stoic until another shape appeared above them. The larger airship they were positioning themselves under, via controlled venting of the balloon above them, bore no running lights of any kind. Its engines were silent.

When a rope ladder was dropped and the lead smuggler from shore offered it to her, Eliza shared a glance with Bill.

He merely smiled wolfishly. This was indeed a test for a couple of new smugglers.

Bill held the base of the ladder steady as two of the crew started climbing up. Bill motioned with his head for Eliza to climb, and so she did. Halfway up her climb, she looked around her—the endless stars above, the cold and unrelenting Atlantic below.

She was back where she belonged—in the field.

Bill had just pulled himself over the side of the airship as its engines were spinning up with some mechanical protest. A crewman manning the rope ladder handed each of them a long leather coat. It didn't stave off the cold completely, but it helped.

"The other two not coming?" she asked, bunching up the leather duster around her. It was ridiculously large on her petite frame.

"No, they were in charge of securing the cargo for hauling. That"—and Bill looked at her—"and they mentioned something about not being paid enough to board this ship."

"An' here I was worried," Eliza said, her voice trailing into her best approximation of an American drawl, "this was all too much excitement for an old-timer like you."

"Are ya done talkin' in tha' moonlight, greenhorns?" someone barked from above them. Bill and Eliza turned to see a squat man advancing on them. He was not as intimidating as his facial hair. It was a beard thick and wild enough to offer a cosy home for a hedgehog, and in the man's glassy eyes was a madness that insinuated he might welcome the company in his beard. "The name's Silas. This is my operation, so my word is second only to the Lord." He jerked his head up and shouted, "Yes, Father, I'll tell 'em!" He shook his head, as if bothered by the interruption and continued. "Do as you're told, you'll leave with coin. Keep with the jibber-jab and lover's talk, and this will be a very short night for you."

Bill looked around at the threadbare crew, then peered down to see only three men tending to the newly arrived contraband. "Mind if I ask, Captain," he began, seeming to steel himself for something unpleasant, "can your direct line to the All Mighty give us thoughts for tonight's run?"

A wild fury filled Silas' gaze as he babbled wildly, *"I won' be toleratin' blasphemy of any kind on this ship!"* Silas blinked, and then looked up. "Beg ya pardon, Father?" He looked at the two of them, then back up to the sky. "Of course. My mistake." He cleared his throat and then addressed both Bill and Eliza in a calm, reasonable tone. "I do not converse with His Lord, but me pap. Captain Elijah Cornwich. Lost at sea, he was"—and Eliza caught in the ship's gaslight a strange twinkle in the man's eye—"which is why I took to the air." He slapped Bill in his arm, and smiled, a sight that made Eliza flinch on seeing the condition of the captain's few teeth. "Welcome aboard the *Sea Skipper.*"

With that Bill and Eliza ceased to be of much interest to the captain. He disappeared deep into the bowels of the airship, leaving them in the middle of the deck with no orders. From here, Eliza observed the *Sea Skipper* was as far from *Apollo's Chariot* as a donkey was from a racehorse. Gaps in the woodwork—that creaked alarmingly—did not inspire much confidence, and its engines did not purr like a kitten so much as they hacked and sputtered like an elderly cat coughing up a hairball. The bladders high above their heads, though, were the largest she had ever seen for such a small gondola as this. Eliza could only speculate the balloons were compensating for heavier cargo when the *Sea Skipper*'s hold, precarious as it was in its construction, was at full capacity. Whatever this airship's spoils of smuggling were, the profits were clearly not invested into the *Sea Skipper* itself, as the craft was clearly held together by string, fencing wire, and faith. As for its captain—

"Mad as a hatter, that one," Eliza said.

"Aww shit," Bill swore, whipping off his hat and running his fingers through his hair. "*Cornwich.* I read this idiot's file. 'Crazy Captain Cornwich,' folks call him 'round these parts. Washington's got a bounty on his head, but thing is no one can catch him on account—"

"Let me take a wild guess," Eliza stated, watching the captain climb out of the hold, shimmy up the ship's rigging, swing over to the ship's wheel, wet the tip of his finger to check for something in the air, and then bark out a few commands. "Aerial evasions?"

"I got friends in the Air Calvary. They told me about this clown and how many times he should have died." Bill replaced his hat, pinched the bridge of his nose, and whispered, "Maybe this wasn't such a good idea after all . . ."

"Too late now," she hissed back.

"If we make it out of here alive, I'm goin' back to Quagmire's, track down this Clayton Mercersion—"

"About that," she said, placing a finger on his chest.

"That's all Felicity," he said, beaming. "Once we got back to the Retreat, she did what she does best. Clayton Mercersion has been the sole visitor of one Jack Flanders. Flanders' last rabble-rousing involved the mayor's son and landed him in jail for an extended stay. Clayton is Jack's right hand, running the operation in Jack's absence."

"She got all that between Merle's and tonight? Nice work."

She felt a tiny twinge of pain in her temples on admitting that.

"It's all about the details, isn't it?" Bill asked before motioning to the poop deck. "Now it's up to us to keep up appearances lest Crazy Captain Cornwich toss us both into the Atlantic."

Grey plumes belched out from the stern, shrouding parts of the sky from view; and with what Eliza could only describe as a battle cry, Cornwich threw a few levers that shot the *Sea Skipper* forwards while the sudden lurch sent her back into Bill's arms. *I should be shrugging him off,* she thought, but she remained there a moment longer. Bill's smile was warm and unnervingly charming. The man gently pushed her forwards, back on her feet.

Silas handed out goggles to them all, barking up a few times to his dearly departed father, which slowed the process. Eliza considered the protective gear, which was as ramshackle as the airship itself. Over the keening of the wind, he shouted from the bridge, "We're meeting another airship just beyond the breakers. Can't risk landing so we'll be working airship to airship." He then pointed to Eliza, "Greenhorn!" He threw her a pair of binoculars. "You're on watch."

"But," she began, fearing the answer, "we're not running with lights. What about our rendezvous?"

"She'll be running dark as well." Cornwich saluted her. "Ye know what ta look for now!"

As Eliza slipped her goggles on over her face, adjusting them as best she could, she wondered idly if Wellington was worried about her. He was aware of Bill's intention to get the two of them into the smuggling channels of the Outer Banks. Perhaps it would bring them closer to agents of Usher. Wellington knew better than any of them what it meant to challenge them. Would he be worried for her?

She hoped he was. It was nice to have someone to worry about you. It meant that someone cared. For a long minute she tried to imagine the expression on his face if something went wrong tonight or—if the worst unfolded—if she were lost at sea.

Then she thought about Felicity. Would she distract Wellington from important things like worrying about his junior archivist? Would she *console* him in light of his loss? Eliza's hands clenched slowly into fists.

"Eliza," Bill called to her, "what's got you all wound up?"

When he motioned to her fists, Eliza felt her skin, even amidst the cold chill of the altitude, prickle with heat. "Nothing. Just trying to stay warm."

Bill shook his head. "Well, save it," he whispered to her, and gave the nape of her neck a gentle rub. "This could be a long night."

Suddenly she was able to direct her anger in his direction. Bill was the one who had gotten them on this stupid, rickety old airship that could well kill them both. If she wasn't the trusting type she might have thought that he was conspiring with Felicity, to keep her away from Wellington.

On that thought Eliza forcibly unclenched her jaw. Now she was starting to think like a giddy-headed schoolgirl—and that only made her angry at herself.

Yes, it was going to be a long night indeed.

"Look lively, lads!" the captain called as he turned back to the crew. "We are meeting some Frenchies out here tonight, willing to part with some of their fine cognac! Just no lighting any cigarettes until we're back upon God's green earth!"

Eliza looked up at the airbags creaking above their heads then back to Bill. "Do I even need to guess what is in those bladders?"

"Nope," he said, cheerfully, "Hydrogen."

"Well, this really shouldn't come as a surprise, now should it? It is after all cheaper to produce, lighter than air, easier for smugglers to obtain . . ."

"And flammable. I know these old ships have a protective coating, but that really doesn't do much."

For a moment, there was nothing else that could be said, until, "You Americans are so quick to see a glass as half-empty, aren't you?"

He shrugged. "Easy to do when you're flying a bomb several hundred feet over the Atlantic Ocean."

Bill has a point there, she thought, turning her gaze to the port side of the ship. She managed to catch the tail end of a lighthouse's beacon before it disappeared into the darkness. Wellington was, no doubt, back in the hotel, fast asleep after Edison's "stirring" talk on science. Fast asleep, in the *guest* bed.

Alone.

Hopefully.

Across the celestial ocean before her, a patch of darkness caught her eye. There were no stars there, and this shadow was slowly growing in size. She brought her binoculars up to make out any kind of detail. Through the lenses, Eliza caught the faint flicker of deckhand lanterns.

"Contact!" she called. "Off the starboard bow!"

"Thar' she is!" called Silas, pointing to the shadow. "Man the grappling hooks and prepare the aeroplanks."

"All righty then, curtain goin' up," Bill said with a cheery grin.

With Cornwich and his crew focusing their attentions on the approaching airship, Eliza returned to the port side to focus her binoculars back to the shore. When the lighthouse flared to full brightness again, she could see tiny details emerge from the dark, such as the tower's unpainted façade. "So that's the Currituck Light?"

"That it is," Bill said. "Time to see if anything about it strikes our fancy, peculiar, supernatural, or otherwise."

A distant thrumming grew louder and louder in her ears as the incoming airship continued to block more and more of the stars above them. Cornwich and crew were not exhibiting any odd behaviours, their preparations typical for a business transaction from the looks of their firearms.

Her attention returned to the Currituck Light, its fixed white-red flash pattern apparently running on a ninety-second cycle. With the commotion growing around her and the drone of the approaching airship growing louder moment by moment, she was thankful for the binoculars. It gave her a bit of focus.

On entering a third cycle, the signal changed. The beacon was now a quickly pulsating scarlet.

"Bill," she called, sharing her attentiveness between her partner and the glowing ruby suspended off port. "Are American lighthouses supposed to do that?"

Bill's mouth had just popped open to reply, when a solid, single beam of light shot out from the tip of the building, lanced out through the sky between the ships and into the distant dark of the ocean. Shadows quivered and trembled across both ships, the shaft of pure energy heating the air across the deck, throwing some of the crew into a panic and Cornwich into a complete and utter fit.

"What the hell is that?" Bill yelled after Eliza.

"Our job!" she shot back.

On the starboard side of the ship, she followed the curvature of the beam through the binoculars. "It's hitting something out there. I can't make out exactly what, but it's glowing white-hot."

Bill leaned in closer to her. She looked over her shoulder at him, catching whispers of numbers. "That beam, if I'm calculatin' right, is reaching twenty miles. Maybe twenty-five."

She offered Bill the binoculars. "A target buoy, maybe?"

"A bull's-eye from this range?" He lowered the binoculars, his face growing as pale as the beam of light between the ships. "That's mighty intimidatin'."

The ships immediately winked back into darkness. The beam was gone. Eliza snatched back the binoculars and ran back to the port side. The Currituck Light was resuming its normal sequence, but she could just make out in the beacon's glare at least two men moving on a platform beneath the light. Both were motioning towards the two airships.

"Bill," she called calmly over her shoulder, "we got to get out of here now."

He looked down the side of the *Sea Skipper* to the dark, churning void hundreds of feet below them, then back to Eliza. "After you."

NINE

❧

In Which Our Dashing
Archivist and Elegant Librarian
Dabble in the Sciences

The resort's modest theatre had been bulging at the seams with its guests, residents of neighbouring towns, and perhaps the odd scientist or two from nearby cities. The reception afterwards, however, was reserved for guests of the Retreat. That included Felicity and a rather anxious Wellington Thornhill Books.

Tonight's presentation had promised its audience—and Wellington could not help but smile into his teacup at the rather obvious pun—an electrifying evening, and it had been just that. The work that Edison and his employees specialised in brought the future ever closer to the present, and the possibilities of that future were limitless. Edison had stood at the front of the theatre, keeping everyone hanging on his words. He easily commanded attention and demanded respect. The talk painted an incredible picture of appliances in the home reducing arduous chores such as cooking and cleaning to mere minutes out of the day. Public transit systems, even personal motorcars, powered by electricity would whisk people across the frontier in a matter of days. For the grand finale of his seminar, the darkened theatre suddenly burst into a brilliance easily outshining what was the customary warm amber gaslight that had started their evening.

As Wellington joined the theatre in applause, he looked over to Felicity Lovelace who, much to his surprise and delight, wore an exceptional outfit for the evening. She was dressed in modest periwinkle blues accented with white lace. Her gloves seamlessly coordinated with her outfit so much in fact that it was hard to find where her gloves ended and the dress itself began. She returned his look to her, and the smile she was wearing brightened his world as Edison's light display had done only moments before. For a moment the archivist was struck by how breathtaking the librarian appeared.

From Colonials to Americans? Dear God, boy, you really are a man of low standards, chided the ghost of his past.

Even fleeing across the Atlantic, he had not been able to shake his father's voice.

Still, he would not let the hauntings of his father spoil this evening. He had a beautiful, intelligent woman by his side, had just heard one of the greatest minds of science speak, and was currently mingling at an event that he might have only dreamed of attending a week earlier.

"It is a shame there are not more people here," Felicity commented, looking around the room anxiously, "but if it increases our chances in having a brief audience with the man himself, I will not complain."

"Indeed, Miss Lovelace." Wellington smiled. It was a little off-putting that she was echoing his own musings. "But as we are guests of the Retreat, it's a privilege that we're getting this reception."

"It really is fortunate happenstance that Professor Edison was presenting here in the Outer Banks," she said softly, and lifted a glass of champagne from a passing server. After taking a sip, she continued, her voice slightly stronger, attracting a few glances from the other gentlemen. "Seeing as I'm here, vacationing from Richmond, Virginia, where I work as a science teacher."

He nodded, glanced quickly around the two of them, and leaned in to Felicity. "A cover works at optimal efficiency when details are not shared openly." He cleared his throat softly. "Or quite so deliberately."

When he straightened up, the blush in Felicity's cheeks darkened. He raised his glass to her to show there were no hard feelings. It was a mistake easy enough to make.

"I'm sorry, Mr. . . ."

She really was new at this. "McPhearson."

Felicity nodded quickly. "Yes, yes, yes, of course. I should have a better handle on our cover identities, considering how often I handle details for our . . . associates," she said under her breath, chiding herself as she took a sip of her drink. Wellington hoped she was not going to drain the whole glass in short order. He did not want to deal with a tipsy woman again. He'd had quite enough of that working with Eliza.

"Tosh. I too am still learning exactly what is involved in this chosen profession of ours."

"So very modest you are, Mr. McFarley."

"McPhearson."

She rolled her eyes. A rather endearing gesture on her part. "What I mean is, you have so much experience, and I can only imagine what additional stories you could tell. The Ministry only made a few choice cases available to us." Her smile widened as she focused her gaze intently on him. "The things you could teach me."

He took a deep breath and sighed. "Truth be told, I find myself trying to reeducate myself on a great many things."

She tipped her head to one side, and blinked at him. "Such as?"

Now it was Wellington's turn to blush. "I had grown quite comfortable in my life in the Archives. Being here as a full field agent?" He forced a smile as he looked at her. "Not what I expected."

Felicity gave a soft laugh and ran her finger down the stem of her champagne flute. "I suppose that is something else we share in common, Mr. Books." And with that she set down her glass, opened her fan, held it up to her face, then quickly switched it from her right hand to her left hand, angled it lower, and then returned her gaze to his.

"McPhearson."

Felicity shook her head quickly and gave an exasperated

sigh. "Yes, yes, yes . . . of course." And then she turned her attention back to her fan, checking her hand, assuring herself it was in her left hand, and that it was low enough that it didn't conceal all of her face.

"Miss Lovelace—"

"Felicity, Mr."—she took a moment, and then spoke with great satisfaction—"McPhearson. Please. You British are so formal."

He began again. "Felicity, is it too warm in here for you?"

"Whatever do you mean?"

"Well, it is most comfortable here in the parlour, and yet you have your fan out." His brow furrowed. "Were you wanting to retire before meeting Professor Edison?"

"Oh, no! No-no-no-no," she protested, collapsing her fan. She then waved the object in her left hand and smiled brightly. "Just a bit flushed perhaps. I will just go on and carry my fan. In my left hand."

"Very well," Wellington replied. "A bit odd, seeing as you are right-handed."

Felicity tipped her head to one side and picked her glass back up in the other hand. "That may be, but I will be carrying my fan—for the remainder of the evening—in my *left* hand."

"All right then," he said, wondering what was driving her conviction in carrying it in such a particular manner.

Felicity gave an awkward nod, and polished off the champagne remaining in her glass. Her elation appeared to be yielding to frustration.

His mother had never lived long enough to educate him on the complexities of women, and his father had certainly never been bothered with the thoughts or concerns of the fairer sex. As for Eliza, she was as complex as she was alluring. On longer consideration, nothing really came easy when it involved the explosive Eliza D. Braun.

Wellington turned towards a bay window overlooking an elaborate light display illuminating the shore outside. The electric diorama, easily covering the same area as two cricket fields, depicted the iconic United States Capitol building, the White House, the Smithsonian, and an American flag. The coloured lights in the flag flickered to another position, and then flickered to a third position seconds later, cycling back to the original. Running between the buildings was a miniature steam locomotive illuminated by amber, blue, and green lights. Normally, such gaudy displays of splendour Wellington found to be a bit pretentious; but in this instance, basking in the brilliance of technology, he found himself breathless with wonder.

He was startled by the feel of a hand sliding into the crook of his arm. He glanced down to find Felicity nestled up against him. She tapped her fan in her left hand and grinned up at him.

Perhaps hysteria was contagious. There certainly seemed to be a lot of it about.

"For my next trick," came a gravelly voice from behind them, "I will create a timer that will run the animation automatically. That way, I won't have to pay someone to sit out there and work the breakers manually. It will cut down on the display's costs."

Wellington felt Felicity's grip on his arm tighten to painful levels as they turned in unison to meet their host for the evening. Even at fifty-three, Thomas Alva Edison carried himself with upright and stern confidence. Two large men stood behind him. One looked as if he had spent some time training for a bare-knuckles boxing match and the other—now taking a moment to really look at the man—was no man at all. Edison's second attendant was completely mechanical in design, perhaps adding to Edison's confidence no harm would befall him. While both bodyguards were opposites in basic nature, they did have one thing in common: a modest silver badge on their lapels that read PINKERTON NATIONAL DETECTIVE AGENCY.

Edison's gaze seemed to read them both, giving Wellington a moment's pause with Felicity as she was obsessively fiddling with her fan once more. Steeling himself, Wellington swiftly placed his empty glass onto a passing servant's tray and extended his hand.

"Reginald McPhearson, Professor," Wellington began. "Words cannot tell you—"

"Speak up," Edison barked, leaning towards him. "The incessant babble of this room is highly distracting."

"Reginald McPhearson," Wellington said a touch louder. "Words cannot tell you"—he looked around with some embarrassment; now he felt he was sharing his adoration of Edison with the entire parlour—"what a pleasure it is to meet you."

Edison's handshake conveyed quite a bit; his grasp was firm, borderline uncomfortable. He used just enough force to let Wellington know that he was, in fact, the preeminent male in this room, and perhaps within several hundred miles. Over Edison's shoulder, the smartly dressed automaton looked at Wellington, then turned with a hiss of steam and symphony of clicks and whirls to look back over the crowd.

"A man of science, are you?" Edison's eyes twinkled with what might have been amusement. He reached over his shoulder and rapped his knuckle against the automaton. "I see you practically taking apart my Shocker here. Do I perceive correctly, Mr. McPhearson?"

"Strictly a tinker," Wellington said, still speaking far louder for polite conversation. "Nothing on the scale of what you do."

"No, I would not think so," he stated firmly. "If you were, you would be delivering lectures, not listening to them." And he waved dismissively to the crowd behind him as if they were merely flies come to sip his particular brand of honey. Maybe they were.

Wellington gave an awkward nod, noodling through what Edison had just said as best he could. Was that a slight against his pursuits? He could not dismiss a distinct impression that he had just been jabbed in the kidneys while his back was turned.

"IT WAS QUITE THE SEMINAR YOU DELIVERED TONIGHT," Felicity bellowed, scattering Wellington's thoughts and, from the lull in the parlour, all of those attending the reception. "I WAS SO GLAD TO BE PART OF IT ALL."

Edison, completely unfazed by Felicity's powerful volume, raised his eyebrows as he turned to look at her. His expression softened considerably. "A woman interested in the sciences? Now *there's* an invention. An oddity in fact. Like a monkey learning to dance."

She gave a polite laugh—which also sounded far too loud to be proper—and gestured over at Wellington as she shouted, "YES, IT HAS BEEN QUITE THE EVENING FOR MYSELF AND MR. MCFERGINSON."

"McPhearson," Wellington and Edison spoke in unison.

Edison snapped his fingers and a waiter appeared with a tray of goblets. Wellington noted this man quite apt in avoiding the other attendees. When he tasted the drink, he understood why. This was, apparently, the host's personal stock.

"Dear lady, while I do appreciate your consideration, I am not completely deaf," Edison quipped. He then patted her on the arm, much like one would a child if they had just skinned their knee on cobblestones in Hyde Park. "Perhaps if you loosened your corset a touch, it might reinvigorate blood flow to the brain." He then gestured to Wellington. "Also might help you remember the name of this polite, dapper gent what's your escort."

"Yes," Felicity stammered. She appeared to be struggling against her blushing, but it was a totally lost cause. "Seeing as I extended the invitation to him for this evening. Highly forward, I know."

"But so refreshing." His eyes did seem to dip a little more than was appropriate away from her face, towards other, more corseted regions. "Thumbing your nose to convention, tradition, and manners, all in the name of science?"

"And progress," she added.

His polite laughter abruptly ended as he suddenly turned on Wellington. "And her forwardness did not alarm your sensitive British manner at all, Mr. McPhearson?"

Wellington started. What a peculiar question. "I beg your pardon?"

"Well, of course you do," Edison remarked. "You Brits tend to do that a lot."

Wellington cleared his throat, fighting a growing prickle underneath his skin. This was more than just an inspiration, but Edison was a pioneer of science. He was also coming across as a complete pillock. "Perhaps, Professor Edison, you can tell me a bit about this Shocker?" he asked, motioning to the automaton.

"A tiny bit, as I have an arrangement with the Pinks." The flesh-and-bone bodyguard glared over his shoulder at Edison. The look did not go unnoticed. "Is there a problem?"

The mountain of a man looked him over from head to toe. "No, sir."

"Didn't think so." He returned his attention to Wellington

and Felicity. "In exchange for their services while I tour, I designed these Shockers for the agency. An idea I have for robot soldiers. Not that you would know anything about what goes into such a concept."

Wellington lifted his eyebrow. "I might surprise you, Professor."

The inventor scoffed at first, but paused on a second look into Wellington's eyes. "Yes, well," he stammered, "I designed these automatons around the Pink's motto."

"We never sleep," Felicity added.

"Exactly." Edison chuckled, patting her on the head. "A perceptive one, you are. How delightful."

Wellington reached his limit with the man's belittling. "Indeed she is. Perceptive as she is progressive. I, in fact, encourage and welcome a woman's presence in the scientific pursuits. We need more women in the sciences. Wouldn't you agree?"

Edison nodded. "I find it admirable to encourage dreams in others"—and he gave Felicity another condescending pat on her shoulder—"even ones as ridiculously lofty as this little lady dares to nurture. The young are so dreadfully unaware of the nature of the world they live in. Never mind—experience will be their teacher!"

That made Wellington and Felicity both blink. The librarian's tone this time was louder, but more with resolution and a hint of anger. "I was particularly fascinated by the ideas of transportation you believe electricity could lead to."

"Were you now?" The inventor chortled. "And here I thought you would be more impressed with the breakthroughs in housekeeping. I think the ladies will be very excited by some of the inventions coming out of my lab. Less time in the kitchen and more time gossiping."

His next masked insult was apparently to be directed to Wellington, but was cut short as a gentleman dressed smartly in colours of black and brown stepped up to Edison with no interference from the Pinkertons, gently took him by the arm, and muttered something in Edison's ear.

"Come again?" Edison snapped, loosing a rather cold stare on the man.

The man looked over Wellington and Felicity for a moment,

shook his head, and talked into his ear. This time, while his words remained muffled, the man ended his message with the word *Currituck*.

Edison did not look pleased. At all. "Now?" he snapped.

"It cannot wait," the gentleman insisted before slipping a small card into Edison's breast pocket.

As the gentleman gave his card another tap into Edison's pocket, the parlour's soft light gleamed off a silver ring. Wellington brought the drink up to his lips before turning back to the light display outside.

"I must away," Wellington heard Edison grumble. He looked back at the inventor, who now held the card and was glaring at the stranger.

Wellington dismissed Edison's demeanour, and said, "I speak for my companion here when I say the brief time you have given us—"

"Of course it is," he blurted, a curt nod ending his conversation with both of them.

"What a complete bombast!" Felicity snapped. If her sharp words had been uttered loud enough for him to hear, he did not react as he walked through the reception.

"He can afford to be, can't he?" returned the archivist, still watching Edison and his companions acknowledge patrons and supporters as they neared the exit. "Perhaps it is the price of genius."

"Hardly," Felicity muttered, slapping her fan hard into the palm of her hand. "Consider your own creation which got us here. It is quite as good as anything he has done, and yet I don't see you primping as Edison did."

The famous inventor and his second slipped free of view, and that was when Wellington grabbed Felicity by the arm and pulled her out of the flow of chattering bon vivants.

"Excuse me?" Felicity squawked, just before Wellington yanked her down to a far side door. They both narrowly missed careening into a waiter, but Wellington twirled Felicity to one side, giving the servant just enough berth to pivot past them. "Whatever are you—"

"Just follow me!" Wellington hissed as they bobbed and weaved through the bustling kitchen staff.

Slipping through darkened hallways, the two eventually

emerged into the Retreat's lobby, where he pushed Felicity back into the shadows and pressed a finger to his lips. The concierge was absent from his desk and the lobby itself empty, but only for a moment. From the other end of the foyer, he could hear Edison and his second, talking over wide strides across the receiving area.

"We have to . . ." But Wellington's words died away as Felicity was undoing her skirts, stepping out of them. For a moment he was struck dumb. Was he in the presence of the American counterpart of Miss Eliza D. Braun? Then he saw what she was about, and he let out a held-in breath. "You're wearing *trousers* under your skirts?"

"Blue jeans, if you must know," she whispered back. "Bill insisted. He said I needed to be ready for anything out in the field." She gave the form-fitting denim a quick rub and shrugged. "At least they are very comfortable."

Wellington looked at his own evening wear, suddenly feeling completely out of place. The truth was, he was far too overdressed for this abrupt outing. Still, following in Eliza's wake had taught him some flexibility in unexpected situations. "Come along then."

He cast a nervous glance to the lobby desk and then to the parlour. There was no one else in sight. They both remained crouching low, just able to peer from the bottom of the lobby doors' elaborate panes of glass. Through the prism created by the ornate window design, he could make out the two men descending the steps to an awaiting wagon. The Pinkertons were notably absent.

"Fortune favours the bold, yes?" Wellington asked.

"What?" Felicity asked distractedly, trying to keep her ornate hairstyle from coming undone following all their ducking and dodging through the resort.

"Just stay with me," he urged while opening the door to the outside.

The wagon was rumbling away, which was exactly the reason why Edison and his attendant did not notice Wellington and Felicity running down the steps after them. Wellington feared his fitted trousers might split, but they eventually got close enough to catch the disappearing vehicle. Felicity was gasping, and holding her sides, which were fairly well corseted.

The archivist took the hint, and grabbing her around the waist swung her up into the cart. While she slid under a tarp covering the cargo, he heaved himself in after her.

Wellington let out a great sigh of relief as he slipped in under the covers with her. It was more than a little warm and close under here. It could also be an awkward situation. He contemplated how much more so had Eliza been in Felicity's place. He made sure to keep his body as far away from hers as possible. "Well done, Felicity," he whispered.

"Thank you," she replied. "If I had known tonight's evening involved running, I might have done without the corset. I am not making a complaint, mind you, but nevertheless, this series of events you have put into motion begs a question."

"Why are we in the back of a wagon under an oilskin surrounded by—" And he took a moment to examine the barrels and crates at their feet. The words "Mineral Oil" were burned in the side of the barrels while the crates bore Edison's company logo, General Electric.

"Mineral oil probably means we're heading to the Currituck Lighthouse," Felicity stated. She peeked out from under the cover to where Edison sat, and then slid back very close to Wellington. "There was talk that Edison was planning to electrify all the lighthouses along the eastern seaboard." She jerked her head to indicate the General Electric crates. "But he was supposed to be starting this conversion farther north, and still hasn't received permission from the Department of Treasury to get started anyway."

"Suffice to say," Wellington observed drily, "Professor Edison does not always play by the rules."

"And you do?" Felicity stared at him, her mouth pursed. "You still haven't informed me, exactly why are we following Edison?"

"Did you not notice the ring his attendant was wearing?" Wellington said, making no attempt to conceal his growing impatience.

Felicity's expression fell slightly. "Ah . . ."

He took a deep breath, drawing from the earlier sympathy he had for her, and hurriedly added, "His ring carries the crest of the House of Usher."

In the dim light under the covers, he observed her slightly

befuddled look resolve itself into understanding. "Oh." Then she blinked again. "Oh!" The second exclamation was exceptionally loud.

Wellington winced, covered her mouth with his hand, while his own finger quickly came up to his lips. Both their eyes turned upwards, to peer through the tiny gap in the cover. Edison's head never swivelled about at all, his lack of hearing now suddenly a blessing. The Usher agent, though, was another matter entirely; he was looking left and right. He stared into the surrounding shadows for a few minutes, drew from his pipe, and then cracked the whip. Their cart lurched forwards again faster.

When Wellington's hand came away from her mouth, Felicity appeared on the verge of panic.

Two quick chirps and then a long, shrill whistle brought both their attentions back to the Usher agent. His call was answered by one chirp, a long whistle, and two more chirps. Wellington could just make out the head of a bearded gent walking alongside the wagon, and the barrel of the rifle he carried. The men tipped their hats to one another before they rumbled onwards.

He tapped Felicity on the arm gently and motioned with his hand to his foot. Slowly, he used it to lift the tarp a few inches. They could just make out the pale sands of the Carolinas and the dark horizon of the Atlantic. Between them, one lone gunman kept his watch. He became smaller and smaller, until their cart turned a bend and he was out of sight.

Wellington motioned for Felicity to follow his lead as he began to slide closer to the edge of the cart. He had pictured in his mind their egress from their stowaway voyage to be far more graceful than what it truly was.

The archivist managed to turn himself around with minimal disturbance to the tarp above them, but tumbled into the sands, his landing knocking the wind out of him. Felicity didn't fair any better; plopping onto the beach on her backsides. However, the sand managed to cushion, as well as muffle, their fall.

He went to stand and suddenly felt a jabbing pain in his hand. Adjusting his spectacles in the moonlight, Wellington noticed three small pods attached to his hand, two on his index finger and one in the heel. Bringing his hand closer to his face, he could just make out tiny thorns protruding from the seed's wall, pointing in all directions. The thorns weren't deep into his skin, but the ones that were not clinging on to him looked quite sharp.

"Sand spurs," Felicity said, reaching around his hand to carefully pull one of the seeds free from his finger. "Welcome to the Outer Banks," she chortled as she removed sand spur number two.

"How utterly—" Wellington winced when Felicity tugged on the last one in his palm heel. Apparently that had been where his hand had hit the hardest. "—charming."

"You should consider yourself lucky you didn't land on one of the larger bushes." She got her fingernail underneath it and pried it out of Wellington's palm, and the archivist marvelled at how the pod, instead of flying off into the darkness, had lodged itself just enough into Felicity's fingernail to remain there. "The seeds are more of a nuisance than anything. The actual plants are quite nasty."

"I see." Wellington stood, quickly inspected his person, and, finding himself absent of any unwanted beach dwellers, produced his pocket watch. "Right then, thirty minutes to midnight. Highly doubtful we will be meeting anyone else at this hour, apart from henchmen of a secret society, a dogged detective agency that is now employing automatons, and one of the greatest minds of science. Should make for interesting nocturnal company."

As he crept further into the brush, he avoided dark shapes—fully grown sand spur plants. Wellington motioned with a free hand, but Felicity bumped into him anyway. He nearly ended up falling forwards into a rather large sand spur bush but a hard tug from behind wrenched the archivist back. Felicity's hold on his waistband was quite the iron grip, and it was enough for Wellington to right himself. He took in a long, deep, but quiet breath.

A "thank you" nearly left his lips, but Felicity turned the tables on Wellington as she slapped her hand across his mouth. This role reversal made him truly long for his proper partner, and he wondered exactly where she was at the moment.

Perhaps she and Bill had returned from their investigation, and she was enjoying the king bed he had arranged for her.

Hopefully, yes.

Felicity was about to say something when her eyes grew wide. She turned Wellington's head to look to his left where he observed a long fence, and an approaching Shocker stomping along its length. They crouched even lower into the surrounding brush, but their concealment he knew was minimal at best.

Wellington shook free of Felicity and moved silently against the sand and brush, remaining low as he followed the length of the fence. The Shocker shuddered to an awkward halt, and its head made a complete, slow three hundred and sixty-degree turn from where it stood. Once the head locked back into place, the automaton stepped back, then to its right, then forwards, heading back in the direction it came.

Motioning with his hand for her to remain still, Wellington took hold of a sizable piece of driftwood. He tested its heft, equal to that of a solid cricket bat. Jolly good. He had only taken five steps before changing his grip on the driftwood, and then hissing in pain.

Embedded in his palm was one of those damned sand spurs.

He looked up to see the Shocker's head spin on its shoulders to look directly at him. Its eyes switched from amber to red as its arms swivelled back and something inside it began to click louder and faster.

Something flew past Wellington and attached itself on the Shocker's head. The disc, perhaps bigger than a crown, popped and sparked against the automaton, bringing the interior clockwork to a painfully grinding stop.

"Hopefully, we didn't just surrender our position," Felicity whispered, looking around them. "Didn't expect the Locksmith to be that noisy."

"The Locksmith?"

"It uses a low current of electricity and magnetism to manipulate tumblers in combination locks and intricate security measures." She shrugged. "I took a gamble it might short out a Shocker."

"Clever girl, you are," Wellington said appreciatively.

"I have my moments."

Distant voices from further down the fence caused them to both crouch low. He whispered to Felicity. "We should be able to remain hidden if we are careful."

She swallowed hard. "Forgive me, Mr. Books. This is usually Bill's office. I'm not one for engagement—particularly if it involves guns."

Wellington nodded, unsheathing from the small of his back a Remington-Elliot three-barrel. After Eliza's comment at the *Delilah*, he opted for a more practical sidearm. "I can empathise." He checked its gauges, then primed the compressor. "If it comes to that, we will have to do our best, now won't we?"

Felicity looked him over. "Exactly what kind of an archivist are you?"

He glanced at the Remington-Elliot and then back at her. "A rather complicated one."

There was just enough light coming from the keeper's house and Currituck Light itself to allow both he and Felicity to make out Edison, along with two other gents, proceeding down the causeway connecting the shore with the compound.

"For the love of God, speak up, man," Wellington heard Edison snap.

"I said, my superiors at the House of Usher are finding your endless tests beyond tedious."

"You want the thing to work properly, don't you?" he barked back. "I suspect, yes, therefore you will want to make certain the targeting array works. Once we perform this test," he said, checking his pocket watch before looking out towards the ocean, "then *and only then* will we proceed to Phase Two."

"If we had employed the man behind the original idea"— Wellington noted the Usher agent's chest swelling ever so slightly as he continued—"we would be further along, I wager."

Edison heard that slight clearly as he rounded on the man. "Let's be perfectly clear, shall we? The Serbian may believe multiple field tests are an inefficient use of time, but if you want something to be durable and above all *reliable*, you throw everything you have at it to try and break it." Edison began to turn away but placed a finger against the Usher agent's chest. "Question my methods again, and this project ends."

Wellington felt a sharp rap against his shoulder.

"Who is the Serbian?" Felicity whispered in his ear.

"I have a notion," Wellington said, looking along the fence's length, "but I need confirmation. Follow me."

Moving as quietly as possible, Wellington and Felicity crept closer to shore, keeping pace with the two men as they drew nearer to the dark, cylindrical tower casting its light out across the ocean.

"Your philosophies and clever idioms may charm a theatre full of admirers, Professor Edison, but to the House you are simply stalling, attempting to distract us from how truly far behind schedule you are."

Edison stopped, the lighthouse flaring to life as if on cue to illuminate the genius' face, showing its kindly façade seen at the reception completely absent, replaced by a cold, hard scowl.

"Is that what your superiors believe?" Edison's grin lengthened at the sight of a young boy and a large man—another Pinkerton possibly?—approaching from the direction of the shore. A large box, slung over the boy's shoulder, bobbed against his thigh as he walked. "Very well then, Gantry. Allow me to show you exactly how far along we are."

"The buoy is ready, Professor," the boy said.

"Excellent." Edison gestured to the Pinkerton next to him and took from the guard two pair of intricate goggles; one pair he kept for himself and the other he offered to Gantry. They slipped the devices over their heads, adjusting them across their eyes, before turning their gazes towards the horizon.

"Get close, Miss Lovelace. If those are Starlight goggles, we could be found." Wellington took her under his arm, allowing her to nuzzle deeper into his embrace. "So, gentlemen," Wellington muttered to himself as he looked over the Atlantic and then back to Edison and his assembly, "what exactly are you up to?"

Judging from the way the boy was attending to Edison, he was some sort of personal assistant. After a curt nod from the inventor, the boy removed the box from his person and opened it, illuminating himself from the faint luminescence emitting from whatever was held within. From inside the box, the assistant pulled out a small listening device that he hung off his ear.

"Telemetry is running," the boy called to Edison. "The signal from both the light and the buoy are steady."

"Then begin the count in seconds if you please," the inventor replied.

The assistant looked in his opposite hand. Wellington could just make out something like a timepiece cradled in the boy's palm. "Five seconds mark." A few moments later: "Ten seconds mark."

It was a strange little scene, but the archivist was sure that whatever Major Brantfield witnessed was about to happen again. Something, he knew, felt distinctly off.

Then he quickly realised something was off. The lighthouse was no longer signalling.

A low moan, somehow reminding Wellington of the bass line's darkness and texture in Wagner's "Siegfried's Trauermarsch," ran ever so subtly underneath the sound of the beach, but only for a brief time. It grew louder, more dissonant. He could feel it in his chest by the time Wellington heard the boy shouting to Edison, "Forty!" The drone became a soft roar, less musical now. More like that of a steam liner's boiler room.

Wellington and Felicity both fell backwards into the sand as, with a sharp clap of thunder, a brilliant beam of white light erupted from the Currituck Lighthouse. They watched this focused energy cut through the inky darkness. He fumbled up to his knees and tried to see what this unimaginable power struck on the horizon was, but could make out nothing at all. With the curvature of the earth his view was limited to only a few miles.

Edison was staring at his assistant, who was twiddling madly with knobs inside the box. Finally, the young man let out a sound that resembled a squeak. "A solid hit on the buoy, sir."

"Now then, Elias"—Edison, the smugness most apparent in his tone, turned to the Usher gent—"your House was concerned about us being behind schedule?"

Gantry was staring out over the sea. "How far out? Ten? Fifteen?"

"Twenty-five miles," the assistant piped up.

Gantry followed the steady beam overhead, then pointed

out into the horizon as he asked Edison, "Target buoys? I thought you lot had been practising on live targets. Why not tonight?"

Edison shrugged. "I was told our little experiments have been gathering curious onlookers. Tonight, I thought to err on the side of caution and not rely on the reputation of the Graveyard." He clapped Gantry on the back. "Nikola may be a reckless crackpot, but I know talent and potential when I see it. A shame he and I could not reach . . ." His words faded. Then, after a moment's reflection, added," . . . an understanding."

My God, Wellington thought, *the rumours were true. The death ray Tesla had on his drawing board is real.*

And now, Thomas Edison had built it.

"As of tonight, targeting and distance are taken care of. We now proceed to Phase Two." Edison began walking away from the Usher agent and his second. His young assistant was close on his heels. "I packed last night for the *Midnight Runner.* It leaves in just over an hour for Chicago. After my show there, we will proceed to Detroit. I suggest you travel light if you wish to accompany me." He spoke over his shoulder to the boy, "And make sure Ford has things ready for me, lest I make things unpleasant for him."

The assistant nodded, then stopped as he put a hand to his ear. "Professor Edison, the watch sighted two ships about a mile off shore."

"Really?" Edison hesitated. "Pirate ships?"

"No running lights." The boy paused, then nodded. "They looked as if they were lining up for an exchange."

Edison looked at Gantry, then back at his attendant. "Signal the Lantern Room. Let them know we're running an unscheduled test." He turned to the Usher agent and smiled darkly. "Last night, we were able to power up for a second shot in five minutes. Let's see if we can break that record."

Wellington turned to Felicity as they watched them return to the Lightkeeper's House. "Fastest way back to the resort?"

"Towards the beach. Follow it in a southerly direction."

"Excellent. A rather successful night of reconnaissance, Miss Lovelace." The sound of a hammer locking back caused his throat to tighten. "Save for that."

"If you got an Ace in the hole," the gruff voice from behind them began, "I'd be getting rid of it. Right about now."

Wellington sank back. This gave him enough cover, along with the surrounding shadows, to lift up the rock in front of them. It was about the same size as his Remington-Elliot, slightly heavier, though. So long as it was heavy enough to sound like a pistol being thrown into the brush and, of course, the man holding them both at gunpoint wasn't wearing Starlights.

"Very well," Wellington said, turning the gun, handle first, to Felicity. "I am armed, sir, and tossing the gun away." He could see the whites of Felicity's terrified eyes. He furrowed his brow, and shot a glance to his weapon. Her still widening eyes jumped from the Remington-Elliot to his own gaze. He lifted the rock and then motioned with his gaze, once more, to the gun. Finally the American got the hint.

Felicity's eyebrows curled up as she slid her hand up to the gun handle. Once the three-barrelled pistol was steady in her grasp, Wellington heaved the rock to one side where it landed with a loud *fump* against the brush and sand.

"That's real good. Now slowly—"

Perhaps the only sound more out of place than the Currituck Death Ray was Felicity's shrill, sharp scream that, Wellington could only assume, was some sort of battle cry. She sprang from her crouched position, the first shot of the Remington-Elliot ripping through the quiet of the night. Then came the second and third in quick succession. Her scream grew softer and softer as she ran out of air, and Wellington looked up at his partner in the field, watched the smoke trail from the triangle of barrels the Remington-Elliot formed, nodded, and then raised his hands.

"Turn around," Wellington said gently as he came to his feet. "And open your eyes."

Felicity did so, and now both of them faced their captor.

"What the hell was that all about?" the gunman, Wellington recognised as the perimeter lookout they had passed earlier on, asked them.

Felicity let the spent weapon fall at her feet. "Sorry," she whimpered. "I hate guns."

Wellington let out a slight chuckle at that, regretting that

Eliza was missing this. That comment would have most assuredly tickled her funny bone. Wherever she was presently, though, Wellington took great relief that she was far safer than he.

INTERLUDE

❧

Wherein a Duke Has an
Unpleasant Dream

Sussex turned over in his sleep, pulling his pillow tight. He had dreamed of falling into a pit, but then being born aloft by a set of massive dirty wings. Perhaps if he slipped back into Morpheus' embrace quickly enough he could capture the dream again.

Dream? That sharp realisation jerked him awake. He could not recall having gone to sleep at all.

He lay still for a moment trying to shake loose a memory of getting here, into his own bed, but for all his attempts, nothing came to him. Had he had too much wine at the dinner table, and maybe Fenning or even Ivy had helped him to bed?

That was the trouble: he had no recollection of drinking *anything*—not even tea.

With his heart beating fast, Sussex sat up and pushed aside his pillows. His head felt lighter than his body, and he discovered that he dared not risk any further physical exertion. He worked his jaw several times, and found his mouth bone dry. It took several attempts, but he managed to croak out, "Fenning . . . Fenning!"

Nothing happened, and he cursed the ancient ears of his

valet. He should have replaced the doddering fool years ago! Shaking, Sussex managed to gather enough strength to lean out of his bed and yank on the bellpull. However, it took so much out of him that he ended up flopping back on his pillows. His own body was apparently about as reliable as Fenning's. What on earth had happened to him?

His gaze darted around his room, trying to find clues, but whatever had happened to his body had also affected his mind. It was hard to hold on to details, put things together, or make sense of anything. He took a deep breath and practised the exercises that his doctor had taught him. Sussex needed to calm himself, and once he was . . .

Rocking. There was a gentle rocking. And that sound. He was on a train.

The curtains were pulled, and in the semi-darkness all his familiar surroundings looked totally alien and a little threatening. What horrors lurked in his wardrobe or lay upon his chair? The mundane suddenly began to appear dangerous when his body and mind were both failing him.

Just before he could sink totally into paranoia, the bedroom door popped open and Fenning finally appeared. *At last,* he cursed inwardly, *earning his damn wages.* The old valet's wrinkled face was folded into concern, but since that was his usual expression, Sussex never read too much into it.

"Sir?" he asked, leaning over the bed, thus enveloping his master in the choking reek of mothballs. "Oh, it is good to see you awake, sir!" A charming sentiment, to be sure; but Sussex didn't have time to spare calming the old man's nerves. The grogginess was taking its toll, making his body slow in responding to his commands. Sadly, it gave Fenning more chance to twitter on. "The mistress was so concerned for you. Of course, she is presently having dinner with the children, but she was assured that you—"

"Fenning!" Both of them were surprised at the volume of his voice when it finally came out. The old man stood as erect as a soldier. Sussex licked his lips before asking, "What happened to me . . . ? I don't remember anything after leaving the palace. Was that today?"

"Three days ago," his valet replied, but his eyes didn't meet Sussex's. The valet then began to adjust the bedclothes, tucking them in so tight that Sussex doubted in his current condition that he'd be able to move them at all. The old man was usually a veritable chatterbox, and yet now he had put a lock on his tongue.

"Go on, man. What happened?" Sussex snapped, feeling some strength return to at least his jaw. "My last memory was returning to the house in order to leave on holiday with the family."

The valet cleared his throat, shifting from one foot to the other. "You. . ." he finally ground out, "You had . . . a fall, sir."

"Stuff and nonsense!" snapped an unseen, but familiar, voice from behind the butler.

Fenning nearly toppled over as Sussex's doctor pushed his way through the door. The valet scuttled out of the room and shut the door behind him with barely a whisper. It was the first time Sussex had seen him break protocol. Fenning had not asked to be dismissed.

Henry shook his head as soon as he was out of sight, but put his bag on the bed and opened it wide. "While I'm sure your man means well, I don't believe in holding anything back from my patients, so I will tell you the truth. You didn't have a fall, Peter. It was another episode. A rather bad one, I might add."

The news dropped on Sussex like a ton of bricks. As he gasped in horror, his whole world slid away. He imagined the hundreds of awful places it could have happened: at the club, at the train station, while he was entertaining any number of foreign ambassadors . . .

Then the worst thought of all crossed his mind.

"Ivy?" he whispered tersely. Fenning could have been trying to spare him the worst of it. "Is Ivy all right? Did she . . . did she suffer?"

The doctor pressed his hand over the duke's. "Don't panic, Peter. Your family is quite well, and no one is the wiser as to your condition. Everyone was preparing for holiday. You were found in your study. So, now we concentrate on making you well," he said brightly, standing up and pulling out the tray of vials holding familiar serums and solutions, "and I take a rather unexpected trip with the Duke of Sussex and his charming family."

"To what purpose and what end?" Sussex asked his physician dully. "With my turns happening with no warning now, surely your treatments can't offer any hope?"

"Peter!" came the sharp reply. "While there is life there is hope, and you, my dear friend, have plenty of life! Yesterday, for starters, you were most enjoyable company. The memory loss could simply be an unfortunate side effect." He peered into his doctor's bag as he assured his patient. "This is promising. I have been working on a regimen with another patient of mine, and I wondered if that treatment plan would serve your malady."

"Really?" Sussex sat up a little in bed. It had been some time since true hope surged in him. Perhaps an end of this madness was truly in sight?

Henry's smile was blindingly white in the semi-darkness as he held up a small vial. "And this is why, my friend, the medical profession is often referred to as a practise. On occasion, I get something right."

It could have been a trick of the eye, but the murky, purplish liquid seemed to gleam as much as his smile did.

"Such a little thing," Sussex croaked out. "Can it really cure me?"

"Cure? That remains to be seen," Henry said with a shrug. "However, I must warn you: the lapses of memory may become more frequent."

"Oh." And that all-too-familiar spectre of despair slipped its clutches around him again. "I see."

"But," he said, handing Sussex what appeared to be a freshly printed photograph, "once we get you better, you will have less of a need for these."

It was his family. Ivy. His sons, John and George. All of them, smiling with wonder and delight. Arching over them was the support struts of Eiffel's engineering wonder. *More of an eyesore,* he had thought when seeing it under construction years ago. Yet he and his family had paid the Tower a visit, and they had been so happy.

However, he couldn't remember any of what appeared in this photograph to be a lovely day.

"We're in Paris?" he asked, looking around the cabin.

"Yesterday," the doctor said, locking the vial into a hypodermic pistol. "We're just outside of Bruges."

Of course it had to be damned Bruges. Ivy and her fascination with canals were to blame. "The lapses of memory don't seem so bad all of a sudden."

"Your body and mind will adjust." Henry placed a hand on his shoulder. "Don't worry, my friend. You won't be alone."

Sussex returned the lost moment back to the nightstand. "A few more memories lost in exchange for a cure? A fair enough price."

"Very well, but I shall have to restrain you again." The doctor's voice was soft and soothing. He had the gentlest of natures. Far too gentle for his profession really. "As a precaution."

The other doses had not been painless, so if Henry was emphasising restraints, then what was coming had to be truly awful. Still, it could not be as painful as living in this limbo, not knowing when the episodes would hit or which of his loved ones he might hurt.

Sussex nodded and closed his eyes, nuzzling his head deeper into the pillow. He heard Henry secure restraints across his body, felt the softness of wool and linen close around his wrists and ankles. The leather he knew was supple and soft. The highest quality, assuring no marks would be left visible. Henry thought of everything.

"Here we go then," his doctor whispered to him, as if they were setting out on a journey together.

The muzzle of the hypodermic pistol pressed against his skin, and the chill raised gooseflesh along his arm.

There was a sharp *pop*, and Sussex learned immediately that Henry was to be trusted without question. His doctor, his friend, had not lied to him.

The pain was quite blinding.

TEN

❦

Wherein Our Colonial Pepperpot
Discovers an Explosion She Doesn't Like

When the Currituck Light's colour turned once again from a typical white light to a pulsating red, Eliza knew their time was up.

For a heartbeat Eliza felt a cool touch of relief when the deadly beam went wide, easily clearing the *Sea Skipper*. That relief faded as the energy sizzled and hissed clean through the French airship's envelope. Rigging around its bladders sparked and flared violently, but it was the fabric bursting into flame that made the airship sag to port. The bow of the French vessel was now a great spear drawing a bead on *Sea Skipper*'s main deck. After plummeting only a few feet, scaffolding and smaller support masts relented to the sudden stresses just before the command gondola burst into flames.

Bill's eyes widened at the sight of what was now a giant fuse for their own floating bomb. The French airship blew apart again, like a bouquet of late-blooming flowers of red, gold, and yellow; but still a section of hull was coming for them. It would have been impressive and rather pretty had it not been for that uncomfortable fact.

"Hard to starboard!" screamed the captain in a burst of sudden sanity. "Hard to starboard!"

"It's not going to matter," Bill spat as the wheel in his hands locked hard to the right. "We're not fast enough."

The French bow careened into their already-unstable main deck, making their gondola pitch and sway dangerously. Flaming debris now struck the gangway and hull, while loose rigging from the destroyed airship threatened to pierce the balloons overhead. Screams of panicked crewmen filled the air, but what caught Eliza's attention was an absence of barks to spirits in Heaven. "Crazy Captain Cornwich" had gone strangely mute.

A swathe of fire fell from the sky, and Eliza sprinted for Bill, tackling him hard as the *Sea Skipper*'s wheel was blanketed in flame and heat.

He looked back, before tipping the brim of his Stetson to Eliza, still wrapped tight around him. "Much obliged. Nice hit."

Eliza was going to say something about her nation's chosen sport when she caught sight of their mad captain dashing for the cabin underneath their feet.

"We need a word with him," she snapped, drawing her pistols.

Some of the crew were attempting to smother the flames, but Eliza saw others sliding down mooring lines and shimmying down rope ladders. What followed seconds later were cries that might have been terror or bravery, before surrendering to the void and the ocean below. Wellington had explained, for some bizarre reason over a rare lunch together on their journey to America, the science of falls to Eliza at some length. *The lucky ones would die on impact,* she thought grimly as they reached the Captain's Quarters. Drowning on account of countless broken bones was not a death she would have wished on anyone.

Bill stumbled into the door. "He's locked it."

"Don't worry," Eliza said, pulling back the hammers of both pounamu pistols. "I have a key."

Two gunshots and a swift kick later, the door flew open. They both ran into the wide-open transom stern; and on locking eyes with Captain Cornwich, all three of them froze.

The metal monster before them took up most of the cabin, so any luxury usually found in a typical Captain's Quarters was absent. It was a massive capsule, conical shaped, lying horizontally on the floor with bat-like wings welded underneath it and, at its base, four similar wings creating an X pattern. A constant, thick plume of steam seeped from the base's centre where a fuse ran from it to Silas' feet. The captain, himself straddling the fuse cord, was holding a long segment of hemp that disappeared into the ceiling in one hand, and a Verey pistol in the other.

"Well this explains a few things," Bill said, drawing his Peacemakers and eyeing the captain's flare gun. "For one, where the ship's money was going."

"I may be crazy, ya greenhorns, but stupid? Hardly. Learned a thing or two when me pap went down with the ship. The important one bein' don't go down with the ship!" He looked up and shouted, "Yes, Father! I will!" before giving the rope a quick tug. Both Bill and Eliza stumbled at the sudden rush of air that pulled them off balance. Eliza shook her hair free of her face and saw that the far wall of the Captain's Quarters had fallen away to reveal the outside world, the single light of Currituck once more its usual brilliant white warning to seafarers. Veils of flame and heat fell across the opening while glowing embers of the airship drifted around them like burning snowflakes. "Me pap tells me to quit with the blabbering and light the goddamn fuse. For once, we are in agreement!"

The flare from the pistol punched through the floor underneath them, but on the way lit the fuse. Silas threw the spent Verey pistol at the two of them and scrambled for the capsule's opening.

"Oh, this one's a keeper," Bill swore, holstering one of his pistols. "Crazy like a fox, he is!"

Eliza had already holstered her pounamu pistols and, with Bill, climbed up the small access ladder. The hatch had almost closed, but the American agent pulled hard against it, ripping the door free of the captain's grasp.

"Get yer own escape pod!" Silas barked, scrambling for its handle.

"On behalf on the United States Government," Bill pronounced, placing his Peacemaker's muzzle against Silas' forehead. "I hereby commandeer this vehicle!"

The captain's eyebrows drew together—but he wasn't as

mad as all that. He pulled his knees up to his chest and scooted forwards in the pilot's chair as Bill slipped in. Eliza came in last, wedging herself in the small amount of remaining space between the two men.

The fuse was now off the floor and nearing the escape pod's nozzle.

"And on behalf of Her Majesty's government," Eliza said, grabbing the hatch and pulling it down on top of the three of them, "I demand you gents make some bloody room for me!"

Bill was behind her. Silas squirmed between her legs. This was a waking nightmare, and Eliza thought quickly that life in the Archives did occasionally offer a perk or two. On securing the hatch's lock, sealing it from the outside, they sat in complete darkness, save for the solitary porthole in front of Cornwich. Their pod lurched. Something roared overhead, from outside. Her grip tightened on the hatch's wheel lock as it was the only thing for her to hold on to as the *Sea Skipper* listed. Were they falling?

Another explosion snarled, then roared, from behind them. Eliza usually found explosions fun, but having them this close took any enjoyment out of the moment.

The space between her, Silas, and Bill disappeared as their capsule shuddered and rocked. They lurched forwards, slipping through burning timbers and debris, and then dropped into darkness. She felt Bill, herself, and Conwich all rise from their shared seat. They were apparently in some form of rapid descent.

Then came from behind them a strange *pop-pop-pop-pop-pop* followed by a deafening roar, and Eliza found herself pushed back into Bill just as Cornwich pressed hard into her, all breath seeming as if it were being squeezed out of her.

Was that Silus' hand fumbling for her thigh? What was he on about, and did he really want to be risking that right now? She would have thought this was a dangerous enough situation. Eliza went to bat away his groping hand when she felt in the darkness a small lever within reach. Was this what he was after? She wrapped her hand around it and pulled, and their coffin lurched upward, the horizon suddenly coming into view. She no longer felt that sensation of free fall nor was it quick acceleration, but they had levelled out and now the Currituck Light was guiding them to shore.

Everything shuddered around her. Eliza thought of home, of the frequent earthquakes she knew growing up in New Zealand, and she found herself missing those in comparison to the ride she was currently taking in the skies of the Americas.

Provided she lived through this ordeal, she was going to demand Wellington take her to these academic lectures he frequented. Perhaps a bit of science would help her comprehend the madness currently enveloping her.

ELEVEN

❧

Wherein Our Agents of Derring-Do
Find Themselves in Absolutely
Compromising Positions

This whole situation was not ideal, and Wellington was guessing it would probably end in some kind of torture. It was part of the basic training for all agents of the Ministry, and he, of course, knew all too well from previous experience: capture eventually led to torture. Perhaps he should start praying for another explosive rescue by Miss Eliza Braun?

On second thought, maybe not.

"Are you just going to let him lead us away?" Felicity hissed.

What. Did. She. Say? "I—I beg your pardon?"

"There's only one of them. Do something!"

From behind them, the Pinkerton barked, "Quiet."

"I *did* do something," Wellington insisted quietly.

"Well, you're going to have to do better this time, now won't you?" she returned.

What cheek!

"Three shots!" he blurted out, rounding on her. "You had three shots—point-blank—*and you missed?*"

"I told you I don't like guns!" she said, her bottom lip starting to quiver.

"And how exactly was I to know that?"

"You could have asked!"

"I said, quiet!" warned the Pinkerton.

"Really? And exactly how do you bring up such a topic in polite conversation?" Wellington couldn't stop the animated gesticulations as he launched into his hypothetical first meeting with her. "A pleasure to meet you, Miss Lovelace. I say, seeing as I am in America, I should ask, as custom dictates, what your disposition towards firearms is? Pip-pip cheerio!"

Felicity's face twisted into a grimace, her voice wavering and high in pitch as she fought not to burst into tears. "I grew up on a farm. Where it's *quiet*. I don't like loud noises!" Felicity motioned to the lighthouse behind them. "You can imagine how I reacted to that monstrosity! I'm trying to do the best I can. I rarely get out of the library. You must know how that is?"

Wellington stared at her hard and repeated. "Point. Blank."

"I said I was sorry!"

"And I said '*Quiet*,' so you both hush," the gunman growled as he stepped in between them. He looked at them both for a moment, his eyes darting from Wellington to Felicity. The man then eased the hammer of his Samson-Enfield Mark II back to a safety position and turned both barrels—still loaded and potentially dangerous, hammers back or in the safe position, regardless—on Wellington. "Being a bit hard on the little filly there, ain't ya?"

"I am not—" Wellington began, then paused. "Come again?"

He shot a quick glance at Felicity as he heard her mumble loud enough for only Wellington to hear, "I hate it when people refer to me as a horse."

"The lady said she don't like guns. Nothin' wrong with that. Ladies ain't supposed to know how to shoot anyways. And as I see it, if you don't talk to each other before doin' what we do here all secret 'n' stuff, then that's not her fault, now is it?"

Wellington cleared his throat. "Am I to understand that I am being handed out a lesson in manners by you? Quite ironic considering that little affair in Homestead."

The thug actually looked uncomfortable at the mention of

the fatal strikebreaking carried out for Carnegie, or maybe he didn't like being identified as a Pinkerton. "Those were Yankees. Not from around here."

"Same agency, I believe," Wellington said with a wide smile.

He shouldered his rifle. "That's enough. Now apologise to the lady."

"I'm sorry. Did you—"

"You heard me." And the Pinkerton motioned with his rifle to Felicity. "You were ruder than a schoolboy after a pot of baked beans. Say you're sorry."

Wellington turned to look at Felicity, who, still with her hands in the air, was facing him, an expression of patient expectation on her face.

He had been right in one respect. This capture had indeed led to torture.

His mouth opened to begin what he hoped would be a satisfactory, insincere as it may be, apology for his rash berating of Felicity when, over her shoulder, the airships exploded again. Judging from the impressive size and power of the distant explosion, one of the ships must have been carrying flammable cargo. His eyes narrowed, though, at something falling from the aerial carnage. Something small and bright that suddenly shot upwards back towards the night sky.

"Well?" insisted Felicity.

"You heard the lady," the guard pressed.

"I know, but—" Wellington couldn't resist craning his neck as he continued to follow the object as it reached higher and higher in altitude. It stilled for a moment—hovering like a bright mote in the sky. It was an impressive display for an object to fight gravity for so long. The archivist wondered what it could be.

In his peripheral vision he saw Felicity finally drop her hands as she turned to see what had caught Wellington's attention. The object plummeted again, but he observed it was not an uncontrolled descent. Whatever it was began levelling out the closer it got to the water. It was rather pretty, and yet . . .

"Wellington," Felicity spoke over her shoulder, "is that shooting star following a trajectory?"

The archivist frowned slightly as the shooting something began a wild corkscrew pattern now, but its course had not changed. He began running quick calculations in his head.

Now a sound could be discerned—a low rumble, like an angry swarm of bees. Wellington knew this sound. He knew this sound *intimately.* That could only mean—

"That's not a shooting star," said their captor, his rifle wavering slightly in his grip.

Wellington glanced at the Pinkerton, his rifle lowered away from them both, and then turned back to Felicity. He could only take care of one, and when he grabbed her wrist and pulled he hoped it was the right choice.

"Run!" he managed to shout before the shock wave smothered all other sounds.

The roar rattled the archivist down to his bones, but he continued to pull Felicity behind him, stopping only to grab the top rail of the fence. Fuelled by fear, both agents cleared it in a single bound. They landed hard on the causeway just before the missile struck both Carolina earth and the Pinkerton agent equally. The impact blew both he and Felicity in the air as if shoved by a giant's hand. Sand and fire flew all around them, and Wellington's senses were thrown into turmoil as the chaos consumed them.

Somehow, improbably, in all of this he managed to keep hold of Felicity's hand.

Sand filled his mouth. He felt what he could only presume was solid ground, and rolled desperately towards the one thing he was certain was there—Miss Felicity Lovelace. He brought his free arm around her, in the hopes that his body could offer some protection while heat, earth, and a blast of super-heated air raged around them.

Yet his thoughts were not of the American that was so close to him. Would Eliza know what had happened to him? Would she care at all that he had died in a strange missile attack? Who would finish the mission and assure her safe return to England?

Then the roaring subsided to a ringing in his ears. He blinked sand out of his eyes, and discovered that he was covered in a thin film of earth with Miss Lovelace tight in his arms. He gave the agent a gentle shake to see if she was alive. Her body was trembling much in the same manner as at the *Delilah*, earlier this morning.

"This is precisely why I don't like loud noises," she huffed, choking back a sob.

Wellington climbed to his feet, feeling himself over for injuries. He would hurt tomorrow morning—of that, he did not doubt—but nothing had been broken or torn. A blessing, to be sure. The only thing damaged was his suit, which was a tragedy since his chances of getting back to Savile Row anytime soon were small indeed. Still, fashion was the least of their worries at this juncture.

The archivist examined the crash site and saw amidst the burning embers of the fence a large trench that the missile had carved into the ground.

A quick tap on his shoulder tore his gaze away from the disturbed earth. Felicity was watching the keeper's house in the distance where a cart rumbled swiftly back in the direction of Swan's Retreat. Edison had made it clear he was booked on the next train out of the area, so by the time they got back to the lodge, Edison and his associates would be well on their way.

Felicity stepped closer to him, wrapping her arm around his. "Thank you, Wellington," she said right before she kissed him sweetly on the cheek.

He looked into her dark gaze and wanted to assure her that everything was well, but he was not that good of a liar. His first assignment in the field would expose Thomas Edison, one of the world's most renowned scientists, in league with the House of Usher, and name him in the deaths of how many in the sea and the air? This mission was far from how he had imagined it would unfold.

"Wellington, you're bleeding," Felicity said, pulling from her back pocket a clean kerchief. She began to wipe at his neck, but her brow creased. "Just a moment. This—this isn't your blood!"

"No, it isn't," he said, looking at the spot on her. "I believe our captor"—and he swallowed uncomfortably as he continued— "vaporised on impact. I think this is—"

"—some of his vapour that got on you?" Felicity nodded

and swallowed hard. "Well . . . you did warn me things would get rather intense once in the field."

"Yes, I had the luxury of undergoing an orientation of sorts with Miss Braun." Wellington observed her slightly glassy gaze. "If you are thinking of a bath once we get to the resort—"

"Perhaps for a week, you think?"

"I'm afraid that would be too much of a luxury at present—we're already losing ground on Edison." Wellington turned back to the smouldering ditch created by the missile. "Perhaps we should ascertain what created this? Take our mind off things."

She shrugged. "I'll still hope for that prolonged bath, thank you very much."

They followed the length of the trench in silence, reaching the battered metal beast that had expelled itself from the mysterious airship. His inventor's interest stirred as he bent to examine it more closely. The starboard wing was curling upwards while the port one had been lost completely. The stabilisers at its exhaust were intact, although with the amount of damage sustained they would need to be replaced.

"Simplistic design," he said, looking down its length. "The hull is still intact, which is quite the accomplishment considering its velocity on impact."

Felicity's grip tightened on Wellington's arm. "I see we found what's left of that Pinkerton fellow," she grimaced as she motioned to the textured crimson streaks beginning at the nose of the missile and running to the rocket's mid-section, just spilling over the edges of the missile's solitary hatch.

Hatch?

They both jumped backwards at the sound of a hard, dull *ka-thunk* from inside the missile. The hatch's wheel started spinning, slowly at first but picking up speed with each second. Reason dictated that a pilot would be required for the changes in trajectory Wellington had observed. Someone was *inside* this thing.

He looked wildly around the immediate area for anything that would work as a weapon. He went to grab a piece of driftwood, but Felicity batted his hands away from it.

"Sand spurs. Sand spurs. Sand spurs!" she said quickly,

bringing her nose close to the wood. "Right, it's clean," Felicity said, thrusting the piece of wood towards him.

Wellington grabbed it firmly and held it over his head. With a quick nod to Felicity, he crept towards the hatch, just as it burst open with a rush of air. Rather foul smelling air. It proceeded to swing idly on its hinges for a moment, the stillness settling in thick and heavy around them.

Fortunately, not for long.

The first body that spilled out of the rocket was a strange-looking man. Wild hair. Tattered clothes. A leather aviator's cap haphazardly jammed on his head, while a pair of filthy aviator goggles covered his eyes. He took no notice of Wellington or Felicity, even with Wellington standing there armed with a large piece of driftwood. The stranger crawled away from the wreck, flopped on his back, coughed a few times, and then started to laugh.

"Ya can talk all ya like, Father," the man shouted up to the stars, "but I'm alive and yer not!"

"He appears to be praying," muttered Felicity.

Wellington agreed. It didn't seem polite to interrupt the conversation but there were questions that needed answers.

However, before Wellington could query this new arrival, as politely as one could when brandishing a weapon, he heard Felicity yelp from behind him as another body—no, *two* bodies—fell out of the rocket's open hatch. Their coughs were rough as well as dry as they landed on top of each other, and if he were not mistaken there was more than a fair amount of cussing going on between them.

Wellington raised his club a touch higher, but it eased down slightly when he finally recognised the woman holding on to the cowboy. She had her head nuzzled into the crook of his neck, her eyes screwed shut as she coughed, then took in a few deep breaths. Her face was covered in soot, her skin paler than usual but colour was returning. Slowly.

Wellington felt like an idiot. Who else would ride a titanic bullet out of a burning airship but his colleague, Eliza Braun?

Bill was stroking Eliza's arm in a most improper fashion, and Wellington's grip tightened on the smooth wood. Maybe he could get in a few whacks on principle, and pretend he hadn't recognised them immediately.

Felicity's voice at his side gave the game away. "Bill?"

Wellington swallowed down his disappointment. "Eliza?" the archivist asked in what he hoped was a similar tone as the librarian's.

His colleague's eyes popped open, and she sat up like a jack-in-the-box. "Welly? Well, I never!"

"Really?" he quipped, tossing the driftwood aside. He motioned to the rocket behind them, and then back to Bill. "I find that hard to believe."

Eliza removed her own goggles and threw them into the rocket. "A most convenient turn of events, wouldn't you say?"

He had other questions, but they scattered from his mind as if the winds of the Outer Banks were blowing through his brain when the wild man by the rocket shouted to the sky, "Will ya shut up, Father, I am trying ta think!" He looked back at the four of them, then up to the Currituck Light. "The ocean is tha' way." He started walking, muttering, "If'n I go left, tha' be Virginia. If'n I go right, South Carolina . . ."

Wellington turned his attention back to Eliza and Bill, now sitting upright and leaning against one another. "As always, Miss Braun, you do choose the most interesting companions!"

"I try," she said, patting Bill on the arm, dust, sand, and soot flying from where she struck him. "They do seem to find me, though, wherever I am. What are you doing here? Wasn't your evening with Edison tonight?"

"One peculiar turn at a time," Wellington replied somewhat testily. "Why don't you start with how a smuggler's name ends with you ejected out of a burning airship?"

With a sweet smile, Eliza ran her hand along her face, but tensed when she saw something over his shoulder. For a moment Wellington wondered if another assailant was coming up behind him, until he realised that it was Felicity. She was now standing close behind him, her arm wrapping gently around his own, and that had drawn Eliza's attention. It was a look he knew very well—she'd last directed it at one Chandi Culpepper. Wellington's mouth went dry.

"Oh no, I think you should go first," Eliza said, one eyebrow arching slightly. "Something tells me you two have a far more cheerful story to tell than we do."

"Well now, I wouldn't say we *didn't* enjoy ourselves, Lizzie."

Bill chuckled. "Good ol' fashioned deep cover work amongst smugglers, topped with an escape from a flying bomb in a devil's chariot." He jabbed her in the shoulder playfully. "I'm trying to think of the last time I had this much fun in one night."

Eliza looked over at Bill's soot-stained face, his smile shining through it, and broke into laughter, nudging him with the shoulder he had just punched. "You barmy bastard," she chortled.

Wellington suddenly wished he had kept a hold on the piece of wood. "Care to explain?"

"While you and Felicity there were out enjoying an evening of the electrical"—Eliza motioned to where the librarian had wrapped herself around Wellington like a vine—"and, from the looks of it, *physical* sciences, Bill and I followed our lead to Captain Silas Cornwich, his fine air-faring vessel, and his even finer personal escape pod." Eliza waved her hand in the general direction of the rocket.

"Wait." Felicity pointed to shore, her jaw hanging slightly slack as she did so. Wellington could almost see her librarian brain running through her catalogue. "Crazy Captain Cornwich?"

"The very one," Eliza said cheerfully.

Bill grumbled, "And he most definitely lived up to his name."

Eliza, whom Wellington knew had quite the affinity for "eccentrics," did not seem as put off as the American. "Well, in our aerial investigation, we discovered the cause of the unexplained shipwrecks," she said, motioning to the Currituck Light behind them. "Case solved." She was very pleased with herself—the archivist knew her well enough to see that.

"Not quite," Wellington said, shaking his head as he looked up at the lighthouse, now sending out its customary signal. "You have discovered the what, while Miss Lovelace and I have unearthed the who and the where." He looked at Felicity, and then produced his pocket watch. "And we're still missing the why."

Eliza's head tipped towards him. "Come again, Books?" It was most satisfactory to see her a little flummoxed and less sure of herself.

"Thomas Edison built this." The next words were going to

sting, especially for the American agents. "For the House of Usher."

As expected, Bill was on his feet, holding up his hands as if to say, *"That's enough."* He fixed his glare on Wellington, and demanded, "You want to repeat that there, Johnny Shakespeare? One of America's greatest minds cannot be working for the House of Usher!"

"It's true, Bill," Felicity added softly. "I heard him speaking openly with one of their agents. It seems that Tesla isn't the paranoid crackpot we were led to believe."

Wellington turned to look at Felicity at the mention of that particular name. The world contained precious few clankertons who the archivist admired, but that particular gentleman was one of them. "So you knew who the Serbian was that Edison referred to?"

"Took me a moment." Felicity bit her lip and glanced over at Bill, and he gave a nod that had to be some kind of permission since he was the ranking agent in the field. The librarian continued, "Edison contacted OSM a few years ago, insisting we open an investigation into Nikola Tesla. He made claims that his ideas and works were being sabotaged, possibly stolen, by Tesla. He also made assertions that the Serbian was dangerous, so we ran a solid two-year investigation into this man. Was he odd? Yes. Particularly if pigeons were involved. Dangerous?" Felicity shrugged. "Evidence was inconclusive."

Wellington found his temper fading a little; it all made a strange amount of sense. He motioned to the Currituck Light, watching its now-harmless beacon. "Well, evidence has now confirmed that Edison took Tesla's conceptual death ray and brought it to fruition . . ." He paused, tilted his head, and muttered, "And yet he's left it behind. Why would he do such a thing?"

"Edison? And the House of Usher?" Eliza said. "Wellington, you realise what you are implying?"

"He's not *implying* anything! This is a confirmed fact," Felicity snapped. "Unlike you two playing airship pirates, we were *here*. Investigating."

"Really?" she said, finally rising to her feet. "Is that what you were doing in your tight jeans?"

Felicity's mouth popped open, and she stepped back from her. "Are you insinuating—"

"Sweetie," Eliza said with a wide smile that Wellington recognised immediately, "I do not insinuate, imply, or suggest. I am stating what is, in my eyes, a confirmed fact."

"Oh, is that so?" Felicity suddenly lifted up both fists in an awkward Queensbury Rules stance. "And you expect me to just let you get away with your sordid insinuations?"

"Really? Do you imagine this will be a fair fight?" Eliza laughed, brushing the sand away from her palms. "Think again, this is a scrap where the hardest, meanest bitch wins!"

"Are you serious, really—you're going to interrupt an investigation with fisticuffs?" Wellington snapped, stepping between the two women. Felicity was still attempting Queensbury Rules while Eliza was slipping back into a stance that resembled a Muay Thai technique. "You're going to make a spectacle of yourselves, and slow us all down!"

"I dunno," Bill said with a shrug, his interest undoubtedly piqued as he leaned against the rocket. "I could go for a show to round out the evening."

"You're not helping, Wheatley!" Wellington barked. "Now ladies, please!" Felicity and Eliza took further measure of each other, then reluctantly relaxed their challenge. "We know Edison was grabbing a train called the *Midnight Runner* bound for Chicago."

"That's the last train out of Chocowinity," Bill replied, his attention still on the ladies, one eyebrow cocked. "Small town on the Norfolk Southern. He might be catching a ride to Richmond, and from there to Chicago. I could confirm that once I get my hands on a schedule back at the Retreat."

"Fine, but we need the fastest route to Detroit."

"Detroit?" Bill asked. "I thought you said he was headed for Chicago."

"He's giving his presentation there first," Felicity said, her eyes still fixed on Eliza, "then heading to Detroit."

"I suggest we go there instead, pick up his trail once he arrives from Chicago." Wellington glanced at Eliza and Felicity, shook his head, and pushed his spectacles upwards on the bridge of his nose. "What are the chances the two of you could find it in yourselves to—"

"Doubtful," both ladies replied.

Uncanny how both of them could read his mind. "Right then, so much for making peace," he muttered. Wellington pointed at Currituck Lighthouse. "I am going to examine the evidence Edison left behind." Then he simply turned on his heel and started in that direction.

"Whoa, Johnny Shakespeare," called Bill. "You mean to let him give us the slip?"

"The lesser of two evils," Wellington replied. "We could give chase now, perhaps even catch up with Edison, provided we can get word to the Retreat." He then motioned to the brick spire in the distance. "And in doing so, we leave Currituck Light with a fully operational death ray apparatus unattended. Aren't you curious as to why he left this technological triumph of terror behind?"

"Good point," Eliza said, brandishing her pistols. "Lead on, Macduff." She motioned to their American counterparts to follow. Wellington noted that Bill mimicked Eliza by wielding his Peacemakers, his own step quickened in order to match her stride for stride. He might not be a gentleman, but the archivist conceded he didn't shirk his duty.

Wellington pulled his journal from his inside coat pocket and unlocked it in the safe and correct manner. He was pleased with himself that he could remember its combination, distracted as he was by this evening's happenings. If he was very lucky he could make some notes before Eliza detonated something useful.

One could only hope.

INTERLUDE

❧

In Which a Prince Is Observed

Sophia del Morte hated waiting. She hated waiting in travel lounges most off all. They were full of weary and angry travellers, and too many whining children for her liking. She would much rather have been scaling the walls of the British Natural History Museum again than sitting on the hard wooden bench wearing what was quite possibly the world's heaviest cloak. Thankfully, as it was chilly for March, no one noticed her attire tonight. She was just another traveller, either awaiting a departure or arrival at San Francisco's International Aeroport.

Barely repressing a tap of her parasol on the fine marble floor, Sophia's gaze darted up to the large clock on the wall. Just like royalty to be late.

Finally, an American in a porter's uniform strode the length of the station, calling out the latest arrivals. "Airship *Continental* from New York City is making ready to disembark."

Sophia got slowly to her feet, and followed the rest of the small crowd over to the entrance where the travellers would shortly make their appearance. She had her hat pulled down and her collar raised against the chill wind. It also helped keep her disguised for the time being.

Though Sophia had been all over the world, been dined and bedded by many of the aristocrats of Europe, she had never yet met Albert Edward, Prince of Wales, heir to the British Empire.

As the passengers began to disembark and were greeted by their loved ones, Sophia lingered near the back. The prince was travelling incognito, which was a wise choice, but still there was no mistaking him when you knew what you were looking for.

The solid frame of the prince stepped into the light, accompanied by a second shadow in the form of an immaculately styled valet. The way he was looking about him, even up at the skyline of the city, said he'd never been to this place before. Not that it was surprising. Based on the dossier, the heir to the British Empire wasn't allowed to go traipsing around, even if his mother hated him. In his wake were quite a few women of questionable reputations, all of whom could easily serve as incubators for bastard princes.

The little smile tugging at the corner of his mouth was strangely endearing, like a child who was easily delighted. It was odd, though, considering the prince's years and his own personal history. Sophia always studied her targets, and information was easy to find on Bertie. He had a wife he had once loved passionately, a son recently dead, and a reckless thirst for the ladies. It was this vice of His Royal Highness' Sophia would exploit. Avoiding the responsibility of carrying an illegitimate heir, of course.

The assassin watched with an eagle eye as the prince and his valet proceeded down the gangplank. Sophia slid her right hand up to work a tiny crank that extended from her thick cloak a small antenna. The antenna was connected to the complicated apparatus resting against her neck, appearing at a glance as a simple, elegant torc; and as she carried the semblance of a woman bundled against the elements, all she needed for the aural-sensitive device was to face in the correct direction. Like all of the Maestro's devices, it was ingenuity realised.

Sophia was reminded of this as she flipped the cloak's hood up over her head and heard the valet, tinny and distant, but still clear, ask, "Your Royal Highness, is there something wrong?"

"No, Morton, merely admiring the view." The prince

sounded calm and assured, even in this foreign place. "Quite different from England, don't you think?"

"You know my thoughts on America, sir."

Sophia tilted the angle of her cloak as smoothly as she could.

"Oh yes, I am quite aware how common you think this country is, Morton, but please, as we are here for two weeks, do try to keep it concealed from our hosts." They were now only ten feet from her, their words so clear she could hear their breaths in between thoughts.

"Naturally, sir." Morton kept pace with the prince, but made sure to stay a foot behind his left elbow. "However, are you also going to inform them about why you do not have a guard with you?"

Out of the corner of her eyes Sophia observed the prince's very slight wince. "I've told you before, I can't be about my work with thugs and louts hanging over me. It makes it impossible to think."

"Perhaps if you had asked Director Sound he could have found more . . ." His valet pressed his lips together, seemingly searching for the most tactful word. ". . . subtle guardians, Your Highness."

"Tosh, Morton, Sound made arrangements. He must trust these people. Besides, don't you find it apropos that an office dedicated to the unexplainable is charged with safeguarding my life?" Albert chuckled. "What did they call me in that broadsheet the other day?"

The valet's mouth twisted. "I believe it was 'the Spare Parts Prince.'"

Sophia fell in behind a family that was making its way to the exit, giving the impression she was part of their group. Luckily, a wailing child was keeping their pace slow.

Albert had come to a stop beneath the clock. "Ah yes, quite clever what with all the tinkering I like to do, isn't it?"

An employee operating a Portoporter came rumbling up to the two Englishmen, just as an ebony-skinned woman came bustling into the marble foyer. Sophia lowered her eyes towards the wailing child, and began to coo at it so as not to catch the newcomer's attention.

The child stared at Sophia, wide-eyed and hypnotised by

her distractions. Sophia smiled brightly at the toddler before shifting her eyes under the cowl to the ebony-skinned woman bowing slightly before Bertie, holding out her hand. "Your Highness, Agent Martha Harris at your service. I am your OSM liaison for this little visit of yours."

"Awesome, indeed," Bertie replied smoothly. "A jewel plucked from the Nubian shores and brought before me, you are."

Sophia smiled in response to the heavy sigh she heard from Harris. "If believing your own poetry makes you more amicable, so be it. It's my job to protect you, Your Highness." There was a pause. "And for the record, my lineage doesn't come from Nubia."

"Oh," the prince asked, still trying to charm the striking young woman, "and what exotic location does your tribe hail from?"

"Baltimore."

Sophia had studied all known agents of the Office of the Supernatural and Metaphysical before setting foot on American soil, and Martha Harris' name had appeared in many OSM reports displaying valour and ingenuity in the field. She was easily among their best and brightest. At this moment, Agent Harris was immaculately dressed in tailored trousers, matching jacket, and a very alluring white frilled blouse—which stood out brightly against her smooth, dark skin. She also wore a set of odd spectacles, which Sophia recognised as serving some other purpose than correcting vision, as she had a similar pair packed in her own luggage. The lenses were scarlet and wrapped fully around her head, giving her a very dire aspect, despite her beauty.

Martha's eyes drifted out the door. "My superiors wish for me to express that they would have preferred you arriving in either an official capacity or covertly."

Sophia smoothed the creases out of her cloak, still remaining within range as well as inconspicuous. The latter had become more a challenge now that a trained operative had intercepted the prince. Discovery by Agent Harris would simply not do, especially with what Sophia had planned for later.

"Since I am presenting at a clankerton convention I could hardly travel incognito for long," Albert said mildly. "I already know half of these people by sight."

"I can understand that, Your Highness, but also please understand I have hired on a few men to help with your security. Strictly as a precaution." When he raised his eyebrows, she raised one hand. "Don't worry. We won't be too obtrusive." She gestured, and a flotilla of Portoporters wheeled in their direction.

On the gesture, the folds of Harris' jacket billowed, and Sophia clearly saw the handle of a sidearm. A slight antiquated Volcanic Repeater but with recent modifications. She immediately darted her gaze down to her trousers. The left hem billowed out a touch wider than the right. Perhaps a Remington-Elliot, considering the lay and cut of her pants. *She favours the left then,* Sophia also noted.

The assassin wandered to a rack of pamphlets by the exit, her gloved hand idly thumbing through information on the cable car network that San Francisco prided itself upon while she watched Harris escort the prince and his valet to a waiting carriage. Once their carriage pulled away, she disconnected the antenna and torc, pushed back her hood, and strode hastily from the station to secure her own transport and then settled into the carriage seat, pulling the folds of the Maestro's cloak closer around her.

"Since I am presenting at a clankerton convention I could hardly travel incognito for long," he had mentioned to Agent Harris.

"Where to, miss?" the driver asked.

"I'm here for the science and innovation exposition," she stated.

He craned his neck to look Sophia over. "You don't look like a clankerton."

She gave a slight nod before extending her arm. The two razor-disc cogs sank deep into the back of the driver's seat, their sharpened teeth most assuredly poking the man just enough to make their presence known.

"My expertise is in personal security," she stated. "Now then, drive."

A single crack of the whip, and the carriage rumbled into the San Francisco evening. She was not a woman rushed or hurried. She knew to where her target was en route. Sophia was committed to achieving the Maestro's goal satisfactorily and efficiently. The carriage soon pulled to a halt outside the smooth white exterior of the Palace.

Her eyes spotted porters struggling with some very fine luggage brandishing tags from the *Continental*. Agent Harris and her charges had obviously already disembarked. Paying her driver, and leaving him the lethal cogs in the back of his seat as his tip, she stepped free of the carriage before the door-man could serve. For the porter in the lobby tending to her cloak, however, Sophia reluctantly tipped in earnest, charging the young man to take care of it as if it were his own.

Inside, the Palace was all soaring white marble arches, gleaming chandeliers, and gilded decoration. On a placard she read a heartfelt welcome from the hotel staff to the attend-ees of the "Engineering the Future: 1896 and Onward" sym-posium. Open to the public, the event promised to be a full week of seminars, workshops, and—more important to the curious—demonstrations from amateur inventors and profes-sional scientists. Sophia spotted the three new arrivals linger-ing by the front desk. She took a seat on an over-stuffed chair facing away from them. At this range, Sophia no longer needed the Maestro's device. Her natural hearing was sharp enough to overhear their conversation.

"I do love your country," the prince commented to the agent. "All the hopes of the new with the style of the old."

Harris replied, her response careful and calculated. "It isn't all this pretty."

"No place is all pretty, Miss Harris. My own country is rid-dled with ugliness on all sides. As individuals, I believe it is a duty for us to endeavour to make it right and beautiful." Albert's footsteps drew nearer, and Sophia bent her head closer, masking the gesture by rummaging through her open purse, perhaps for powder or a mirror. "I see you are doing your own bit with your service to your country. May I call you Martha?"

Sophia smiled slightly to herself. The Spare Parts Prince did enjoy the ladies.

The agent's reply, when it came, was surprisingly chilly. "You may call me Miss Harris or Agent Harris. As for my service to my country, it is not for my own betterment, nor is it some charge put on me. It is to understand the unknown and protect our shores from it, if necessary."

"Precisely," he returned, "and thus you endeavour to make things right and beautiful." Sophia dared a glance from her chair to the prince. His brow was creased together. "Whatever did you think I meant?"

She eased back into her chair as Harris, her tenor now peppered with embarrassment, said, "I understand there is a reception for the convention currently under way in the Garden Court. Shall we?"

Sophia saw Harris leading the prince into the Palace's Garden Court, a breathtaking display of grandeur consisting of a huge vaulted ceiling made entirely of glass, supporting gilded ironwork, and teardrop chandeliers. She stood slowly, and kept a wide berth between herself and her target, allowing her eyes to surmise the people around her. There were ways of finding a spy's tell, and with an agency as young as OSM, those tells could be quite pronounced.

Concerning tells, Bertie's reaction to the Garden Court was quite surprising. She expected him to be underwhelmed by the attempt at splendour, just as she had been; but he took all of the artistic touches with relish. It must be the way of a clankerton to find the wonder in everything and anything, even the audacious.

Adding to this comical farce of wonder were strains of "God Save the Queen" blaring out from a hidden steam organ. She heard some of the people around the prince joining in the chorus while others showed a bit of cheek and sang the alternative American lyrics, which did make Bertie's cheek ruddy with laughter. From where Sophia stood, shadows seemed to move of their own accord as chandeliers dipped, swayed, and twirled overhead to the laborious beat of the music. It was a ridiculous affectation.

"Not the best tune, is it?" came a familiar voice, heavily buttered with Scottish brogue, making Sophia turn with a start.

"Hamish!" she exclaimed, rising to her feet. "Of course I would find you here."

The smell of machine oil and Macassar oil should have warned her. Lord Hamish McTighe travelled in a veritable cloud of it, merely feeding the image he perpetuated of the quintessential Scottish mad scientist. "Mad McTighe," with his crop of wild, yet still receding at the brow, red hair, his clan tartan displayed both proudly as his jacket and his kilt, grinned broadly at Sophia before making a rather spectacular bow.

"Contessa," he wheezed when he stood up. "Nah' this is a most wonderful surprise."

Sophia smiled. "I am a firm believer in the joy of surprises."

"Well," McTighe said, blushing a red that rivalled his beard, "I can hardly wait to share this one. A very good friend of mine has just arrived for the convention, and I would love ta introduce you."

Smoothly, Sophia cast her eyes over the fine French silk satin dress she wore, knowing full well the white stood out against her olive skin, and made it gleam in contrast. "I am sure any friend of yours, Hamish, will be delightful."

She had not lied when she told McTighe she was a firm believer in the joy of surprises. Sophia had not counted on his presence here. The Scotsman was as erratic as he was brilliant. She had met him at an event that was a far more intimate affair than this event, taking place in a tiny Tuscan village. Under her Contessa guise, she had been there to win over the trust of an ambitious French biologist. Along the way, she also made an impression on this madman.

Now that would serve her well. She took his arm and allowed herself to be led into the Garden Court. Just as she had anticipated, McTighe led her straight over to the OSM agent and the Prince of Wales.

"Albert," McTighe called across the ballroom, "I have someone ya must meet."

Before he could mangle her alias with that vicious accent of his, Sophia introduced herself. "Contessa Fiammetta Fiore," she announced, her full, crimson lips fixing into a smile as she held out her white-gloved hand. "And you are?"

"Albert Edward Saxe-Coburg-Gotha. People call me the Prince of Wales, but you can call me Bertie"—and Sophia feigned a mock gasp of surprise as he kissed her hand and added—"provided you call upon me."

With the exception of Agent Harris, they all burst into laughter. Sophia placed a hand on her chest and caught her breath. "Oh, I feel so silly not showing honourable deference."

"Worry not, madame," Albert said, "in the eyes of St. Patrick, we are all humble engineers."

McTighe gave a gruff laugh. "Bertie and I have enjoyed a few of these soirées together, I canna tell you!"

Between McTighe's dark chuckle and Bertie's blushing, the evening was promising to yield many stories, possibly around many drinks. That would have been the direction of things had redoubtable Miss Harris not stepped in. "Unfortunately, Your Highness, there is an urgent message from home waiting for your attention in your suite. From your *wife*."

Really, the American knew just how to kill a mood, and Sophia was becoming more and more unhappy with her presence.

Bertie broke the sudden silence between them with a bit of nervous laughter. Through a tight smile, the prince asked, "Miss Harris, exactly what do you think you are doing?"

"My job, Your Highness," she replied pointedly, her gaze fixing on Sophia.

The assassin did not return the glare, lest she engage in a staring competition with the American. After all, she wouldn't be much of a lady if she did. However, she did take note of the woman's opening tactic. Sophia wanted to know this adversary's tell, and she was getting her wish.

McTighe cleared his throat before making a rather spectacular bow to the agent, and then followed it up with a, "If you don' min' me sayin', you are a bonnie lass to be guarding this old fool."

"Now, now, McTighe, don't attempt to turn the lady's head," the prince said cheerily, looking between the women. "She'll get quite the wrong idea about you."

"Gotcha eye on her yourself?" McTighe whispered none too quietly to him. "Can't say I blame you there . . ."

Albert winced, as if he would rather not be having this conversation. With a gentle shake of his head, he implored, "My dear friend, when are you going to learn at least some of the social delicacies? Not all of them, mind you, but just a spattering?"

McTighe shrugged and grinned. "I got thro' fifty-eight years without 'em. Why bother now?"

Sophia chuckled at his rather poor joke as if it were the most amusing thing she'd heard in months.

Once again, Agent Harris interjected, "Watching His Royal Highness is my duty, Lord McTighe, and I made a promise to fulfill my duty to the letter." Her eyes returned to Sophia. "No exceptions."

"Your guard is most"—Sophia paused to lick her lips—"enthusiastic."

The prince shrugged. "I fear you are right, and that the only way to calm her is to do as I am told." He smiled wickedly, seemingly ignoring his own advice. "As if I am a very naughty schoolboy."

Sophia knew she was walking a fine line between McTighe and the prince, but she dared an askance look. "Perhaps that is what she likes."

Both men nearly choked on her wickedness.

Harris went to retort, but this time Sophia spoke first. "The pleasure has been all mine." She paused, then smiled wide, making the prince gasp as she said, "Bertie." She tapped her hand just briefly on the prince's arm, earning a flinch out of Harris. "We shall leave you to your amazon. Another time, I hope, we may enjoy one another's company under less chaperoned conditions?"

McTighe, taking his cue, led her deeper into the Garden Court, with the prince falling behind her.

Sophia's smile was content as they went. She knew one thing about such men as the Prince of Wales: they always wanted what they couldn't have. Such dangerous passions could also be used to lead them as if there was a ring in their nose.

She felt within the next few days she would have exactly what the Maestro wanted. That would make putting up with Lord Hamish McTighe almost bearable.

TWELVE

❦

Wherein Our Intrepid Heroes
Ascend a Spiral of Madness

Eliza tried the door, and found it surprisingly unlocked. Perhaps someone up above—be it Heaven itself or just the chap manning the top of Currituck—was trying to make up for her rather marginal evening. She took a deep breath, and pushed it open slowly. Beyond was the interior of the lighthouse, lit by a series of incandescent lightbulbs. Once through a stone archway, they all stopped just before a circular alcove, a spiral staircase winding its way up to the summit of Currituck Light, its flash only visible through the cracks of the access hatch.

"This ain't good," Bill muttered softly behind her. His grasp of the blindingly obvious was still intact, and just as annoying as it had been on the *Sea Skipper*.

"Oh, come along, Bill, where's your sense of adventure?" Eliza asked brightly. "Entering a potentially hostile environment with no intelligence whatsoever pertaining to who could be here? What could be better than this?"

"Yeah," Bill breathed nearly in her ear while matching her step for step, "what could possibly go wrong?"

"We know at least one person is up there," Wellington whispered. "Edison's assistant was receiving data from Curri-tuck. Best-case scenario: there's a difference engine up there, sending out a simple, rudimentary signal the assistant was reading."

Felicity asked, "Worst case?"

Wellington looked at Eliza. "Don't worry," she replied. "I have plenty of bullets to go round."

"The longer we stand here," Bill grumbled, "the worse it gets."

He had a point. Many times while on assignment Eliza had been in similar situations, and she had discovered there was a certain point where waiting began to eat at confidence: ears began to hear things that weren't really there, and nerves began to fray. She took the lead, but paused after taking only four steps. It was bloody nigh impossible for anyone to climb these stairs silently. The sounds of their footsteps on the iron staircase reverberated throughout the brick spire. If there was someone up there, they were practically announcing their ascent through.

On reaching the first landing, "This lighthouse," Felicity whispered, "is quite tall, isn't it?"

"Just keep climbing," Eliza returned, continuing up the next flight.

At the top of the stairs, all four of them trying desperately to catch their breaths quietly, they reached the Watch Room. It was crowded with all the trappings of lighthouse keeping, but also, and far more importantly, the bottom half of the clockwork that kept the light turning. It was still working, and the whirring of its cogs and gears was somewhat soothing.

Eliza turned to Wellington and Felicity. "You two, stay back. We don't know how many are out there." She then looked to Bill. "What do you think? In, or out?"

Bill's eyes considered the door leading to the Watch Room, and then looked over the heavy hatch that led to the Gallery.

"Out."

"In for a penny, in for a pound," Eliza muttered, holstering her pistols. Gripping the handle, she disengaged its lock and pulled. Obviously the light keeper had not been so careful in his maintenance of Currituck's details as the door's hinges let out a scream like a terrified cow, a scream that echoed throughout the tower.

Yes indeed, stealth was no longer an option. "Taking the left," Eliza said, bringing out her pistols.

"Goin' right," he replied from behind her.

Eliza crept around the barrel of the lighthouse in a low crouch. She had only travelled a few feet before she saw the figure ahead of her, dressed in black. The man was not looking in her direction. Instead, he was leaning over the railing, looking down. *That would not do,* Eliza thought. They had many questions to pose.

Still, she and Bill were moving in on him like pincers of a crab. Now there was no other escape, but that was the worry.

Just as she was deciding how best to work this, she heard her OSM counterpart speak from the other side of the stranger. "Easy, partner. It don't have to end this way."

Darkness swallowed the man whole, but there was just enough light for Eliza to see the movement of shadows in front of her. When the intermittent light returned and pierced the darkness, Eliza felt her chest seize up when she saw the man's leg clear the Gallery. He was leaning out over the abyss; only his arms wound into the iron railing kept him from slipping off into the night.

"You won't stop the House," the man warned, and his voice cracked on that assertion.

"Look," Bill spoke gently, "I'm unarmed, see? How 'bout we jus' talk, okay?"

"Do you really think talking will make things better?" he replied, his eyes flicking up to the stars as if they had some answers to offer.

Eliza took a few hesitant steps forwards. Between the fall underneath him and Bill on the other side of the deck, she remained unseen to the Usher agent. She had seen plenty of people driven to the edge of terror before. So long as Bill kept calm and kept him talking, it meant time. Time for people to consider their actions.

"It could," Bill insisted. "Come on—is the House of Usher worth throwing away your life like this?"

"You think I'm going to let go?" The man started laughing

in a deeply unsettling fashion. "That *would* be insane. No, this is my insurance. If you do not do as I say, I let go. Then, we all die."

"We all die?" Bill asked.

The light came up again, and Eliza got a better look at the young, bearded man. What she had first thought was terror causing the henchman's voice to waver now appeared to be conviction. Conviction of a fanatic.

If needed, Eliza knew she could catch the henchman's forearm or bicep before he took that lethal fall. He had interlocked his arms with the railing, and clearly showed no intention of letting go.

Her eyes narrowed on one of the Usher man's wrists—there was something odd about it.

"I know you don't want to die," the American agent said, "and while this may sound odd coming from this side of the railing, I can assure you that I do not want you to die either." Eliza heard the soft sound of a boot heel against the iron platform, marking Bill's cautious approach. A gust of wind ripped through Eliza's leather duster as if it were not there. She could also hear the flapping of the Usher henchman's long coat and even Bill's duster.

When the gust subsided, the Usher man continued, "You leave. Your compatriots leave. We all live. One more step, and I take us all."

"Not sure if I can do that, partner," Bill replied in a conversational tone.

Currituck's light grew brighter again, and a thin steel band wrapped around the henchman's right wrist gleamed for only a moment. Eliza also caught a glimpse of wires running underneath the man's shirt cuff. Eliza leapt, grabbing the man's forearm in a vice-like grip. Bill was not far behind her.

"I had this under control," Bill grunted, struggling with the Usher thug who was now attempting to wriggle free of his coat.

Eliza thought a little pepper was needed on Bill's attempts to keep the man still. "He's wearing a dead man's switch. He's either dropping, or trying to disconnect the leads."

The American agent immediately changed his grasp on the Usher man. Eliza tightened her own grip, but with the thug's feet dangling in open space, gravity refused to be ignored. She felt the railing of the lighthouse Gallery press harder into her chest as the man kicked and squirmed.

"Goddamn it, Bill, pull him up or we die!" she shouted.

Apparently that was the just the inspiration he needed. Both agents heaved, and the man bounced hard into the railing. Eliza thrust her head forwards to plant a Glasgow kiss between the Usher agent's eyes. She got a bit of a nasty shock in return, but the blow was hard enough to stun the man. Feeling him slacken, Bill and Eliza readjusted their grip and pulled him over the railing.

"Nice move," Bill grunted. "You're quite the lady!"

"Shut up and get him on the landing," she growled through clenched teeth.

The Usher agent suddenly became lighter, easier to manage, and Eliza felt another pressing against her. With the help of a newcomer, the limp body cleared the railing and fell against the iron landing. The henchman lay groaning against the light tower, bleeding from where Eliza's forehead had connected with his nose. She turned to see Wellington standing over the thug, his hands on his hips, examining their prisoner as if he were a prize fish he'd just helped land.

"Any idea as to who this rather enigmatic gent is?" her partner asked.

"He," Eliza said, ripping the man's shirt open, "is one highly dedicated git."

The small box strapped against the centre of his torso continued to tick merrily into the darkness and Wellington gaped at it with a pale face and wide eyes. Eliza bent down and pulled the thug's right sleeve back to reveal the steel band and set of wires she had seen in a flash. It was the House of Usher's sophistication that always unnerved and alarmed her. Their shadowy rival appeared to have unlimited resources, and technology paralleling the Ministry's own. She knew these kill switches intimately. She and Harry had worn them when running highly sensitive documents from city to city, country to country. This was uncommon technology, or so Blackwell and Axelrod had told her.

"Wellington!" an all too familiar voice called from inside the lighthouse.

Eliza pursed her lips. She'd been rather enjoying some quality time with her partner, and didn't appreciate Felicity's interruption.

"Once we heard the struggle, Agent Lovelace and I dared access to the Watch Room," Wellington said, adjusting his besmirched cravat. "You should come have a look at the inner workings of this light."

Eliza turned to Bill, who waved his hand dismissively. "Don't you worry your pretty little head. I'll keep an eye on our friend here, make sure he don't go nowhere."

Another wave of light swept across their balcony scene and that was when her eye caught something tucked into one of the kill switch's chest straps. With a frown, she peeled back the strap and found what appeared to be a key.

"Curiouser and curiouser," she said. The key had no markings, and didn't look a regular size. So rather than show it to her partner, she tucked it into her waistband. "Come along, Wellington. Let's go look at the pretty clockwork of Currituck."

Eliza followed Wellington inside the cramped cylindrical chamber housing the magnificent clockwork running the Fresnel lens. *Feels as though we are trapped inside a glass grandfather clock,* Eliza mused. She pulled apart the top two buttons of her shirt, since the temperature here was actually warm, almost stifling. She didn't need to look to know that Wellington was more fascinated by the clockwork than her own external workings. That irritated her more than she could express at present.

"Over here," Felicity said, her eyes not leaving the light's clockwork arrangement. At least, for once, she was not ogling Wellington.

They walked around Currituck's huge movement together, coming to an abrupt halt on seeing what prompted Felicity's earlier cry. Six sticks of dynamite were strapped in among the clockwork, the multitude of fuses leading back to a small metallic box that ticked and blinked in time with a rhythm similar to a heartbeat.

"Now there's a design I can respect," Eliza said with a smile, though her heart began to race just a little.

"Miss Braun," Wellington hissed, "have a care."

"Oh, give over, Welly. You have your Archives where you

rule, but this? This is *my* element." She bent over to examine what they were up against. The kill switch relay she identified earlier, if she were lucky, would be the most complex component of this bomb. "What I need is—" Eliza looked over to Felicity and said, "Do you happen to have one of those fancy half dollars on you?"

Felicity patted about all over her tight jeans, before finding and handing over a single coin. It was amazing she could fit anything in the pockets at all.

The coin easily served as a makeshift screwdriver, and within moments Eliza had removed the cover of the relay, revealing an even more wild array of lights, gears, and wires. She carefully ran her fingers along the wires leading from stick to relay. The tiniest pinprick of sweat began to build on her neck as she gently gnawed on her bottom lip, each *tick-tick-tick* testing her patience. Then finally Eliza muttered, "There you are."

"There what is, Eliza?" Wellington asked, leaning forwards—curiosity getting the better of him despite the situation, despite his constant fussing.

She smiled slightly. For the first time on this mission, she held Welly's undivided attention.

"That," she said, pointing to a small brass box lodged behind two slow moving cogs, "is the cypher to the puzzle."

Eliza tucked her thumb underneath the silver dollar, sent it skyward, and then caught it on its fall. She slipped it underneath the small metal box connecting all the sticks of dynamite to the relay. The box's internal metronome continued to tick, but now the coin vibrated in time with the ticking.

Wellington beamed. "Fantastic."

"What?" Felicity asked—completely out of her depth in this situation—and glancing at Wellington and Eliza for clarification.

It really was most satisfactory to have all of his attention in this way. "The kill switch works on the principle that a second signal must continuously send a sequence that keeps the fuses dormant. Without that second signal, boom." She then turned to Felicity. "I've created with that half dollar a false signal. When the relay attempts to detonate the bomb, the coin disrupts the sequence, resets the timer, and the sequence begins anew."

Felicity looked back and forth between the two of them, but stopped on Eliza with a decided glare. "You did what?"

"I gave the bomb a bad case of the hiccups." Eliza motioned to Wellington. "So have a look at your clockwork, Welly." She then began to remove the fuses from each stick. "Take all the time you need."

Her victory over the librarian, she discovered, would be a short-lived one since Felicity nuzzled in closer to Wellington as they studied these modified inner workings of the Curri-tuck Light.

"This is all rather ingenious," Wellington said as he flicked open his journal and began to sketch. "The targeting works with the timing of the lighthouse itself, and the beam powers up from this source."

Felicity narrowed her eyes on the generator. "A rather small generator to carry such output, don't you think?"

Eliza seethed quietly as she stepped away from the clock-work engine, giving Wellington and Felicity more room, but neither one taking it. *Of course he knows it's a small genera-tor. I'm sure Wellington is smart enough to deduce how Edi-son was able to focus more power for the beam.*

"Well, yes, but do you not see these additional optics? I believe that assists in creating a more narrowed, focused out-put," he said, motioning to a configuration of two large glass lenses mounted on arms, lowered to the right and left of the main clockwork chassis. He continued to scribble notations and draw rough sketches of the device as he added, "I'm cer-tain this is the death ray's targeting system."

See? Eliza thought proudly. *I knew Wellington would have the answer.*

"There is something in this array," he whispered, gestur-ing to the extra lenses, "that is completely different than what one would find in a typical design of Edison's." He pressed his lips together, and stared off into space in a rather charm-ing gesture. "Good Lord, what's the word I'm looking for?"

Felicity considered both the targeting time and power source. Then, on looking at the lenses again, she stated, "Economical."

He looked down at her, and Eliza was alarmed at how his eyes sparkled at the librarian. "Brilliant. Yes, that is exactly the word. Economical."

When the archivist returned his attention back to his sketching, Eliza snapped a look over at Felicity. The American was smiling far too appreciatively at Wellington, before happening to catch Eliza's eyes. She crooked an eyebrow ever so slightly at her just before she returned her attention to Wellington and the death ray.

That little strumpet, Eliza raged inwardly, *she's playing Wellington like a Stradivarius!* If not for being in this peculiar situation, Eliza would demand the American's guts for her finest garters.

"Most of Edison's designs are quite complicated, both inside and out," Felicity continued. "This, you can tell, is so wonderfully simple."

"At least on the outside," Wellington added. "If this is truly one of Tesla's designs, it could be a rather complicated enigma on the inside."

Amazing no one was pointing out the obvious. "And Edison wanted to blow it up?" Eliza asked.

Wellington and Felicity looked at one another, back to Eliza, and then to Edison's invention. "Well put, Eliza," her partner answered.

Eliza happened to catch Felicity's gaze. She made sure the smile on her face was not too proud, but definitely self-assured.

"It's a prototype," Wellington said. "Build it to see if it works in the first place. Test it. And then . . ."

Felicity finished the thought. "Rebuild it. With improvements."

Sinking down to the floor to get another perspective on the device, Eliza looked at the array's housing, then at the device's base. "Any idea if we can help ourselves to this prototype so we can understand what we're dealing with?"

Wellington looked back at Eliza for a moment, then pushed his spectacles up higher on his nose as he leaned closer to the moving mechanisms. "It would make sense that the device would be portable. This was built, after all, as an addition to what was already here."

Eliza's hand immediately went to the waistband of her trousers as she remembered what she had found on the henchman. "Wellington, I found this key . . ." She ducked under the low-hanging lens and ran a hand along the pedestal underneath the machine. Her fingertips slipped over a crack in the base. "Here's where it splits."

"So we need to find a keyhole?"

"Exactly." She looked on either side of the optics' base. "It doesn't appear to be here."

Felicity tapped Eliza on the shoulder and pointed to a small indention by Eliza's left foot. "What about there?"

Eliza looked at the key, then back at what appeared to be a matching keyhole. She fixed her grip on the key, slipped it into the slot, and turned. The sounds that softly echoed all around them suggested some kind of large and intricate pulley-lock system built within the lighthouse. A loud hiss emanated from beneath them, and the agents scampered back as the base slid away, parting in two. With a slight clang, it stopped, and then retracted into another segment that widened the part in the pedestal. This pattern repeated twice more, leaving the death ray optics and targeting system mounted on what looked like a reinforced crescent-shaped base. With the pedestal open before all of them, they could see a metal column, no more than two feet in height, perhaps a foot thick, decorated with tiny valves, pipes, and gauges.

This was Wellington's domain, but Eliza had some experience with mechanics. She could easily read not only boiler pressure on the gauges, but could make out there were also stored volts and amperage displayed, as well as firing solution and estimated range. Mounted on top of this pillar was the firing mechanism. She had rather a lot of experience with firing mechanisms.

Another loud groan and the floor beneath the targeting device opened. Slowly, the lighthouse mod began a slow descent on pulleys towards the base of Currituck Light.

"And now we know how they intended to transport it," Eliza said, watching it lower to the ground. "Shall we see if Bill's found out anything new?"

With a final look at the progress of Edison's creation, Eliza led them back to where Bill had remained. He looked cold, but still not as miserable as the Usher henchman, who had his hands now bound behind him. A gust of wind attempted to claim Bill's Stetson and send it off into the darkness; but the quick gust only toyed with the flaps of his duster.

"I got to admit," he said on seeing the three of them, "Cornwich's crew jackets are pretty good at keeping the wind off you."

"How's our guest here?"

"This cuss really hasn't been good company," Bill said, giving him a nudge with his boot. "Not pleasant company at all. Got quite the mouth on him."

Eliza's gaze narrowed on the prisoner. "Why don't we all go back to the resort together then? Maybe a nice warm fire and some time alone with me will make him more social."

"Do take care, Eliza," Wellington said, pinching the bridge of his nose, "we need him to be able to tell us as much as he can about the weapon. If his jaw is broken that might prove difficult."

Even with as dark as it was, Eliza could see the hench-man's face grow paler. "You have the death ray?" he asked.

"Not the optics, sadly. Those are built into the proper mech-anisms of the lighthouse." Wellington motioned back to the Watch Room. "At least with the targeting array confiscated, you shouldn't be able to fire it again."

"I'm certain the residents of the Outer Banks will be pleased with that," Eliza said, turning to her partner. "Just as I'm sure the science behind it will keep you—"

The Usher agent pushed hard against the balcony, catching Bill off-guard and sending him against the railing. What hap-pened after that, none of them could move fast enough to stop. The henchman, with his hands still bound behind him, stepped back and then jumped, his waist catching the top of the Gal-lery's railing. He thrust his torso downwards while kicking his legs behind him, propelling himself feet over head out into space. His head clocked against the outer railing with a sick-ening, dull thud before he toppled silently into the darkness.

Eliza, Wellington, and Felicity leaned over the railing just as the Usher operative impacted against the ground, sending sand and dust around him in an odd halo effect. Felicity stum-bled back from the railing to brace herself against the light-house, her bosom heaving as she tried to catch her breath.

"All right," Bill groaned as Eliza pulled him up from the iron platform, "this evening has officially stopped bein' fun."

"Suicide?" Wellington managed to gasp out. Eliza glanced

at him, noting he was now looking as ashen as the Usher hench-man only moments before. They had seen many things in their adventures together, but this had shaken him to the core.

"Since he'd failed on a mission," Eliza said, stepping away from the railing, "there would be retribution. It was quite obviously a retribution he didn't care to face."

Bill slapped his hand against the railing, then turned back to his partner. He placed a hand on her shoulder and spoke softly, "You gonna be okay, Felicity?"

"I—" She covered her mouth and screwed her eyes shut. When they flicked open, her eyes looked glassy. "I don't know."

"Well then, let's get a move on," Bill said. He looked over his shoulder to Eliza and Wellington. "We got a mad scientist to catch and not a whole lot of time to do it."

Bill was right. They couldn't afford to dillydally over one man's final choice. Eliza watched Bill whisper a few choice words to his partner, put his arm around her, and lead her to Currituck's stairwell.

With no horse cart or motorcar in sight, it looked as if it rested on the four of them to carry the targeting array back to the Retreat. A good deal of walking was in store for them. She anticipated there would be sore arms and legs by the time the sun came up. They would have to follow the causeway to shore, and then follow the beach back to the Retreat. It made the most sense, and if Edison were the showman he prided himself to be, the dazzling light display would still be on, eventually guiding them back to the resort. It would be pretty, at least. However, if the Americans thought they were getting away without doing their fair share, then they were in for quite the nasty surprise.

Eliza looked over at Wellington and managed to squeeze out a smile. For his first sanctioned mission, her partner was managing quite well. Since their shared free fall from the Cul-peppers' airship, she had suspected his talents were wasted in the Archives.

"You all right there, Wellington?" she asked softly.

"I will be," he said, his mouth setting into a grim line. "Quite a notion, this fieldwork."

"That it is, Welly, that it is."

She stood there for a moment, the words hanging in the air. Was that all he had to say? It was a moment's peace alone between them, and this was all he had to say?

"What is it, Eliza?" he asked, his expression blank.

Eliza went to say something, paused, then began with, "While I was up there, tumbling to what I believe could have been a certain death. . ." This was harder than she thought it would be. "I was—"

He just stared at her. Confused.

She shook her head and smiled. "I'm just tired, so the sooner we get that back to the resort, the sooner we can get some proper rest. Come along, Welly," she said, turning towards the stairwell.

Once down the spiral staircase of Currituck, together with the Americans, they lifted Edison's targeting system with only the slightest of grunts. It was not as heavy as she first feared, but hefting this thing for miles was not her idea of a good night out.

Outside the lighthouse, the four set off to the sound of the crashing waves on the shore. Eliza and Wellington did not share any words on their long walk back to Swan's Retreat, although she watched him march ahead of her, his hand wrapped around the handle for the longest time. Was he even happy to see her alive, after the mad ride she and Bill took amongst the stars? Could he not have spared a quick kiss, a hug, or even just a pat on the back?

Eliza turned her eyes back towards the direction of the Retreat. Perhaps for a moment like this—carrying a targeting array for a death ray along the shores of the Carolinas— silence between them was best.

THIRTEEN

❧

In Which the Paris of the West Calls

Wellington Thornhill Books had never expected to see the great lakes, never imagined that he would see the very north of America, so as their train pulled into Detroit he was, despite everything, rather excited. He leaned forwards in his seat and peered out the window.

New places were always a delight to him; it was just that he didn't show it as much as his partner. He was enjoying this quiet time in the dining car, watching the sun sink below the horizon while he wrote in his journal.

When a woman took the seat opposite him, and it was not Eliza, he was somewhat relieved. Felicity with her sweet smile was far easier to understand than his partner, who had of late become rather volatile.

"Anything of interest?" the librarian asked, folding her hands on the table between them. "Anything about me?"

With a dismissive wave of his hand and a light chuckle, Wellington shrugged. "Just some general observations on America and my experiences here. I've only visited New York before, so this mission has been quite an immersion into your culture. The things I have seen already."

She looked faintly disappointed. "Like what?"

He was caught out for a moment. "Oh, well . . ." And then a recent memory popped into his head. "Back in North Carolina, I caught sight of a lady who had just missed the train. She was a priest. A woman priest. Fascinating! Particularly as she gave chase with the train. A shame. I would have loved to hear about her parish and diocese. Quite revolutionary."

"That was rather funny," Felicity replied. "Still, not a whole lot of trains running out of there." She leaned back. "I hope she didn't have to wait too long to catch another."

"But in between the case-sensitive matters, I've been enjoying the countryside. America is a nation of layers, isn't it?"

"Indeed." Her smile widened. "Perhaps, if time allows, you can take in a few of our other fair cities. Boston, perhaps?"

"Anywhere but San Francisco. Apparently, Miss Braun has suffered there and would prefer not to return and tempt fate."

Felicity nodded. "I know San Francisco very well. Lovely city. I would love to show you its wonders."

She was very charming, and Wellington couldn't help but smile back. Perhaps he could convince Eliza to stay for just a few days longer, or perhaps his new colleague would offer to sponsor him.

That was the moment Eliza chose to reappear, with Bill close behind her.

His partner's smile was by contrast a little forced. "We're pulling in soon, so I hope that automobile of yours is ready." And with that she strode off. Bill only grinned and followed in her wake, and Wellington could have sworn he was chuckling to himself.

Further down the carriage they began talking in low voices. Wellington had observed that ever since they'd fallen from the sky, Bill and Eliza had become as thick as thieves. He barely got two words out of her since that night, which maddened him to no end. He had been so relieved to know they were leaving the Outer Banks safe and secure, and that she had walked away from such a harrowing ride. But with her new-found compatriot, Wild Bill Wheatley, there were no secrets. Never a dull moment.

It was not a development he found himself very comfortable with.

When the train pulled into the station, Felicity followed him out chatting non-stop about things he didn't really listen to. On his mind was the rather rude manner with which his partner was treating him. Wellington was more than accustomed to her dismissive attitude, but this silence that seemed to border on anger was something that had seldom been between them.

Further down the platform Bill and Eliza appeared once again, though this time in coats and undoubtedly better armed—if the bulges were anything to go by.

When Eliza strode over to him, Wellington worried for a moment she was going to punch him, but instead it was Bill that spoke.

He looked quite happy with the turn of events, and even with the air itself. "Miss Braun, Johnny Shakespeare." Wellington flinched. He was now missing Eliza's pet name for him. "Welcome to Detroit, Michigan, the Paris of the West. You folks are in for quite a treat. Detroit is one of the prettiest, most modern cities in America."

"I hardly think we are here for fun," Wellington replied, pulling his coat tighter against the cold. This continent certainly had all the seasons in abundance at the same time. He was sure March ushered in *spring*.

"Bill was born in Detroit," Felicity chimed in. "He likes to play at being a cowboy but really . . ."

"These folk don't want to hear about that," Bill said, hooking his thumbs in his belt, and seemingly embarrassed by his partner exposing his origins. "The first order of business— hell, the *only* order of business—is getting handcuffs on Mr. Edison."

Eliza's smile deepened as if she knew a rather unpleasant secret. "That is why we're going to catch a carriage and scout out his company. Since he's in Chicago tonight, this might give us some time to watch his base of operations."

"Just a moment," Wellington began, his eyes jumping between her and Bill. "You and Bill are going ahead?"

"Considering the eyeful Edison got of you two at Swan's Retreat"—and for an odd reason, her gaze lingered on Felicity in a somewhat accusatory fashion—"he'll be up and away if he spots you here. So Bill and I will go on ahead, wait, watch, and see how the mice are running things when the cat's away."

A simple enough plan. A shame she had not shared any details of it with him. "And what of Felicity and myself?"

"Having you two in such a hostile environment, Wellington, could serve as a hazard. Just check us into the hotel and pick us up later tonight, there's a good chap."

She called him "Wellington" but this time she wasn't angry. Eliza was pulling rank.

"Understood," he conceded, but then added, "considering my lack of hostile environments. After all, the Phoenix Society was nothing more than a posh outing in the country. Provided you looked beyond the underground weapons factory, mad scientists, and—"

"Just—" Eliza pursed her lips, took in a deep breath, and began again, her tone softer now. "Have the automobile ready to go."

"What if you need something better to back you up that doesn't involve bullets?" he asked her.

"You English aren't the only ones with the gadgets," Bill said over his shoulder and down to them. "Our own R&D haven't sent me into the field without a few mechanical tricks."

"What a pity," Wellington quipped. He turned back to Eliza. "What if we find ourselves in need?"

Her patience, from the tightness around her eyes, was thinning. *Welcome to my world, Miss Braun,* he thought with a smirk.

"We're in the Americas. Send up a smoke signal."

Wellington did not care for her tone, but liked even less when Bill handed him a map and gave him instructions as though he were a chauffeur. "Pick us up here. It's on the corner of Washington and State, pretty easy to find. Look for a building a block or so away with the name Edison on the side."

"Really?" Wellington asked pointedly. "Guess I can't muck up something that elementary, now can I?"

Bill shrugged. "Day's still young."

With that the two of them strode away, and it was not lost on the archivist that Eliza slipped her hand under Bill's arm as they went. Wellington felt a cold, familiar knot in his stomach start to build—and it had nothing to do with the chilly weather. He was also half expecting the ghost of his father to give him a warning.

Nothing.

Bloody good, Wellington seethed. *The dead are best when silent.*

As if mimicking them, Felicity put her gloved hand into the crook of his elbow and patted his arm. "Don't mind Bill, Wellington," she whispered, "he's just excited to be home I bet."

"Perhaps," he grumbled.

"And I think it quite charming how Miss Braun has put her differences with him behind her. They are two peas in a pod, they are," she tittered.

Wellington stiffened at her implication, yet he couldn't be consumed by thoughts of Eliza. He had important duties too. "I do hope your American porters handle our cargo with care."

The archivist led the librarian to the rear of the train so they could supervise the unloading of the car, with particular attention paid to the large crate that had conveyed the prototype with them from the Outer Banks. It was well packed and nailed shut, but Wellington was a little nervous as they lowered it down to the platform.

"The vehicle we will take," he told the admittedly competent-looking stationmaster, "but I will need the crate stored at the station until we call for it." He paid the fee, took the green docket, and watched as the array was wheeled away by a Portoporter.

"It will be fine," Felicity assured him, gently caressing his arm. "We can hardly be very covert lugging that huge crate with us."

He nodded stiffly, but found once he got behind the wheel of his automobile, he felt better and more relaxed.

As they entered the city proper, Wellington was quickly educated on why Bill referred to this American city as the Paris of the West. Towering high above them were breathtaking works of masonry art. In the distance, he could see one impressive building—or "skyscrapers" as the Americans coined them—reaching ten stories easily. Felicity cracked through the quiet of their car to point out the Queen Anne–style Schwankovsky Temple of Music, which featured an electric elevator.

"Since we are not on duty as it were," Felicity said, "perhaps we could pay a visit to Randolph Street. From what I've read, they have some wonderful architecture from the antebellum period."

"As lovely as it would be to take in the sights, we are still on a mission. Now where exactly are we staying?"

"A few more blocks. We're nearly there."

Wellington eventually found himself on Monroe Street. Felicity pointed ahead at yet another splendid work of art, this time constructed in a European Renaissance Revival style. Reaching eight stories and decorated with iron balconies, the Hotel Ste. Claire was quite a picture of luxury. Once his motorcar came to a halt, a team of valets appeared to open both his door and Felicity's. His eyes glanced down Monroe and Randolph, noting restaurants of various cuisines, all of which looked busy for a crisp afternoon in the city. When the front doors opened for them, Wellington caught details of bird's-eye maple, marble accents, and the finest crystal everywhere in the interior. The Hotel Ste. Claire believed heavily in making a lasting impression.

"Will this suffice?" Felicity asked. "The Russell was all booked up."

"Paris of the West, indeed," Wellington said with a nod.

Felicity led the way to the main lobby where, as dutiful agents to their colleagues currently in the field, they checked themselves in and secured their luggage. Agreeing on a time to meet in the lobby, and refusing yet another kind invitation to venture out and see what was playing at the Detroit Opera House—tempting as that was, considering the last time he'd attended a performance—Wellington stretched out on the queen bed he had reserved for Eliza, and let his mind wander.

Did it really matter if she was off on her derring-do with the American agent? After all, he'd protested mightily when she'd dragged him into the brouhaha with the Phoenix Society, not to mention the business with the Culpepper sisters . . . So he should be happy he wasn't included in her exploits now.

Shouldn't he?

When he was awakened by Felicity knocking on his room door, Wellington realised he had nodded off.

Rousing himself, he donned his bowler and jacket, and joined his counterpart, who was waiting in the hotel lobby. Navigating the city streets turned out to be not nearly as fearsome as he might have thought because of a series of wonders that were a delightful union of architecture and science. In fact, it was his consistent craning of his neck that nearly made Wellington wreck his prized possession.

"Eyes on the road, Books," Felicity snapped.

Twice.

The moon had hidden her face, but a line of tall towers punctuating the city brought light to the streets. On his third near miss, Wellington decided to pull the car over to admire these local marvels.

"I've read about them," he muttered, "but never thought I'd see them." He wished Eliza was here to enjoy them with him. He doubted Bill could possibly appreciate such wonderful constructions.

"The moonlight towers?" Felicity said, holding on to her hat and peering up the length of the tower reaching nearly one hundred and fifty feet into the sky. "They are impressive, aren't they? Thanks to them, Detroit is one of the best-lit cities in America."

"A marvel," Wellington agreed, but knew very well that his chances of examining the arc lights was minimal given the current urgency of finding and apprehending Edison.

They gave the streets a strange pattern of light and deep shadow in among the buildings, but it did make navigating much safer. They found Washington Avenue easily enough, and it was there—as Bill had so cheerfully commented—Wellington found a large brick building with the title "Edison Illuminating Company" emblazoned on it.

The roads were full of streetcars, carriages, and the odd hiss of an automobile, a welcome sight to Wellington. One or two of the motorists gleefully waved to him, as if welcoming him to the brotherhood. Many, though, cast lingering glances at his motorcar.

"It seems," Felicity whispered to Wellington, "your ingenuity might not suit keeping a low profile."

"Yes," Wellington said, giving a clumsy wave of his fingers

at curious onlookers. *Eliza,* he lamented quietly, *perhaps you were right.*

Eventually, the onlookers became fewer and fewer, but in these later hours, Edison employees were still coming and going from the building. It seemed the Paris of the West and its industry did not sleep.

Wellington removed his spectacles and rubbed lightly at his eyes. Much as it bit, Wellington knew Eliza had also been right in having he and Felicity remain out of sight. Both Edison and his hired Pinkertons had seen them. Parked in an alley between the Illuminating Company and the Cadillac Hotel, they still managed to stand out on account of Wellington's unique motorcar design. However, he had a responsibility to the mission and a promise to keep to Eliza. The boiler still hummed and purred, since he knew Eliza and Bill could at any moment demand a quick getaway.

He was uncertain how long he and Felicity had been sitting in what he suddenly realised was a strangely awkward and dark silence, but from Felicity's query it must have been prolonged.

"Wellington?" Felicity asked, peering after him. "Is everything all right?"

"Yes . . . certainly." He wrapped his arms around himself to try and keep a little warmth. "Just getting a little . . . stiff sitting still. I'll do a bit of walking up and down—that should help."

He strode up the alleyway a little, still keeping the automobile in sight. It was not the gentlemanly thing to do, leaving a lady alone in the dark. Standing in the shadows, he felt almost blanketed by it, looking out into the white light provided by the towers. For a city still bustling in the evening, it was a remarkably peaceful moment.

Until the yelling began.

"Get your goddamn hands off me!" a male voice boomed. "I'm not going to help. He damn well owes me money and I—"

Wellington peered around the corner just in time to see a group of men struggling to stuff a tall, lanky man into a large truck. Badges flashed in the light from a nearby tower. Wellington could not be sure if the gents were Pinkertons, but then

three Shockers, just like the ones they'd seen in the Outer
Banks, appeared from the nearby building, their clockwork
innards gleaming through poorly fitted human clothes strain-
ing at the seams.

"Just get in the truck," a Pinkerton separate from the struggling party implored. From his manner, he sounded as if he
had better things to tend to than this man. "We don't want this
to get ugly."

"What?" the man barked. "Getting ugly is new to you Pinks?
Thought it came naturally."

"Fine," he said, spreading his arms wide. "Back off, boys."
The Pinkertons, struggling with their quarry, as one, released
him and took several paces back. "Back off a bit more."

The tall man kept looking to each of them. He looked ready
to bolt.

"Number Twelve," the Pinkerton leader spoke suddenly,
"fire."

The Shocker closest to the tall man extended its right arm.
From there, a tendril of blue-white electricity connected with
him. Seconds later, the man collapsed to the ground, a slight
smoke rising from his limp body.

"As you were, boys," the leader said, motioning to the man.

Wellington glanced back to check on Miss Lovelace's safety,
but his concerns scattered on hearing the motortruck's boiler
engine winding up. Before he reached his own vehicle, the truck
was already lumbering away. For a large steam-powered vehicle
he admired its acceleration.

He leapt into the driver's seat, released the hand brake, and
brought his boiler to full.

Felicity let out a muffled squeak, "Is it Bill and Eliza?"

"Pinkertons. Heading out with a captive." Wellington
spoke louder as his creation lurched forwards and roared out
into the street. "I am making a field decision to follow them."

Felicity did not complain. Indeed, her eyes narrowed with
delight. She clutched onto the side of the automobile as they
spun around the corner, and braced herself against the frame.
As soon as Wellington caught sight of the truck, he slowed
the vehicle.

"Why are we slowing?" Felicity called to him.

"It would not do to be spotted," Wellington replied, allowing the truck to rumble far ahead. "I'm not looking to engage. Not yet, anyway."

The truck emblazoned with the Edison name continued for another five city blocks, and then Wellington noticed he was closing distance again. He allowed his own speed to drop until finally he pulled over to watch the truck roll to a stop outside a small brick building located by what appeared to be a series of massive generators.

Glancing around them, Wellington secured his motorcar and motioned Felicity to follow. The two of them crept down the lightly illuminated sidewalk, sticking close to the few shadows available.

Granted, Felicity's pinks, whites, and light beiges were offering challenges of their own.

When the Pinkertons appeared, Wellington and Felicity ducked into an alleyway and peered around to watch the man, groggy but alive, lifted from the motortruck's bed by a Shocker. With a quick look around the truck, the remaining Pinks and Shocker disappeared into the building.

"Arc Light Power Plant?" Wellington read off the building where the truck had parked. "From death rays to power plants. Your summation, Agent Lovelace?"

"This is bad," she replied.

His mind was racing with what the Pinkertons and their captive could be doing in such a building. Above the plant were two tall smoke stacks, and out in front was the far more elegant, but just as tall form of another moonlight tower.

"Who do you think that poor fellow is?" Felicity asked.

"I'm not sure," Wellington said, adjusting his cravat. "Shall we go and find out?"

Wellington took a step towards the building when another motorcar came around the corner at the end of their street. Grabbing Felicity, he scrambled for the front of the truck and crouched low. This new motorcar parked close behind the truck. From the driver's seat emerged a silhouette resembling Elias Gantry, Edison's Usher contact. Wellington and Felicity remained crouched as they countered around to the other side of the truck. Gantry joined his passenger at the door of the

Arc Light Power Plant. There was a moment's hesitation when Gantry made a silent *"After you . . ."* gesture to the door. Wellington dared to peek around the truck for a better look at who the second person was.

"Wellington," Felicity whispered when he whipped back around to join her. "The passenger!"

"I know. Edison was supposed to be in Chicago," Wellington said, patting the pistol Eliza insisted he carry alongside the Nipper. "Just to make sure we are clear on this—our respective partners are waiting for Edison to arrive from Chicago, and we have him here presently in a power plant specializing in high voltage electricity."

"And," she added, "Edison has a prisoner."

"Yes," Wellington said, looking Felicity up and down. "Miss Lovelace, I need to know something about your undergarments."

"What!?" she said, far too loud for Wellington's liking.

"Do you have a weapon of some sort concealed there?"

She stared at him, swallowed hard, and after careful consideration, blushed as she replied, "After North Carolina, yes, I have a weapon."

"Then I believe it is our duty to go in after that man and offer whatever assistance we can."

She pressed her lips together. "Yes, Wellington, that is our duty."

Together the librarian and the archivist crept out of hiding and slipped quietly into the building. Inside, there was a distinct humming noise that cast a foreboding in the air. *Rather unpleasant,* Wellington thought. Deeper inside, he experienced sensations that made him somehow more relaxed: the rumble of steam engines at work, and the smell of oil. This was the heart of the city's lighting generation, and thus the perfect place to find the inventor. They were in the heart of Edison's empire where, Wellington supposed, he might make mistakes out of overconfidence and arrogance.

Just ahead came echoes, shouts that Wellington recognised straightaway. The mysterious prisoner was awake and fully aware. They followed the rantings into the boiler house where machines fed hungrily on the precious steam created here. It was hard to make out any words, but apparently a change of location and a Shocker's wrath had not altered the captive's outrage. The engine room was impressive in size and score, an array of spinning dynamo wheels at its centre, driven by engines that were laid along the floor in rows. These half dozen metal brutes made perfect hiding places for Wellington and Felicity as they crept closer to the commotion.

Daring a peek over their chosen shelter, the archivist could make out in front of the power plant's main control panel a group of five Pinkertons huddled around Edison as if they were his personal rugby team and he the coach. The tall man was now seated in the middle of the group, unable to protest on account of the beating he appeared to have taken. Even with blood streaming down his face he did however look unrepentant, and was in fact waving his finger in the direction of the nearby steam engines.

"Mine," he panted. "That is my invention, and you can have it when you damn well pay me the agreed price." His voice remained firm, though his posture was not.

Edison held his hand up to his ear, as if he could not hear him. "What's that, Henry? I could have sworn you were making demands."

"This is bad business, Tom. Very bad," he said, shaking his head. "And I'm not one to indulge in it."

"Are you telling me you've developed a conscience about this?" Edison guffawed. "Well, a conscience with a price? Allow me to give you a counteroffer."

He gestured to the Shocker, who stomped over to Henry. The automaton lightly touched its metal hand against his arm. The man lurched in his chair, his yelp echoing throughout the power house.

"So that's your second sampling of a Shocker tonight, Henry. Do you really think you will survive a third?" Edison tilted his head, as if he was a father delivering a lesson. "You are still under my employment, and simply need to finish the task I set for you."

Wellington's engineering brain began to become very curious indeed. A new kind of dynamo to generate electricity would be most fantastic with many applications far beyond lighting.

Edison bent over a device in front of Henry. It could have passed as a younger brother to the many engines surrounding them. "You solved the problem of size and portability, but you're not telling me everything. You're not telling me the breakthrough, are you?" His gaze hardened as he considered Henry, then motioned to the onlooking Pinkertons. "Is this some kind of bid for negotiation? I do hope not. You know how much I hate negotiation."

Henry wiped his hand over his moustache, clearing away some of the blood. "Oh, I know full well, Tom, but I also know how important it is for you to understand how things work. You can figure it out. I have no doubt." His mouth formed a smile, albeit a painful one. "I also have no doubt you don't have that sort of time. Just pay me our agreed upon sum, conclude our business, and we both walk away from this as happy men. We agreed on ten thousand—"

Edison barked out a laugh. "Henry, I was making a joke when I mentioned such an outrageous number. Sometimes, I'm beginning to wonder if inventors simply lack a refined sense of humour." The surrounding Pinkertons joined Edison in a chuckle. Henry merely scowled. "You should remember who you are, and remember your wife and son. I really don't think you want to go back on our agreement."

"All right . . . all right . . ." He took in a long, shuddering breath, and then looked up at Edison. "The dynamo is not running on steam. It's a completely different kind of engine. It runs on a new fuel source. Not as clean, but it's got more kick to it. A petroleum-derived oil called gasoline."

"Gasoline?" Edison asked.

"You're going to need a lot of it. The dynamo's a thirsty little sonofabitch."

Wellington felt raw panic swell inside of him. With a portable dynamo, using a fuel source as volatile as gasoline, Edison's death ray could be transported anywhere, constructed at a moment's notice, and possess output far more lethal than seen in the Outer Banks. Nowhere would be safe.

"I wish to change my assessment, Mr. Books," whispered Felicity. "This is *really* bad."

"I agree," he said, ducking back into full shadow of their dynamo. "Obviously, we cannot allow Edison to get away with this portable dynamo. This leaves us with only one thing to do."

Felicity's brow furrowed.

"We must attract Eliza's and Bill's attention."

"But how—oh you cannot be serious."

Answering her with a single, crooked eyebrow, Wellington braced the Remington-Elliot Eliza had loaned him against their hiding place.

Three bullets. Too many Pinkertons, especially when you factor in the Shocker.

Wellington took his aim to the right and fired. A hose snaking along the outside of a nearby dynamo exploded, engulfing two Pinkertons. Their screams were barely audible over the high-pressure bombardment.

Everyone, save the Shocker, who took a step towards Henry, ran for cover behind spinning engines surrounding them. Once the pressure was spent, a silence fell over the plant.

As good a time as any. "Hand over the portable dynamo," Wellington called out, "and present to us Mr. Edison."

He hoped the "us" would be taken as more than just himself and a librarian. The rattle of bullets on the other side of their sheltering engine was all the answer he was going to get, and didn't bode well for his bluff. He fired off the remaining shots of his Derringer . . .

. . . and then realised Felicity was crouched tight against their hiding place.

"Feel free to join in," Wellington barked at her, and the look he got in return did not fill him with any confidence.

"I said I had a weapon," she confessed. "I never said I had a gun."

"I could not care if it is a slingshot, now would be a good time to employ it."

He glanced around the corner to see the Pinkertons creep free of their hiding places.

Wellington turned back to Felicity, who was reaching up her skirts and yanking free of her thigh a frilly, peach-coloured garter decorated by a small metallic cylinder. It looked like a Locksmith.

Felicity hurtled the garter at the Shocker. The *clang* echoed into the power plant.

The Shocker slowly turned in their direction.

"Right then," Wellington said as the Shocker began walking towards them.

Frantically gathering up her skirts, Felicity muttered, "Working on it."

From her other thigh, she tore free another matching garter. This one, however, had attached to it a small box. Flipping a sole switch on its side, lights flickered on.

"After North Carolina," Felicity said, shoving Wellington aside to peer around their hiding place, "I took a Locksmith and modified it."

"To do what? Explode?"

"To do this."

The Shocker froze in place with Felicity's pressing of the box's green button. Her thumb then pushed at the small handle, turning the Shocker to face the remaining Pinkertons.

"And . . ." With a wicked smile, she pressed the red button.

The Shocker raised its right hand and waved.

"Tarnation," she swore as she pressed the yellow button.

From the Shocker's waving hand, a surge of electricity shot out, tossing the hired guns out over a row of dynamos as if they were rag dolls thrown by an angry child.

Wellington was about to commend the librarian on her ingenuity, and not her comely thighs, when a man dropped down next to them. Wellington cocked back his arm, preparing to use his spent pistol as a club, until he recognised the bloody moustache.

"Thank you for the assistance," he gasped out, shaking the archivist's hand enthusiastically. "Henry Ford. Inventor."

Wellington, remembering the importance of introductions, returned the handshake, then motioned to the librarian. "Miss Felicity Lovelace of your American government. I'm Mr. Wellington Thornhill Books, Her Majesty's government." He thought that pretty much covered the situation. "That portable dynamo of yours—how portable is it?"

Henry went to answer when they heard from the other side of the power plant a door burst open. All three of them stepped out of hiding. The Shocker was still waving in the direction of the downed Pinkertons. The dynamo prototype Henry had been interrogated over was no longer in front of his rickety chair.

"Very," he grumbled.

With a little grunt of frustration, Henry stormed over to the plant's control panel. One by one, levers were shoved by the inventor to maximum. He did not hesitate for a moment when he picked up a nearby iron bar and began smashing it into the control panel. Each strike was paired with a sharp cry from Ford; his attacks against the controls were fuelled by the energy of a madman. Eventually, Ford's angry cries became a dull roar that was eventually drowned out by the increasing scream of the dynamo array.

Wellington hastily did the calculations in his head, and knew that this overload Ford was unleashing would be quite spectacular. The dynamos were already spitting out long streams of sparks that struck nearby walls and bounced fiery rain against the floor. The inventor's desire to cause a delay or distraction for Edison was admirable, if not the actions of a man pushed too far.

Wellington grabbed Felicity under her elbow and dragged her past the still-waving Shocker and up to Ford, now stepping back to admire his maniacal handiwork.

"Work your magic now, Wizard of Menlo Park," Ford howled, grinning at his revenge.

"Huzzah for you, Mr. Ford. Now, if you please"—and Wellington grabbed him as well—"run!"

As they pelted past them, the boilers began shuddering on their foundations, but it was the foreboding scent of electricity in the air that was most concerning. Even after they left the main array behind, every hair on Wellington's body was telling him something catastrophic was about to occur.

The door leading outside burst open just as the motortruck carrying Edison and Gantry rumbled away from the power plant.

"My dynamo!" Henry howled.

"This way," Wellington shouted, motioning to his motorcar.

Wellington knew it was vital that they get to his automobile, not only to catch Edison, but for safety's sake. The overload Ford created was only moments away, and on their sprint to his motorcar, the light—and the surrounding shadows seeming to retract more and more around them—caught his attention.

The moonlight tower looming over his car grew brighter and brighter, an ominous hum from high overhead slowly becoming an undulating growl reminiscent of the wild cats Wellington remembered from his time in Africa. The boilers of his car had just reached full pressure when the lamp burst apart, showering glass, smouldering carbon, and white and gold sparks over everyone. They lurched forwards to drive into the brilliant glare of the next tower light, it too reaching to an inevitable death. As the moonlight towers were a network, every one of them would give way or simply wink out to darkness once the power plant failed.

"There!" shouted Felicity, pointing ahead of them.

Rumbling just ahead of their car was the truck carrying Ford's prototype dynamo. The street suddenly popped into view in a glow of scarlet, orange, and yellow as the Arc Light Power Plant erupted behind them. For a moment, it was only the burning building that provided them light as the towers around them dimmed and then went dark.

"Don't worry," came Henry's voice from the tumble seat. "We have another power plant on the other side of town. It will take a few minutes for the towers to alight again."

Wellington thrust the accelerator forwards as the truck continued undeterred by the destruction of the power plant. The farther from the inferno, the heavier the shadows grew around them.

Then, for what felt like a short eternity, the darkness consumed them.

"Dammit, I can't see them!" Wellington cursed.

"Why not turn on the headlamps?" asked Felicity.

Oh, how utterly daft of me, he thought. *Of course!*

Wellington flipped the switch for the headlamps, and then heard Felicity and Henry scream.

He removed his foot from the clutch, stomped hard on the brake pedal while yanking back hard on the hand level. They shuddered to a halt as, appearing pale in the light of the motorcar's headlamps, four Shockers stomped out into the street between them and Edison's truck.

He cleared his throat as the front-most Shocker lifted a single hand in their direction. "Miss Lovelace, Mr. Ford, would you kindly stay low? I think this is about to become a rather sticky wicket."

FOURTEEN

❧

In Which Mr. Edison Proves to Indeed Have Friends

At first Eliza thought it luck—good or bad depending on how the situation was exploited—when the moonlight towers outside started to dim and brighten at odd intervals. It was the most exciting thing she and Bill had seen all afternoon. They were just about to break into their third building of the evening when the explosion four blocks away ripped through the night. This could have been just the diversion she and Bill needed to continue through Edison Illuminating Company's headquarters undeterred, as attention would be directed to greater priorities.

"Goddammit, Johnny Shakespeare," Bill swore. "We should have known better than to leave him alone with Felicity."

"Wellington?" Eliza said with a fierce frown. "You think Wellington is behind this happenstance?"

"Lizzie, in our profession, there's no such thing as happenstance. 'Bout as possible as an honest politician on Capitol Hill."

Eliza removed her picks from the door and jabbed Bill in the side before slipping them back in her belt compartment.

"Could just have easily been Felicity, considering that girl's penchant for stumbling into trouble."

"The good news is we should blend in," Bill said, his eyes looking out the window to the open campus below. "Looks like those workin' the late shift are runnin' like cats hit in the ass with a boot jack."

She had to think about that odd turn of phrase for a moment, then took it as a good sign. "Little blessings. Come on."

Both secured their sidearms before joining a stream of line workers and what appeared to be scientists, if the lab coats were any judge of occupation. The rush of Edison employees were all headed for the main gate of the campus where security guards—Pinkertons, on a glance at their badges—were motioning everyone to run. She had just reached the large wooden gates when a Pink paused and locked eyes with her.

He had only taken two steps before Bill's meaty fist clocked the man hard, sending him to the ground.

"Our chariot awaits," Bill said amidst the chaos, motioning to the open doors.

"And they say Americans lack a sense of chivalry." Eliza chuckled, grabbing his arm and pulling him to the exit.

They were out in the open only for a moment before their world began to wink in and out of existence. "It's going to get very dark soon," she commented to Bill, looking back at the glow of the fire, blocks away.

"All the better," he replied. "All this light ain't good for the likes of us."

Rounding the Illuminating Company to where Bill had arranged for Wellington to meet them, the moonlight tower in front of them flared into a blinding white light and then blew out, the sparks falling around creating the illusion of a strange, ethereal beauty against the dark of night, but the explosion had partially blinded Eliza's eyes as if she'd stared at the sun a moment too long.

"He had—*one*—job!" she heard Bill shout.

The odd grey, purple, and black splotches appearing in front of her eyes finally dissipated, and she finally saw what Bill was railing against.

Wellington's fabulous motorcar was nowhere to be seen.

The Detroit skyline was abruptly stained again with red

flame, a ring of thick pearlescent smoke spreading wide and high into the air above them. As annoying as it was knowing he had disobeyed her, the senior partner and primary on this liaison, a little stir of pride filled her. That was quite an impressive explosion; and whether intentional or not, Wellington had, upon reflection, followed her orders to the letter.

"You were right, Bill!" she admitted, her smile wide and as bright as the moonlight towers struggling to stay lit. "It is Wellington!"

"How do you know?"

She pointed above them. "He sent us a smoke signal." Eliza couldn't help but laugh now. Maybe she had rubbed off on Wellington a little, after all. "Come on, Bill," she said, drawing one of her pistols. "We've got to hoof it from here."

"Hell with that," Bill huffed. "Think you can manage one of those?"

Behind Eliza, a motortruck, similar to the ones they had seen ferrying objects and people in and out of Edison's factory during their afternoon surveillance, sat motionless and silent.

"Of course," she lied, holstering her pistol.

"Well, as you folks like to say," he chortled, running for the truck, "tallyho."

Eliza glanced over to the glow in the distance. Four city blocks. How hard could this be?

Pulling herself into the cabin, her heart sank. Eliza had hoped to mimic the actions she'd observed when Wellington drove, but this truck had none of the elegant simplicity of his motorcar. This dashboard was an array of clunky levers and knobs with no clue to their purposes.

Where to begin here?

"What are you waitin' for, Lizzie?" Bill asked. "An invitation?"

"Just a moment!" she snapped.

There was something spinning in the motor when Wellington pushed the starter. Something spinning. So for this monster . . .

She looked under the steering wheel column and found the crank.

"Gotcha!" she said as she started turning the handle.

Within seconds, the boiler gauge jumped to life and the truck began to shudder.

Wellington's car had three pedals, just like this one. He pressed the centre pedal upwards to accelerate. She began to slowly bring the pedal up higher, and higher. The engine was snarling angrily, sending thick steam everywhere.

"Lizzie, we ain't moving," Bill stated.

She wanted to punch him again.

The handles on the wheel, she suddenly remembered, were also key. She vaguely recalled Wellington mentioning "opening the throttle," which was just under her right fingertips. It only moved perhaps two inches under her feather touch, but those two inches were enough to slingshot the two of them in this metallic leviathan out of David's sling.

"Wall!" Bill screamed.

Eliza jerked the wheel and threatened to tip over the truck, but on account of the narrow alley they were thundering down, their vehicle bounced hard back on all four wheels. They burst out into the open street, and this time Eliza turned the wheel more slowly, which turned them in the direction of the burning building.

"Clever, this," Eliza said brightly.

Then the moonlight towers around them went completely dark.

This would be the longest four city blocks of her life.

"I think this motorcar has headlights," she said, "somewhere."

"Think you can fi— TRUCK!" Bill screamed again.

She saw the twin pair of headlamps appear in front of them, perhaps coming around a corner she could not see in the pitch darkness. Both cabs clipped one another, and the wheel jerked hard in Eliza's hands. She allowed the wheel to turn one way, then when it went slack, she turned it the opposite direction. The moonlight towers were now growing brighter, and she found herself in the middle of an intersection, taking a turn far too wide than would have been acceptable had it been daylight. Their motortruck was now facing what appeared to be a power station, the source of the fire.

It was not the burning building however that caught her attention. First she saw Wellington's car, slowly moving in reverse, and then the man himself, standing up in the driver's seat. Felicity was apparently holding the wheel steady as they slowly retreated from the four Shockers spanning the street. He was taking aim . . .

. . . with that damn unreliable Nipper gun.

"Bill," she called, shoving the clutch upwards while opening the throttle a few inches more, "jump now!"

"Are you—"

"JUMP!"

Bill was out of the cab, hopefully safe with no broken bones, and she just had to hope this truck would have enough momentum.

"Come on, Wellington. Trust me on this . . ." she whispered, as she centred the motortruck for the space between the inside Shockers.

She saw Wellington lower the Nipper, then draw aim on her.

"Oh, you clever boy." She chuckled just before throwing herself free of the cab.

Eliza landed hard against the road, but she rolled into it, as if she were jumping from a moving cart. The fall was half that of jumping from a hansom or carriage, but the landing still hurt. A lot.

The low, powerful thud reverberating in her ears reminded Eliza of an explosion underwater. This had to be the Nipper. She looked up to see the odd blue wave of energy strike the coasting motorcar, blowing apart the vehicle. Parts of the vehicle flew in all directions, ripping into the surrounding automatons as if it were made of straw and paper. They tried to continue walking, but instead collapsed into nothing more than scrap metal.

"Eliza?" Wellington called out. "Eliza, answer me!"

"All's well," Eliza groaned, pulling herself up to her feet. "Could use a driving lesson or two."

"Make that three," Bill muttered from behind her.

The motorcar rumbled forwards now, coasting to a stop where Bill and Eliza stood. "Get in. Henry Ford in the tumble seat. Introduce yourselves," he spoke quickly as she and Bill climbed into the back with a battered and bruised stranger. Before she or Bill could say anything in reply, they were all thrown back into their seats as the motorcar sped off.

She looked around her quickly and wanted to scream in frustration. "He's heading back the way we came," Eliza exclaimed.

Bill drew his Peacemakers and clicked his tongue. "I hope your partner knows what he's up to."

Her pounamu pistols were also out and at the ready. "Wellington has . . ." She wasn't going to express any doubts in him now. That much was certain. How could she describe this to Bill without him losing his temper, or his faith in them? ". . . hidden depths."

The stranger—Ford was his name?—leaned forwards and shouted over the surrounding din, "I told your partner to drive back to the Illuminating Company."

"Wellington, a bit more of an explanation . . . Who is this?" she demanded.

"Henry Ford, an inventor under Edison's employment," he said over his shoulder.

Eliza looked the poor man over. "I had no idea science could get so . . . physical."

"He's invented a portable, highly efficient dynamo." Felicity was the one who replied. "That's a kind of power device."

"I know what a dynamo is, Miss Lovelace," Eliza snapped.

"Edison now has it," she continued undeterred.

"Edison's here right now?" Bill asked. "In Detroit?"

"Yes," Felicity said, glancing over at Wellington with a broad smile, "and it is up to us to prevent his escape. Correct, Wellington?"

This librarian always did love to have all the answers. She was not impressing Eliza at all. Not in the least.

Their car rumbled into the campus, Henry Ford tapping Wellington's shoulder and guiding their motorcar through the campus.

"Stop! Stop! Stop!" Ford shouted, directing them to a four-story building similar to a warehouse. "Here. He's here."

"How do you know?"

"I was always barred access to it," he grumbled, "but I would catch ends of conversations where if something were to go ass-end up, Tom and his hired guns were to meet here."

"Welly, keep the car running," Eliza said, looking up at the surrounding structures. "We need to be ready at a moment's—"

The garage suddenly blew at the door's joints, the door itself not sliding up or down so much as it collapsed on itself. Henry was screaming like a wild man as a gigantic craft— something appearing as a boat turned upside down, a baffle running the length of the hull and inflated to a solid shape. They could see in the cockpit of this creation Edison, Gantry, and a handful of Pinkertons. Hovering a few feet above the ground, this compact, personal yacht sported Edison's touch in the electricity dancing wildly between the baffle and the ground. The craft slipped by them in a lazy, leisurely manner but then launched forwards as if released from invisible tethers, leaving their motorcar in a swirl of dust, dirt, and ozone.

Then the shooting began.

"Drive," Eliza shouted as she returned fire.

Bill joined Eliza in the firefight as their motorcar roared through the campus once more. "Keep them shooting at you," he shouted to her. "I don't want to wait for the local police to show up. I bet Edison has them in his pocket."

"I've got a limited water supply," Wellington said on turning a corner and coming in view of the main gate. "Where exactly am I going?"

"The train station!" It was Ford. "He's headed to the Arizona Territories! Flagstaff! There's a twilight hypersteam Edison mentioned booking before he and his Pinks started 'negotiating' with me," he said drily, motioning to his face. "That hovercraft of his serves only as an emergency egress. Not what you would call subtle."

Eliza went to ask why this town of Flagstaff piqued Edison's attention, but all thoughts scattered on the motortruck lumbering around a corner.

"Never mind, Eliza," Wellington said over his shoulder. "I can—"

"Drive! You can drive!" Eliza said, opening fire alongside Bill. "We will cover the escape."

Good Lord, she simmered inwardly as she emptied her pistols in the motortruck. *I know he's a crack shot but he can't do it all!*

She flipped open her pistols and started feeding them more bullets. "Any idea where we should be shooting?"

"Right now," Bill said, holstering his spent Peacemakers

and drawing out the Winchester-Edison 96X, "I'm just trying to keep these varmints at bay."

Once her pistols were loaded, Eliza took one of Bill's Peacemakers, pulled the hammer back to the loading position, and worked the lever underneath the barrel to eject its spent bullets. "Suggestion," she said while slipping bullets into the cylinder. "Knock out the engine?"

Bill lowered the 96X for a moment, then grinned. Several pops drove him back down to the tumble seat where Ford and Eliza were crouched. After muttering a few choice words, Bill threw open the rifle's generator. As it started to spin up, he said, "You're going to have to provide cover. Once the generator is activated, the lever action is locked."

"You owe me, Bill," she said, pulling the hammer of his Peacemaker back to a firing position.

"I look forward to collection," he quipped, loosing a devilish wink at her.

Eliza popped up from her hiding place and fired. A gunman toppled from the back of the truck.

The truck that was now only a few feet from them.

"Wellin—"

The truck slammed hard into their motorcar's bumper. Eliza clearly heard from the driver's seat her partner screaming. Whether it was in rage, agony, or a bit of both was impossible to conclude.

They lurched forwards as Eliza continued to fire. Another bullet sent a Pink to the back of the truck's cab. The victory was brief as three gunmen popped up from the rear of the truck. She caught glimpses of a Winchester and perhaps a Browning rifle before diving into the back. Over the gunfire, especially when bullets struck at the motorcar's frame, she also thought she could hear Wellington howling again.

"What are you waiting on, Billy?" Eliza quipped. "An invitation?"

The red light in the rifle's Edison modification flipped to green, a single chime just audible within the mayhem.

"Get ready for some fireworks," he said.

Bill popped up and pulled the trigger. She shielded her eyes from what she thought would be a massive blast but the resulting blast was more akin to a photographer's flash pot than the promised fireworks. The electric assault lasted for only a few seconds, but it was enough to remove the pursuing motortruck off their back bumper.

"I hope making promises to a girl like that isn't a habit for you, Bill," Eliza quipped.

He flipped the rifle's generator off, shaking his head. "Stick with what ya know. That's my motto."

"We have two problems!" Wellington shouted as they continued through Detroit. "The car and our crate back at the station! How are we going to take them with us?"

Bill reached into his satchel and handed Ford a card. "Mr. Ford, you take this contraption and the crate we have stored to this address. Tell them to ship 'em to Flagstaff."

"At this hour?" Ford asked.

"Don't worry," Bill insisted. "Someone will be there."

Wellington thrust a green luggage docket towards Ford. "I cannot overstate how important and delicate this piece of equipment is. It is of utmost importance that it is handled with care."

The inventor fixed him with a stern look, tightening his hand on the claim ticket. "After saving my life like you did tonight, you have my word I'll take good care of both."

"Bill," Eliza said, slipping a final bullet in his Peacemaker. She placed the gun back in his holster and brandished her own. "The Pinks are back for another round."

The headlamps Eliza first saw in the distance were growing larger and larger with each second. She steadied her hand, drawing a bead in the dark space between the two approaching lights. Somewhere in between them was an engine.

She lost her breath as their motorcar lurched suddenly to the right. She pulled herself out of Bill's lap to see they were pulling into Michigan Central Station. Eliza and Bill leapt free of the tumble seat and advanced as one while Wellington and Felicity scrambled to switch places with Ford.

"Right then," Eliza began, "your plan?"

"I'm usin' the word 'plan' kinda free and loose here, Lizzie," Bill admitted, "but I'm thinkin' you get out of here with Felicity and your boy, Wellington, stop Edison in Flagstaff, and I'll keep them busy here!"

"And let you have all the fun?" Eliza asked, peering into the darkness. "I don't think so."

He looked at her askance. "You're goin' all in with me then?"

"As you all say in the Americas"—and she switched to a languid drawl—"reckon I am."

Bill lowered his rifle. "Then now's as good a time as any." And before she could ask what he meant by that, he grabbed her and planted a kiss on her mouth.

It was not the first kiss Eliza had experienced in the midst of battle, but she was sure it was intended to be the most well remembered—mostly because of Wellington Thornhill Books, whom she heard calling out to them, and his call cutting off rather abruptly.

Still, there was no time for Wellington's feelings—whatever they might be.

"While the thought of a last stand and dying in a hail of gunfire sounds just ripping good fun," Wellington shouted as his motorcar with Henry Ford at the wheel rumbled away behind him, "we could instead catch the hypersteam which is still on its platform?"

Their lips parted, and Bill was grinning from ear to ear. "Want to pick this up over dinner? It's a long ride to Flagstaff."

Her lips went to form either an answer or an invitation for another kiss—yes gods, but did she ever need that—when something flashed in her vision. She holstered her pistols and grabbed the 96X in Bill's relaxed grasp. From the ease at which she disarmed him, that kiss had been building up for some time.

Eliza dropped to one knee, fired, pumped the rifle's action, then fired again. On her third shot, the motortruck swerved and then toppled over.

"We have a train to catch," Eliza said, tossing the rifle to Bill as she sprinted to Wellington and Felicity.

Once on the platform, the conductors called out, *"All aboard!"* Shrill whistles blew out into the night.

"We'll buy our tickets on board," Felicity suggested. "Just run."

Eliza felt the iron grating underfoot of the joining car's observation deck when she heard the gunshot behind them.

A sign suspended above the platform delineating their

current platform as a hypersteam line swung free and clobbered Wellington, landing him flat on his back.

"Wellington!" Eliza screamed.

Two Pinkertons trotted up to the archivist. The lead Pink, wearing an horrendous tweed that clashed spectacularly with his striped pants, pulled his pistol's hammer back into a firing position.

Eliza knew that look, and from Bill's hissing behind her, so did he.

Another bullet sent the thug spinning to one side. The second Pinkerton brought his gun around, but his knee exploded. He too fell to the platform, his cries drowned out by the building whine of the hypersteam engine.

Wellington scrambled to his feet and sprinted for the train, but it was already travelling at ten miles per hour within his first few steps.

Eliza turned to Bill. "He's not going to—"

Bill drew from the small of his back what appeared to be a Derringer. Before Eliza could stop him, Bill fired. The coil appeared to be emanating from his belt, a belt that Bill was rapidly removing from his person. On the other end of the rope, Wellington's left wrist had been ensnared, and he was now being compelled to run faster.

"How I do love intricate ironwork," he said as he hopped on the deck's railing and threaded the belt through its awning. "Ladies, hold on to me on three. One-two . . ."

Eliza and Felicity both grabbed Bill and pulled him to the deck. Something in the belt locked, and Eliza heard a yelp from the platform. She looked up to see Wellington dangling off the observation deck from his wrist as if he were an English piñata.

"Howdy, partner," Bill said, tipping his hat.

"If you dare to make a joke about me hanging around," Wellington began, "I swear I'll kick you."

"I might let go," he mused.

"Might be worth it," the archivist returned.

"Would you mind posturing inside the hypertrain, you bloody nincompoop!" Eliza screamed as she grabbed Wellington by the waist.

The archivist still managed to glower at Bill, even as he tumbled onto the metal platform. His glare switched over to Eliza. They could hardly afford an argument at the moment, and Wellington was smart enough to realise that.

"Look! Out there!" Felicity called, pointing into the darkness.

Out in the dark void, a shimmering blue patch of light bolted across the open plains. Edison, it appeared, was making excellent time in his hovercraft.

"He's gonna have himself a chore on his hands once he reaches Wisconsin," Bill chortled.

Eliza turned her eyes away from the fleeing Edison to her partner. She expected him to be working soreness out of his arms or checking his wrist for abrasions, but his eyes were still looking back at the train station.

Eliza caught a glimpse of the one figure still standing at Michigan Central's hypersteam platform.

"Welly," Eliza asked, her brow furrowing. "Is that . . . a priest? A female priest?"

"Yes," he answered. "The same one I saw in North Carolina. Trying to catch the train."

She shook her head. "Not the train, Welly. Not the train."

INTERLUDE

❧

In Which a Priest Giveth a Lesson

Quite a trail of destruction these people were leaving on the flesh of America—that much was certain. Who were these folks, anyway? First there was the strange goings-on out at the Currituck Light, the odd wreckage of what could be best described as a gigantic rocket and a dead man apparently wired with some sort of transmitting device to his wrist and chest. Then she arrived in Detroit to find Pinkertons, both of God's and man's creation, also on the hunt. She had so narrowly missed her bounty in the Outer Banks, and now she had him on the Michigan Central platform only to have him literally yanked away from her.

She still couldn't understand why she hadn't taken a shot. It wasn't like her to hesitate, and something didn't feel right. The Pinkertons, one of them healing up in a hospital while the other sat across from her, were evidence of that; but every instinct in her screamed to hold fire. This bounty and the company he kept were giving her far more trouble than she was accustomed to.

And considering the mayhem in their wake, no wonder the House of Usher wanted this man, Wellington Thornhill Books, so badly. The smoking ruins and destroyed moonlight towers she could see from the window of her modest lodgings were testament to the real need to apprehend this man—even beyond the demands of the House of Usher.

The large number of men roaming the streets, brandishing their badges and asking questions in a somewhat animated, intimidating manner, immediately worried her. Whether flesh or clockwork, they were Pinkertons. They'd broken up riots, killed innocent people, and generally bullied the population of whole towns. Usually that meant poor folk, or those born without the correct skin colour. The fact that they were here complicated the issue considerably and she knew she'd have to find out why. The House of Usher had employed her to find Wellington Books, and butting heads with the Pinkertons was just the kind of complication she didn't need.

Yet their presence both in the Carolinas and here meant they were involved in whatever business Mr. Books and his band of ne'er-do-wells were engaging in, and that meant she was at least one step closer to her bounty. When the knot of Pinkertons underneath her window broke up and dispersed, she drew the blinds and curtains.

She turned back to the man secured in a chair. The bleeding had stopped in his shoulder, and as she had placed that bullet right where it needed to be, the shot was clean through and through. No surgery needed, unlike the second Pink. Between the two men she had removed between her and Books, this one was the easiest managed.

Opening her current read to where the bookmark rested, Van was instantly whisked back to where Edward Prendick was rousing himself from what he had been told was a troubled sleep. Edward was far more rational, and clever to distrust what he had seen in the jungle the previous night. There is a foreboding in the air—not a far cry from the one Van currently found herself feeling—that manifests into something sinister as he reached an open operation theatre. Van held her breath upon reading what poor, innocent Edward saw: something human, yet altered. Transformed, somehow. Edward dared a closer look, but then he appeared . . .

The snort caused Van to start. *Dammit,* she thought to herself. *Just when it was getting good.*

The Pinkerton blinked, then sniffed. He appeared relieved that he could do as much. Maybe he thought his nose had broken. He licked his lips and registered the remains of ether still lingering there. Ether intended for Wellington Books. He looked to his left first, seeing only the far wall, the shaded window, and a dresser. When he looked to his right, he froze, his eyes locked on the collar of her office.

Van learned something new today. Pinkertons felt fear.

It was only for a moment, but that moment would be enough for her to utilise.

"I don't know who you are, lady," he grunted, "but if you're looking for trouble, you got plenty."

Van said nothing. She continued to sit there, her eyes boring into him, much as she would do with her sons if she caught them in a lie.

"Fine," he said with a huff. He then struggled for a moment against the ropes. He didn't budge, and Van knew he wouldn't. Farm life taught her many lessons, one of which was how to tie up an animal properly so it couldn't escape. He stopped struggling, then took a deep breath. "So what do you wanna do here, lady? Just sit here and say nothing?"

She was as still as a statue. Her eyes watched him. She didn't have unlimited time, but all she needed was patience. Pinks were used to being in control. The trick here was to assert dominance. Much like with her dogs back at church, they had to respect her as the alpha. She had to bring them to heel.

"Look, lady, you should let me go," he finally said, his voice sounding slightly tighter than when he first spoke.

"Should?" she asked, raising an eyebrow. How she hated that word. "That is not a word in my vocabulary. You've got to decide what you're going to do and then commit to it. That word suggests hesitation."

The Pinkerton grinned wryly. "My boys are probably looking for me, so let's try this again. You should—"

Van's fist was probably half the size of this Pink's but she knew where to strike to get his attention. She knew how hard to hit. She understood the science behind a powerful, efficient physical blow. It was the difference between a martial art and brawling.

His head snapped back then forwards. He could still breathe. The nose was bleeding just enough to remind him of who was in control.

"You are going to tell me what I want to know," Van said, easing back into her chair, "and then I'm going to leave you here to consider what you've done and how to best atone for it."

The man nodded. "Look, I'm not sure how you think—"

This time her fist struck his bottom lip, this time a fraction harder. It was not hard enough to break skin or draw blood, but it was hard enough to give him a lingering shock.

He looked up at her, his brow knotted in pure confusion. "What the hell kinda priest are you?"

With a flick of her wrist, one of her treasured Smith & Wesson revolvers slipped into her waiting hand. "I'm the last person you want to test. I believe in what's just, I believe we treat our fellow man with honour and dignity, and I have faith that we all can do that." She leaned in and asked, "Can you say the same?"

He went to answer but Van raised a solitary finger.

"I suggest," she offered in a low voice, "you consider your words before a servant of God. Are you going to tell me you have treated your fellow man with dignity and honour?"

He went to answer, but nothing came from his rather puffy lips.

"To enforce the law, you broke the law, didn't you?" she asked him.

"It was the right thing to do, you know? They were bad people, see?"

"They were fathers." Van paused, then added, "Those women, they were mothers. Loving, doting mothers."

The Pink wanted to refute her words. She could see it, but he averted his eyes, fixing his gaze shimmering with tears at a point on the wall. Van, at times like this, cursed her judge of character.

"I don't doubt you thought you were doing what you thought was right, but can you truly pass judgement on your brother or sister—for we are all connected in God's eyes—when you know only one side of the story? At home, the home of your brothers and sisters, there were children. They wondered why their father came home hurt." She leaned in, her gun still in one hand but the free hand coming to rest on the man's striped pants. "They wondered why their mother never came home at all."

He suddenly burst into tears. The Pink was coming to heel.

"I just wanted to do what was right," he blubbered. "I'm not a bad man."

Van nodded, her finger still avoiding the gun's trigger but close enough if she needed it. "What's your name?"

"Seth," he managed to say between breaths.

"It's a whole new world out there, Seth," she replied gently. "You can be anything you put your mind to so long as you got faith."

Perhaps it was facing a person with faith that scared him, that was breaking him down to the basics of human compassion he had forgotten on his journey. His eyes darted to his Pinkerton badge, then up to Van.

In his tear-welled eyes, that piece of tin didn't mean a thing here.

"Someone blew up Mr. Edison's power plant," he said holding up his hands, "and took off with one of his clankertons."

Van frowned. Edison, she had found out when she was in the Outer Banks, mysteriously disappeared immediately after giving a talk. Without explanation, authorities had shut down Currituck Lighthouse. Then Edison, who was scheduled to deliver another presentation in Chicago, had instead come to Detroit. All of these events had one person in common: her quarry, Wellington Books. Could Edison have some kind of vendetta against him? If so, that would mean wherever Edison went . . .

She let out a slow breath. "Seth, I need to know where Edison has gone."

Whatever the reason, his shoulders sagged. By chance, Van had chosen a Pink carrying quite the burden. "He's gone to Flagstaff in the A.T. He's got business there."

She nodded, extended her arm again, and the Smith & Wesson retracted back inside her sleeve. Van then gave the ropes a few strategic tugs, and just like that Seth was released.

He looked at her, a touch confused with the newfound freedom.

"You got two choices now," Van stated, her eyes staring

deep into the thug's gaze. She could see a war of wills raging there. "You can either jump me, kill me, and return to the world you know. That's an easy way, to be sure, but it's a coward's way. The other"—Seth's eyebrows raised slightly; it was hard to tell if he was still heeling or waiting to go rabid—"is to challenge yourself. Be a better man to your fellow man, not just in the eyes of God but in your own." She placed a hand on Seth's cheek. Her instincts were warning her to pull away, but this time her faith prevailed. "Walk in wisdom toward outsiders, making the best use of the time. Let your speech always be gracious, seasoned with salt, so that you may know how you ought to answer each person."

Seth nodded, and he smiled, sniffling a bit as he felt himself calm.

"I left a Bible there on the bed," Van said, picking up her other read. It was going to be a long trip to Flagstaff, even by hypersteam, and she wanted to know more about this island poor Prendick found himself on. "Room's paid for the night. Get your bearings first. Then tomorrow morning, decide your path."

"You're not going to need your Bible, Preacher?"

Van looked back at him. It was a sincere question. He truly does work in mysterious ways.

"What I am called upon to do, it's best left behind," she said.

Van was already calculating the fastest route to the Arizona Territories. The tracker provided by the House had been helpful, but instead of waiting until his signal stopped, knowing Books' destination increased her chances a thousand-fold. Saved time between hunting down details and making up for lost ground, which summed up both Detroit and Currituck. The rest now being just travel, Mr. Wellington Books could continue planning his revenge upon Edison for the time being. She'd take him in, collect her bounty, and be back in church by Sunday.

As she stepped into the morning light, searching for a cab to shuttle her to Michigan Central straightaway, Van couldn't keep back her smile of pure satisfaction. She could practically hear the choir welcoming her home.

FIFTEEN

❧

Wherein Eliza D. Braun Gets
a Dressing Down

Eliza remembered a long and painful hypersteam trip from York to London. It had been an excruciating journey, bouncing between the window and the shoulder of her then-senior partner, Wellington Books. The innovations of steam power had lessened the time it took to go anywhere, but it added this uncomfortable shimmy to the carriages that always left her feeling dreadfully shaken.

Now here she was in America, waking up to another bright morning on the *Excelsior*, this nation's first hypersteam train. However, it unfortunately still had all the same bumping and jostling of the one back in Britain.

Travelling with Felicity Lovelace in tow was certainly not improving her mood, and because Eliza knew why she was so miffed with the American librarian, it made it even worse. She hated being jealous, because it was not her natural state. Yet, every time Wellington so much as glanced at Felicity she could feel the serpent chew on her insides.

Is that why she let Bill kiss her? Was it because she wanted him to do so, or because it would make Wellington equally jealous? Maybe it was retribution for how she was feeling?

Perhaps they would finally find an opportunity to talk about what was happening between them, as Felicity had pushed Eliza and Wellington together, thanks to a favour the OSM had unintentionally done. Due to their mad dash for the hypersteam, the American agency had purchased for its agents the only remaining tickets on the *Excelsior*—first-class tickets. Additionally, as their luggage had been left behind at the Hotel Ste. Claire, OSM had opened an account with the *Excelsior*'s on-board establishment. Eliza knew full well that the Ministry would not spring for such luxury.

Accommodations on the train far exceeded her expectations; with a separate washroom on board, including tiny rose-scented soaps, and their very own waiter who came round whenever they fancied a little something to nibble on. Then there was coffee on tap, and most blessedly of all, tea. *Proper* tea. It was bliss!

This bliss was short-lived, however, as Wellington also took his place in the *adjoining* cabin.

She could still recall the previous night, both of them lacking sleep on account of their wild escape from Detroit, watching him wrestle with the cabin door, probably having trouble managing the key. After muttering, *"Good night, Miss Braun . . ."* he had left her then as she was now—alone in the room, her delight over such treatment deflated like a balloon pricked by a pin.

Falling back into her bunk, nearly wide enough to be considered a bed, Eliza suddenly felt like she was twelve years old again. The boy she liked didn't like her . . . even if he had kissed her first.

And to complicate matters all the more, the new bloke recently moved into town had kissed her, and it was hard to tell who was the better at it.

Eliza picked at the pretty pink quilt with one fingernail. Well, she wasn't twelve anymore, and she was damned if she was going sit around waiting for either Welly or Bill. She just needed to get a clear idea on where each of them stood.

She slipped out of her bunk, crossed to the adjoining door, and finally after a few tries—Eliza needed to have the Porter service this lock—opened the door to stick her head into Wellington's room.

He jumped on seeing her head poking into his room. On recovering himself, Welly frowned. "Miss Braun, is there any reason you are appearing in my room like a big game trophy mounted on my wall? Is everything all right?"

Eliza opened her mouth twice without success, trying to decide if she should have it out with him then and there, but the knock at his door and Felicity's voice from outside announcing, *"Ten minutes, Wellington . . ."* kept her silent. Everything, words and otherwise, dried up immediately.

"Quite fine, Welly," Eliza muttered.

"Well, do get a move on then. We're expected for breakfast in the dining car." And with that, he gave her a gentle push with two fingers back into her own cabin, and then shut the adjoining door firmly between them.

Eliza rubbed the spot where his fingers had placed a feather touch. He could not have hurt her more if he'd punched her in the face.

Eliza then clenched her teeth together so hard, she believed they might crack. *Get a move on? Oh, I promise you, Welly,* she thought to herself as she took a seat in front of the vanity, *I will do just that this morning!* After all, if they were about to have breakfast, perhaps Eliza could look her best for someone who would appreciate it. Namely, "Wild Bill" Wheatley. She certainly understood his advances better than Wellington's. When the man she wanted was making absolutely no effort, it was tempting to have a very attractive one that was nearby.

Eliza flipped the switch that retracted the bed into an overhead compartment. *Now that's an ingenious contraption; Southern Pacific and White Star lines should take a page from them,* she thought idly as she slipped into her morning wear. She decided that trousers would be appropriate this morning. Something about long pants always made her feel more comfortable and ready to face danger and disaster.

And she knew, as she was displaying her assets, Bill would notice.

Turning back and forth in front of the mirror, Eliza took a measure of pride in her figure and how she enjoyed using it to her advantage.

"A dash of makeup perhaps," she whispered to herself, and pulled out her mother-of-pearl lady's case. After a moment's consideration, she picked out a little rouge, and a touch of deep red lipstick.

A thought came to her as she began. Her hand paused in applying blush on her cheeks. He was her partner-of-many-secrets, for he'd never spoken of his family nor much of his past. She knew he'd been in the army, but apart from that how well did she truly know Wellington Thornhill Books?

"Things need to change in Arizona," Eliza told her reflection sternly. "If they do not . . ."

Eliza shut the compact with a snap and spent the next few minutes wrestling her hair into a neat French twist. The final touch was her strapping into the Ministry-issue Mark II corset. Once the hooks running down the front were secured in place, Eliza commenced with "proper adjustments." When she was satisfied, particularly as to having a "good corset day," she exited her cabin, ran her palms along her tight trousers, and strode confidently towards the dining car.

The smell of eggs and bacon did make her stomach rumble with thunder, but it tightened when she laid eyes on Felicity. Eliza thought she had taken plenty of trouble with her attire this morning, but she was suddenly seized by the urge to run back to her cabin. The American agent was dressed in a lovely deep green dress, topped off by a perfectly sized hat with a flourish of feathers pinned to the side. Quite the polished, refined lady she made.

She looked like a damned Parisian courtesan, complete with wares on display.

Bill was sitting next to Felicity, seemingly watching the countryside race by, a rather pensive look on his face. His plain attire only served to enhance his partner's.

This scene of fashion and elegance irritated her so badly, Eliza had to stand still for a moment in order to gain control of her own expression. That was her style. Conservative. Reserved. *Dull.* It was ridiculous to think about turning around and going back to change—this was her style. Bold. Expressive. Independent.

Damn it all if her mind did wander longingly to the stunning red satin evening dress that she had packed in her luggage.

Eliza placed a single hand across her corset, and hoped that her new trousers didn't have a hole in them somewhere.

While she was doing so, Felicity caught Eliza's eye and waved cheerily to her. The agent knew why the woman annoyed her so much—she wasn't that foolish. It was that she did make such an effort to be pleasant. Felicity Lovelace was like a veritable splinter trapped under Eliza's skin, one that she'd need a hot needle to get out.

She loathed this pettiness getting the better of her, and had never thought of herself as a nasty person, so she would try her very best to keep her thoughts from showing. Forcing a smile onto her lips, Eliza waved back and joined them at the breakfast table.

"Good morning . . ." And Felicity stared blankly at Eliza, biting her bottom lip while her eyes darted around the car. Was she picking up *any* subtleties of fieldwork on this mission?

"Eliza," the agent said, her reply a bit too sharp. "We're not travelling incognito for the moment so we can use our real names."

"Right," the librarian said, laughing in relief as she picked up her cup of coffee. "The pot is still fresh. Would you care for a cup?"

"Yes," Eliza said with a nod. "Maybe that is what I need." She would much rather have had tea, but she wasn't going to yield the advantage to the librarian.

In truth, Eliza did find the aroma of fresh coffee appealing, and after applying the appropriate amount of cream and sugar cubes, the morning drink did begin to soothe her tensions.

She was just about to relax when Bill turned to look at her. "Whoa!" he exclaimed. He then settled into his chair, his grin reminding her of when they met at the beginning of this mission. "Didn't realise I'd ordered eggs sunny-side up this morning."

With all the maturity of a schoolboy, Eliza seethed. "They are called breasts. I have no doubt you've seen them before."

She glanced over at Wellington. He was consulting his journal, making notations concerning . . .

That.

Bloody.

Car.

"Many thanks to OSM for the accommodations," Eliza said, toasting the two of them as if it were a champagne flute rather than a plain white coffee cup. "It's been a while since I have travelled so comfortably."

"This isn't the way to see the States," grumbled Bill.

Felicity rolled her eyes and leaned into Eliza, as a dear friend would do when wanting to engage in some scandalous gossip. "Don't mind Mr. Grumpy-Chaps over there. He's not one for progress. His idea of transcontinental travel is on horseback, with baked beans, sausages, coffee for breakfast, lunch, and dinner, then arriving at your destination with a sore behind."

Did she really call "Wild Bill" Wheatley *Mr. Grumpy-Chaps*?! And had she really talked about his rump in such a fashion, before breakfast?

Perhaps that was another reason she did not care for Miss Felicity Lovelace. The two of them were very much two peas in a pod.

Eliza looked over at Wellington, still jotting down notations in his journal.

"Yes, Wellington, I slept spectacularly. And you?" Eliza took a sip of her coffee, and then added, "Oh, I am famished as well."

Wellington looked up and gave a start at seeing Eliza's provocative fashion. "Oh, I say!"

"No, you didn't," Eliza stated flatly.

"It's just that you are . . ." And he seemed to launch on an epic quest for just the right words. ". . . quite the picture."

"But not quite eye-catching enough to tear you out of your beloved journal."

Wellington looked to his fellow agents and awkwardly cleared his throat. "My apologies, everyone. Last night, I had an idea what is causing that damnable backfire in the motor-car. I'm just making a few notations to myself so that I can remedy it."

A loud snort came from across the table. "And when you finish with that," Bill said, still talking to Wellington as he topped off his coffee, "maybe you could do something about that annoying noise it's making." He tilted his head as he mimicked the sound. "*Chittity-chittity-chittity-chittity.* Does wonders for workin' your last nerve."

Wellington fixed a hard gaze on Bill that Bill did not

bother to return. The cowboy's gaze was, once again, directed to the countryside speeding by them.

Their waiter, in immaculate black and white, stood at a fair distance from his new diner, greeted the table with a warm smile . . .until his eyes fell on Eliza. The arched eyebrow suggested that, obviously, her rugged attire was not meeting the *Excelsior* dining car's dress code.

Eliza returned an arched brow of her own. "If there's a problem, mate, then out with it."

"Tea, if you please," Wellington interjected, disregarding the sniff from the waiter. "And if you would just bring us all your standard breakfast menu?"

With a nod and a polite smile, the waiter disappeared.

"Are you sure you wish to go on with this meeting?" Eliza asked, motioning to his journal. "We really cannot afford distractions . . ."

"Says the woman in the Mark II corset," Bill jabbed. "Two targets clearly out in the open."

"And if I were a lesser man, I would be distracted by such a fashion, but alas, I am not," Wellington retorted.

Eliza honestly didn't know if she should feel flattered or disappointed by that.

"I knew there would be severe consequences and challenges introducing a prototype in the field without proper testing," he said with a faint sigh, "but nevertheless, I will bear this responsibility as would Odysseus when returning his soldiers home."

Bill tipped his head to one side. "Was that English you just spoke?"

"Yes, Bill," Felicity began, "there's this incredible resource at OSM headquarters called a library. You should indulge in it sometime." And Bill bounced in his chair as Felicity flinched in hers. Eliza had delivered a few kicks under the table to Wellington in her time, and knew the signs very well. Bill cleared his throat, loosing a dark glare at Felicity. "Now then"—and she laid out a napkin across her lap as two porters appeared with fresh breakfast plates—"shall we begin this morning's agenda properly?"

"Yes, let's." Eliza glanced over at her partner, who immediately began cutting into his ham and eggs. His eyebrows popped upwards as he took in what was sure to be the smoky taste and delicate texture of a robust cut of meat. "Not my usual breakfast, but when in Rome, yes?"

Wellington took a sip of tea and then dabbed at the corners of his mouth just before addressing the table. "Upon reviewing my notes and cross-referencing them with Felicity's, we've taken a closer look at this 'Extravaganza' Edison has been conducting. Its stops, so far, have all been along the eastern seaboard. Cape Henry in Virginia, Ocean City in Maryland, the Rehoboth Beach Camp Meeting Association in Delaware—"

"What the hell is Edison doing?" Bill asked, his interest piqued. "Collecting seashells?"

"Coastal towns offer a variety of variables and elements," Wellington offered. "Air currents, water currents . . ."

"Potential targets, both stationary and moving ones," Eliza interjected.

"Exactly. Edison is truly a genius, and as geniuses go there is a methodology to his own brand of madness." Wellington took a quick bite of eggs, a quick sip of tea, and flipped forwards a page. "Following his appearance in the Outer Banks, he was scheduled for a stop in Chicago, yes?"

Felicity nodded, adding, "But shortly after North Carolina, Edison cancelled that appearance."

"Understandable," Eliza said.

"And now we are headed to the Arizona Territories," Felicity replied. "Flagstaff, to be precise, and that just so happens to be the last stop for the Extravaganza. No pomp. No circumstance. No dates or appearances after Flagstaff."

"So he hightails it to Detroit after the Outer Banks, and then heads to Flagstaff." Bill scratched his beard, mulling over the notes shared. "Guess the original plan was head on out to Chicago, do the dog-and-pony show, meander over to his base in Detroit, pick up the dynamo. Remind me what we found at Currituck again?"

Felicity motioned to Wellington, and flipped a few pages back in his journal. "It was the prototype targeting system. As Edison left it behind so callously, we can only assume that it was more of a proof of concept. They just wanted to see if it could be built . . ."

Felicity's words faded as Eliza's attention turned to the fact that Felicity was reading from Wellington's *private* journal. She flipped through it as if she knew it intimately.

"Lizzie?"

Someone asked Eliza if she was dizzy. She was feeling a little lightheaded now that she thought about it . . .

"Eliza?"

It was Wellington. What the hell did he want?

"Eliza, are you well?" he asked.

There was . . . real concern in his voice?

"I beg your pardon?" she asked.

"Bill asked what your thoughts were on why Edison would be going to Flagstaff. He went to a variety of coastal cities to read variables affecting firing solutions. Then he went to the Outer Banks to perfect a targeting device. Detroit was where Edison procured a power source. What does he need from Flagstaff? A desert town, yes?"

"The A.T. is beautiful country, but Flagstaff seems a bit out of the way, even for A.T. standards," Bill said. "It's a far cry from Phoenix, but it's not Glenwood Springs, Colorado, either."

"So," Wellington said, pressing his fingers to his lips, his eyes still studying his Currituck sketch. "What do we do now?"

Eliza closed her eyes for a moment. She needed to clear her mind. She needed to stay focused.

She so desperately wanted to kiss Wellington. Bill was a mistake. She knew that now.

Bill tipped his head to one side. He looked at Wellington as if he'd suddenly sprouted a third arm out of his forehead and was offering to pour Bill a coffee with it. "Well, how about we take this train to Flagstaff, find Edison, and stop him?"

"The four of us?" Wellington asked.

"Naw, I was thinkin' just Lizzie and me. You and Felicity can watch."

"Bill," Felicity chided, "is there a problem?"

"Yes, there is. I don't appreciate Johnny Shakespeare here telling me that we can't do our job."

"That's not what he's doing, Bill." Eliza could feel tensions of all kinds rise suddenly; and with everything that had unfolded since their meeting in Norfolk, they all needed to be working together. Even with her differences, she knew that. "Wellington is simply—"

"Too cautious for this line of work," Bill bit back.

"Mr. Wheatley," Wellington said, giving a curt nod and returning to the ham and eggs remaining on his plate, "have you ever faced the House of Usher?"

"The OSM ain't no stranger to these Ushers."

"I'm not asking OSM. I'm asking you." His eyes were still on his breakfast as he said again in an affected drawl, "Jus' little ol' you, *pardner*."

Looking up from his plate, Wellington held his gaze with Bill for what seemed like a small eternity. Felicity looked back and forth between them nervously while Eliza fought the urge to reach underneath the table and touch his leg. Wellington was apparently pushing back. Hard.

He finished the last bite of ham and with a small piece of bread began mopping up the remains of yolk on his plate. "So I thought," he said.

Wellington shot a look at Eliza. She was still trying to clear her own head, so that she could offer some help. Where was this sudden venom coming from?

Of course. He had seen them kiss.

The archivist gave her a pained look before turning his focus back to Bill. "The House of Usher is an organisation not to be taken lightly in any way. Their resources appear limitless, and from what we can tell, their reach is everywhere."

"Not everywhere," Eliza said, giving Wellington a playful nudge. "They are not in Antarctica. Not anymore."

Wellington chuckled, and Eliza suddenly realised how long it had been since she had made him smile.

He gathered himself by taking a sip of tea and continuing, "With the exception of Antarctica, they have a global reach, and their goal is to plunge the world into an unholy chaos. We still don't know if they intend to place themselves into power or if they are simply a living contradiction as organised anarchists."

Felicity laughed this time, but as no one else found Wellington's words amusing, she coughed and busied herself folding her napkin on the table. The rosy blush on her cheeks was far too fetching in Eliza's estimation.

"Whoever they are, they're damn crazy," Bill growled. "Who would want the whole world turned into hell?"

"Some look forward to a world lost in fire and madness." Wellington waxed, stirring his tea, staring into its depths. "They picture a bigger, better world, rebuilt from the ashes. This, Mr. Wheatley, is what makes Usher far different from other secret societies."

"How so, Johnny Shakespeare?"

"They have no vision of a better world, or even a Utopia. Their Nirvana is seeded with wild mania." Wellington looked across at Eliza, and she felt as if the words were meant for her alone. His hazel eyes were the most serious she had ever seen them, and that chilled her. "The House of Usher simply have nothing to lose."

Bill finished off his coffee, and then looked at Wellington. "All the more reason we need to move on Edison the minute we get into Flagstaff."

"But we still have no idea what his endgame is, Bill," Felicity spoke suddenly. She was, apparently, on the side of the Ministry. "Even if we get him back to Washington to stand trial for his crimes, that still doesn't take into account his political connections. He is a man of influence, as you well know."

Bill didn't look at her, but Eliza saw him tense up on that. "I most certainly do."

"We can't play our hand so quickly," Felicity replied softly but firmly. "We need to find out why he is doing all this."

"Perhaps," Eliza began, "this would be a good time for reinforcements."

Bill's eyes darted up to hers. "You calling in the Calvary, Lizzie? How's that not playing our hand?"

"Before we pull into Flagstaff," she said, now looking over to her partner, "I think we can send an æthernet to the Ministry. We're going to need additional logistics."

"Oh. Yes, of course." Wellington pushed his spectacles higher up his nose, cleared his throat, and gave a tiny sigh. "Thank you for the warning."

"Sounds fine to me," Bill said, rising from his own chair,

"but if Edison gives me a reason, I will not hesitate to bring him in—with whatever force is necessary."

"Agreed," Felicity replied.

"Just give us until meeting our reinforcements before you do anything rash," Eliza said, batting her eyelashes just a fraction and angling her chest appropriately. "Please."

He pressed his lips together and squeezed out an, "All right then." Bill put his hat back on, tipped it to the ladies with a wicked little smile to Eliza, before shouldering his bag, and leaving the table without another word.

Wellington rose from his seat as well. "I believe I will see to my own appearance. Miss Lovelace here makes me feel quite in the shade. Ladies, if you will excuse me." He closed the journal and, after locking it, made for the exit.

"You are most fortunate, Miss Braun," Felicity said, watching him leave with a little gleam in her eye. "He really is such a charming individual." She pushed her plate forwards slightly and said, "Well then, I suppose I should get ready for Flagstaff."

"We have some time," Eliza said, quite impressed her own tone was so pleasant. "I'd like to talk to you for a moment."

"Oh?" Felicity asked, "About our case?"

"It pertains to our case. In a manner of speaking."

Eliza placed her hand in her lap and fixed her gaze on Felicity's. She was quite beautiful, quite pleasant to the eye, and rather sweet. This acknowledgement left Eliza with two options: a right hook to her jaw or just blurting out what was on her mind.

"I am a bit concerned of your intentions concerning my partner, Wellington Books."

Felicity blinked a few times, then made a quiet "Oh . . ." as she sat back in her seat, glancing down. Her cheeks grew slightly red and her posture deflated as if she wanted to sink into the floor. She appeared most embarrassed.

"Come, come, Felicity. No need to play the blushing maid with me. It's just us girls, after all."

The blush then, as quickly as it arrived, disappeared. Her eyes grew slightly darker, and suddenly the librarian was a statue of cold civility.

"You are quite right," Felicity said, leaning forwards into a far more assertive posture. "Miss Braun, my intentions are only of interest to myself and Mr. Books, and should hardly be of concern to you."

Eliza could now easily see her behind a fine oak desk, tomes stacked high on either side of her, demanding payment for late returns with the same stare that bore into her now. It was fortunate that Felicity's dark eyes were not daggers for Eliza would have thought herself in imminent peril. This librarian, perhaps a novice in the tactics of spycraft, had been hiding this particular spine of steel beneath all that charm, demureness, and benevolence. It was one of the few times that Eliza had misjudged a person. An error she would not make twice.

Perhaps she herself was not as educated as a librarian or even an archivist, but she had just as much pepper in her personality. She leaned forwards on her elbows, her own eyes narrowing. "Oh, but they are, make no mistake. I am very solicitous of Mr. Books' feelings and his well-being. If his confidence or trust is compromised in the field, then our partnership is working at only half-strength. We cannot afford such a risk when dealing with the House of Usher. I assume you cross-referenced that much just now."

Felicity crooked an eyebrow. "We're still talking about Wellington, correct? Because it sounds as if you are referring to yourself."

Eliza tipped her head a bit lower. "If you want to play hard, then I can play hard. What's your real game?"

"My *game*, Miss Braun?" Her expression remained composed, but Eliza noted the librarian's hands were turning white as they clenched on each other.

"Oh, dearie, you really have no idea who you are facing presently, do you?"

"If this is a battle of wits, Miss Braun, then I would say, for the first time, you may be outgunned."

"But this is a problem with you and I competing for the same man. Only one of us is aware of the competition." She would not lose her temper on this ninny of a girl. At least, not yet. "Stay away from Wellington. He is not for you. Not now, not ever."

Felicity's lips pursed. "Is that a fact?" She unlaced her

fingers from each other, and made a steeple with them as she asked, "And you know this from the close company you two have been keeping?"

"We've been through a lot together." Eliza's eyes narrowed. "I've known Wellington a bit longer than you."

"So then if he knows you so well, he expected you to enjoy Bill's affections back in Detroit, yes?"

Eliza remained stock still. That mistake was now costing her.

"I find it very sweet that you are so protective of your partner." Felicity leaned back in her chair, the morning sun lighting her face up like an angel's. "It is quite a surprise, I must admit, seeing as how you talk to him as if he were a petulant child."

"I do nothing of the sort!" Eliza snapped.

"So you did compliment him on that amazing motorcar of his, didn't you? Or for his investigative work in Currituck? And what of his rescue of Henry Ford? How did you address him when we arrived in Michigan? 'Just check us into the hotel and pick us up later tonight, there's a good chap.' Spoken like a true lady of the manor, yes?" Felicity's smile had no mirth or well-being behind it. "Your words. Not mine."

Eliza's mouth opened to reply, but she had nothing to fling back. Her mind raced to recall exactly when the last time it was that she had said anything nice to Wellington since arriving in the Americas. A compliment, a kind word, anything . . .

"So Mr. Books really has not expressed an interest in you in a romantic way, Miss Braun, since our first meeting in Virginia. This, I would say, makes him fair game. I find his deportment, his wit, and his intellect most appealing." She smirked, and then added, "His backsides are quite nice as well. I presume you've noticed?"

Felicity could not have rocked Eliza back more convincingly if it had been her delivering the right hook.

"The final decision as to where Mr. Books casts his attentions resides with Mr. Books. Not his partner in the field. And as I am in the field and charged with making notes of this case, upon my word as a fr . . ."—she was going to say "friend" but thought better of it—"colleague, I will not make any record of this conversation, unless you are concerned about the security of this mission. Are you?"

"No," Eliza replied drily.

"Excellent. It would be terrible for you to be relieved from your duties on account of your judgement being clouded. That would leave Wellington to complete the mission alone." Felicity leaned in and whispered, "You needn't worry. I'd look after him."

For a moment Eliza wondered why she didn't sod manners, decorum, and international goodwill, and just throttle this bitch only scant inches from her?

Because the bitch was right.

It had been one kiss with Wellington. Glorious and delicious as it was, it had been only one kiss. She had no idea where she stood with him, and here she was, dismissing him as if he were a rookie agent fresh from training, and paying no mind whatsoever to what he had laboured over in their continental progress specifically for this mission and for her.

And the irony wasn't lost on her. Another solitary kiss had now thrown all of this into turmoil.

Eliza took a deep breath, and then looked around her. Somehow, the dining car managed to clear of people without her noticing.

Losing time. What sort of field agent was she that she was letting this get in her way? Eliza rose from her seat, dusted crumbs from her trousers, and strode off towards her cabin. Maybe somewhere in there she could find the old Eliza D. Braun, the Eliza D. Braun in full control of herself.

INTERLUDE

Wherein Blackwell and Axelrod
Become Quite Excited

Doctor Basil Sound stepped into the lift, tucking the æthernet missive from Agent Braun into his jacket pocket, and pushed the chadburn to Research. The lift rattled and banged its way there, but it was not the only noise to be heard. The doctor winced as the retorts shook the shaft. It sounded like more than small arms fire, perhaps shaped charges of some kind. Research and Design had been established in a strengthened portion of the building; but at such moments as these the director did wonder if builders had quite managed to get those specifications up to snuff.

Still, the lift lurched to a stop, and Sound stepped out—with a hint of genuine relief. The main hatchway vibrated as one more explosion sounded from behind it. For an instant the director thought on how Miss Braun loved visiting this particular division of the Ministry.

She was however one of the few hardy souls that did.

As Sound grasped the handle of the R&D cast iron blast hatch and began to spin it, he watched the light above carefully. The more he spun, the more the light above turned from red to green. He just hoped that those on the other side noticed someone attempting access.

A final retort sounded—making him leap just a fraction—but the hatch had merely shuddered. The blast from the other side must have remained controlled. Or at least as controlled as R&D would make it.

Sound let out the breath he had been unconsciously holding, and levered the door open. It was a relief that there was no smoke to greet him when he stepped into the most peculiar of the Ministry's various branches.

Bearing down on him from behind the blast wall that stood directly in front of the hatchway was none other than the incomparable Doctor Josepha Raven Blackwell. Several other researchers were just straightening up from the shield, but Blackwell was first out of the gate as per usual. Sound had dealt with all sorts of powerful women in his time at the Ministry, from the explosive Miss Braun to the sometimes unnecessarily combative Lady Caroline, but the head researcher of the development team was an entirely different sort of bird.

"Director," she said, peering over her glasses at him as she removed the corks from her ears, "your timing is excellent. I was just about to head up to your office to demand an explanation. This shipment of blasting caps is far below an acceptable standard for my new project."

Movement from behind the director brought him around to her colleague, Professor Hephaestus Axelrod. Apparently, he had been behind a blast shelter by the hatch. Currently, his mouth was opening and shutting, as if trying to find the right words but giving his face the resemblance of a fish. Sometimes there were no "right words" with these two.

At first it was impossible to tell what the researchers had been doing since there was a contained but dense cloud of smoke at the far end of the long room. As if sensing the query forming on his tongue, a battery of fans spun up to full speed and cleared the room. The hazy curtain suspended before the target of Blackwell and Axelrod's research slowly rose, along with Sound's eyebrows at the sight of man-sized, brass riveted armour.

"I take it this little creation," he began, pushing back the lapels of his jacket as he looked the MechaMan from top to bottom, "is based on the designs we salvaged from the Phoenix Society?"

"With a few modifications of my own," Blackwell replied tartly. "I found that there were a couple of weak points when we scaled down the design of the MechaMan Mark II . . ."

"I don't remember signing off on any armour development," Sound cut in. Had he missed some mandate stating his orders were to be regarded as "light suggestions" to Ministry personnel?

"Last month, Director," Axelrod, his voice finally found, began, "if you recall I asked about beginning automaton development based on those plans and—"

"And I realised that it would make for a most suitable protective armour for our agents in the field," Blackwell interjected. She motioned to the target, the metal not even showing signs of burns or abrasions from the explosives. "Scaling it down makes many of the seals stronger and the welds a little less likely to burst under pressure."

"That is why we need a higher quality of explosives," Axelrod said, his smile bright and confident. "We must test our model thoroughly. Find out what its limits are. I wouldn't want to send our brave lads and ladies out in something not up to snuff."

Doctor Sound was always unnerved by Axelrod as he carried himself as if he knew far more than Sound did, but was far too charming for Sound to be offended by his superiority complex.

Granted, Axelrod was brilliant. In an eccentric sort of way. So was Blackwell. Individually, they created an odd assortment of gadgets and weapons that could be best described as ridiculous and outlandish. Together, they brought agents home alive.

His gaze considered both of them for a moment, trying to decide if his mad-scientists-in-residence were working from a place of genuine concern for their fellow Ministry workers, or just attempting to get hold of more ordinance.

Blackwell wants a bigger boom, a tiny voice in his head warned.

Josepha's perpetually wide eyes really made it hard to tell. He was going to have to be politic.

The director ran his hand across his belly—which had grown larger in recent years than he might have liked—and spread his hands wide. "Unfortunately, I don't think the test room is certified for taking anything larger than the charges that you've been supplied, Doctor Blackwell." Both Blackwell and Axelrod appeared crestfallen. Rather endearing. "I find alternatives come to me quite faster when stepping away from a project." He leaned in, a wry smile across his face. "I have need for you in the field."

"A field assignment?" Blackwell and Axelrod chimed in together, and there was no mistaking the notes of excitement in their voices.

Sound straightened. "Delighted to see you are so excited to be providing support to Agents Books and Braun."

Blackwell sighed, appearing disappointed, while Axelrod's eyes lit up with delight. "Wellington Books," he said brightly. "How fortuitous!"

"As a matter of fact, yes, they are handling a most delicate case," Sound said, his smile widening as he added, "A delicate case that directly involves one of our off-site consultants. One I believe you have been petitioning me to bring on-site for the last three years."

The two researchers glanced at each other. Blackwell's eyes were so large they almost threatened to engulf her whole face. Axelrod was now rather pale.

"You mean," his voice broke a little, and he had to stop and clear his throat, "Nikola?"

"We have to get ready," Blackwell uttered to no one in particular. "We have to finish proposals."

"We have to finish a few prototypes."

"Quite a few," she agreed. "Testing?"

Axelrod shook his head. "We can always run trials at a later date. Worth the risk."

Sound raised an eyebrow at that, but both Axelrod and Blackwell were lost in preparations. "Yes, I will send a reply immediately then, shall I? Oh, and due to urgency, we will need to employ the æthergates. Are you all right with that?"

Axelrod, fit to burst, slapped his hands on top of his head. *The hair had grown back rather nicely there after the last incident,* Sound thought. From their collected enthusiasm, the æthergate option made this assignment practically a visit from Father Christmas. The technology was a convenient way to travel, but not without its dangers. Still, it was the only means to reach Agents Books and Braun before it was too late.

Doctor Sound clapped Axelrod on the back, knocking him onto the tips of his toes a fraction. "Calibrate the gates on their Ministry ring signal and all will be ready."

It was catching sight of Doctor Blackwell checking her appearance in the reflective surface of a nearby centrifuge that made Sound's breath catch in his throat. There had been an incident four years ago where Josepha had met Nikola while visiting Europe. The weekend in Vienna to this day was still referred to as "The Lost Weekend." Working together again opened the door for dangerous outcomes, but it was just the kind of chaos that might tip scales to their advantage.

Sound wrapped his hand over Axelrod's shoulder and guided him to one corner of the laboratory. "I am relying on you to be"—the director paused for a second, glancing over to see Blackwell now turning in place to inspect her fashion, not quite able to believe what he was about to say—"a voice of reason over there."

The researcher blinked at him for a couple of moments, as if he couldn't quite believe that either. "I will try my best," he managed to grind out.

"Good man!" Doctor Sound slapped his back again. "Just make certain your compatriot Blackwell keeps her wits about her, respect Tesla's idiosyncrasies, and you should be fine. Once you are packed, pop up and see me."

Axelrod gave a curt nod and returned to what Sound could only assume was a checklist of items for the journey. Just as Sound reached the iron hatch, he heard the scientist call out, "Sir, might I ask, what will you be doing in preparation for the journey?"

Sound gave a long, low sigh. "I'll be enjoying what may be the last good cup of tea for a spell."

SIXTEEN

❧

In Which Our Dashing Archivist, Colonial Pepperpot, and Friends Old and New Walk in the Footsteps of Giants

The town of Flagstaff reminded Wellington of his time in the Queen's Calvary: hot, dry and unwelcoming. Immediately on exiting the hypersteam, Wellington exchanged his spectacles for ones with tinted lenses, and breathed deep of the warm Arizona air. He removed the heavier coat he had needed for Michigan, and hoped their luggage would arrive tomorrow as promised by the hotel they'd not enjoyed fully in Detroit. He was feeling the lack of his portable analytical engine and his car.

As America—Detroit, in particular—was deep into the embrace of industrialisation, the town of Flagstaff looked as though it remained stranded in the past. During their carriage ride from the hypersteam terminal, Wellington wondered if they were riding through the picture books of his youth depicting the rough and tumble world of the Wild West. They reached their hotel, the Royal. Hardly the splendour of the Hotel Ste. Claire but civilised enough. The four of them followed their porter up polished wooden steps to their rooms.

As Bill and Felicity disappeared into their respective rooms, Wellington decided now would be the best opportunity to discuss the current status of the mission with his partner, without the Americans being involved.

Perhaps, if things went smoothly, he could also share with her opinions of a more personal nature. Again, free of American interference.

Sharing a room—even if it was in fact a suite—was something they'd done before, but he wondered if it was going to be even more uncomfortable now. They opened the first door to the bedroom and went in. It was light and airy, painted a duck-egg blue, with simple dressing furniture and a large bed. A door to the right led to their parlour, while one to the left led to the bathroom.

Eliza was just heading in that direction, when he managed to forestall her. "If you wouldn't mind, I'd like to debrief, I think," he said, in what he hoped was a cheerful manner.

His partner frowned slightly, but came out into the bedroom once more and folded her arms in front of her.

The room itself might be far more modest than the Carolina resort, but as Wellington strolled to the window he realised the view was just as marvellous.

Instead of brilliant gold and ivory beaches and a serene Atlantic expanse, the view from the suite in the Royal looked out over a small grove of trees, and a range of red rocks reaching up into a bright blue sky. He took a moment to admire it before turning to Eliza; she was still wearing that eye-catching corset-trousers ensemble that she had worn at breakfast. Staring at him, one hand on her hip, the other already clasping a glass of water, Wellington completely forgot what he wanted to talk about.

After she'd taken a sip, she looked him up and down. "Well, what sort of briefing is this then? Something hush-hush for our ears only or some such?"

His mouth was abruptly dry. He wanted privacy. Now he had it, and he had not a clue what to do with it. "A lovely view, don't you think?"

After carefully placing her water down on the table, she smiled. "Look, Welly, it's been a long trip and I'd like to clean up. I'm not terribly interested in the Oak Creek Canyon at present, but I know the sandstone is quite lovely, and also there is a very nice vantage point for a sniper on the lower ridge facing east."

"Oh," he whispered, as understanding washed over him. He had wanted to brief her on his assessment of the mission and, perhaps, his own emotions, and yet it was she who was schooling him.

Eliza smiled lightly. "Remember, this is an assignment, not a holiday."

"Of course," he muttered, feeling particularly dense.

"And as I am the senior field agent, please, tell me what you can about our current locale."

With a quick nod, Wellington cleared his throat and looked out over the property. "There is a solitary entry point in the back, a servant's entrance no doubt. That means the Royal has one door at the front, exiting into the street, and another leading to this modest grove behind us. A small stable with room for at least ten horses. No surprise as this is the largest hotel in Flagstaff. The establishment probably caters to the needs of professional gamblers."

"Very good, Wellington," she said, sitting on the large bed and crossing her legs.

He went to continue, paused, and tried not to look at Eliza. She did have very fine legs, which were especially noticeable in the current outfit. Such an evaluation was highly inappropriate. Wellington yanked his mind back to the task at hand. "Well, there is my motorcar. Once it arrives from Detroit, I need to make sure it receives attention, preferably when it is not high noon as the heat can be rather unpleasant here."

"Rather," she agreed.

"Out of the ten stalls, there are seven occupied. That would mean the Royal is not full to capacity but quite well-off as I'm sure being one of the largest buildings in the town, it could serve many people on their way west."

"So are you insinuating that if the corral is full, so is the hotel itself?"

"Hardly," Wellington said, shooting her a satisfied grin. She was trying to trip him up, but he would not disappoint. "The corral is but a courtesy offered from the Royal. Once the tenth stall is occupied, I have no doubt that patrons are offered, for a reduced rate, accommodations for their steeds at the stables we passed only five doors down."

"Excellent." She got to her feet and went to the window. "And the rooftops—what did you note about them?"

Wellington frowned. He glanced through the curtains, parted them slightly for a second, longer look, and then shrugged. "Some are flat, some are at angles. Quite common for modern American architecture."

Eliza motioned to the continuous row of wooden structures. "The buildings are far enough apart that anyone cannot simply leap from one rooftop to another. Until we get closer to the centre of Flagstaff, it is not a concern for us." She glanced to either side and then to the ground. "We are quite secure in the Royal and should not have any issue if under siege."

Wellington's eyes fell on the trough of water. That area, far enough from the horses so as not to disturb them, could serve as the best to park his motorcar. He would need to fill the boilers, just to be certain they were ready for any unexpected occurrences. Around Eliza, the unexpected was rather to be expected. He wanted to be ready, ready as she was. This was, after all, the world he had been bred and trained for, but turned his back on, those many years ago. How his choices had disappointed his father.

There is always room for redemption, a whisper echoed in his mind.

"If you must know, you're exceeding my expectations, Wellington," Eliza said, bringing him back to Arizona and the here and now. "You handled yourself with exceptional aplomb in Detroit."

"Thank you, Miss Braun." He checked his watch and caught his breath. "Oh dear, I do believe we only have a few minutes until our meeting with Doctor Sound. Shall we head down to the reception area in ten minutes?"

Could he say what he wanted to in ten minutes? He didn't want to part company at present. It was rather nice having Eliza next to him. He wanted to let her know how he felt, how he felt about seeing Bill kiss her. That was his fault, he wanted to admit, spending too much time getting the motorcar ship-shape and Bristol fashion, as it were.

"Right then," Eliza said, her smile oddly mirthless, her voice definitely cold. "Off you go."

Wellington turned to leave the bedroom, however each step felt completely wrong. He needed to talk to her. Desperately.

"Tosh, man," he chided himself, as he prepared the small, curved couch in their parlour into something that he might be able to sleep on. *This is Eliza. She is back in her element. Let her do what she has longed to do, and then, on the way home, perhaps you can discuss things over tea. Now is not the time.*

Tea. He did so long for a proper cuppa, but sadly this country did not seem to regard the ceremony of tea with the same reverence as the Empire did.

He took a moment to splash some much-needed water on his face, take a breath, and then changed his shirt. He opened a pair of small windows opposite one another in the hopes to encourage a cross breeze. The Arizona Territory was hot, but at least there was very little humidity in the air.

Eliza emerged from the bedroom, giving him a silent *"Are we ready?"* glance. She too had changed, by placing a fresh white blouse over her corset, accenting the new look with an ivory, long-line jacket. She had gathered her hair into a bun at the base of her neck. From underneath the coat, he could see her two pistols.

"Eliza . . ." And again, he was at a loss. Why was this so hard? Stiffen sinews, summon up the blood, and all that. "I know this has been a delight for you . . . returning to the field . . ."

His partner sighed dramatically. "Wellington, we had ten minutes, yes?"

Most assuredly, on the voyage home, Wellington pledged to himself silently as they made their way down to the Royal's reception area.

Bill and Felicity were waiting for them in a small atrium of circular couches. Settled into wide-back chairs, both of fine wicker make, Bill was reading the newspaper while his colleague enjoyed, with outward, obvious interest, her new surroundings. Felicity, rocking back and forth on the chair slightly, made eye contact with Wellington and smiled at him brightly.

"You all settled in?" Bill asked, as he folded the newspaper and tossed it on the wicker table before him. His smile, Wellington noted, was aimed squarely at his partner.

"Quite," Eliza replied with an inclination of her head that hid the tiny smile on her lips. "The Royal is a lovely establishment."

"I apologise for the room sharing we've had to do," Felicity said. "Apparently, Flagstaff is booming so much they are struggling to keep up with demand."

"No need," Wellington said, waving a hand dismissively. "We will manage."

"I'm sure you will." Felicity looked between him and Eliza. "But if an inconvenience arises, do let me know. Straightaway."

"Certainly," he said, furrowing his brow slightly. What was Felicity implying exactly? Dear Lord, when it came to women, sometimes he felt all at sea. "Learn anything from the paper, Bill?" Wellington asked, desperate to steer the conversation in another, safer direction.

"These local rags?" Bill shook his head with a snort. "Barely worth the ink. No, I'm reading what is happening out west. But I do have some great news: unexpectedly our luggage—and that motorcar of yours—is all arriving this afternoon." Wellington gave a sigh of relief as he continued. "And the prototype from the Outer Banks is already here. Our people expedited it as they deemed it 'real important.' It's at our safe house. We also had a message waiting for us at Reception." Bill took the telegram out of his pocket and read, "'Anxious to see you in Flagstaff. Keep your shadow close. Cheers.'" He looked up. "Well, that makes as much sense as a lawyer running a church."

"I know the code seems a bit much, but we were using the open wireless, Bill, so we had to be careful." Eliza touched his arm in an entirely too familiar fashion. "The House of Usher has a wide reach, and they probably know by now we're on their trail." She checked her pocket watch and gently bit her lip. "So 'Keep your shadow close' is in reference to when they want to meet. Your shadow is closest to you at noon. Which it nearly is."

"Then let's get goin'." Bill nodded to Felicity and rose to his feet. "Follow us."

The Americans led Wellington and Eliza out into the warm streets of Flagstaff. The desert sun was strong, and so many were seeking shade underneath the awnings of the various buildings and stores. Traffic along the main causeway was very different from the traffic of London, mainly stagecoaches that Wellington had never expected to see for himself. As a young man on the grounds of his father's estate, he was being groomed for a life in the Empire, not serving at the Queen's pleasure in the United States. The dust from the road didn't seem to hang long in the warm air of the desert territory, but it was immediately kicked up again even by the slowest moving of carts.

"Poor idiot," Bill muttered as a third wagon slowly ambled by.

Wellington looked up sharply at the American agent, but noted that the man's eyes were not cast on him. Instead an older, portly gentleman, his rotund belly seeming to bounce and tremble with his own cart's cadence, had caught his eye. The white in his beard was a brilliant, shocking white, popping against his own darkened, weathered skin. With the older man were some folk that surprised Wellington—two other men, perhaps a decade younger, and of African descent.

"I beg your pardon?" Wellington asked in a whisper to Bill as they walked down the street a little further.

He motioned with his head to the passing cart. "Miners. Even though the Rush ended years ago, we still got those optimistic few out here, convinced there's another mother lode just waitin' to be found." He shook his head. "It's amazing how a few tall tales told around a campfire to pass the time can suddenly become a legend people are willing to cash in their life's savings for."

"Esteemed guests," Felicity said, motioning to a small variety store apparently closed for business, "we've arrived."

He turned his attention to the storefront in front of them. "A five-and-dime?"

"This is our safe house," Felicity hissed theatrically.

"Well, the Ministry has a need for it," Eliza whispered back in an identical matter. "Do you mind?"

Earlier in the mission, Felicity would let such a slight pass, but it appeared that the librarian was catching on to Eliza's slights. She looked ready to throw a punch.

Bill gave a little chuckle and held up a key that granted them access to the unassuming store. Proceeding into the darkened room, Wellington crossed over to the store's sales counter and lit a single lantern located by the register. As he moved to the other end of the counter, he heard Felicity ask, "Shall I pull down the blinds?"

"That would be lovely," Wellington said, striking a match and lighting another lantern.

A few sharp tugs later, the five-and-dime plunged into darkness pushed away only by the warm, golden light of two kerosene lamps.

"The prototype's over here," Bill said, lifting a tarp that covered a table near the back of the store.

Wellington's vest pocket softly chimed, making him start slightly. Eliza's own fob chimed as well. The archivist pulled out his pocket watch, and then looked around. "Right then— eyes open, everyone."

"Why?" asked Felicity.

"Well, if you happen to feel a strange, queer feeling like the floor is slipping out from underneath you," he began, his eyes still looking around the general store, "then you may be in danger of being either torn in half or possibly having your flesh flayed . . ." His voice trailed off as he caught Eliza's hard stare.

"Not in polite company," she said under her breath.

Felicity and Bill glanced at each other, and then quickly hastened over to where Wellington and Eliza stood.

A clean scent, as if a summer storm had just breezed across an open field of freshly cut grass, wrapped itself around them. However, that pleasantness soon passed as the scent grew sharper, colder. Felicity let out a strangled breath, and it formed itself into a fog just in front of her nose. She shuddered, and stepped closer to Wellington, cuddling against his side.

The floor beneath them vibrated but it was not being torn apart. A good sign. Wellington let out a breath of his own, and by the time it evaporated in front of him a low drone thrummed in his ears. It grew louder and louder, until it finally resolved into a white light in the far left of the shop. It lingered in the air above the floor, shimmering in the crisp cold.

Felicity gave a slight gasp as the world rippled—like a

stone breaking a placid lake—around the suspended flare, slowly becoming water rushing into the brilliant pinpoint as if it were an open drain. Reality itself slipped towards the light in a mad rush, feeding this ravenous vortex. The undulation grew to a low groan as this vortex stretched apart from its centre, its sapphire blue edge burning with a fire that gave off no heat. The portal grew larger and larger, growing beyond the open space and sinking into the floor while its top just brushed the five-and-dime's ceiling. On the other side of this rip in space and time, another world appeared. It was night on the other side of the portal. Stepping into view was a small party of four, a familiar face leading the way. The other three people from the other side proceeded carefully, minding their heads— although there was no real need to—while a small covered trolley rolled between them and their leader.

"Bill, Felicity, reinforcements have arrived." Eliza extended a hand to Doctor Basil Sound. "Welcome to the Arizona Territories, sir."

SEVENTEEN

❧

In Which Wellington Books Suffers
a Bout of Hero Worship

"Agent Braun," Doctor Sound said cheerfully as he stepped out of the glare of the æthergate and glanced at his own fob, "I must apologise for our tardiness. It took a moment to lock onto your rings. Must be something in the air here. How go things in the field?"

"Better than I could have hoped, Director," Eliza replied, motioning to Wellington with her head, "what with a new partner to initiate and all."

"Indeed," he said before turning to Wellington. "And you, Books—adjusting well I hope?"

"What Miss Braun does here is par excellence, sir," Wellington answered. "I do have a great deal to learn."

Doctor Sound gave a chuckle at that. "Intriguing choice of words there."

Wellington's brow furrowed. "I'm sorry, I don't understand . . ."

"Those were the same words that Agent Braun here used to describe her time with you, weren't they?" he asked, looking over to Eliza. He then turned to the Americans and stretched out his hand. "And these must be your counterparts? William Wheatley, or 'Wild Bill' as you prefer?"

"Howdy, Professor," Bill replied. "Heard a lot about you."

"Tosh, man," he said, waving a hand, "I'm a doctor not a professor. I'm afraid moulding young minds is beyond my purview." A twinkle came to his eye as he glanced at Felicity. "And this must be the tenacious and talented Felicity Lovelace, head librarian of the Office of the Supernatural and Metaphysical."

"Doctor Sound," she spoke quickly, "it is such a pleasure to finally meet you, after all the research I have done on your organisation."

"You flatter me, madam." He enveloped her hand. "I know that both our organisations are steeped in secrecy, but if you wish to discuss details about what we do across the pond, I would be thrilled to discuss such matters. Over dinner tonight?"

Eliza nudged Wellington in the small of his back, and motioned to Sound with her head. "Look at that," she whispered under her breath to him.

"But he's . . ."

"By a few years, yes." Eliza could only hope that the director would draw Felicity's attentions, but she knew that was highly unlikely. The strumpet was far too smitten with Wellington. Still, Felicity revelled in the flattery. An older man, yes, but a man in power, nonetheless.

"So this is what the fabled æthergate travel looks like?" Felicity asked breathlessly, turning her gaze to the gaping hole suspended in space behind them.

"Yes, but we must not abuse this technology as we still do not fully understand its side effects upon the human condition," the director warned, in a tone a schoolmaster might have when chiding children.

"Oh, now come along, Doctor Sound," the haughty voice spoke. "Knowledge and discovery always contain an element of danger."

Eliza shot a glance at Wellington, who had flinched ever so slightly. He too had recognised that voice.

"There is risk," Doctor Sound said sternly to Professor Hephaestus Axelrod, "and then there is foolhardiness."

"You and I are never to agree on that point," he returned tersely.

Axelrod held up what could have been confused for a snow globe set in a marble base; but on closer inspection, the "snow" was actually pinpoints of energy floating within the globe. When Axelrod's hand grasped the globe, the energy turned pink, creating tendrils that danced along the inside of the glass between it and Axelrod's palm. Punctuated by a rush of air, the globe traced the edge of the portal and gradually closed it.

Eventually, the chill gave way to the surrounding heat of the Arizona Territory.

"Doctor Blackwell and I are here to help," Axelrod began, setting the æthergate generator on one of the shop's empty shelves. "We have made a few improvements to our armoury since our agents have set foot in the Americas."

When Axelrod's eyes landed on Wellington, Eliza was rather startled by the professor's reaction: he was elated.

"Books!" he bellowed as he crossed over to shake his hand. "You know, I was *thrilled* to find our paths would be crossing like this." Axelrod rocked gently on his heels as he proclaimed, "Your commission is ready. Shall we try it out here in front of your colleagues?"

"I think *not*, Professor," Wellington replied, his smile tight and forced. "Perhaps when we finish here, yes?"

"Oh, yes," he replied, his words coming out as a whisper. "Discretion is the better part of valour."

Wellington would never hesitate to trade barbs with Axelrod. It could have been over the extravagant design of his experimental weapons. Sometimes, it could be about his choice of fashion, which Eliza thought was unwarranted. Dressed as Axelrod was, polished in a fine-tailored grey suit, a crisscross pinstripe pattern of black and silver that seemed to shine in the dim light of the five-and-dime, it could not be denied the man's fashion sense was impeccable.

Civility? With Axelrod? The mystery of Wellington Thornhill Books deepens . . .

Eliza rapped the archivist lightly on his shoulder. "A commission?"

"It is a personal matter," Wellington answered flatly, "best kept between gentlemen."

Eliza felt a breath catch in her throat. What was Axelrod holding over her partner?

"Agents Wheatley, Lovelace," Axelrod said with a grand flourish, doffing his top hat and motioning to the small trolley that had followed him from the other side of the portal, "we at the Ministry's Research and Design are here to provide you with the latest tools of our exciting trade."

On the mention of "we," Wellington's eyes immediately went to the other two people in the shadows, working on arranging an array of weapons and accessories. One was immediately recognisable as Axelrod's counterpart, Doctor Josepha Blackwell.

Eliza glanced over to Wellington. He looked as if he were ready to bolt.

While Axelrod was a man of fashion and impeccable style, Blackwell was a woman cut from a rather gothic cloth. She had such a penchant for black attire it would have been a safe assumption that she was in mourning, had it not been for the plunging neckline that bordered on the scandalous.

The other contradiction of Blackwell's consistent fashion of mourning attire was her personality. Unlike Axelrod's put-upon civility, Blackwell was effervescent, much like Agent Lovelace, only far more anxious. Far more volatile. And also unlike the American librarian, Blackwell's enthusiasms embodied themselves in more terrifying behaviours.

"It is such a delight to be in the Americas!" Blackwell spoke, enthusiastically pumping the arm of Felicity Lovelace. When she grasped Bill's hand, Josepha gasped. She then reached up and gently squeezed Bill's forearm with her free hand, making an interested noise in the back of her throat.

"You really do not want to know," Wellington said, making eye contact with a bemused Bill.

Josepha blinked, and then turned to look at him. "Ah, Agent Books, so excited to see you here in the field!" She leaned forwards with a wicked grin. "We have a few surprises for you."

"From you, Doctor Blackwell, I would expect nothing else," he replied warily.

"So you won't be here for long, Director?" Eliza asked.

Doctor Sound was now all business. "Yes, Agent Braun. We do have other cases happening here and within the Empire. Your telegraph, however, demanded use of the æthergates."

"Yes, what with the House of Usher possessing the technology of an electroacceleratron, we found the need to up your arsenal, as it were," Axelrod said.

"I'm sorry," Bill asked, "the technology of a *what*?"

Axelrod considered Bill and then shook his head, stroking his thin, tightly groomed goatee. "An electroacceleratron. The device you procured in the Outer Banks."

"You mean, the Death Ray?" he asked.

"The proper term is *electroacceleratron*, thank you very much," he said sharply.

"Therefore," Blackwell chimed in cheerily, "we have a few items for your consideration as well."

"Mighty kind of you, Doc," Bill said, tipping his hat to Josepha, "but my Peacemakers are serving me just fine."

"We did lose a Remington-Elliot in North Carolina," Eliza said, shooting a cold glare in Felicity's direction.

"Oh, excellent!" Blackwell exclaimed. "Then you will be *obligated* to take our experimental weapons!" Eliza and Wellington both groaned in alarm. Josepha, in reply, held up a hand. "They are in need of field-testing. You are in the field. *Quod erat demonstrandum.*"

Eliza leaned over to Wellington. "I really don't care for Latin." She then returned her gaze to Josepha Blackwell. "I like it even less coming from her."

"Come, come, don't be shy, my dear Eliza," Axelrod said, his smile chilling to the core. "To the table."

Eliza could see the remaining figure moving in the shadows—but exactly what he was doing remained unanswered. They now all gathered around a table offering the oddest pistols that she had ever seen. Perhaps the strangest trait all these guns shared was that none of the barrels were open. They all appeared sealed.

"Welcome to the exciting future of armament." Axelrod beamed.

"Interestin' gadgets here, Doc," Bill said, picking up a smaller model close to him. The pistol was just a hint larger than a twin-barrelled Derringer. "What exactly do they shoot?"

"They don't shoot." Axelrod's chest swelled with pride. "They excite and vacillate."

Bill furrowed his brow, held the small gun up to his face for a closer look, and then pointed it at the five-and-dime's covered cash register. The gun emitted an undulating growl like that of a lion as successive rings of fire shot across the room, burning a hole through the shop's tender that Bill, if he removed his hat, could easily fit his head inside.

"Sweet hell on earth!" Bill swore, releasing the gun's trigger. He held the Derringer-style pistol close to his face again with a wild grin spreading on his mouth. "This thing ain't putting off any heat."

"Internal cooling systems. The gauges on the side will give you a full diagnostic and will warn you in case of imminent overheating." He glanced over to his counterpart, and after she shrugged, he added, "At least it is supposed to."

"We call that particular model the Dragon's Breath." Blackwell motioned to the other offerings before them. "Each of these models offers a wide array of options."

Wellington cautiously picked up one closer to the size and grip of the Remington-Elliot. This gun was easily twice the weight, though, and while it did look capable of slipping into a standard holster, the glass tube protruding from the top appeared alarmingly fragile. "So if this were to shatter," he began, tapping the glass gently, "exactly what would this liquid do?"

Blackwell's smile disappeared, and Axelrod shook his head, disappointed. After a moment, Blackwell said in a heavily rehearsed response, "The solution in the vial is vital to Jack Frost's effectiveness."

"You named the gun—"

"The exciter," Blackwell interjected.

"—Jack Frost?"

"It was either that or the Axelrod-Blackwell-Olszewski X-2. Jack Frost seemed far more elegant in comparison." She motioned to the gun and added, "After working closely with our Germanic colleague, we can offer a safety tip that should be sufficient for you."

"And what is that?"

"Don't break the glass."

Wellington nodded. "Lovely."

"At least you have a replacement for your '81," Eliza said. "I must admit these exciters of yours are . . ." She looked up at both scientists and forced a smile. "Compact."

"We did have one particular creation—the Annihilator— set aside for you specifically, Agent Braun." Axelrod shot a look to Doctor Sound, who returned the glare with an elevated eyebrow of his own. "We were told you needed to keep a low profile on this mission."

"Obviously she didn't tell you about Detroit." Bill chuckled.

Eliza picked up a pistol roughly twice the size of her pounamu pistols. It was bulbous, its shape and size resembling a sheep's heart—which, as a New Zealander, she was very familiar with. There were several small pipes running from a circular vent cut on one side of it. She flipped over the weapon to find on the other side a dial offering several settings:

INTERRUPTION—VULGAR DISPLAY—
PUB BRAWL—TYPHOON

"The Brouhaha," Axelrod spoke when Eliza looked up to him. She crooked an eyebrow. "Please tell me you're having a laugh."

He sniffed. "I never joke about my work, Agent Braun."

"I am sure you do not," she replied, extending her arm fully to feel its balance. "Surprisingly light," she commented. Just how she would she carry it? Perhaps in a large handbag or satchel.

She drew aim on the half-melted remains of the cash register, but Axelrod scuttled over to her and lowered her arm before she could even slip a finger around its trigger.

"Eliza, my dear, please," he breathed, his face quite pale, "I would prefer you not discharge the Brouhaha in here."

Wellington was slipping the Jack Frost into its fashioned holster as he said, "Well, we did ask for reinforcements, and these exciters should give us just what we—"

His words were cut off on account of a rather odd giggle from Blackwell, and a pronounced eye roll from Axelrod. He gave Eliza a sincere look of sorrow, as if saying silently to her, *"It pains me to see someone of your calibre tethered to such a one as Books,"* but he drew himself together, plastered a sickeningly civil smile on his face, and replaced his top hat back on his head. "My fellow Ministry colleague, you once again underestimate the scope of our services to you in the field. We were charged to bring you reinforcements, and so we have."

"What Professor Axelrod is trying to tell you, Books," Doctor Sound began, "and you all, is that with the developments of your mission, both the Ministry and OSM agree that an addition to your party is required."

"Another agent?" Eliza asked, stepping forwards with a dark expression on her face.

Sound stroked his moustache with his thumb and replied, "More of a consultant, a scientific resource for questions you all will no doubt have."

"Now, hold on," Bill said, raising his hands. He was looking at both Sound and Axelrod, casting only a few nervous glances at Blackwell, who was still, for some bizarre reason, sizing up his forearms from a distance. "We're trying to move all secret-like with four in our party, and—to be honest—our stealth tactics as a group are in need of some attention. You're saying you and OSM want to add on a fifth?"

"Doctor Sound," Eliza said, echoing Bill's concern. "I'm training an agent in the field already—"

"Books is an agent possessing skills that could even rival your own," Sound stated, waving his hand dismissively. "Besides, we have worked with this consultant on several occasions, and are in need of his services. Particularly now, considering—"

"I honestly could not give a toss, Director, if this fifth wheel is bleedin' Sir Isaac Newton, Louis Pasteur, and Marie Curie all rolled into one. He's a complication we really do not need!"

"Agent Braun, you have been only recently reinstated to the field," Sound warned, his voice even and controlled. "I sincerely hope we do not have another disagreement that has you removed from it again."

"This isn't about following orders!" Eliza snapped. "This is about personal safety."

"Agent Braun," Axelrod cooed. "You must not work yourself up so."

"Stuff it, you git!" she barked. "You're not the one riding inside of rockets with mad airship cannons while death rays—"

"An *electroacceleratron*," Axelrod snapped, rolling his eyes again.

She wasn't sure if she wanted to direct her words or a solid right hook at Axelrod, but it was Wellington who stepped up to him. "Remind me how the electroacceleratron device works again?"

"It launches focused, charged energy elements at designated targets, decimating said designated targets utterly and completely."

Wellington nodded. "So the device shoots rays?"

"Yes," Axelrod replied.

"Of imminent death?"

"Yes."

"Then why don't you call it a death ray, you popinjay?!"

"I beg your pardon," came a calming voice from the shadows, "but that is what I told Professor Axelrod in so many words. Electroacceleratron, at least to me, seems a bit extravagant."

All of them turned as the man once concealed in shadows stepped into the shop's flickering lights. His features could be best described as angular, and his fashion unquestionably European. His eyes studied them all intently, and a curious grin remained on his mouth. It was not the condescending mannerism that Axelrod had down so well. This was a grin one would make when learning something new.

The man was dashing and—from the wide-eyed expression on his face—familiar to Wellington.

Doctor Sound cleared his throat. "Agents, may I introduce to you . . ."

"Nikola Tesla," Wellington said, taking a few steps forwards. "This is a great pleasure." Now it appeared that Wellington would be in need of smelling salts.

"Of course it is," the new arrival said, his tone conveying it was more a statement than a jest. He wrung his gloved hands as he looked to both Wellington and Eliza. "I am afraid you have me at a disadvantage, though."

"Wellington Thornhill Books, Esquire, Chief Archivist for the Ministry's Archives," he said.

Eliza cleared her throat, and added, "And recently promoted field agent."

"A man of many talents," he stated coolly, "if what I was told back in England is true."

Eliza cleared her throat again.

"And my partner," Wellington stammered, "Eliza D. Braun."

"Mr. Tesla, a pleasure."

"From the briefing I received, you managed to disarm the bomb attached to the Outer Banks prototype." He gave a tiny bow to her. "Thank you."

"The creator behind Tesla Knuckles?" Bill gave a gruff laugh as he inserted himself between the Ministry and Tesla. "Now here's a man I'm happy to meet," he said, sticking out his hand.

The scientist's smile faded on looking at Bill and Felicity. "I think you and your organisation are well acquainted with me, considering your surveillance of me, yes?"

Bill's hand lowered slowly as Tesla walked by him. He greeted the blushing Felicity with a curt nod, and then turned quickly on Eliza. "I know my involvement in your quaint adventure is slightly unexpected, if not unwelcomed, but the death ray is, simply put, my responsibility."

"Nikola here hardly needed persuasion in joining you all in the field," Doctor Sound said, his mouth crooking in a sly smile, "once he heard of Edison's involvement in this."

The bad blood between them was well-known, even beyond scientific circles; and from the look on his face at Edison's name, Eliza did not know if Doctor Sound was practising best judgement in bringing up the man's name.

Wellington picked up one of the lanterns on the main counter. "Mr. Tesla, if you would follow me, please." He led the man to the back of the shop. Wellington set down the light at one end of the table, and then pulled away the tarp. "I believe this is what you risked the æthergates to see."

"Well now, look at you," Tesla whispered, removing his gloves.

When the scientist's bare fingers touched the mechanical device, he sighed. Eliza was convinced he would burst into tears at any moment. It reminded her a bit like Wellington's behaviour around that damnable car.

"Yes . . . yes . . ." muttered Tesla, his eyes seeming to dismantle the device in his mind. He suddenly winced. "No, that part there is Edison's handiwork. Crude, but I can see the reasoning. I suppose." He tilted his head to one side and then looked up at Wellington. "So he managed to stabilise the current. Admittedly, using the lighthouse's optics was a stroke of genius." His fingers continued to skim along the edges of various mechanisms and alternators as he spoke. "A hundred different ways to make the power distribution more efficient, and yet he just blunders on through, more worried about upsetting one of his precious fuses. I told him he needed to make those blasted things sturdier. Like trying to support an ocean liner's hull on an eggshell." Suddenly, Tesla's voice displayed real emotion: bitterness. "My design, but very much Edison's style. If you can call it as much."

"Don' know if this trinket will mean anything to you," Bill spoke, pulling from his satchel what Eliza recognised as the dead man's switch from the Usher operative. "He did have one of his boys wired with one of these."

Tesla looked over the jumble of wires and clockwork, clicked his tongue, and grabbed the suspended magnifying glass from where he had been laying out tools. He positioned the device on its stand, suspending it over the breastplate of the dead man's switch and studying the array as would a biologist over a dissected frog.

"You're welcome," Bill huffed.

"It appears that Edison is making his new pastime taking my ideas and bringing them to fruition." He looked up from the kill switch and said, "Stands to reason. He has plenty of resources that I, unfortunately, do not. He has spent all his life capitalising on the ideas of others, granting him the ways and means to create all this," he said, motioning to the portable death ray and the kill switch.

"We know Edison's been a step ahead of us," Bill said gruffly. "So how does you coming along with us help the situation exactly?"

Tesla fixed his gaze upon Bill, and Eliza felt a shiver dance through him, thankful such a look was not aimed in her direction.

The scientist brushed off his hands, though there was nothing apparently on them, before answering Bill. "I understand these concepts and contraptions better than you, and I know Edison far better than anyone else in this room. If he has not deviated too dramatically from his bombastic manner, I can provide you insight on what he is doing next."

"Valid points, Mr. Tesla," Eliza spoke, her tone as pointed and focused as his had been, "but you are hardly a trained field agent and able to defend—"

"Madam, I am capable of defending myself." He then turned to look at her. "Do you really believe the gentleman behind the Tesla Knuckles to be a shrinking violet?"

Eliza arched an eyebrow. "Touché."

The scientist took his jacket off and returned his attention to the death ray contraption. "I am going to need some time to study this unintentional Tesla-Edison collaboration. Doctor Blackwell, would you be too troubled in assisting me on this endeavour?"

There was something genuinely endearing in watching Blackwell transform from scientist to giddy schoolgirl in an instant. From underneath her massive hoop skirts, Josepha Blackwell danced on the tips of her toes, and softly clapped her hands together. The woman practically bowled over both Felicity and Bill in order to get to the Serbian.

"Mr. Books, could I trouble you to remain here, simply to walk me through your eyewitness accounts." He gave an awkward nod to him as an apology.

Wellington smoothed out his coat, more out of a nervous gesture than attempting to press out the wrinkles within the fabric. "I am more than happy to assist." He was determined not to spin a pirouette as Josepha had done, but Eliza could tell it had crossed his mind.

"Excellent," Tesla said, beginning to roll up his sleeves. "Professor, I know your time is limited, but if you have a moment?"

"For a colleague and peer, of course I do," Axelrod replied brightly.

"Excellent." Tesla's smile widened as he fished in his coat pocket and produced a small slip of paper. "If you would not mind, I am in need of libation. From my briefing of Flagstaff, I understand there is a purveyor of juices in this town, perhaps two establishments west of here. Would you have them make a drink following these specifications?"

Axelrod stood there, staring at Tesla, who slipped the paper between his fingers and then turned back to the death ray device, where Blackwell eagerly awaited.

"Yes." Axelrod glanced at the order again and then back at Tesla. "Straightaway." It was a rather strangled affirmation.

As the head of Ministry's R&D proceeded out into the Arizona sun, Eliza caught a glance of Wellington, who'd never looked happier.

"And why are you smiling so broadly?" Eliza whispered to him.

"Just savouring one of the best moments during my time with the Ministry," he replied with a slight sigh. "Ever."

EIGHTEEN

❦

Wherein Our Dashing Archivist and
Our Colonial Pepperpot Survive
a Moment Interrupted

Eliza, still dressed in her morning robes and desperately
craving a strong cup of breakfast tea, stared out of the window at the panoramic view, one she was certain was best
shared from bed with a warm lover lying beside you.

And now I am thinking of Wellington.

She pinched the bridge of her nose, and screwed her eyes
shut. "Gods, I have been away from home for far too long."

"Beg your pardon?" the voice came from the doorway.

Eliza picked up the drinking glass from the bedside table
and brandished it aloft. It was most satisfying to see Wellington dive to the ground.

"You're right," he said quickly waving a hand, "I should
have knocked!"

Her grip tightened on the makeshift weapon. She still
wanted very much to throw it.

"Just thinking aloud," Eliza said, finally curbing her desires,
and lowering the glass to her side.

Wellington looked up from the floor. "Thinking?" He

chewed on his bottom lip for a moment. "Don't you think better when being shot at?"

She tossed the glass up in the air and caught it, trying her best not to let her mood show. Still, at least she knew he remembered some things. "I do, but as it is the morning, and I have not partaken of breakfast yet . . ."

"Neither have I," he said, getting to his knees.

That was when Eliza noticed the grease and oil smudges on his shirt. She wondered how much sleep he had got last night.

"I know, I am quite a sight," he said, adjusting his glasses on his nose. "Just give me a moment to change out of this work shirt."

"Wellington," Eliza said, crossing her arms, "a moment if you please." She was no trembling maid or delicate thing. She was a woman of *Aotearoa*. She was better than this. Eliza drew in her breath and looked squarely into his eyes. "I want to have a word with you."

Wellington cleared his throat and returned her gaze. "Yes, Miss Braun?"

She blinked, as he got to his feet. Sometimes she forgot he was taller than she was.

"I am assuming you wish to test my observations, assess how I am handling the field, yes?" Wellington frowned at her silence. "What would you have of me, Eliza?"

"I—" she began. He was as close to her now as he had been in the Archives. She could smell the combination of sweat, oil, and steam on his skin. She wanted him to kiss her like that again. Why didn't he? Why didn't she for that matter just grab him? Lost, she ended up blurting out. "I must know what your game is."

His brow knotted and that charming look of befuddlement flickered across his face.

But only for an instant. "*My* game?" He rested a fist on his hip as he added, "You and that brash git Wheatley are attempting to perform an emergency tonsillectomy on one another while Pinkertons are bearing down on us, and *you* want to know what *my* game is?"

Eliza had steeled herself for that, although she had not expected Wellington's depiction of Wheatley's unexpected kiss to be so graphic. Still, she ploughed on. "Trust me, Doctor Books, your own surgical skills were quite impressive in the Archives, yes?"

A hit. A very palpable hit. *Don't you agree, Johnny Shakespeare?* she seethed.

"Ah, yes, in the Archives . . ." Wellington said, nodding. His hazel eyes darted away from hers as he removed his spectacles. "Is this something really appropriate for public discussion?"

"No, it's more suited for a private discussion, a conversation stymied by either demands of the mission"—and then she flicked the tail of his work shirt—"or that ruddy contraption of yours!"

Perhaps it had not been the right thing to bring the motorcar into this, because he was as sensitive about it as if he was its damned father. He raised a finger. "Now just a moment, there's a reason I've been working on that 'ruddy contraption' as you so eloquently put it . . ."

"One would have thought you kissed the motorcar instead of me," she said, feeling her annoyance rise with each word that passed between them.

"But there's a *reason* for—" Wellington caught his thought in mid-speech, and averted his eyes once more. Apparently he was trying to calm himself by taking in the view of the mountains. "You want to know why," he snapped, his words clipped, "why I kissed you in the Archives?"

"No." Eliza stepped closer, and that brought his eyes back on her. "I want to know why you kissed me *like that* in the Archives?"

Wellington tilted his head. "Like what?" He thought about it a moment and then nodded. "Oh. Like . . . *that.*"

"Yes, Welly." She longed to just lean forwards and kiss the hell out of him, but this moment was strung on a knife edge, and Eliza would not upset the balance. She wasn't sure if Wellington had been struggling with this also, but they were going to see this to the end. They were going to have this talk.

He fidgeted with the stained cloth, wringing it between his hands.

"You have to understand," Wellington began, "this is . . . difficult for me."

"I was the one getting kissed, and then left dangling for days upon days," Eliza said. "You're not alone on this, mate."

"Yes, I know. I—" And he shut his eyes tight. Then, following a long, slow draw of air, Wellington blurted out, "Eliza, if you must know—"

Knock-knock-knock.

Both she and Wellington leapt apart. Whoever was behind that door had better be frightfully important. She eliminated the possibility of Sound, Axelrod, or Blackwell. They had returned to England the previous night. It couldn't be Tesla, since they'd left him at the five-and-dime, working on the death ray device.

Before she could stop him, Wellington had opened the door. Eliza clenched her jaw shut and managed to hold back the expletive that trembled on her lip. It almost burst out when the knocker was revealed.

Felicity Lovelace's smile matched her outfit. It was bright, cheerful, and a picture of sweet perfection. Decked in spotless pastel pink and green and liberal accents of lace and bow, she looked absolutely darling. So darling, in fact, that Eliza longed to punch her square in the nose.

What was more, Felicity was carrying a tray bearing orange juice, the miracle of proper tea, ham, eggs, toast, and as a centrepiece a modest vase, a single red rose in it. A proper breakfast to be sure.

For one.

"Good morning, Wellington!" Felicity said cheerily. "I was bringing you breakfast, and on the way I intercepted the bellhop; he had a message for you." She nodded to the slip of paper tucked under the glass of juice. "It simply reads: 'Come at once if convenient. Breakthrough. N.T.' Pretty safe assumption that we are now needed at the five-and-dime."

"A lovely meal you have there," Eliza said, drawing closer to the door, almost like a panther bearing down on a deer.

"Oh dear me," Wellington spoke suddenly. "Your arms must be tiring. Please, do come in."

Eliza continued to locate any and all vulnerable points on Felicity's person as the American made her way across the suite. "No matter. I made the bold assumption you were awake as I heard movement." She looked over to Eliza as she set the tray down. "The walls here are so thin."

You. Bitch.

"Breakfast is served, and by the time you finish and Eliza"—Felicity looked over to her, motioning a hand from her head to her feet—"dresses, we can all be off to the safe house, yes?"

"Of course," Wellington said with a sigh.

Eliza gave the librarian a tight smile as she walked over to the breakfast. "Give us—"

"Twenty minutes," Wellington interrupted her.

"Excellent!" Felicity beamed. "Bill and I will meet you downstairs."

She turned to leave with a rustle of silk, but Wellington stopped her. "Felicity?"

"Yes?" the American asked softly. "You need me?"

Eliza was now looking for objects to throw.

"I am in need of a favour," he began, and then motioned to Eliza. "As we are on official business now, I am in a state, and time is a luxury, would you mind fetching a hotel maid? My partner is in need of assistance in getting ready." Her smile faltered for a moment. Wellington appeared not to notice, but Eliza did. "It would mean a great deal to me if you would do so."

"But of course, Wellington," Felicity said, her cheeriness now sounding slightly forced. "I shan't be long." With a glance to Eliza, she turned and disappeared out the door.

As soon as she was gone Eliza spun on him. "In the field you usually make sure I am laced up."

"I don't think that is very appropriate at the moment," Wellington muttered, snatching up the glass of orange juice.

"Welly—" She hated the tone of her own voice immediately.

"Eliza, I suggest partaking of breakfast," he interrupted, motioning to the meal intended for him. "Your maid will be here in a few moments."

Wellington gave his hands another wipe down, gingerly grabbed a fresh shirt and vest, and disappeared into the washroom.

This was, most certainly, not over.

She had only made it two steps when a soft rap sounded at the door. Eliza nearly tore the door free from its frame, her free hand cocked back and ready to indulge that earlier urge—

Her fist remained locked and suspended by her head when she saw the Royal maid, her bright, pleasant demeanour suddenly replaced by abject terror.

"My apologies," Eliza muttered, dropping the fist to her side. "I'm not a morning person."

The young lady who came up to tend to Eliza was waifish but had the pull of a team of oxen. On the third pull, Eliza gave a sharp grunt. She thought absently how this girl could give her maid back home, Alice, a run for her money. On the fifth tug, she wondered if Felicity had paid the woman extra for this abuse.

Once dressed, Eliza stepped out and met Wellington in the parlour. Just behind the archivist was a valet. The attendant must have come in while she and the maid were engaged in suiting up for the day. Slipping what appeared to be a generous tip to the valet, Wellington discharged the man and turned to offer his arm to Eliza. He was, much to her delight, dressed impeccably, as usual.

In fact, he appeared taller. The outfit was lying quite handsomely on him.

"Wellington—"

"As you told me, this is an assignment, not a holiday." He motioned in the direction of the exiting valet. "This morning, I thought to indulge. Shall we?"

She'd been so close to getting a straight answer from him. If it had not been for . . .

"There you are!" Felicity declared brightly from the base of the staircase. Bill stood behind the librarian, loosing a stunning smile at Eliza. "I take it the maid I sent up was satisfactory?" she asked. With a wry grin, Felicity then added, "I wanted to make sure you were properly attended."

And there was the confirmation. "Well," Eliza said, running her hands along her stomach. "I feel quite secure. While I can normally take a bullet wearing this thing, I believe now I could take a cannonball."

"And you look great in it too." Bill delivered the compliment so easily as he hooked his thumbs in his belt. "Belle of the ball, you are."

At her side, Eliza could feel Wellington shift uncomfortably. She needed to disarm this straightaway, let Wellington know where Bill stood in her eyes.

Before she could reply properly, Bill spoke. "Edison's here. After we left Tesla with the death ray, I took a night watch, keeping an eye on the station and all. Not sure where he caught the train, but it wasn't a hypersteam. The Wizard, the Usher fellah, and the Pinks all shuffled off the train at four this morning. I overheard him say something about limited range and next time they'll find a hypersteam station."

Wellington nodded. "I'm surmising that clever escape craft of his has restrictions."

"You could be right about that," Bill said, rubbing his beard. "He didn't look none too pleased when he checked into the Concord hotel across town."

"So he's still keeping the pretence of a tour?" Eliza asked.

Bill held up a local newspaper. "Front-page news. He's talking tonight at the Town Hall. No announcement of any cancellation."

"So we know where Edison is: his hotel, asleep. Bill, keep an eye on the Concord. Anything changes, come get us."

He nodded. "Sounds good, Lizzie."

Eliza motioned to the doors, slipping on a pair of sun spectacles. "Let's get going. Tesla's waiting on us."

The three of them were soon strolling in Flagstaff's morning light. Wellington leading Eliza on one arm, Felicity on the other. To curious eyes they must have just appeared as one lucky man with two attractive ladies, but Eliza instinctively kept her eyes moving from building to building. Casing the town was the only thing keeping Eliza from throttling the librarian.

"A death ray able to pick off ships from the sky," Wellington mused, "a portable dynamo powering this weapon, and one of America's most innovative minds at the centre of it all." He looked at Felicity. "We're missing something."

"Well, yes," she said, "intent."

"No, I mean, we're missing something that could help us draw a conclusion and decipher Edison's intent," Wellington said as they reached the five-and-dime. "If we could just find that missing piece, we may be able to have a stronger grasp on this investigation. We still don't know why he's in Flagstaff."

Felicity chuckled softly as she pulled out the small key and disengaged the lock. "You make it sound as if the clue is right in front of us."

"There is a good possibility it is," Eliza said, still checking corners and side paths. "Personalities like Edison tend to show off. We have dealt with our fair share of maniacs with the flair for the dramatic," she added as they entered the dim general store, its display windows still covered and interior illuminated with lanterns.

"You got my message? Excellent." Tesla was standing at the counter, his gaze focused on a small component no longer than his hand. He was fastening the two parts together. When a hard *click* sounded, he said, "Follow me."

He strode to the back of the five-and-dime where three lanterns were casting more concentrated light for the table. The array's components were displayed in precise rows. Eliza strolled over to the dismantled array for a closer look, picking up one of the death ray's mechanisms—perhaps this was a timing disc of some fashion—for a closer look. The hiss escaping from Tesla froze everyone in place, making it easy for the scientist to slip between them to snatch the part from Eliza's hand. It was as if he were handling a piece of Ming Dynasty china how Tesla returned the palm-sized disc back to where it had been originally placed.

If Tesla had not done that, Eliza would have never caught the pattern.

The items removed from the targeting array were lined up in three long rows extending from either side of the array's case. From the edge of the table, the three rows were only three items deep in width.

"Welly?" she whispered.

"Yes, the pattern," Wellington replied. "I think you're looking at the price of brilliance."

"Mr. Tesla," Felicity began, her hand hovering over the three-by-three pattern of mechanical devices and parts, "have you . . . slept?"

Tesla blinked, and then gave a forced grin, perhaps an attempt to appear civil. "I . . ." He blinked again, seeming to notice Felicity as if for the very first time. "Miss Lovelace, I sometimes prefer not to sleep in matters of importance such as this."

The three agents looked to one another, the silence threatening to smother them all before Wellington spoke up with a slight cough. "So . . . you said you had a breakthrough of some kind here?"

"Yes, I did." Tesla walked over to the opposite side of the table where the parts had been arranged and held out a hand over a group of rows. Eliza swallowed hard as she noted the three rows and columns had also been segregated into three groupings. She took a deep breath, pushing back her own impulsive thoughts, as Tesla began. "This group controlled the input of power. The second group here was more centric to calibration, coordinates, and targeting. And this group," he said, holding his hand over the final group of components, "is for regulating output. Based on Mr. Books' notes, I can attest that Edison has a fairly impressive but rather inelegant replica of my design."

Eliza stiffened. "That's your breakthrough?"

"No," Tesla said, returning to the husk. "This prototype is Edison's ridiculous method of operation realised. He loves to say, 'If I find ten thousand ways something won't work, I haven't failed. I am not discouraged, because every wrong attempt discarded is another step forward.' A rather slapdash approach to science," he scoffed. "Therefore if we make the assumption that Edison is remaining true to his past methods, I believe the Currituck death ray was meant to be broken. Test it to an inch beyond its endurance, then build on the failure. The final test, according to your accounts, Mr. Books, was more about power levels. You will note here," Tesla said, motioning to several of the devices in the "output" group, "the pitted and scorched condition?"

Wellington adjusted his spectacles and nodded. "These components are burned out."

"The death ray was only sustainable for one small, concentrated burst," Tesla said, tapping on a small stack of papers next to the death ray casing, his eyes wildly darting over each component, each grouping. "One short burst of energy, while impressive, is hardly worth the risk of discovery. He now needs to sustain the beam's integrity."

"So Edison has a targeting mechanism," she repeated. "He also has a better dynamo for increased output. What are we missing?"

"Better optics," Felicity whispered suddenly, looking over to Tesla.

"Exactly," Tesla said.

"That's why we're here in Flagstaff," she added, her pale skin now turning an unhealthy shade of green.

Eliza leaned forwards. "Care to enlighten your guests?"

"A pair of scientists—Lowell and Douglass, I believe their names are—petitioned a few years ago to build an observatory in the A.T. The designs were ambitious, and they got their wish. The observatory went active just two years ago." Felicity looked at both Eliza and Wellington. "Care to guess where it is?"

"And that's why we're here," Wellington said. "The optics of a telescope are hardly the same cut or curvature as the lenses used with a lighthouse. However . . ."

Eliza drew to his conclusion quickly. "Those optics could easily be manipulated and modified. We're talking about Edison and he has been looking to increase everything. Efficiency. Output. With the right optics and the proper mods, he could easily increase range."

Wellington shook his head. "We are still no nearer in deducing exactly what his ultimate plan is with the House of Usher."

"You could always ask him." All eyes now turned to Tesla as he took them all in, one at a time. "He established an office here not more than a year ago. The other end of town. Edison has never been very concerned with secrecy."

"Right then," Felicity said, "I'll fetch Bill at the Concord, and we can pay Edison a visit."

"Just a moment," urged Wellington, "if we go in with guns blazing, we may very well fail in discovering Edison's ultimate intentions for this death ray."

"Which is why we are going to go collect Edison properly," she replied. Felicity then turned to Eliza. In the woman's eyes, that rivalry had been set aside. She was all business. "I know you understand what needs to be done, Eliza, yes?"

"I think Wellington is right," she insisted.

"You do?" Felicity asked, stunned.

"You do?" Wellington asked, equally stunned.

Ye gods, Eliza swore silently, *I cannot afford to do anything else stupid from here on out!* "Yes," she repeated through clenched teeth, "I think Welly is right. All we know is Edison has a death ray and that he's come to Flagstaff for improved optics. This means he's building an even better one, yes? Where? We need to proceed carefully.

"Felicity, if you and Bill help Tesla here pack up the death ray prototype, Wellington and I will case the Red Rock Theatre, where Edison is speaking tonight. We will note known entrances, exits, possible abduction spots." Felicity went to contradict her, but Eliza immediately cut her off. "You are a clever girl, I would never question that"—Felicity arched a single eyebrow on those words—"but this is the mission and you are quite green concerning spycraft. Four people are far more likely to be spotted in a simple casing of the location."

She looked between the two of them, and then gave a reluctant nod. "Fair point."

That must have been painful.

"We will meet you and Bill at the Royal"—Eliza checked her pocket watch—"at three? We have the upper hand at present. Best not to lose it."

"Agreed," Felicity admitted.

Eliza gave a nod, then motioned to Wellington. "Let's go take a closer look at this theatre, shall we?" she asked as she replaced her sun spectacles over her eyes. "See you at the Royal, Felicity."

Once outside, Wellington offered Eliza his arm, and they began a slow stroll along the main street of Flagstaff. They continued in the shade of shop awnings until the cover ceased, stepping into the sunlight and open space before a grand building advertising tonight's audience with Thomas Edison. Eliza smiled up to her partner, and then gave his arm a light tug. They continued past the wide building and took a moment underneath the awning of another row of storefronts.

"There's the Red Rock Theatre," Wellington said, motioning with his head.

He didn't point. Good. He was learning.

Still, he had a bit to go before he was ready to be out by himself. "Excellent observation. Now, follow me."

His head bobbed between the building and Eliza. "I thought we were going to the theatre to case all access points?"

"We will," she said with a little smile. "Once we return from Edison's workshop, the only other establishment in a town like Flagstaff that would hold the interest of a cad like Edison."

Eliza had just made it to the front of a hardware store when from behind her, she heard the rhythmic *thump-thump-thump* of Wellington's feet against wooden planks.

"Aren't we trying to keep the peace with our American counterparts?" Wellington asked under his breath. "You told Felicity—"

"I know what I told her." Yes, their goodwill presence was supposed to be as only "observers" in this investigation. Considering everything up to this point, some New Zealand initiative and British ingenuity was needed. "I think that the Americans are ready to charge in with guns blazing, as Americans are wont to do. We need a closer look at this workshop."

Wellington blinked. "Eliza, these sorts of decisions should be cleared with the director."

"Well, he's back in London," she hissed. "And how long do you think it will be before Edison decides to turn this invention against the Empire? One man should not have that much destructive capability at his whim."

"A noble thought," Wellington said, looking around them for a moment. He leaned in closer, unsettling Eliza for a brief second. "So how are we to go about doing this?"

Now they were firmly in her territory. "Follow my lead. I should be able to get us in and out without anyone noticing, not even our delightful American companions."

Eliza then slipped her arm into the crook of Wellington's and gave him a tug. Together, they made for Edison's workshop, the time for protest behind them. The time for action, ahead.

INTERLUDE

❦

In Which Miss del Morte
Learns about America

Being Madame Fiammetta Fiore was no great hardship, but being on the arm of a mad Scotsman was. Sophia allowed herself to be led around and have her feet trodden on by McTighe for several days. Most of his conversations were about things that she couldn't understand one bit. The meaning of freckles, the movement of cloud formations over the Isle of Skye, or the history of copper coins. Rantings of a brilliant lunatic. Now she understood that the "Mad" moniker he had earned was entirely appropriate. Albert was going to be the harder target, since that OSM agent assigned to him, Martha Harris, never let him out of her sight.

It was always the women, Sophia mused, watching her over the rim of her morning cup of tea. The assassin took the female of the species far more seriously than the male. She knew all too well that one of the "weaker sex" had to work much harder to rise into any position of power. Despite the recent advances in technology and society, women were still seen as creatures that needed to be protected. But Sophia's mother, the renowned courtesan Francesca del Morte, had taught her daughter that strength did not merely lie in weapons alone. It was also in the mind. This Miss Harris required some assessment.

Hamish McTighe was up in his suite today on account of a rather severe cold, thanks to an additive Sophia had dropped into his nightly single malt. Now she was freer than she had been in a few days.

A lucky thing for Hamish too. Sophia had reached the stage where she was quite willing to risk bloodshed just to be free of him. It was her preferred modus operandi, but since joining the Maestro's employment, she had stretched her skill set to its utmost. Assassinating nobility had been a pastime for her. *Kidnapping* nobility? Something new, at least when it came to royals. A fact she had to remind herself again and again as she loaded the dart gun that morning.

Sophia took a sip of her tea and smoothed down the rather plain bronze-coloured day dress she had picked out this morning. The only concession to luxury was the narrow trim of fur at the neck and on the trailing edge. It was as simple as Sophia's wardrobe got.

The prince's American agent, in Sophia's observations of her, was more than competent at keeping an eye on him, but she didn't appear to be heavily armed. Sophia's assessment was that this Martha Harris had been chosen for her assignment because of her looks. The prince appeared charmed with her, her dark skin and shapely figure most becoming to him. Bertie's lingering gaze insinuated that he desired a more intimate adventure with her. Like all men, it was not the head on his shoulders that led him.

Sophia stirred her tea, and drank another sip. She was proud of the fact that anyone observing her would never have been able to tell she hated the stuff. Far too much time in England had forced her to drink lakes of the dishwater beverage, yet without it a lady often had nothing to mask her intentions while seated.

So when Miss Harris came downstairs, and walked to the concierge desk, Sophia was careful to be busy about adding more lumps of sugar to her cup. She watched with her peripheral vision as Harris stood at the desk, waiting impatiently for someone to tend to her. The concierge in his very fine dark green coat continued whatever menial task held his attention at the other end. Sophia knew this was a trivial thing as she had seen two other hotel patrons approach the concierge, both patrons receiving the man's undivided attention. Martha Harris was the exception, even when he completed whatever was at his desk. The agent was visible to him, and yet he did not seem ready to acknowledge her existence. He sat there for a moment, his eyes darting in the direction of Miss Harris for a brief instant, then set to stacking some papers. Something about the set of Harris' shoulders suggested that she was used to this.

America was a strange creature to Sophia; always talking about liberty for all, and yet failing so miserably to provide it. Their recent war might have proven a point, but its good intentions were still some way from filtering down to the actual people.

An immaculately dressed red-haired woman approached the desk at the other end, also ignoring Miss Harris. Immediately, the concierge was on his feet, tending to the lady, standing mere inches from Harris. Sophia managed to hide a smile. She would have laid odds that the agent was having trouble repressing the urge to smash the man's face into his own counter.

The red-haired woman and the concierge were talking about travel plans, and sights to see in the area. From the look of the travel brochures in the woman's hands, Harris would be waiting for some time. This would leave the prince unprotected for, at the longest, thirty minutes, depending on how many places this patron wished to visit.

She recalled McTigue's comments earlier when he had first introduced Sophia to the prince. He would be on the fourth floor. Before the lift came to a halt, she pulled back the inner gate, opened her handbag, and pulled out her compact.

This early in the morning, especially after a night of carousing, there would be few people in the hallways, and those in their rooms asleep or groggy. Her chances of moving undetected were all in her favour. Still, she kept her footsteps light as she crept down the row of suites. She opened her compact and held the mirror down low and angled out in order to peer around the corner. The way was clear. She looked over her shoulder, and then swept as quietly as possible back the way she came. Reaching the end, she repeated the manoeuvre.

The man currently standing in front of the prince's door appeared remarkably alert for this time of the morning. He was also quite large. If he were the *first* line of defence for her to face, his counterpart would be even more formidable.

She put her compact in her purse, and took out a dark mask of hard leather, with two small cylindrical filters fixed on either side of it. Once the mask was secured around her mouth and nose, she fished out a silver ball that fit quite nicely in the palm of her hand. She then glanced at the fob dangling from her dress, checked the time, and gave the sphere a slight twist from each side.

On hearing the sphere click, Sophia began a silent count to ten as she tossed it towards the man and then disappeared back around the corner flipping up the mask's eye shields. Sophia calmly walked around the corner, her carriage confident and hardly rushed. Perhaps her fashion was bizarre, at present, but she would wear it with all assurance.

The guard had seen the sphere first as his eyes were cast downwards. When he looked back up to see a woman of pleasant proportions, her stunning outfit topped by a monstrous visage of brass, leather, and glass, he drew his sidearm. The weapon had cleared his jacket when the sphere tapped at his foot. He disappeared in a rush of greenish gas that enveloped him, turning whatever warning he attempted to shout into a sickening retch. The guard was already dead considering how his body collapsed onto the fine-carpeted floor underneath them.

A second guard, alerted by the sound of dead weight falling in the hallway, appeared in the door. Sophia knew the first burst was lethal, but once dissipation occurred it was nothing more than an irritant.

That did not mean it was a *mild* irritant.

Sophia was only a few steps away when she caught sight of tears glistening against the guard's cheeks, his pistol faltering in his grasp and his breath audible in excruciatingly harsh, dry coughs. A quick flick of her wrist, and the concealed stiletto shot out of its hiding place under her very respectable sleeve and stabbed the guard's forearm twice, releasing his grip on his weapon. The other arm came around in a wild left hook that Sophia ducked under. She leapt on the man's wide back and drove the stiletto deep into his neck. He stumbled back, but Sophia continued to ride him as if he were a fine performance horse until he joined his compatriot on the floor.

The bloody stiletto still in hand, Sophia stepped into the prince's suite. The man she recognised as the valet was on his feet, a modified blunderbuss braced against his hip.

"To arms!" the man screamed just before Sophia dove to one side.

An explosion ripped through the mêlée, but she was a moving target and this man was not an experienced shot. Sophia stood from her roll and shot her other arm out forwards, sadly ripping the respectable sleeve and cuff there, and two razor-discs sailed across the suite and knocked the valet to the ground. Unlike her, the brave servant to the prince would not be getting back up.

Sophia took a few moments to get the tingle of excitement running under her skin back in control. She had not enjoyed this sort of kill for quite a time, and she found that she had missed it. Scooping up the fob hanging from her waist, she noted the time, the second hand also helping her rein in her thrill. She still had time, but could not kill the man in the final room. The Maestro wanted him alive.

She kicked open the door with a well-planted foot and immediately dove for the floor on hearing the generator. A wild, frantic display of lightning bolts reached above her and singed the walls, shattered wall fixtures, and destroyed a breakfast setting where the valet had originally been. From her purse, Sophia pulled out the small dart gun, leaned out from her hiding place, and fired. Prince Albert hefted his unique rifle but no second volley came. Sophia's dart had landed square in his chest. By the time Bertie got his hand on it, he was already falling.

She ripped the mask free, tasting fresh, unfiltered air. He landed hard, but he would get no compassion from her. Soon enough, under her care, he would be earning more bruises. Heaving from underneath Bertie's armpits, she dragged the unconscious prince through the servant's door, hefted him into the lift, and then joined him in a ride down to the laundry. The convenient carts on the ground floor she could use to push his not-inconsiderable bulk to the rear entrance. There, her driver could manage the prince into her carriage. This morning's abduction was about keeping things simple.

The lift doors shuddered open.

"Room service!" Martha Harris spoke cheerfully just before punching her hard in the nose.

This was not the first time Sophia had taken a blow there, and so she avoided the natural reaction to clasp her face. Still hurt like the devil, but she managed to stay standing. Her vision flared white for an instant, and yet through the glare she could see a form she knew was Harris. The thing in front of her lolled and shifted in her eyes, and then snapped into focus. Harris' second jab was coming straight for her. Sophia's hands came up and landed a strong hold on the American, yanking her into the lift, sending her chin into Sophia's elbow, and pushing the black woman back into the hallway wall.

"Between the wait for the idiot at the concierge desk and all the lovely reflective surfaces downstairs," Harris said, pulling herself off the wall, "you didn't think I spotted you, did you?"

Sophia did not respond. Her own body was flush with the joy of battle now. The punch to the face had been unexpected. That meant Miss Harris was formidable. And as she loosened her skirts and stepped free of them, she recalled how she preferred being up close and personal like this with opponents.

Harris did not enjoy it as much when Sophia's knee stopped her charge. Martha struggled to catch her breath, leaving herself open for a kick, but Sophia's leg was in Martha's iron grasp before it could reach its target. The assassin found herself thrown hard into the wall and then, a moment later, on the floor. She attempted to roll out of the way as Harris unleashed several kicks to her rib cage.

"Nice corset," Martha quipped. "Before I turn you in to the authorities, I'm going to want the name of your tailor."

Getting her feet under her, the assassin returned her stiletto back to her grasp. She feinted right, but Harris ignored the bait, trapping then twisting her arm, driving the blade between the door and its frame. She then pushed hard against Sophia, and the blade snapped free of its hilt.

Sophia loved that blade.

"Puttana!" she spat, charging forwards. Elegance and technique were both supplanted by all-out brawling, both women landing what blows they could. Sophia, through the flurries of punches, jabs, and slaps, caught sight of a stairwell, perhaps leading to a basement. She grasped tight to Harris and pushed her to what she hoped would be her death on the narrow staircase.

Unfortunately, her opponent was far too clever for her to get away with that.

Harris wrapped a free arm around Sophia's waist, and together they slammed against the stairwell. The assassin landed on top of Harris, and proceeded to strangle the life out of the agent who had broken her favourite stiletto. Harris brought the heel of her palm straight up into Sophia's lip, breaking the Italian's hold on her.

Sophia scurried back away from Harris, just as the prince moaned from the floor of the lift. This was not going as planned. She should already have been out of the building with her prize, instead of roughing it with this harlot. This scuffle was costing her time. Time she didn't have as the commotion in the prince's suite would have assuredly alerted others by now.

The door to the first floor rooms popped open and a maid appeared with a stack of towels in her hands. At the sight of a coloured woman standing in a martial challenge stance, an Italian lady dressed in the top half of a day dress and tight trousers, and the heir to the throne of England lying in the servants lift, she apparently did what came naturally. The ear-piercing scream Sophia seized as her opportunity, quite literally. The assassin threw the still-shrieking woman into Harris' direction, then scrambled for the door where the maid had appeared. The exit led to an access hallway to the street. Sophia dashed down the length of the hotel, reaching the open alleyway where the hired driver was waiting.

"Andiamo!" she yelled to the cab.

The man jerked awake and urged the carriage forwards. Not waiting for it to stop, Sophia pulled herself up into the moving carriage, and secured the door just as she disappeared into the bustle of San Francisco.

As she leaned back in the seat, she let her racing heart

slow. She had underestimated Agent Martha Harris of the Office of the Supernatural and Metaphysical. It would not, however, be a mistake she would repeat.

The mark of a good assassin was to know when to retreat, and how to change the approach for the next opportunity. She knew. There would be other ones.

She would simply have to find a moment when the odds were more in her favour.

NINETEEN

❧

Wherein Our Colonial Pepperpot
Takes Advantage of What Precious
Time Remains

"You know," Wellington observed, "usually our mad scientists have their lairs hidden underground, or in desolate wastelands, or, in the case of the Culpeppers, at a country home with convenient escape airship handy. But Edison has to be a first."

"Oh, come along," chided Eliza. "Do you think death rays, evil henchmen, and raw materials come free? Man's got to earn a bob or two to pay for all these marvels of technology."

"I suppose that's one way of looking at it." Wellington and Eliza continued walking, at a slower pace this time, casting occasional glances to Edison's not-so-secret hideout.

Wellington was in desperate need of a drink, and while a chilled white wine sounded like a delightful option, he knew in Flagstaff he would be hard-pressed to find such a thing. Most especially right now as he and Eliza stood across from the Edison Illuminating Company workshop, their American counterparts completely unaware of what they were doing.

"How do we know he's not there?" Wellington asked,

shifting against the post to get comfortable. His back was to the building, but the dry goods shop window in front of him offered a clear reflection.

"Bill mentioned that Edison's train arrived very early this morning," Eliza replied, her own eyes scanning left and right. Her gaze lingered only for scant moments on Edison's workshop. "He's speaking today, so he's bound to be napping, just to make certain he is well rested for his personal appearances." Eliza reached for her fob watch dangling by her dress, flipped open the cover, and nodded. "I'll wager he won't be rising from his bed at the Concord for another hour or so, then off to tuck in with a late breakfast or early lunch, depending on his perspective."

"Are you suggesting," he said, trying not to notice how close she was standing to him, "that you have somehow gained insight into Mr. Edison's personal habits without ever clapping eyes on him?"

"Not at all," Eliza said with a chuckle. "I am simply relying on one of the most accurate of timekeepers—a man's stomach."

As if answering to her voice, Wellington felt his own grumble. He regretted not partaking of that breakfast Felicity had so kindly fetched for him earlier.

She took a few steps away from him, nodded for no apparent reason, took in a breath, and then said, "Shake your head, Welly, and spread your arms wide as if you are completely in the dark as to what I have apparently asked of you."

Wellington did so, adding in a hushed tone, "And we are performing this pantomime because . . . ?"

"Because, my newly promoted fellow field agent, just in case we have any curious eyes, either inside or outside the Illuminating Company, we are two people having a conversation." Eliza stood, smoothing the creases in her dress. "Part of the scenery."

"Then may I," Wellington asked, slipping a hand into his coat pocket, "suggest this accessory?"

The two magnifying lenses swivelled on a single hinge, and the tiny apparatus was fastened to a clip, which Wellington secured on one arm of Eliza's sun spectacles. She lowered one lense in front of her right eye and then gave a little start. Lowering the second one in place, she gave a small giggle as she looked over to the workshop.

"Seems that Edison should have someone tend to the windows. They're filthy." Eliza returned the second lense to a vertical position, keeping the first in place. "Quite clever, Wellington."

"I know jewellers, clockmakers, and clankertons use these ocular enhancers for precision work," the archivist replied. "I thought they would serve our own endeavours admirably."

With Eliza's fingers tightening on his arm, Wellington and his effectively accessorised partner continued on under the guise of a stroll. Even with his sun specs, the Arizona glare was quite intense. He was reminded of his time in the bush, the African sun bearing down on him and his men with only pith helmets to stave off the light.

Eliza's words broke into his reverie. "All clear, it seems," Eliza said, flipping the final ocular up and out of the way. "Are you ready to move?"

"Yes, it would seem so," he replied as quietly as possible.

"Let's just wander another two storefronts down, cross the street, and then find our way in."

Wellington hesitated, considering the woman on his arm. "That's the plan then?" He gave his bottom lip a gentle nibble. "We have no idea how many are in there!"

"Details, Welly, details," she said as they continued past Edison's workshop. "But you should know there is one Pink keeping watch upstairs, and two more just visible in the lower right window."

"Very well then." Wellington licked his lips. "You've done this before, so I'll follow your lead."

"Tosh," she scolded, "it's not like we haven't been on a case before. Just this one is—"

"Sanctioned," he interjected drily.

The fact she had chosen the moment a horse-drawn wagon rumbled by to cross was not lost on him. They slipped into the gritty veil of dust and sand, the sun specs shielding their eyes a bit as they continued into the alleyway. Eliza slipped her hand into the open fold of her skirts and produced her

Remington-Elliot. Wellington could see each barrel indicator was green, providing an odd comfort as they crept closer to the rear of the structure.

Eliza held up a lace-gloved hand, stopping him in his tracks as she peered around the corner. Wellington stared at her fingers, noting that such delicacy was better suited taking a high tea or perhaps a spot of cross-stitching, not taking part in clandestine operations in the Americas.

"All clear, Welly," she whispered as she continued around the corner.

Just as he followed her, it became apparent she had pulled back the hammer on her weapon.

"What in God's name are you doing?" he hissed, pushing the gun down just as she raised it.

"We have to get in here," Eliza said, with a determined twist of her lips, "and the '81 here serves as quite the skeleton key."

By Jove, she was at it again! "Not to mention an attention getter," he said desperately.

"Time's not a luxury we have," Eliza bit back, "so unless you have another idea, or a key on your person perhaps?"

"Well now you come to mention it," Wellington said, reaching underneath his coat, "I do have this." The Jack Frost, once out in the sunlight, looked even more complicated in its design. It also looked larger, for some odd reason. "Shall we see if this bloody thing works?" he asked, giving the heavy weapon in his hand a slight shake.

He knew her grin should have been more disturbing to him. "Let's play with Axelrod and Blackwell's toys then." Eliza motioned to the door.

"Watch the window," Wellington said, as he studied either side of the gun. "I believe there is a setting lever here." Indeed on the inside surface of the weapon, there was a small switch that offered two options:

FROSTBITE—POLISH WINTER

Eliza peeked inside the window, then glanced back at him. "Any ideas?"

"Not like Axelrod to provide instructions for his overindulgent engineering feats," he grumbled. He flipped the switch to "Frostbite" and shrugged. "If I need more, I'll unleash the Polish Winter."

Wellington splayed his fingers around the butt of the exciter, and squeezed the trigger. It made a soft snapping noise reminiscent of ice cracking underfoot, or when trees and plant life struggled against the elements following an ice storm. However, this gentle creaking and cracking was coming from the door. From the Jack Frost itself, a cone comprised entirely of blue iridescence covered the doorknob and keyhole, blanketing the metal and surrounding wood in a thin sheet of ice that even the heat of Arizona could not melt. The ice went from a crystal clear sheen to a faint grey to a stark white within seconds.

The odd crackle stopped when Wellington released the trigger. A tendril of cold mist rose from the invention's muzzle. "Anyone notice anything?" he asked.

Eliza peered inside the window. She shook her head.

He stared at the now-white doorknob, fascinated by the fact that the pearlescent wisp rising off it was not coming from heat but the exact opposite. Wellington positioned the butt of the gun immediately above the doorknob and rapped it lightly. The knob popped out of its housing and shattered against the ground.

"Now I admit," Wellington whispered as the door swung open, "that is impressive."

Eliza held her Derringer at the ready, and gave Wellington a nod. He opened the door quickly, and she stepped in, her small pistol ahead of her. When she motioned with her head, they crept together into Edison's workshop.

The door thankfully did not creak open or shut. Both of them remained light of foot, taking wide strides, not placing their heels down hard against the wooden floor. Wellington was afraid to take a breath, in case anyone would hear it. The archivist turned as quietly as he could—but froze when a plank creaked underneath him. He dared to peer down the hallway to his left.

Two people were talking but from the opposite room, an open doorway separating Eliza and himself from Pinkertons.

Didn't Eliza say there was a man keeping watch upstairs?

"I still do not see the point of carrying out tonight's show with what happened in Detroit," the unseen man stated.

The next voice that followed was one Wellington recognised from the Carolinas. Gantry, the House of Usher man liaising with Edison. "What part of 'stick to the script provided' fails you, Sutherland? Any more deviation will only cast more suspicion, and considering how you all blundered the Currituck Experiment—"

"*We* blundered it?" Sutherland growled.

"The Pinkertons were in charge of security. Had you done your job, we could have continued operations under the myth and mystery of the Graveyard of the Atlantic, thereby maintaining our secrecy." There was a pause, and then Gantry guffawed. "The United States government is not that hard to hoodwink, but still they came. Didn't they?"

Wellington held his breath. No one was moving in this standoff between Pinkertons and the House of Usher.

The front door opened, flooding the hallway with light. Wellington ducked back into hiding with Eliza. She kept her attention on the nearby stairwell while he leaned back towards the room where Gantry and Sutherland were talking.

"He's awake," the newcomer said. "A bit more pleasant than when we got here, but not by much. I left him ordering lunch."

"Are your men ready to go?" Gantry asked in a tone that spoke of his annoyance.

"Of course they are, Elias," Sutherland bit back.

"Good. The sooner we put on a show for these trappers, the sooner we can get the optics we need and then leave."

The sound of feet scuffling against the dusty wooden floor reached Wellington as, one by one, they began walking away. Sutherland called to another Pinkerton from what he surmised was a second staircase, and footsteps above soon descended. Wellington pressed himself harder into his corner when sunlight poured into the hallway. The door closed, then locked. Neither he nor Eliza moved for a moment.

"Right then," Eliza said, returning her Derringer into its concealed holster, "I think we have the place to ourselves."

"At least for an hour, maybe two," he agreed, holstering the Jack Frost. "Edison will want the details of tonight to be completely flawless."

He poked his head into the room where Gantry, Sutherland,

and Pinkertons had been. The table was clean, apart from a small stack of papers. The top sheet spelled out tonight's agenda, a handwritten collection of lighting cues and notes, all of which he recognised as the same key points of emphasis from Edison's lecture in North Carolina. Wellington's eyes looked all over the room. Nothing more than a room for meetings such as what they overheard.

Wellington crossed the hallway over to where Eliza stood examining the next room. This one was twice as large as its counterpart, with various-sized crates bearing the General Electric logo all pushed up against the far wall. *Recent arrivals,* he thought quickly. Long tables with workbenches on either side waited for what Wellington imagined would be future projects.

His gaze followed along the ceiling the two rows of ceiling fans wired with lamps, presumably to allow the staff to work at night. Instead of the usual belt system accompanying a cooling system like this, the motors and mounts were simply housed in the ceiling, independent of one another, save for a network of coils that ran from their mounts, along the ceiling, and down the wall where the crates were stacked.

"Keep the workers cool during the day," Wellington said, motioning to the fans above. "Provide light for when you make them work into the evening." He looked around the empty room. "Rather sparse, considering this building's been here for close on a year."

"Crafty old bastard, isn't he?" Eliza suddenly blurted out.

He stared at her in disbelief. Where did *that* come from? "I beg your pardon, Miss Braun?"

"Look at how he operates. He visits cities and towns, puts on a fancy show for the locals, and then sets up a permanent business for himself. With all the excitement this codger is cooking up, he will bleed communities dry supplying them with all his latest baubles." Eliza gave a bark of a laugh. "Edison's no mad scientist. He's a shrewd businessman wrapped in the sheep's clothing of an innovator."

With a final look of disgust at the wall of crates, Eliza walked past Wellington and headed for a staircase leading up to the second floor.

"Sounds as if you do not approve of Edison's business

ethics," Wellington ventured as the two of them ascended the staircase.

"Wellington, when you grow up in the farthest reaches of the Empire, you meet many an opportunist who manage to cloud your judgement with a delightful turn of a trick or two." She shook her head as she stepped back before the closed door in front of her. "Edison's bringing the promise of a brighter tomorrow, at a cost that may send some honest people into ruin."

This was something Eliza apparently had seen before as the kick she dealt the door carried a good amount of fury behind it. The hatch and its frame did not stand a chance as it flew open, revealing an office with two desks, one at each end of the room. By the window, spent cigarettes littered the windowsill and floor.

"And there's where the lookout man had stood," Eliza said.

The floorboards creaked underneath him as he walked around one of the desks, his eyes moving from it to the chalkboard hanging between the two desks. He stood mere inches from the slate, reaching up to touch the board.

"Eliza," Wellington said, looking down at the eraser and two sticks of chalk resting in the board's cradle, "this has been cleaned recently."

"Why wouldn't it?" she asked in reply. "I'm sure the workers here need to wipe down their boards after a week or so, if Edison's the slave driver that I think he is."

"Yes, but . . ." His voice trailed off. There was no dust even in the cradle. He expected to see, at the very least, sketches for incandescent lightbulbs, lamps, or other conveniences he would not have recognised. "This is a workshop. Where ideas are realised."

"Welly, what are you getting at?"

Something was tickling the back of his brain. "Eliza, both desks are clean. Impeccably. Nothing in the desks' boxes—in or out. We heard the meeting room underneath us also in use, but there was no outward evidence of any work currently in development." He held his hands out wide. "Eliza, you have seen the basement of my home. Even R&D at the Ministry is more cluttered than this."

"The workroom—" Eliza began.

"Boxed up? No sign of any bother or toil whatsoever?"

"I put this away too soon," she grumbled, pulling out the Remington-Elliot. "Shall we see what is waiting for us up here?"

Wellington stepped behind Eliza, who was slowly crossing over the one threshold to stand before the other. If the layout was consistent, this would be a second production room of some kind as it would be directly over the other one they had seen. With her free hand, Eliza tried the doorknob, which turned freely in her hand.

"And Wellington?" Eliza whispered, looking at him over her shoulder. He shrugged in reply, earning him a groan. "You're in the field, in a hostile setting. Are you going to arm yourself?"

"With what?" he said, feeling a dry prickle in his throat. "The Jack Frost? What shall I do, give our Usher opponents a cold?"

"A second gun?"

"From where?" He then followed Eliza's gaze to the folds of her skirts. "Oh."

"No booby traps down there, I assure you," she said, her smile quite unnerving.

"Right then," he said, clearing his throat, "as I am a field agent now . . ."

His hand fumbled along the folds of Eliza's skirts until he found the opening where she could access a second Derringer. His hand reached forwards; but instead of touching the butt of the Derringer straightaway, his fingers grazed by a butt of an entirely different kind. He continued down, and found Eliza's thigh far softer than he imagined. How low did she keep this gun?

"A bit to the left," she said with an arched eyebrow.

And there it was. With his thumb, he flipped the strap from the holster and slipped the second pistol free.

Wellington gave the Remington-Elliot a cursory glance. Indicators were at green. And the gun was warm. Delightfully warm.

Hoping he wasn't blushing too hard, he pulled back the hammer, hearing the internal compressor hiss to life. "Ready then."

The door groaned from the hinges as Eliza pushed. They both heard the door knock against the inner wall, but neither of them moved.

"Eliza . . ." Wellington whispered, not in order to keep his voice down, but because his throat had suddenly gone incredibly dry.

"Yes, Welly, I know," she whispered back. She splayed her fingers around the butt of the Derringer and swallowed. "In for a penny?"

The room was completely barren, save for a single crate placed in the centre of the room. In front of the crate, a crowbar had been set. Eliza lifted up a hand, and both of them froze halfway across the room. Wellington knew his partner was still breathing, although she moved more like an automaton as her eyes swept the room, her head moving slowly from one side of the room to another.

"It's all right, Wellington," Eliza said, lowering her weapon. "It's just us and whatever is in this crate."

"This crate and its phonograph, you mean?" Wellington asked, eyeing Edison's creation as if it were his Archimedes curled up and peering down from the top of his dresser. "So what would this room be, the dance hall?"

"And the crowbar? I suppose that's needed to motivate people to relax and be social?"

"Or pry apart couples too amorous with one another," he quipped.

Eliza gave a laugh and proceeded to walk around the crate, while Wellington crept towards the window. He peered out over the street. Wagons and carts continued past while townsfolk strolled along the streets.

He cleared his throat. "No one appears to be lingering outside."

"And no sign of any activity in this—"

He heard the board creak under Eliza's step. Then it clicked.

That was when the door slammed shut on its own accord. It locked itself, as well.

Wellington knew this all served as one grand, ill omen when the phonograph on top of the crate suddenly came to life, and Edison's voice echoed in the room.

"Well hello there. Now I must first give you all my most

heartfelt appreciation for your tenacity, whoever you are. I always regarded myself as being driven, on the verge of stubborn, but for you to follow me all the way from the Outer Banks, to the Paris of the West, to the Arizona Territories?" Edison's laugh was genuine. Even the cylinder's recording made his admiration quite clear. "That truly is impressive. I applaud you.

"However, I cannot abide your pursuit of my person—flattering and inspiring as it may be—any longer . . ."

"Wellington," Eliza spoke, "crowbar."

Edison's words were drowned out as the iron wedge dug into the wood. Together, Eliza and Wellington pried open one corner, drove the wedge lower into the opening, and continued to force the opening until finally the wooden panel ripped free.

Once the crate panel settled on the floor, Edison's voice was now audible. ". . . made this detonator a bit more layered than the one in the Carolinas. I've connected it with the crates downstairs which have enough collected explosive agents and incendiaries to level this building and, I am afraid with the amount of wood structures surrounding my workshop, its neighbours too."

"The old bastard's right," Eliza said to Wellington as she studied the interior of the crate, its complicated array of wires, gears, cogs, and pins slowly ticking in time with the phonograph's cylinder. "This is going to take some time."

"If my theory about your skills is correct," Edison's recording continued, "and I have no doubt that it is, judging from how you not only kept Currituck Light intact and disarmed my first security system, I gather it would take you roughly twenty minutes to crack this enigma of mine—"

Eliza snorted. "Tosh. Fifteen minutes if I take my time."

"—which is why I have the timer—this recording—set to send a charge to the detonator in ten."

"Bugger," she swore. "That means we have roughly seven minutes."

"Seven?" Wellington asked. "But Edison said ten."

"Yes, but he's been talking for roughly three minutes. I'll wager you Edison's timer started the moment that phonograph started playing."

Edison sounded very smug. "So we all have our gates to

pass through, I suppose. My only regret is that we did not find the opportunity or means to work together. Seeing as I really can't afford the final phase of my project to suffer another delay, off you go."

"All right, empty your pockets," she said, removing her watch fob and primary belt pouch before the crate. "It may take a miracle to manage this, but I think I can make do."

"Make do?" Wellington asked, unsheathing the Jack Frost and placing it next to Eliza's belongings alongside his own watch fob and a few coins. He rummaged his pockets as he added, "This is your speciality, isn't it?"

"Yes," Eliza said, looking over the items, "provided the gent or lady who built said explosive device didn't go from his thumb to his pinkie via his elbow which is what Edison did." She picked up the nail file from Wellington's items and gave him a wary glance.

"Manicured nails are a trait of a gentleman," he stated.

She palmed it, along with one of the American half dollar coins, and both their watch fobs. "Let me see what I can do with these."

"Fine, I'll tend to the door," Wellington said.

He picked up the Derringer and checked its indicators, but he knew they were green. He would have to make the angle count. As this was hardly an armoured hatch or a heavy bolt, each bullet ripped through the wood. He stepped back once the '81 was empty, and gave the door a kick. It budged but only a little. Wellington took a step back, growled, and kicked again, this time freeing the door.

"Right then," he huffed, "one dilemma solved. Your turn, Eliza. Disarm the bomb."

"No," she said, returning to her feet and facing him.

Wellington ran over to Eliza. "Eliza? What's wrong?"

"I want to talk," she insisted. "About us."

The phonograph suddenly spoke up. "Three minutes, if you're wondering."

"You want to talk about us? *NOW?!*"

"I want to finish this morning's chat." Eliza's calm was utterly terrifying. "I want to talk about our feelings. More to the point, your feelings. About me. About us."

"Do we really need to do this at this *precise* moment?"

"I think we do," she stated. "And I suggest you make it quick because you're wasting time."

"ELIZA!" Wellington screamed, throwing the spent '81 to the floor.

"OUT WITH IT!" she shouted in return. "I'm done with these silly games, the distractions from that tart Lovelace, and you skirting about the issue."

"And if I tell you, you will turn the bomb off?"

"Of course, but I need to know. Now." She took a step forwards, crossing her arms. "Why did you kiss me? Like *that*?"

"Because I wanted to," Wellington stated. And it was true. He did want to kiss her after that business with the Culpeppers. Badly.

"And that's it?"

He blinked. "You want . . . more?"

"You just wanted a kiss?" she asked, tapping her fingers against her biceps.

"I'm not very good at this," he whimpered.

"Whatever you're doing, better make it count," Edison's voice said from the phonograph. "One minute to go . . ."

"I'd start getting better at it then." Eliza sighed. "And with the way you kiss—"

"All right then!" Wellington blurted out, "I wanted more than just a kiss. I wanted *you*. I wanted you so much in that moment, and I still do."

"Even after my blunder with Bill?"

"Yes, about that," he said, waving a finger in the air. "Did that hurt? Yes, deeply. Has anything changed in how I feel about you? Don't be ridiculous. No."

"So why not show a little interest on the airship?"

"Because I wanted the car to be perfect."

"Oh, that sodding car!" Eliza swore.

"I made it for me, but I wanted it to be perfect for you. Perhaps you would not appreciate the lost time, but I wanted to assure that we would have a return trip. And there would be a return trip assured, provided I had the car properly assembled and operational. I wanted to show you that regardless of the adventurers, the nobles, and the oil and rail barons you have loved, whether for Queen and Country or just as a passing fancy, I was just as resourceful, just as worthy of your attention. I am!

"And, yes, I am horrible at this because the one person in my family that I loved unconditionally, the people I have trusted in my military days, everyone I held dear has been taken from me, and I don't know if it was on account of the monster my father created inside of me or just my bad luck, and I couldn't take that chance with you. You awakened passions in me without unleashing what my father attempted to engineer since birth. I discovered that I could actually embrace life and not be terrified by it, terrified by what I was supposedly destined for. I was truly in control of my fate, and I could not, nor would not, risk losing you." He was rambling now, and he just didn't give a toss. "Yes, it was selfish, but I did not want to lose you too. I just couldn't bear it, Eliza. And that's why I wanted the sodding car to be perfect! So we could enjoy a return trip together. I wanted to show you that I could keep you safe, and I was worthy."

"Ten," Edison counted, "nine . . . eight . . ."

And I was just getting the hang of this, Wellington thought sadly.

Eliza's eyes softened, and the touch of her skin against his cheek made him shudder. "Wellington . . ."

So this was how it was going to end? Fine.

He pulled her close and kissed her, his embrace tightening with every second that Edison counted down. She moaned softly, and that was what he wanted to hear. Not Edison's blasted voice counting down the final seconds of life. He wanted Eliza to know what he hadn't the time to tell her. He wanted to grant her just a touch of pleasure, a final passion before shuffling off this mortal coil.

And he would, with this final kiss, this final embrace.

Her fingers raking through his hair felt exquisite. Her lips were soft, warm. Her kiss tasted sweet, and he caught the whiff of roses and tea in her skin. She was not close enough. He wished to see her naked; and he along with her, intertwined like ivy, losing sense of time and space, descending deeper into their . . .

Hold on.

Wellington pulled away, drawing in a deep breath. From the bomb there came a soft, steady hiss. The hiss wasn't from the bomb but from the phonograph that had, as far as he could tell, finished its countdown. Several seconds ago. His eyes jumped back to Eliza, who was still standing there, her lips parted slightly and bending into a very contented smile. When her eyes flicked open, she looked around, trying to gather herself.

"Well, very good then," Eliza said, stumbling back a step as she touched her hair to make certain it was still secure and in place. "Most impressive, Wellington Thornhill Books, Esquire." Her eyes fluttered, and then she brought a hand to her chest that, try as she might, would not stop heaving. "I say, old chap, what do you use to practise kissing? I remember in my youth my friends and I using a broom—"

"Eliza," Wellington said, pleased he still had a voice with which to speak, "what—" and then he motioned to the bomb, "what—?"

"Oh yes, the bomb." Eliza's smile widened, and she motioned to the Jack Frost, a faint wisp of frost reaching up from its muzzle. "I froze the detonator's battery, essentially crippling the bomb."

"And you did this—"

"I actually took care of this while you were breaking down the door." She took in another deep breath, her eyelids fluttering as she said, "So, now that we've cleared the air, shall we go?"

Eliza took up the Jack Frost and handed it to Wellington as she passed by him. He watched her leave, and then looked over at the bomb that was smoking ever so slightly. *No,* he thought, *the vapour isn't rising. It's heavier than air. Perhaps . . .* And then he lifted the Jack Frost up to his eyes. The vial he was told not to break was nearly empty. *Liquid nitrogen perhaps, or the other breakthrough of Olszewski's that he knew more intimately . . .*

"Coming, Welly?" called a voice at the bottom of the steps.

With a nod to no one in particular, Wellington holstered the exciter and proceeded downstairs to where Eliza awaited him.

"Do we exit from the front or back?" he managed to ask without bursting into a fury.

"Wellington," Eliza spoke gently, and he knew in her tone that whatever she would say to him presently, he was not going to like it. "Thank you. I know what you said up there was not easy."

"Not easy?" Wellington shook his head. "Front, it shall be then." He walked by her and spoke over his shoulder. "Miss Braun, obtaining the girdle of Queen Hippolyta, retrieving the Holy Grail, or perhaps—"

"Stealing Thor's hammer?" she offered.

"—would all have been far easier for me than what happened upstairs, if you must know." He stopped at the door and turned to face her. "And before you ask—Case 18740614NOHT. The bloody hammer weighs a ton."

Eliza blinked. "Really? I'd love to read that file . . ."

Wellington felt his jaw twitch. This was not how he had envisioned professing his true intentions for Eliza to be. Not in the Americas. Certainly not on assignment. He screwed his eyes shut and counted silently to himself. "Please, Eliza . . ."

"No, really, Wellington," she said gently, "I understand, and yes, perhaps my timing was . . ." Her words trailed off.

"Terrible?" Wellington asked.

"Awkward?"

"Inappropriate?" he ventured.

She shrugged. "All right, I will grant you that one."

He nodded, opening the door. "Well, let's see what other surprises await us out of doors."

Wellington turned, and stood eye level with a pair of pistol barrels. Smith & Wesson Revolver, .38 Calibre. The dark metal still managed to gleam in the sunlight, showing a good deal of maintenance and—without mistake—love. He dared not move, even when Eliza brandished her own Derringer and drew as clean a shot as she could from behind him. Wellington felt his brow crease as he contemplated what dumbstruck him harder—the two pistols only scant inches away from him, or the fact that their owner was a priest.

"Wellington Thornhill Books," the woman spoke coolly. "You are one hard man to catch up with."

TWENTY

❦

In Which Science Saves the Day

Eliza now knew beyond any doubt that if she were given the choice between America and Australia to establish residence, she would choose Australia. Americans were mad. All of them. It was the only rational explanation for the tableau now before her.

On the other side of Wellington was a priest—at present, denomination unknown. This priest, however, brandished a pair of .38 Smith & Wesson pistols, pointed at the forehead of her partner, Wellington Thornhill Books. The metal was a polished black and the visible handle of the firearm was a lovely, dark wood. These were exquisite firearms, to be sure. They were sidearms she would proudly add to her private arsenal, second only to her own pounamu pistols. Eliza would have appreciated these pieces far more if they were in her own hands instead of in the hands of a priest who apparently knew Wellington. At least by sight.

As for herself, she was not fully prepared for this outing. Her own signature sidearms were stowed safely back at the hotel where their American counterparts agreed to meet them later in the afternoon. They were on their own, and as Wellington had only the Jack Frost on him, this meant she had three shots from her Remington-Elliot for this standoff. Three bullets, and Wellington Books presently in the line of fire.

As the priest reminded her. "You have three, my child. I have six. You look like an educated sort." Her eyes shifted back to Wellington. "Do the math."

"Wellington . . ."

Her urging went unanswered. "Eliza, I have a better vantage point here, and I can assure you, with her vestment robes, I have no clue if there is another weapon under there. I am also getting a good look into this woman's eyes. Quite frankly, I could very well find a bullet in my brain if I so much as flare my nostrils impolitely."

"I really don't want to make this already awkward setting worse, but I have the strictest orders for you to come back with me alive, no exceptions." One pistol retracted back into her robes while the remaining one pressed into Wellington's arm. "That means I can apply my grasp of anatomy and physics to make sure my bullet goes through you in order to get to her. You'll be bandaged, but still alive when I hand you over."

Eliza's grip tightened on her pistol. "What kind of a priest are you?"

"Episcopal," she replied. "God works in mysterious ways, especially when it comes to the sciences. We get that."

She placed her own elbow on Wellington's shoulder, steadying her aim on the priest. "Even if your Smith and Wesson goes through his arm like a hot knife through warm butter, what makes you think I couldn't squeeze off at least one round before hitting the ground?"

The priest gave Eliza a cocked grin. "Do you really think you're going to be able to hit me when my shot sends you down the hallway?"

"While you ladies argue the finer points in outbluffing one another," Wellington quipped, "might I remind you both that I'm standing right bloody here?"

The priest crooked an eyebrow. "So much for manners."

"Promise me you will not harm her," he spoke quickly, "and I will go with you. Without argument."

Eliza did not take her eyes off the priest, but oh did she want to. "Wellington, what the hell are you doing?"

"Negotiating, Miss Braun, with an Episcopal priest armed with a Smith & Wesson .38 calibre pistol, or are you not paying attention?" Wellington licked his lips and said, "And would you be so kind as to give me five minutes with my partner here?"

"Look," the priest began, "my business does not take into consideration tearful good-byes. We got places to be."

"I just need a moment." Wellington then tipped his head and said pointedly, "Look carefully then how you walk, not as unwise but as wise, making the best use of the time, because the days are evil."

The priest's eyes widened, but her mouth bent into a pronounced frown. She then stepped back a half step, her gun still pointing at him. "I'm giving you two minutes." The priest held up a finger to each of them. "Right here. In the doorway."

Wellington tipped his hat. "Thank you."

"Step out of the way, Welling—"

His hands had slipped around Eliza's wrists and brought the Derringer up and away from the priest. She felt her trigger finger squeeze, but it only felt air now. Her partner of many secret skills had effectively and effortlessly disarmed her.

"I have two minutes," he said, handing the small pistol back to her, handle first. "I intend to make the most of it."

"What are you doing?"

"This woman is hardly a master assassin or we would be dead, now wouldn't we?" he asked. "If she is taking me alive, whom do you think she serves?"

Eliza gave him a shove. "Come off it, Wellington, this is not proper procedure."

"No, it isn't, but it is buying you time." Wellington glanced over his shoulder and then turned back to her. "Eliza, I just confessed my heart's desire to you, and part of that desire was to assure that no harm befell upon you. This woman is exactly what I speak of."

"One minute," the priest spoke.

"You will make sure you stop him. Stop Edison from reaching San Francisco at all costs. What he is planning cannot bode well."

Whatever was he on about? "San Francisco?"

"Just promise me that you will do this and then, when you find a moment," he said, smiling quite sincerely, "come fetch me."

"Wellington—"

His lips were on her again. Second time in one day, in rather close proximity of the previous engagement, and Eliza found she preferred it to the waiting she had done earlier. She wanted Wellington to say something clever or perhaps slip her a clue as to where he suspected the House of Usher was whisking him off to, but he had said to her that Edison was heading to San Francisco. How did he know this?

When he parted from her, his eyes danced with the bits of light coming from outside. She got a good, long look at his eyes. She wasn't committing them to memory. She would see them again. Hazel was a colour that truly suited him, suited his nature—ever changing, chaotic, and yet sincere and reliable.

"You ready to go?" the priest asked. "The minute was up a few seconds ago."

"Coming to your rescue is threatening to become a habit," Eliza said. "Are you ready?"

"I am," he spoke, loud enough for both of them to hear.

Wellington straightened up to his full height, gave his vest a slight tug, and adjusted his bowler. "I will lead. Shall I? Train depot."

The priest lowered her pistol, concealing it in her robes. "If you make a scene, I'll put you down, you hear me?"

"You don't want her. You want her masters," Wellington reminded Eliza. "Remember that."

Why, oh why, did Wellington have to be right? "The mission first, then I come find you."

"Let's go," the priest said, slapping a hand on Wellington's shoulder and guiding him down from the stoop of the Edison Illuminating Company.

Eliza followed them out, determined to watch them for as long as possible. Wellington's logic was sound—the mission had to come first. If she found him in Antarctica, there was no place on God's Earth the House of Usher could hide him from her. Eliza would find him again, but every hour—every moment—away from him was an advantage for the secret society. There was also the possibility that Doctor Sound would sequester her from any kind of rescue mission and carry out with another agent his original orders to eliminate Wellington Thornhill Books on sight.

The mission had to come first, though. He was right in that. Regardless of the House of Usher making this personal, the mission—apparently now taking her to San Francisco— had to come first. Then, once the job was done, she could take a leave of absence, starting straightaway.

Dammit, she should have risked the shot. Eliza should have worked harder to get the priest inside the building. Once in here she could have figured out how to distract her, how to disarm her, or how to turn Wellington's disadvantage into a strength.

Perhaps the madness of America was rubbing off on her. She needed to get home.

Home suddenly flew from her thoughts as a board creaked from behind her. She turned around to be face-to-face with the man sneaking up behind her, the garrotte constricting around her neck as he pulled his crossed fists in opposite directions. Her head reeled in a queer sensation, as she could not draw a breath, could not scream. She could feel her own hands on the man's wrists, but it took all of her strength just to do that. Eliza should have been able to kick at the very least. Something was turning her feet into lead weights. What was happening to her?

I'm dying. Slowly, she assured herself when she tightened her grip on the killer's wrists, *but I am dying.*

The harder she tried to take a breath, the more her head swam. His face was blurring now, and she could hear his grunts and her own pathetic whimpers, and she had a vice grip on his wrists. She knew where the man's crotch was. Why didn't she kick? Why couldn't she kick?

The stinging in her neck was finally subsiding. At least that was some cold comfort.

Coming to your rescue is threatening to become a habit, she had said to him. *Are you ready?*

I am, he had replied. Wellington had shown such bravery. He was ready to face his fate, sacrificing himself for Queen and Country. For her. Such courage. Such . . .

Eliza pulled against the man's wrists, and when her head drove into the man's nose, she felt something give.

That wasn't good enough. Not for her. Which is why she did it again.

He let go, and Eliza felt the floor. She pulled the rope free of her neck, coughing and wheezing as she did. Eliza was also finding her balance again, shaking her head as she brought herself back to her feet. Whoever this cad was, he was kneeling away from her, trying to fix his nose as best as he could. Eliza buried her hand into the man's scraggly hair and drove his face into the closest wall, smearing it with a streak of fresh blood. If there were any teeth in her human brush stroke, she didn't bother to look. When she released him, he collapsed in front of her on the floor.

There was his crotch.

Her kick sat him bolt upright and that was when she delivered a sidekick to his blood-covered face.

Eliza took a few more deep breaths, watching the man for a moment, noting the right foot twitching slightly. That being the only movement on his person, she looked over his clothes.

When she flipped the lapel, the badge caught sunlight.

He had been keeping watch from the lower right window on the first floor. She recognised the blue bandanna wrapped around his wrist. Her eyes narrowed on the Pinkerton shield before tossing the lapel aside and relieving the man of his pistol. A fully loaded cylinder. Good omen.

With one deeper draw of the dry desert air, Eliza stormed out of Edison's workshop, fumbling for her sun specs.

Her strides were wide as she made her way down the centre of Flagstaff. A cart and rider saw her from a distance and wisely veered out of her way as her gaze jumped from her right to her left. They could not have gotten far.

Two buildings ahead of her she saw them. Eliza lowered the ocular magnifiers still attached to her sun specs, bringing them both closer to her. Wellington's second shadow, the priest, walked barely two paces behind him, a Holy Bible in her grasp covering her mid-section. No one could get between them, barring any break for freedom Wellington could make. Eliza focused on the Bible. It was bowed slightly. A weapon of some kind had to be behind that book.

Now how could she convince the priest that she, Eliza Braun, was *not* the problem.

She now looked ahead of them, then across the street, the distant windows and rooftops jostling back and forth alarmingly close in one eye. A dizziness threatened to knock her off balance, but she focused, the dry warmth of the Arizona Territories reminding her of where she was, what her priority was. One for her, so there had to be someone for Wellington. There had to be. Her eyes went to the higher windows of surrounding buildings and rooftops.

And there he was. One building down, from a rooftop vantage point, a marksman was lining up his shot.

Then came the shot. Apparently, the sniper had his target.

Wellington toppled back into the priest. They hit the ground as people around them screamed, and another bullet shattered a window where Wellington and the priest had once stood. Couples walking in their direction now ran in the opposite one. A mother walking with her children behind the priest scooped up her crying daughter and shielded her in a crouch before the storefront.

"Move for the alley!" Eliza shouted to the priest as she grabbed hold of Wellington's limp arm. Ye gods, he weighed far more than she'd realised. "We have to get to cover. Now!"

Eliza took aim in the direction of the sniper. She knew the Pink's gun lacked range, but her blind fire was more for effect. So long as they thought she was armed . . .

The priest fired several shots across the street before hefting Wellington from the other arm. His feet bouncing lightly against the cracks between boards, they scrambled for a narrow gap between buildings as glass and wood shattered and splintered around them.

"Dammit!" Eliza swore. The alleyway was not a complete pass-through but simply an alcove. While out of the line of fire, they were still trapped. She needed . . .

Wellington had not moved. Even the priest was looking him over, confounded.

"That was a Winchester," she said. "I know that sound intimately. He should have a hole the size of a fist in his chest."

Eliza had always pictured tearing open Wellington's shirt in the heat of passion. However, that passion's aim was not to check for an entry wound dealt by a Winchester. She grabbed his shirt and pulled it apart . . .

The impact point caught her eye immediately. It was difficult to miss as the flattened bullet gleamed against the pine green suede. Eliza's hand hovered over his torso, but she couldn't see it. Because he was wearing . . .

"Is he wearing . . . ?" the priest began.

Eliza cocked her hand back and slapped Wellington across the face. His eyes flicked open as he rolled to one side and wheezed. It hurt to hear him take in a breath, but the hacking cough and his movement were confirmation that Wellington Books was, indeed, alive.

"You're wearing a *corset*?" Eliza screamed, driving a fist into the garment. *"You're wearing a bullet-proof corset?!"*

"What's good for the goose . . ." Wellington growled as he pushed himself deeper into their alcove. "Taking back everything I've said about Axelrod, I promise you, does not pain me as much as that bullet."

Bullets struck the ground where his feet lingered. He bolted upright, and then took stock of where they were.

He was probably about to state what Eliza already knew, when he noticed. "Good Lord—your neck!"

"Later!" she snapped. Her eyes returned to the priest. "So maybe we got off on the wrong foot. Consider that as we're currently pinned down by Pinkertons. They're working for Edison. He wants us dead."

"Wait," the priest said. "Edison wants *you* dead?"

"But, Eliza," Wellington said, "he's in league with the House of Usher."

"He is?" the priest asked.

Eliza gave the priest a quick nod before taking aim, driving back two gunmen daring to cross the street.

"I'm beginning to think the relationship with Edison and Usher is a bit . . . complicated," Eliza grumbled. "How many, Welly?"

"I can only be sure of the sniper at present, but if I were to guess?" Wellington quickly poked his head out from their concealment, and immediately lost his bowler to a bullet. "Judging from the amount of gunfire, ordinance damage, we're looking at five at the very least."

Eliza gave a nod and returned to the priest, who was looking at them both wide-eyed. "Are you with us?"

"Who are you people?" she asked with a shake of her head.

"We serve at the pleasure of the Queen," answered Eliza. She glanced at the window above their heads, and turned in the direction of the bloody mess she had left behind in Edison's workshop shambling up the main road. Eliza felled the man with one shot, but was knocked forwards when a bullet slammed into her back. "Bugger me"—she winced as she crawled back to her hiding spot alongside Wellington and the priest—"that stings."

"Just be glad it didn't hit you in the lacing," Wellington chided. "The armour there is not quite so reinforced. Roll over." She felt his fingers against the outside of her dress, stopping where it stung the hardest. "That sniper is going to be a problem."

She looked at the slug in Wellington's hand. "You were right," she said to the priest. "A Winchester." In one hand she held the now-dead Pink's pistol, two bullets remaining. Turning the small pistol handle first to her partner, she shrugged. "Make it count, Welly."

The priest slapped her own pistol into his hand. "Make *them* count, Wellington."

Another rain of bullets pushed them farther back into the limited noon shadows; but Wellington remained still, watching the direction of the larger splinters. "Right then." And he stood and fired the Pink's pistol in the direction of the sniper, the .38 at the storefront barricade of the Pinkertons.

One man's scream could now be heard just across the street.

"Right then. Two down. One wounded, right shoulder. I wanted to make sure I didn't kill him outright." He looked to the priest who was moving a hand underneath her robes. When it reappeared, her hand held six bullets. "We needed a target. I saw three hostiles over there. The sniper." A scream came again. "Counting the wounded man, five total."

The priest shook her head, reloading her pistol. "Now, just back up a moment. How are you so sure?"

"The House of Usher wants him alive, no exceptions, you're seeing him do this," scoffed Eliza, now drawing her remaining '81, "and you have to ask?"

"You shot my brother!" came a voice from across the street, just before a new storm of bullets.

The assault appeared to slow, and that's when the priest emerged from her cover, the second .38 in her other hand, responding with a firestorm of her own. Her robes caught the desert breeze, making her a far wider target than she was truthfully. The billowing fabric gave the Pinkertons a target, but that also meant stepping out from their own hiding spots. Her .38 gave good report to the gunfire ripping harmlessly through the robes.

It was the single gunshot—Eliza knew it was the sniper—that sent the priest to the ground.

Wellington grabbed a handful of vestments and pulled while Eliza fired her pistol. On the *click-click-click* of dry fire, she shuffled back to where Wellington was removing the vestments from the priest.

"You'd better not leave that .38 behind," the priest snapped once the robes were free, her expression quite stern. "You don't know how hard I prayed for a pair of guns like this."

"We have more pressing matters upon us," Wellington said, ripping off his cravat. He wadded it over the shoulder wound and pressed. "Lean forward."

She gave a groan, and Eliza saw what Wellington no doubt suspected. Against the wall, where the priest had propped herself, was a patch of blood. Eliza fished from Wellington's inside pocket his kerchief and pressed it against the exit wound.

"At least the bullet passed through," Eliza said, gently easing the priest back against the building. "Keep pressure on it."

"Not my first time seeing a bullet wound on the battle-field," he said while attempting to help the priest sit up, perhaps find even the slightest comfort for her. "So what do we have?"

"I got on my belt . . ." the priest panted, opening her hand, and groaned, "Aww, fuck!"

Both Eliza and Wellington gave a start.

"It's a perfectly acceptable Anglo-Saxon word," the priest stated quite factually. "Ruined by the French, if you must know." She then hefted the gun. "And I said it because we're down to three bullets."

Eliza patted around herself for any option that could present itself, and her hand fell on the bulbous chamber strapped in by a makeshift holster she had created out of strips of leather. The slipknot parted easily and she held up the odd weapon before them both. "I have this," she said, referring to the Brouhaha.

"All right, I'll go on and ask," the priest said, hardly impressed with Axelrod's creation. "That is what exactly?"

"It's—" The weapon's name stuck in her throat. She simply could not call it by name without chuckling. "It's the exciting future of armament."

Wellington gave his brow a quick wipe, glanced out into the street, and muttered, "We're what I believe Americans would call 'easy pickings' for that sniper." He looked around him, licking his lips as his eyes went from the end of the alleyway to the rooftops above them. "We need a distraction of some kind."

"And then what?" Eliza asked.

He motioned to the exciter in Eliza's grasp. "Give that thing a field test, I suppose."

"So what's the distraction?" the priest asked.

Eliza shook her head, until a thought came to mind. "Welly," she began, not entirely certain whether she should feel anxious, dreadful, hopeful, or all of the above. "That method I employed to keep the bomb from exploding . . ."

"Using the Jack Frost to disarm the detonator? Yes, what of it?"

"I didn't say 'disarm the detonator,' now did I? I said, 'keep from exploding.' There is a difference."

He arched an eyebrow. "Eliza?"

"When the ice eventually melts, which it has been doing steadily since we left Edison's workshop, the battery leads should become active again." She bit her bottom lip. "And the phonograph was still playing when we left it."

"Which means what, exactly?"

Eliza brought up the exciter. "We might get that distraction after—"

A savage frenzy of fire, glass, and wood erupted several buildings down, the mushroom cloud of smoke casting ominous shadows across the street and storefronts around them. Eliza stepped out of her hiding place, held out her arm in the direction of the sniper, and pulled the trigger of the Brouhaha.

A whistle emitted from the exciter's vent, its sound quickly growing from a shrill cry into a wild scream over a matter a seconds. The wild scream became a wild roar, and then something launched from the exciter's muzzle. It was a transparent sphere that roiled and rolled towards the sniper's rooftop. When the distortion reached her intended target, the sphere cut like a fine blade into the wooden building, peeling its timbers back like the skin of some exotic fruit. Eliza could see the shooter swept into the sphere, spinning like a child's top and then cast aside in the distance.

She looked down at the indicator dial to read the Brouhaha's current setting:

TYPHOON

Eliza jumped at the sound of gunfire, but this time coming from her side of the street. Two more Pinks fell as "Wild Bill" Wheatley strode up alongside her and held out his Peacemakers at the remaining two.

"There's been enough killin' for one day, boys, doncha think?" he called out to them. Neither man dropped their guns. Bill gave a rough laugh and said, "Look, either it's my Peacemakers or Lizzie's little gadget here. Your choice."

The remaining Pinks glanced at one another and then dropped their guns, raising their hands above their heads.

"And how are things at the Red Rock Theatre, Lizzie?" Bill asked her. "Got all those entrances and exits sorted?"

"Wellington and I got a little sidetracked," she returned, lowering the Brouhaha.

"This is what you call 'sidetracked' in Jolly Ol' England, huh?" He gave a laugh as the two men stepped out and then got to their knees, placing their hands on top of their heads. "The minute I heard the gunfight, I knew you were jus' having a good ol' time without me." He looked over Eliza to see

Wellington emerge out of hiding with the priest draped over his shoulder. "Care to explain why you got yourself a wounded—*lady*—of the cloth there?"

"I think," Eliza said, "we're all in need of a drink."

TWENTY-ONE

❦

Wherein a Priest Takes Sabbatical
and Plans Are Made

The priest winced as she sat in the bar of the Royal Hotel, the high-back chair hardly allowing her to prop up her arm as the doctor had ordered. Wellington looked around for another cushion; and on relieving one from a nearby chez lounge, he added it underneath her arm. Her face twisted in pain, but settling into the chair once more she closed her eyes, took in a breath, and colour returned to her face.

Her eyes betrayed a lack of sleep, though. Wellington, glancing around at the rest of them, wondered if any of them had got real rest since Detroit. His own night had been frustrating. He had slept quite soundly, even though it had been in bed. With Eliza Braun. Hardly in the manner he had pictured, though.

The priority of Flagstaff had been dousing the fire at Edison's Illuminating Company. True to his word, Edison had created a bomb that not only turned his workshop into a gigantic torch, but also began a dangerous chain reaction with the surrounding buildings. Many had been lost in the conflagration. What the inventor had underestimated was the tenacity of those men and women living in the Arizona Territories. The fire would not claim Flagstaff once the townspeople rallied and began working to stop it from spreading. The sun had begun to set when the last of it had been extinguished.

Wellington remembered returning to the suite, Eliza gently guiding him to the bed, and wrapping his arms around her as they fell asleep on top of the blankets, still in their day clothes. It was a strange combination of sweat, dust, smoke, gunpowder, and perfume that tickled his nose; and it was the last thing he remembered before falling asleep. He had awakened three times before the morning's dawn, but never left her side. *That,* he thought, *would be most improper.*

The next morning, he and Eliza repeated their morning routine as per usual, saying very little to one another. They descended down the staircase to meet Bill, Felicity, Nikola, and the priest, whom they found over a light breakfast to be Van Sommerset of Virginia.

Wellington had already sent for a specific case from his luggage, but there was another matter needing his attention. He sat down next to Van. "Thank you."

"Shouldn't I be the one thanking you?" Van chuckled, with a slight wince. "I'm the one you dragged off the street."

"You at least wanted me alive," he reminded her.

"Edison wants us dead," Eliza pointed out.

Wellington nodded. "So I am thankful for the House of Usher's tenacity, for once."

"Not only are they tenacious, but they know when to make the most of an opportunity," Bill said. "I heard some folks talkin'. Seems that while the town was fightin' the fire, there was a break-in at that fancy telescope."

"They got the optics," Felicity said.

"Speaking of Usher," Eliza began, looking down at Van, "exactly how were you able to keep a track on us?"

Van gave a little snort. "I would love to say it's because I'm part Indian, but I've got a soft spot for gadgets." With her good hand, she pulled up what appeared to be a square pocket watch. Flipping up its cover, Wellington and Eliza looked not at a clock face but a map of Flagstaff. It was something similar to the Ministry's ETS.

"We've got a tracker on us?" Eliza asked.

"Your rings." Van looked to each of them. "Usher apparently had a man tinker with your rings while on your trip over here."

Wellington's eyes went to Eliza's. She too had reached the same deduction. "That bloke on *Apollo's Chariot*. That's why he had no valuables in his haul," she said.

Wellington motioned to Eliza's Ministry ring. "Looks like I have a new project to complete before I can return to the car, yes?"

"Actually, Welly," she said, removing the Ministry ring from his finger, "I can take care of them." She took her own ring off and placed them together on the floor. Her heel came down on them once, then twice. Eliza narrowed her eyes on them and then struck their remains once more. "There," she said with a quick gasp. "Fixed."

A tall, black case landed with a dull thud in front of Wellington. "Your luggage, sir," the young porter huffed.

"Excellent, thank you," Wellington said, sliding it at an angle for he, Van, and Tesla to see what he would be presenting. "I suggest you all come around here."

He pulled a footrest closer to him and flipped back the latches on the black case. From its top section, he pulled out what would have appeared to passersby to be a large book completely constructed of gears, mechanics, and glass, and not paper and leathers as books usually were. Wellington turned the odd contraption one way, then the other, feeling a bit embarrassed that he could not find the valve straightaway. When he finally found the round, blue handle, he gave it three twists, then disengaged a tiny latch. This unlocking parted the device's "covers," instantly changing the mechanical book's appearance to a large central hub of machinery attached by a hinge to a small screen. Sliding out from the front of the hub was a keypad of letters, numbers, and symbols. Wellington then stretched out from the array two coiled cables that hung from the back of the monitor.

"Now let me think," he muttered as he began pulling out the smooth, black bricks that were housed deeper inside the case. "Memory Block Gamma should be it."

The plugs at the end of the coiled cables fit neatly within Gamma's sockets. He then checked the hub's tiny pressure gauge, flipped two switches, and with a puff of steam, the screen flickered to life with a soft amber glow, one word coming into focus for the group.

COMMAND?

Wellington cracked his knuckles and typed.

DISPLAY MAP OF UNITED STATES.

Gears and cogs turned while small puffs and hisses of steam sounded angrily as they waited.

REGION? TYPE "A" FOR "ALL."

His fingertips danced across the letters in reply.

SOUTHWEST REGION AND WESTERN COASTLINE.

"What's that about?" Eliza asked.

Wellington spoke as he typed. "It was Edison's message to us. Remember what he said?"

"Not particularly, as someone had charged me to disarm a rather nasty incendiary device."

"He said that we all have our gates to pass through. If ours was to be the Pearly Gates, then what exactly could his gate be?"

Eliza gave a slight gasp. "San Francisco. That's why you mentioned San Francisco. Edison's heading there?" she asked, turning her eyes to the screen.

Wellington held up a single finger and then added to the screen a new command.

OVERLAY RAILROAD NETWORK.

A few clicks and whistles later. "And there you are," he said, motioning to the lines appearing almost as cracks in the screen's glass. "As you can see, there is a direct line from Flagstaff to Sausalito, where a ferry picks up passengers and takes you off to San Francisco. That's where his endgame will take place."

"It has to be," Tesla replied. "There must be lighthouses in the vicinity, yes?"

"Oh, there are, partner," Bill interjected. "Lighthouses and fog signals aplenty. Can't spit without hitting one."

"Do you have that information in here?" asked Eliza.

Wellington tapped a quick command into the engine and several small dots now appeared on the screen.

Bill gave a slight whistle. "This ain't looking easy, folks."

"How are we going to narrow down which one is Edison's?" Felicity asked.

"Wellington," Eliza said, staring at the dots decorating the West Coast, "can your analytical engine narrow down the signals to those within a thirty mile radius?"

"I believe I can."

With a few punches of keys, the image winked away from view and then vertical lines of light gradually rendered with each pass a map of northern California, the bay city at its centre with smaller dots representing remaining signals. Wellington pulled at his bottom lip with his top teeth during this sequence and then glanced at the array of finger-sized boilers to the left of the monitor. Already, two of them were empty while Tank Three was almost at half-full.

Wellington looked up from the back of the display to his partner. "Why thirty miles?"

"Don't you remember Edison's test back in the Carolinas? The target buoy Bill and I saw was roughly twenty-five miles offshore."

He nodded. "So we are working with a range of thirty miles in either direction, and the further he is away from San Francisco, the better of a lead he will have from the mayhem." He tapped in another command and the list of signals on the display whittled down to two:

```
POINT REYES, CA, USA
MONTARA, CA, USA
```

"Well now, ain't that something? Cute little contraption there, Johnny Shakespeare." Bill guffawed. "Time to saddle up, head to San Francisco, and shut down Edison's anarchist agenda."

Wellington and Eliza blinked, then looked over to Felicity.

"I think he's been sneaking peeks at some of my political science volumes," Felicity quipped.

Tesla cleared his throat, and everyone turned to him. "It might help you to know that this isn't an anarchist's agenda we're disrupting. Edison would never intentionally ally himself with the House of Usher unless he had something to gain from it. To Edison, Usher is a resource. An end to a means."

"Excuse me," the priest spoke suddenly.

Wellington had forgotten that Van was sitting there, in the midst of this. She looked wide-eyed and perhaps a touch overwhelmed, but her eyes went to each and every one of them for a moment. "From what I gather, you all serve at the behest of the United States or British government, so maybe you can tell me, why would anyone do something so terrible?"

A very valid question, Wellington realised. "The House of Usher, from our previous interactions with them, has but one desire. They are bent on plunging the world into—"

"Chaos and disorder, yeah, I know that," Van interrupted. "I have worked with them on two other occasions, so I understand them to an extent. It's Edison himself that has me pondering. You all are smart people, especially you," Van said, motioning to Tesla, "but no one here has asked or answered a simple question: why is he wanting to destroy San Francisco?"

They all looked at one another. They still didn't know the "why" behind this grand plot of Edison's.

"How long have you all been working on this case again?" Van asked.

"Hold on a second," Bill said, reaching for his pockets. His right hand landed on a folded-up paper and he unfurled it. He let out a hearty laugh and slapped the newspaper. "I've been reading up this morning on what's been going on out west."

Everyone looked at him blankly.

"Oh, right. Sorry," he said, turning the *San Francisco Chronicle* to face everyone:

CLANKERTONS COLLIDE
San Francisco to Host Scientific Exposition

"Seems there's a clankerton convention in San Francisco and it's a pretty big shindig from what I've been readin'."

Felicity's hand flew to her mouth. "The leading minds of innovation, all in one place!"

"He's intending to wipe out potential threats. Then he'll offer this device to the highest bidder." Eliza looked at the image on Wellington's screen. "It's not mad at all. It's simply business."

"That's okay." Bill shrugged. "We got him dead to rights. Just send out a wireless, and we'll have him—"

"No, we won't," Felicity insisted. "Bill, this is Thomas Edison."

"I think I see Miss Lovelace's reasoning," Tesla chimed in. "Edison will have considered a number of variables that could affect this experiment. One of those variables, I would speculate, is discovery. He will have a plan for just that contingency."

For a moment, no one moved. Wellington felt as if there needed to be a rallying cry of some sort that would get everyone moving; but they all just sat there. Edison was on a train. Had been since last night. Even if they were to stock Wellington's motorcar with enough water to keep its boilers at full, their speed, while faster than a stagecoach, would never close the gap between them and Edison.

"You all have to get there."

All heads turned to Van, their unexpected ally in all this.

"Look, Padre—" Bill began.

"If Edison is going to destroy San Francisco, you all need to get out there." She held up a finger at Bill, who looked ready to say something. "There are always options."

Bill's mouth shut. Wellington looked at Van, mulling over her words. He looked at his engine, the amber-coloured map of California beginning to fade in front of him.

"Fort Huachuca," Bill said suddenly. "If I can get to a wireless, we can get in the air in an hour, two at the most." He did not seem, however, comforted in any of this good news. "But if I recall, Huachuca is more like a supply base now. The only airships they may be able to spare won't be battleship class. Maybe cargo transports, but they're the fast kinds designed to ship equipment coast-to-coast."

"That's just what we need, Bill, and a transport means we can take the car," Wellington said, glancing at Eliza. "I suggest also getting in contact with a base in San Francisco."

"Fair enough," he said with a shrug. "Come on, Felicity. I need that whip-smart brain of yours for clearance codes and such."

The two of them headed for the front desk, producing for the desk clerk credentials that acted as his call to action. They watched in silence as Felicity and Bill were hastily led behind the hotel desk into a back room.

"And what of me?" Tesla asked.

"It will be a tight fit," Wellington said, sizing up Tesla, "but you will be coming with us. If the death ray is in a final firing sequence, we will need you to deactivate it."

"You will be able to add 'field agent' to your repertoire," Eliza quipped.

Tesla nodded, albeit, rather timidly. "I'll return to the workshop meanwhile. Fetch any tools I may need." He took a deep, shuddering breath. "In my youth, I avoided a life in the military. It seems fate has brought me back around to it. If I believed in fate that is . . ."

The analytical engine collapsed on itself as Wellington gently brought the monitor down. Once again, the device resembled a huge book of gears, cogs, and mechanics. He turned to the priest, Eliza taking a seat next to him.

"And then there was one," Van said with a crooked smile.

"Thank you," Eliza began, "with coming forward about Usher. Knowing that there are two agendas at work here provided plenty of insight with Edison."

"And thank you for not taking me into custody after our tussle with Edison's men," Wellington added. Van looked at him incredulously. The archivist shrugged. "Well, it needed to be said. You could have remained committed to your bounty, even after we had saved your life."

Van chuckled. "When I took this job, I had a bad feeling about it." She reclined her head and rolled her eyes. "I'm beginning to think that maybe I have been at this for too long."

"Won't the House of Usher come after you?" Eliza asked.

"No, they are much smarter than that. I heard they tried something like that with a hunter they felt left her job incomplete. They lost six of their order that night." Van paused and then asked, "If I may be so bold to ask, exactly why have they made you such a priority?"

Wellington cleared his throat, hoping his skin was not turning scarlet. He could feel a sudden sweat on the back of his neck. "It's a long story."

"I know I'd like to hear it as well," Eliza said brightly, shooting him a look.

"It is also very complicated," he retorted. Wellington rapped his fingertips lightly against his analytical engine and added, "I have certain skills that the House of Usher deem invaluable."

"You're a crack shot, I'll give you that," Van attested.

"It goes a bit deeper than that," Wellington replied gently.

The priest nodded. "I won't say I understand because quite frankly I don't. The things I've heard and seen since being around y'all has provided quite the yarn. I'm thinking I should just retire with the notion that San Francisco is going to be okay."

"But," Eliza said, "we haven't done anything yet."

"No, but you will," Van said with a warm smile. She then took up Wellington's hands with her good hand, and the squeeze she gave surprised him with its strength, as well as with warmth and sincerity. "I have faith."

The archivist smiled. The plan unfolding in his mind offered so many variables for failure, but it was all they had. However, when he looked at Van, felt her grip on his, something—no, he was not certain of what it was, but something—assured him that this was the right path to follow.

TWENTY-TWO

✦❦✦

Wherein Wellington Books, Eliza Braun, and New Friends Drop in to Say "Hello"

Wellington awoke to a poke in his sides. The engines of the USAA *Sherman* that droned in Wellington's ears had lulled him into a deep sleep. His motorcar's tumble seat, it seemed, was more comfortable than he had realised.

The waking jab had been dealt by Felicity, and her expression was not nearly as friendly as it had once been. Mending fences with Eliza had in turn broken them with the librarian.

"Thought you might like to watch the birds launch," she said in a cool tone, before marching off. Despite that lackluster offer, Wellington was interested, stretched himself awake, and moved further aft towards the loading ramp. He checked his pocket watch. They had been in the air for several hours.

His eyes immediately fell on the row of gleaming brass eagles perched inside the hangar bay. Each was an immaculate example of craftsmanship. Bill was watching him examine them with a grin on his face, and Wellington was well aware he liked having one over on him.

"Elegant design," Wellington conceded. "Some kind of aerial surveillance I believe?"

Felicity was the one that answered however. "Indeed,

Wellington. Our R&D department has spent quite some time on them."

"If there's something within thirty miles of San Francisco that isn't supposed to be there," Bill said, "they'll find it." He threw a lever, making a huge lamp to one side of Wellington switch from green to red, and tilted his hat down over his eyes as sunlight and wind poured into the bay.

On feeling sunlight, the metallic eagles opened their wings, caught the breeze, and set off in their particular direction. It was a surprisingly serene moment.

"Magnificent," Wellington muttered as the aft bay doors closed.

Felicity dealt one more chilly glance towards him before excusing herself from the bay, leaving him alone with Bill.

Bill tucked his thumbs in his belt as he strolled over to him. "That Eliza, she's a fine girl." He chuckled, and then his eyes locked with Books. "I might have hoped you two didn't sort out your differences, but . . . well . . ." He appeared to be tasting something bitter in his mouth. "I just hope you appreciate the hell out of her, Johnny Shakespeare."

Wellington was not quite sure what to make of this genuine moment, but he was thankful that they would go into battle in a better frame of mind. He held out his hand, and Bill shook it. "I do. More than you can imagine." His smile turned wry. "Tex."

"What's happening?" Eliza's sudden arrival made both men start.

Bill rubbed at his chin. "Eagles are on their way. Felicity should have an answer in the next couple of hours."

"When should we be in that thirty mile radius?" Eliza asked.

"Late afternoon. Somewhere between three and four o'clock."

"Excellent," Wellington said. "Would you mind helping me back the car to the ramp?"

Bill followed him back to the motorcar and, once blocks were removed and gears were released, his engineering feat now rolled freely back to the ramp that had been open mere moments ago. Wellington was trying not to think of this section of metal and scaffolding as the only thing between his motorcar and several thousand feet of open space. The thought lingered in his mind as he crawled underneath the chassis to check supports, shocks, and axels. This was going to be his creation's final field test, and the nerves in his stomach would not calm themselves.

When he emerged from underneath the motorcar, he jumped back with a yelp on finding Felicity in the tumble seat. She appeared ready for action, dressed in tight leggings and a modest top with a corset that bore a striking resemblance to Eliza's own. The tracker she and Bill had used in the Outer Banks was open in her lap, its tiny pencils sketching over various points of map depicting Wellington's designated search area.

"Telemetry is coming in," she stated. "So far, all the signals are strong. Nothing out of the ordinary yet."

Felicity's eyes remained fixed on the tracker with deadly intensity. Wellington took a strange comfort that her gaze was not aimed at him. "I didn't hear you climb into the tumble seat. You are quite stealthy."

He felt a chill run through him as she looked up from the OSM tracker. "I'm a librarian. Silence is more than golden. It's a way of life." She then leaned in and whispered, "And you'll never hear me coming."

Wellington suddenly felt the need to know where Eliza was. Hopefully, within shouting distance.

Thankfully, the tracker in Felicity's lap started chirping. "I'm getting a small encampment north of Montara"—she glanced at a pair of maps next to her—"that isn't supposed to be there."

Eliza and Bill appeared in the bay. "Felicity, you get the same hit I did?" the cowboy asked.

"Montara, California," she returned.

"That's where he will be," came the voice from over Wellington's shoulder.

Again, he jumped with a yelp, turning to see Tesla. Did this man ever sleep?

"With unlimited resources," the scientist continued, hardly bothered by Wellington's reaction, "that is where I would be. Someplace isolated where I can work uninterrupted."

"That's good enough for me," Bill said. "Lizzie, Wellington, what do you think?"

Wellington and Eliza shared a look. *God help San Francisco if we are wrong,* Wellington thought. In the end, both of them nodded agreement.

"I'll let the captain know," Bill said, heading forwards.

Tesla, once Felicity gathered up her maps and the tracker, took a seat next to her, his eyes awkwardly looking the librarian from head to foot. Even after he noticed the sticks of dynamite strapped across Eliza's thighs, the scientist-turned-field-agent looked as if he were settling into what was about to unfold before him until he saw Bill return to the cargo bay.

Bill now wore crossing bandoliers full of bullets, two Peacemakers strapped to each hip, and a pair of Winchester-Browning-Worthingtons Model 1895. "We needed some extra punch on this trip and so I figured I'd bring out what OSM was recommending."

Wellington did not think the Serbian could look any paler. He was wrong.

"Captain has got a lay of the land. The *Sherman* is going to do a pretty fancy maneuver. The pilot said there is a small . . . well, you can barely call it a road, but that's where he's dropping us off. I hope your automobile there can take a low flyby."

As if the *Sherman* was a living, breathing beast responding to Bill's word, the airship began a sharp descent, its engines on each side whining in protest.

"We best load up then," Eliza shouted over them. She did not look in the least worried.

"Ten minutes," called Bill. "Time to get this chariot of yours started, Books."

"Yes, all right," he stammered.

Wellington went to his automobile and motioned to the backseat. Bill scrambled into the back with Tesla and Felicity. Eliza climbed into the front seat as Wellington turned the small crank just by his right thigh until he heard the engine rumble to life.

Adjusting her own baldric of bullets and bundles of dynamite, she pulled down her goggles and then turned to him. "All set, Welly?"

"Ask me that after the mission," he said, securing his own door and slipping the rose-tinted goggles across his own face.

Eliza chuckled at the sight of him, but he was determined to finish this mission as he started it—confident in pink goggles. "If you are looking that far ahead," she returned, her own confident smile lifting his spirits, "I think that is a good sign."

"Here we go!" Bill called out as the large lamp in front of them switched from green to red.

Before them, the floor split, revealing the outside world inches at a time. The road was barely even a goat track, but there was no going back now. Wellington wrapped one hand around the brake, the other gripped the steering wheel as the opening grew larger and the airship dipped lower. He could see the ground fifty feet below coming up quickly to meet them. The ramp extended lower and lower, until it locked into place thirty feet above the ground. At twenty feet, the *Sherman* began to tip upwards, the outside engines roaring angrily just over the rhythmic sound of his motorcar.

The timing was crucial.

He was just able to make out Eliza calling *"Wellington!"* over the wind, the engines, and the odd shuddering from *Sherman*'s gondola as the front of the airship continued to rise upwards. He disengaged the brake—Bill's and Felicity's signal to pull the ropes attached to blocks in front of the wheels—as he opened the throttle and pressed the accelerator forwards, sending them down the ramp. They covered the distance between their launch point and the end of the ramp faster than he had calculated, but the lip of the ramp had just managed to touch the ground, giving their front wheels no time in the air. *Sherman*'s engine power, though, was far greater than the motorcar's, and the back of the car fell hard to the ground as they sped forwards. If any of them reached up, their fingertips could have grazed the stern of the airship, but the *Sherman*'s steep ascent continued to lift the airship upwards like a curtain.

On the horizon was the compound of Edison's modified lighthouse. Apart from the seemingly harmless white beacon that towered ahead of them, the area consisted of a large building that appeared to be a barracks of some kind. It was currently expelling men like ants. These troops were running for two barns on the opposite side of the base. Within moments, motortrucks and motorcars were rumbling out of the stables.

There was another structure in the distance, too small to be the keeper's house but still connected to the lighthouse by what appeared in the distance as a webbing of cables. Wellington focused his eyes on it and accelerated.

He called out to Eliza, pointing to the small array of buttons on the dash. "Time for the field test!"

Her finger hovered over each of the buttons and switches before she shook her hands in exasperation. "Dammit, which one do I pick?"

"Indulge yourself!" Wellington shouted, turning their car in the direction of their closest enemy. "But do it fast!"

Eliza pressed the top blue button in the array. From behind a small panel in the dash closest to her right hand appeared a small stick with a trigger set within it. When she pulled it towards her, the motorcar's internal mechanics rattled to life. Wellington allowed himself a self-satisfied smile seeing the headlamps of the car rotate upwards, just as he intended.

"The trigger," he shouted. Eliza was exchanging glances between him and the stick in her hand. "Now would be good."

Wellington's smile turned into a delighted laugh, not that anyone could hear it over the sudden firestorm that erupted from the front of the car. The oncoming motortruck fought to keep control, but Wellington countered as Eliza squeezed the trigger hard. Their opponent disappeared in a thick cloud of steam, and then the truck exploded. Wellington turned their car to the left as the remains of the other tumbled aimlessly behind them.

"That's one!" he said, bringing another enemy in front of them.

The two morotcars once advancing on them were now turning back towards the compound. He could make out, though, two gunmen leaning out from their backseats, attempting, it seemed, to get balance on their motorcar's runners.

Eliza went to make quick work of one car, but bullets striking their hood caused Wellington to swerve.

"Hold her steady, Wellington!" shouted Bill. "Nick, hold on to my belt!"

"I beg your pardon!" Tesla stammered. "Did you just call me Nick?"

"Hold on to my belt," he repeated, hefting the Winchester-Browning-Worthington in his arms, "unless you want to be shot at!"

Wellington cast a quick glance over his shoulder to see Bill hanging out of the backseat. His upper body, as Tesla was apparently following his order, was perpendicular to the ground. He cocked the lever of the rifle, and then came a sound Wellington could only describe as a quick gasp of breath which he knew was a silly analogy as it was coming from the Winchester-Browning-Worthington.

Rifles make sounds distinctive from pistols, and rifles themselves are quite distinguishable between one another. The Winchester-Browning-Worthington Model 1895 was unique, even among its own ilk; after the sudden intake of air, the firing sounded like a whip crack rather than the concussive signature of a rifle. The Winchester-Browning-Worthington shells, on account of the steam-assisted velocity, dealt more damage than a normal caliber Winchester.

Seeing both gunmen toppled out of the second car, Wellington marveled at the weapon's efficiency in the hands of a master.

Eliza's own efforts on the lead car were not as quick as on her first target, and then the firestorm from the front of the car stopped abruptly.

"Welly?"

"We've run out of bullets," he shouted back. Wellington stretched over to where Tesla was holding Bill's waistband, grabbed hold, and heaved. He felt Tesla follow his lead. Bill's expression to both of them told him he was not quite finished. "Just hold on!"

Wellington flipped a few switches by his own steering wheel and then pushed a red button under his left foot, and suddenly a high-pitched whine screamed from underneath the car. He felt himself thrown back into his seat as the car leapt forwards, its wild banshee wail drowning out what he could

only assume were the curses of Bill and Eliza. If Nikola and
Felicity were also screaming, he hoped no unpleasant flora or
unfortunate insect were to find their way into their wide-open
mouths.

With a small pop, the shrill sounds from the undercarriage
ceased and Wellington turned the wheel hard to the right while
pulling up the brake. Their motorcar began to slide across the
sand and grass, turning laterally and stopping with the rear end
facing the smaller house connected by an array of heavy cables
to Edison's lighthouse.

"Tesla," Wellington shouted, "get in there! Eliza, switch
with Felicity."

"Wellington!" Eliza and Felicity both snapped.

"Yes, Felicity, I know how you feel about guns. Yes, Eliza,
I know how you feel about Felicity sitting next to me." Gunshots bounced off the ground and struck the building behind
them. *"Now switch!"*

Felicity and Eliza scrambled around the car, exchanging
cold glares at each other as Tesla slid across the tumble seat,
out of the car, and landed in a run for the door.

"It's locked!" Tesla shouted, struggling with the doorknob.

Bill cocked the Winchester. "I got a key."

Tesla returned back to the car as Bill fired, splintering the
door lock.

"Thank you!" And with that, Tesla ran inside.

"We have to supply cover," Wellington said, releasing
brakes and revving the engine.

"With what?" Eliza shouted as they shot forwards. "Even
with Bill's Winchesters, we are a bit—"

"Trust me, my darling," Wellington sang as he centred
their vehicle on their remaining foes. "Felicity—"

Felicity shook her head wildly.

"We are out of bullets in the front cannons, so if you
would—" The lone motorcar in front of them closed the distance fast, its driver steering with one hand while aiming a
Peacekeeper with the other. "The yellow 'Number One' button, if you please."

Felicity swallowed, took a deep breath, and pushed the
button while cowering in her seat.

Wellington followed the rocket's trajectory from his car to

the oncoming vehicle, which, seconds later, was not so much of a motorcar as it was a fireball hurtling towards them.

"See?" Wellington shouted as cheerily as he could when one is shouting. "No guns."

Felicity watched with wide eyes as the car coasted by them. The fire completely covered and consumed it so that as they watched, the wheels collapsed from underneath it.

"Would it be forward of me to tell you that I think I am falling madly in love with you, Wellington Books?" she panted.

"What can I say, Eliza, other than you inspi—"

His words abruptly cut off as a barn to their left exploded. From the dark, acrid smoke lumbered out an armoured monster. It came towards them on treads that ran underneath its length, giving it no challenge in terrain as was made evident when it successfully scaled the first motortruck wreckage without effort. Mounted on a cylindrical turret, a single, ominous cannon came around to bear on them.

Wellington turned the wheel sharply to one side, checked the gauges on the dash in front of Felicity, and tightened his jaw. He knew that if he kept this type of driving up, there would not be enough water left in the boilers for their escape. From behind them came a hard, concussive explosion, and a moment later the shell's impact sent dirt and rocks flying around them.

"You only have one yellow button!" Felicity screamed at him.

"One button, one rocket." He heard another cannon shot from behind him, and immediately turned to the right. The shell impacted harmlessly to the left. He wished the miss had instilled confidence but alas, it hadn't.

Then his eyes fell on the white and black buttons, set apart from the others.

"Welly," Eliza called from the backseat, "bring us around. Bill and I can slow him down."

"A moment, if you please," he answered back, opening up the throttle even more as he turned the car around and drove straight for the tank. "I'm having a thought."

"Wellington," Felicity began, "this thought of yours—is it a happy one? It's not at all suicidal, is it?"

He waited for the turret to come to bear on their motorcar. Once the barrel stopped, he jerked the wheel to the right. He was flanking the armoured truck by the time it fired. "The white button! Now!"

From behind them, a plume of thick smoke billowed out. He motioned for Felicity to strap on the mask by her own seat as he ripped free his own from under his seat. They continued their wide arc around the tank, completing a circle only to retrace their path by remaining within the smoke billowing all around them. Wellington kept throwing quick glances over his shoulder at the blurry silhouette of the tank now in the eye of their smoke ring. When he saw the cannon swing by them, he cut the wheel to the inside, driving them up to the rear of the tank.

He had counted on Eliza and Bill to pick up on his plan, and thankfully they had.

Eliza was sprinting for the tank with Bill, shouldering the modified Winchester, behind her. Wellington saw Eliza free from her bandolier one of her clockwork fuses and jam the device into a single stick of dynamite. As she ran up to the tank's auxiliary hatch, located in the rear, she removed a few more sticks of dynamite just before heaving the door open. Her lethal package delivered, Eliza dashed back for the car. The top of the tank turret flipped back, and a man appeared with pistol in hand. He was quickly felled by Bill's Winchester.

Wellington honked the car horn again and again, aiding Eliza and Bill in the growing haze around them. Once they both landed into the tumble seat, Wellington opened up the throttle and pushed the accelerator forwards, returning them to the wall of smoke. From behind them, a sharp explosion threatened to lift their car off its wheels, followed immediately by a second explosion that did. Their motorcar shuddered on hitting the ground but it was holding together without fail.

Then the world disappeared in a blinding flash. Wellington engaged the brakes, attempting to shade his eyes against this light that came from everywhere. This California sea cliff, it seemed, was being bathed in blasts of brilliant white and cerulean blue emitting from the air itself . . .

. . . and Wellington could no longer smell the ocean, dirt, steam, or smoke. All he could smell was a scent that made his mouth water. It was the smell of metal baking in the sun, a bitter taste of copper on his tongue. It was a scent Wellington had caught before being snatched up by the Culpepper twins.

When the flashes subsided and his vision returned, the sky above him now yielded a massive airship, one that would easily dwarf *Apollo's Chariot*. It would have to in order to compensate for the gunports running along its hull.

"Where the hell did *that* come from?" Bill swore.

Wellington went to answer when the sight of another car speeding from the lighthouse caught his attention.

"Hold on, everyone," he shouted, the motorcar's engine snarling like a wild cat on the hunt, "we've got an airship to catch!"

Their motorcar shot across the dirt and grass, quickly closing on this new car that made a mad dash of its own for the titanic aircraft descending just ahead of them. Wellington could just make out a driver, and two men in the car. The passengers kept looking back at them as they closed the distance.

A gunshot rang in his ear, and Wellington's attention switched to his side mirror. He flinched as a second bullet shattered it but not before he recognised the reflection as a motortruck he had lost track of during the battle. They had to catch the airship in front of them, but they also needed to get rid of the motortruck behind.

"Wellington?" he heard Eliza call from the backseat.

"Eliza, Bill, hold on tight!" Wellington motioned to Felicity what appeared to be a smaller version of the car's brake handle. "Pull that back please! Hard!"

He could see Felicity didn't quite trust him after the rocket launcher, but with a grumble, she slapped her hand around the handle, squeezed, and growled as she yanked it towards her. Both Eliza and Bill let out startled squawks as the tumble seat collapsed on itself, then burst back open, only this time the backseat was facing the opposite direction, giving its occupants a departing view of their journey. Eliza and Bill, having been tossed and turned during the transformation, ended up sprawled out across the cushions. The shock was slightly mitigated, Wellington hoped, by the handle and triggers that sprang up from the centre of the floorboard. Eliza would know what to do with those.

"What! The! Hell?!" Bill might have been laughing.

"Tumble seat," Eliza scoffed as she took hold of the stick. "Clever boy, Welly."

Wellington threw the accelerator forwards as the call of a Gatling roared in his ears. Yes, indeed, Eliza had figured it out.

The car ahead had reached the airship's ramp. Above the sounds of his own motorcar, Eliza's Gatling, and the car behind bursting into flames, Wellington could just make out the thrum of the airship's engines spinning up for a quick ascent.

"Wellington," Felicity called, "we're going to miss our flight!"

There was just enough time. "No we're not."

He pushed the red button by his left foot again, and their car jumped forwards. He heard a commotion behind him from the tumble seat and hoped he hadn't lost Eliza and Bill.

The airship's ramp could not retract fast enough to keep their motorcar from boarding. He had some room to manoeuvre in this massive landing bay, which he did as soldiers in uniforms he did not recognise took positions to make a stand. They were, however, outgunned as Eliza brought the Gatling around, mowing down any opposition present. Any fortunate enough to avoid Eliza's Gatling found misfortune from Bill's Peacemakers.

Wellington powered down the motorcar, and took a deep breath as the echoes from gunfire faded into nothing.

"So, Eliza," he asked her, "your thoughts?"

"I love this sodding car!"

He nodded, "Thought so."

"All righty then," Bill said, jumping out of the tumble seat, "any ideas who this monster belongs to?" he asked motioning to the airship around them.

"Not a clue." Wellington looked at the whole of the landing bay. "No flags. No markings. A pirate ship, perhaps?"

"Since when do pirates wear uniforms?" Eliza asked,

motioning to a pair of fallen soldiers. "Felicity, have you on record—"

"A moment, if you please."

Felicity was sitting stock still in the motorcar. Wellington was not sure if she was going to burst into tears, scream in terror, or simply succumb to vapours. She took a deep breath, so deep her delicate frame seemed to shudder, and then Felicity let her breath out easily and slowly.

Wellington looked to Bill for some kind of insight. He shrugged.

"Forgive me. Loud noises," she said. "No, Agent Braun, we have no such member in our Rogue's Gallery that insists his minions follow this particular dress code. Anything else?"

Eliza did not seem moved at all. "No, but if something comes up, I'll ask."

"Right then," Wellington said. "What now?"

"Control room?" Eliza asked, holding up her pounamu pistols.

"I'm in," Bill said, pumping the action of his modified rifle.

Wellington turned slowly to Felicity, who was, once again, loosing that cold stare on him. "Felicity, I have a charge to ask of you." She crooked an eyebrow at him, but Wellington held his hands up in defence. "I need water."

"Water?" she asked.

"Yes, water. For the motorcar. Without it, we're going to have a problem in making an escape that doesn't involve us plummeting to our death."

"Ah," she replied with a light nod. "I'll try to keep that in mind."

"Very well then," Eliza said brightly, returning to the motorcar, "let's go save San Francisco."

From the floor of the tumble seat, Eliza produced a pair of fine, polished wooden cases. The smaller one revealed the Brouhaha. Wellington stopped Eliza as she held it up in her hand. "Are you sure about this thing?"

"Considering Arizona," she began, motioning to the other case, "I think you should share the same faith in Axelrod and Blackwell as I presently do."

Wellington looked into the case to see the Jack Frost resting securely in its cushion of crushed velvet; two full vials of its mysterious coolant were nested in velvet next to it.

"Fair enough," he said, lifting the weapon with one hand while taking its holster from Eliza with the other.

TWENTY-THREE

❧

Wherein Our Agents of Derring-Do Find the Balance of Power a Delicate One Indeed

The three of them began their ascent to the bridge of this massive airship, the constant rumble of the engineering section nothing less than unnerving. They would not hear any oncoming personnel; and with limited lighting, sightlines were impossible to ascertain. Wellington suddenly felt this deep-seated loathing. For airships. What was it about creeping through enemy airships? Was this something that field agents did often? Once was more than enough for him.

He looked over his shoulder at Eliza, who shrugged. "You know how I hate repeating myself?" she whispered, as if reading his mind. "Welcome to the life of a field agent."

Bill signalled them to step back as a pair of guards, again in the enigmatic uniforms no one seemed to recognise, walked by, weapons drawn.

One of them commented, "Do you know what's going on?"

The other shook his head as they passed where the agents were hidden. "Probably another drill."

Once they were safely out of sight, Wellington, Bill, and Eliza continued deeper into the gondola until they reached a

door. Eliza nodded to Bill, and they slipped out of the dim
engineering section into a well-lit hallway.

Actually, it was a rather smart, pristine hallway that again
reminded Wellington of the luxury he was introduced to on
Apollo's Chariot.

A thought raced through Wellington's mind as they
walked through the narrow, silent hallway: What if Edison
was not here? What if he had convinced the House of Usher
that, on account of their discovery, it would have been better
not to proceed? This meant that the technology and application behind the world's most devastating weapon was now
underground and there would be no way for either the Ministry of Peculiar Occurrences or the Office of the Supernatural
and Metaphysical to stop him until after he struck, until after
there had been more deaths.

Then he recalled the man he had met in the Carolinas.
This was Edison's opportunity not only to provide the House
of Usher with a final display of awe and power but also to
eliminate any additional competition in the field of invention
and practical sciences.

Edison was here. He knew it.

Bill put a finger to his lips. Just ahead, there were footsteps
and voices, coming closer. Bill placed a hand on the door in
front of him. Locked. The one behind them was also locked.
The last door, however, opened without fail. He motioned
with his head for everyone to go in. Wellington hoped this
apparent passenger's quarters would be empty.

What he saw he was hardly prepared for.

The room itself wasn't a room but a giant chamber with a
smaller chamber inside it. A room within a room.

"What the hell is this?" Bill asked quietly.

Eliza approached the solitary door and dared its doorknob,
which turned freely in her hand. Bill gave her a curt nod. The
door slowly creaked open, revealing absolute darkness. There
was no outside light whatsoever from their antechamber leaking into this room. Bill slowly stepped forwards as Eliza
reached into the room, and then seconds later gaslight illuminated the room.

Wellington furrowed his brow as his head slowly tipped to

one side. "Well now, this is something you don't see every day, now is it?"

The room was an impressive replica of a first-class train compartment: a delightful parlour connecting to an adjoining room that was reserved for sleeping purposes. Out of the windows there appeared a countryside, painted in an incredible detailed fashion. There were details showing signs of occupation. A recent newspaper from London. A glass of water, nearly finished.

"Now I'm not normally a man who would admit something like this," Bill said from the parlour, "but you're way smarter than me, Books, when it comes to certain things. And I'm looking around, thinkin' this is one of 'em certain things."

"Bill, your guess—"

Both of them started as the parlour and bedroom began trembling, swaying back and forth as if . . .

Outside the window, the landscape was now in motion, passing by the window in a blur. Before Wellington could ask Bill for an opinion, he heard it—the sound of a steam train, just loud enough to drown out the drone of the airship's engines.

"Oh, this is clever," Eliza said, entering the parlour. "They really are going for the whole experience, aren't they?"

When neither of them answered her, Eliza smiled and beckoned them to follow her. Once back in the antechamber, Wellington could see the entire mock-up was shaking on some apparatus built underneath it. Both he and Bill followed Eliza to a large phonograph that was playing an abnormally large cylinder. When Eliza removed the needle, the unseen apparatus deactivated.

"How much would you care to wager the scenery outside the windows is painted on a conveyor belt?"

"Ten pounds?" Wellington asked hopefully.

Eliza pursed her lips. "Nice try."

"So what's all this for then?" Bill asked. "For people who aren't keen on flyin'?"

"Perhaps we should table this mystery for another time? I believe we were heading for the bridge."

Bill crept up to the closest door, opened it a crack, and gave a nod to Wellington and Eliza. The three crept around the hallway, and they continued their way up to the stairwell.

The stairs led up to a deck similar to the one they had just left. Wellington wanted to check and see if there was another illusion behind one of these doors. Perhaps another train journey across a countryside, or maybe a simulated airship journey over Paris or Frankfurt? Instead, they pressed on towards what they hoped was the bridge.

This landing led to a single door, presumably to whatever remained forwards.

"We're not high enough for this to be a bridge," Wellington whispered. He pressed his ear to the door. "There are voices on the other side. Hard to say how many. What do you think this room could be?"

The seasoned field agents both shrugged. "Control room."

He looked back and forth between them. "You both sound confident."

"After your fair share of mad scientists," Bill said, "you notice a theme."

"So how do we play this?"

"We are the least of their worries, apparently," Eliza said, motioning to the door. "Control room or not, this is an access point and there should be a guard here."

"That actually gives me pause, Eliza," Wellington said. "It means either Edison is far more arrogant than we believe, or—"

"We're expected." Eliza reached into a small pouch hanging off her belt. "Ready, Bill?" She sent the coin spinning upward. "Call it!"

Bill watched the coin intently as it reached an apex. "Heads."

Eliza pulled out her pounamu pistols and kicked open the door.

"Or we can just barge in with guns blazing," Wellington grumbled as the coin bounced against the floor. "Right then, mind if I borrow a Winchester?"

Bill tossed it to him. "Right behind you, Johnny Shakespeare."

He had only just shouldered the rifle when a Pinkerton appeared with his gun drawn. Wellington's shell knocked him back, giving him a moment to join Eliza sheltered behind a vacant control panel.

"Quite a large control room, don't you think?" Wellington asked.

"Bit larger than I had hoped for."

A hard, grating yell erupted from the stairwell as Bill came in firing round after round from his Peacemakers. He managed to get all the way across the room before return fire drove him to his own shelter.

"Awful place you find yourselves," a voice spoke. Wellington was certain that was Gantry. "Pinned."

Bill looked over to Eliza, flashed two fingers, and pointed quickly in opposite directions. "Can't see that I'm too worried," he shouted from his hiding place, "seein' as you're not gettin' a lot of help from your boys in grey."

"I would hardly call those men reinforcements," chortled a voice Wellington immediately recognised. Edison wasn't mad nor was he deranged. Wellington could hear it in his voice. This was all part of his strategy for today's business. "My Pinks were sent to slow you down. Which they did. Adequately."

"Welly," Eliza whispered. "You will need to preoccupy Edison while Bill and I move into position."

"Time to maximum charge?" he heard Edison ask.

"Ten minutes," someone replied.

Eliza crawled low, away from their hiding place to another terminal. Wellington looked over to Bill, who was also attempting the same kind of flanking manoeuvre. Wellington took in a deep breath and checked the rifle as best as he could under cover. Wellington could see by the lights on the Winchester that he had three rounds left. All he needed to do was keep Edison and the Usher henchmen busy while Eliza and Bill reached their positions.

He pumped the stock in his grasp as he emerged from his hiding place. "I must ask that you stand down, Professor Edison."

His rifle switched from soldier to soldier, a variety of pistols and rifles now pointing in his direction. Silently, he took stock of the control room: two Usher henchmen, two guards dressed in the military greys of those they met in the aft bay, a sole technician, inventor Thomas Edison, and Elias Gantry of the House of Usher.

"You?" Edison said, his eyes wide with surprise. "I thought that present I'd left you back in Flagstaff would have ended this cat-and-mouse game."

"What?" Gantry spluttered. "I told you we would handle the archivist our way. The death ray was supposed to be your business. Books was supposed to be ours."

"The moment he meddled with our affairs in Currituck, he became my business," Edison replied, his eyes fixed on Wellington in a manner that Wellington found less than pleasurable. "You understand, Mr. Books, that this is a business. Nothing personal?"

"Likewise, I hope you understand," Wellington answered, splaying his fingers along the Winchester, "that stopping you is merely business for me as well."

"Books," Gantry said, "I can see three greens on your Winchester." He motioned to the guns around him. "There are four bullets trained on you, and I can make it five."

"And you know all too well what I am capable of," Wellington hissed. "So who cares to volunteer themselves?"

The two soldiers guffawed, but went silent as the two Usher men lowered their weapons.

"By the Order of Her Majes—" Hold on, he wasn't here in that sort of capacity. He would have to word this delicately. Wellington cleared his throat and proclaimed, "On behalf of your United States President Grover Cleveland, *serving the interests* of Her Majesty Queen Victoria, I order you to power down your death ray and step free of the controls."

Dammit, it seemed as if Bill and Eliza were taking their bloody time getting into a flanking position!

"Hold the countdown," a voice—a strange voice that sounded airy, metallic, and cold—ordered from behind Edison and Gantry. "Keep the generators powered up, but hold the firing until my mark."

The two men parted to grant room for what Wellington swore, upon first glance, was the ghost who had haunted him for so long. He nearly fired before the creature could enact its revenge for his transgressions, but he hesitated. Whoever or whatever the man-machine was, Wellington could not be completely convinced it was human. One arm was encased in a massive boiler, the metal limb ending not in a hand but in a

Gatling gun similar in size to the one he used on his motorcar. It was seated in what appeared to be a throne constructed of tubes, wires, boilers, and pistons that pumped life into the chair. This throne, like the tank he had destroyed outside, was rolling on treads, but he could see legs dressed in a fine pinstripe pattern that did not appear frail or weak. Half the man's body was visible, and adorned with dark furs and folds of a cloak that seemed to blend with the mechanical throne he rode. His jaw rested in a shiny brass encasement while his eyes were hidden behind darkened lenses. Topping this bizarre, macabre sight was a gentleman's top hat from which underneath it, dark raven's hair flowed like an ebony curtain down his shoulders, losing itself in the texture of his furs.

When the left eye suddenly flared with a menacing red glow, Wellington tightened his grip on the Winchester.

Then he got a look at the monster's valet, and Wellington lowered his rifle slightly. That taller figure he recognised straightaway. His weekend with the Phoenix Society had left quite a few impressions on him. "Pearson?" he managed.

"Mr. Books," the man-machine spoke, and Wellington felt a shudder pass through him when he heard that voice. So very, very cold. "I feel the time has arrived to introduce myself. I am the Maestro." He turned his head unsteadily from side to side. "I require a moment of your time. I take it I have your attention?"

INTERLUDE

❧

In Which the Good Doctor Is
Up to No Good at All

Nikola Tesla was not a man unfamiliar with physical exertion. Unlike many in his chosen profession, he believed passionately in remaining fit. Abstaining from stimulants such as tea and coffee, a proper regimen of exercise, sleeping only when his body demanded it—as opposed to habitually, as society deemed necessary—were only a few disciplines that kept the fine fibres of his brain in excellent working order with the rest of his body. He discovered in his youth the importance and relevance fitness had in relation to successes in the laboratory.

However, that Nikola Tesla was a young adolescent burgeoning upon manhood, exploring the mountains of Croatia, attending classes in Austria, or advancing the technology of Budapest's Telephone Exchange. Perhaps that Nikola Tesla would have barely bothered with the short flight of stairs leading into a building of unknown purpose or occupancy. Perhaps that younger, arrogant upstart Tesla would not feel his heart pounding through his rib cage on hearing the sounds of warfare outside. Would that Tesla have felt, as he did now, the debilitating flashes of thought, inspiration, and power familiar to him when he was a child? He screwed his eyes shut and took in great, hollow breaths through clenched teeth, the stench of a diesel engine threatening to choke him. He needed to control the images of the lighthouse, of the death ray, of the inner mechanics Edison had so clumsily assembled, or, more likely, had his people assemble as per his sloppy, slapdash specifications.

The lights behind his closed eyelids were now fading. He placed his face in his hands and took another deep breath, the gasoline fumes causing his head to reel, and shouted out to the darkness around him, "No!"

Tesla pulled himself off the wall and opened his eyes. His vision was normal once again. The stench from the diesel dynamo was tolerable. And before him, at the far end of the building he was told to run into, unescorted and armed only with his intellect, was a wall of machines. Tesla turned back towards the door and felt for something resembling a light switch. On finding a knob, he slowly turned it to the left.

Of course he had to turn it *slowly* considering how absurdly fragile Edison had made his lightbulb design.

The illumination was just enough to reveal more details of the various control stations before him. Yes, that Englishman Books was quite correct in his assumption that this building was the auxiliary control for the death ray. Tesla rested his fists on his hips as he deduced exactly what individual function each station served. Difficult as it was to grasp, Edison had finally managed to impress him with this contingency plan. Having a redundancy in order to carry out or prevent the death ray's firing solution if something were to happen in the main control room displayed the signature of a logical, rational mind he could respect.

Still, Edison was behind this architecture. *This should be effortless,* he thought with a grin. *Perhaps a bit of fun, as well.*

While he wouldn't see Edison's face when he took control of the death ray, Tesla would know without fail that it would be he who would foil his counterpart's grand plan for San Francisco's destruction.

An explosion from outside caused him to start. That had been far too close for his liking. He needed to cease this diabolical plot with haste. Later he would savour the moment.

"Let's see then, this column would be power input, power output, and output stability. Good." He went to the next bank of controls. "Targeting X coordinates. Targeting Y coordinates. Targeting Z coordinates. Very good." On these controls, Tesla felt a tightness well in his throat, as he muttered, "Turbine speed. Boiler level. Optical alignment."

They were all like this. He took another step back and counted the individual banks of gauges and readouts. Fifteen in total. He then saw the six lights blinking in sequence in three of the stations. In three other banks, the lights were flickering on and off, but Tesla noted that nine lights were always on at one time.

"A thing of beauty," he whispered.

The flash hit him so hard he stumbled back, the world disappearing in a sea of brilliance. He steadied himself, placing his hands on his knees; but again he was blinded by the image of the death ray, new coordinates, the output exceeding safe levels, the focus of power travelling westward . . .

Then he saw Edison. The sentence handed to the judge, and the word "Guilty!" and proclamations of victory rising and falling like waves of the Pacific as he sat in the gallery, watching the Wizard of Menlo Park fall from grace.

On the final flash, he opened his eyes, and to his alarm he found himself on one knee. He hadn't felt himself come in contact with the rough planks underfoot.

He looked up at the auxiliary controls towering over him, the sacred number repeating in various calculations, various connotations, over and over again. "Of course," he whispered. "It would be wrong of me if I ignored it."

Tesla reached over to the lever on the far end of the mechanics, and brought it down towards him. Once it locked into place, he heard a distinctive crackle of electricity from behind the controls. Still the pattern remained. He knew it would. This would solve so many problems, not only for himself but for the sciences in general. For one thing, this preposterous debate concerning currents could finally be laid to rest.

He looked at the current coordinates, and began to run

calculations in his head. Perhaps there would be casualties, but not nearly as many as if San Francisco were to remain the target. No, this way would be the only way to still show what *Edison* had created, how dangerous *Edison* was to society, and what *Edison* was truly capable of. Deaths, if any were to occur, would be acceptable, as San Francisco would be saved.

A few more adjustments and the new firing solution would be set. Tesla would finally be free of Edison. The bombast's influence would disappear into the mist.

All would be well.

TWENTY-FOUR

❧

Wherein Things Go Unexpectedly Awry

From Eliza's vantage point, there was no way she could get a clear view of this gent calling himself "The Maestro" as he was blocked by that behemoth Pearson.

"I don't know who you are, sir, and quite frankly I don't care," Wellington began. "I am here to apprehend Mr. Edison and stop the House of Usher, as a courtesy to the United States government. I mean no offence, sir, but I do not know you from Adam."

That's it, Welly, Eliza thought. *Keep this crackpot talking. Bill and I need to get an idea of whom we're dealing with.*

"No, you do not, but I am well aware of you, Mr. Books. Since your first insertion into my affairs, I have made you a bit of a pet project of mine." The Maestro chuckled, and Wellington winced as he had heard coughs from sucking chest wounds less painful. "I should thank you, now that I reflect upon it. Doctor Devereux Havelock was a bit of an incompetent. It was your interference that brought this to light, and for that I am indebted to you."

Wellington managed a meek grin. "You're welcome, sir?"

"And once I became aware of your involvement in the

Outer Banks of North Carolina, I knew it was most imperative I became involved in this delightful scheme."

This was when Gantry blinked. "I beg your pardon?"

"When it was brought to my attention that Agents Books
and Braun from the Ministry of Peculiar Occurrences were
being sent to the Americas on a goodwill mission for the
Office of the Supernatural and Metaphysical, I made it my
business to find out why.

"This is why your original pilot for this plot bowed out, Mr.
Gantry, whilst you were enjoying the sights of Detroit, Michigan. As much of a hold you perceived to have upon him, mine
was greater. You will be happy to know your pilot has reunited
with his family." He cast a casual glance towards the ocean.
"As close as a father could ever imagine to be with his wife
and children."

"Dear Lord, Elias," Edison spat, "what kind of lunatic
have you gotten us in league with? I trusted you to take care
of the resources needed for this venture."

"I would daresay, Mr. Books, we are of the same mind
here," this Maestro prattled. "I have an agent on the ground in
San Francisco, an agent of immense value to me, and I would
care not to have such an asset lost in the mayhem and destruction that Edison would bring about."

Edison's demeanour suddenly changed, and Eliza did not
care for the inventor's sudden swagger. "You have stepped
into the middle of a final experiment which, if successful,
should prove to be the next step in the evolution of electricity,
science, and warfare. Do you really want to bungle that?"

"That is exactly my intent, Mr. Edison." The Maestro settled into his mechanical chair. "Pearson, proceed."

Eliza's grip tightened on her rifle as Pearson drew from his
belt two mammoth knives. She recognised them as Spanish
facóns, but a brief glimpse of them was all she could see
before one sailed across the control room and felled the Usher
agent. The other Usher man had glanced at his mate, and that
moment's distraction was enough for Pearson to move. Eliza
would have never imagined a man of Pearson's height or
stocky build to move as swiftly or gracefully as he did. The
hulking butler was on top of the gunman in seconds, and

when he stood Eliza saw not a trace of blood on him. He was dangerous *and* neat.

She had seen a lot of things in her time in the field, but a showdown between a pair of megalomaniacs? This was a first.

"So that settles the matter of being ambushed by your men, Gantry, doesn't it?" asked the Maestro.

"I do crave a pardon," Wellington interjected. "I still have a Winchester. Your man there is fast, but I would not recommend him challenging his agility to my shooting."

"Quite inspiring, Mr. Books," the Maestro said with a chuckle. "Such grand nobility for Queen and Empire. Admirable, but wasted. Regardless of what you may believe, I have the situation well under control."

When Eliza heard the sharp clicking behind her of a gun's hammer being locked into a firing position, she comprehended the Maestro's confidence. "Very slowly, madam," the voice warned.

Eliza set her pounamu pistols on the control panel in front of her, and then she rose to her feet. Very slowly. The man countered around her, keeping the Smith & Wesson trained on her. On the other side of the control room, Bill stepped out into view, hands raised with another of this ship's crew behind him.

"Now that I have made it clear to everyone present who is in control," the Maestro began, settling comfortably in his mechanical throne, "do I have your attention now, Mr. Edison?"

Edison looked over to Gantry, then back to the Maestro. "Five minutes," the inventor said.

"If you would?" the Maestro asked Wellington, his Winchester still trained on him.

Wellington lowered the rifle, but Eliza could see he had no intention of powering down.

The Maestro also noticed. "Even as I hold your colleagues prisoner?"

"My father raised me to live with caution," he said, his fingers splaying around the rifle.

"Indeed," he replied. He then placed his good hand across his Gatling forearm and looked up to Edison. "I am afraid, Mr.

Edison, Mr. Gantry, as entertaining as I find your experiment, I must call a halt to your proceedings. They are a distraction I cannot afford."

Edison blinked. So did Eliza. She was certain others around her did so as well. "Exactly who do you think you are, sir?"

"I have two agents, one from Her Majesty's government and another in the service of your President, under gunpoint. I have also removed the immediate Usher threat with the aid of my valet here. Finally, your base of operations is located on my airship. All of these things make me the man in total control of this scenario."

"Very well then, Maestro," Gantry said, marshalling his courage even though he stood tall over the man confined to a monstrous wheelchair. "Exactly what do you want from the House of Usher?"

"Him," he said, motioning to Edison.

Edison straightened his posture slightly. "What?"

"I am in need of your services for a project that demands a special touch. Your touch, as it were. Therefore, I have come for you."

"Just like that?" the inventor asked, his eyebrows rising as his mouth twisted into a wry grin.

"Yes," the Maestro said. "I intend to take you with me, pick up my agent from San Francisco, and then be on my way."

Gantry scowled. "You expect the House of Usher, after everything we have invested in this operation, to simply allow this?"

"Of course I do," the Maestro said, laughing slightly. "You have what you wished of Edison. Perhaps I have delayed your outcome, but I have no intention of taking the death ray. I just need to collect Edison and my agent in San Francisco before you are on your way."

"*Collect* me?" Edison said with a snort of derision before motioning to Gantry, "Will you please do something about this nuisance so that we can carry out our—"

"Thank you, Mr. Edison," Gantry began cordially, "for your time and expertise, but our contract with you has come to a conclusion." He turned to the technician. "You're relieved."

The technician nearly bowled over Edison as he made for

the exit. Edison stepped back only to bump into one of the Maestro's men that had closed on him, taking him firmly by the arm. "I beg your—?"

"If you were expecting some sort of loyalty for services fulfilled," Gantry began, "I believe you've demonstrated a severe lack of judgement in regard to us. As you made it clear earlier, your agenda is far different from our own."

"But you need me!" he barked at Gantry.

"Not as much as the gentleman here does," he replied, motioning to the Maestro.

Wellington suddenly shouldered his Winchester. "I am sorry to be rude and point a primed rifle with repeating action at everyone, but even the *attempted* destruction of San Francisco can hardly be dismissed, as well as the delivery of a dangerous weapon to a known criminal organisation and the abduction of a fugitive." Wellington motioned with his head to Edison. "The fugitive in question would be you, Edison."

"How noble of you," the Maestro said. "Parker?"

"Yes, sir?" spoke the guard behind Eliza.

"Kill her."

Eliza swallowed hard, fighting back her smile. Even at that close range, her corset would protect her. She would be winded but alive.

He pulled back the hammer of his pistol, then raised it to her forehead.

"All right, stop!" Wellington said, bringing the rifle up with one hand, the other held out to one side. "Stop, please!"

The Maestro held up his good hand. "So very noble, Mr. Books," he wheezed.

Wellington laid his rifle gently on the deck. With a swift kick, the Winchester was now out of his reach. Parker extended his foot and slid it beyond Eliza's as well.

"I have one more sidearm," he said, raising his hands back in the air. "Shall I?"

"One word. That is all Parker needs," the Maestro warned.

Eliza looked over her shoulder and saw it in Parker's eyes. It was over. The Maestro didn't bluff, and he would illustrate that once Wellington was disarmed and truly unable to help her.

I'll die looking at him, she thought, turning her eyes to

him. *At least this prat is too close to miss. It will be quick.* Wellington, however, looked as if he had never been farther away. *I'm sorry, Welly,* she lamented. *I'm so sorry.*

Slowly, Wellington reached behind him and pulled out the Jack Frost. He looked at Eliza, holding up the exciter, and then tossed it in the air.

I love you, Wellington Thornhill Books, she thought as she watched the weapon fly up in the air only to have gravity take hold.

Eliza twisted and jumped as the Jack Frost fell just past Parker's waist, and what happened next all seemed a lifetime crammed into a single heartbeat. There was a shattering of glass immediately followed by a gunshot. Then came the cold, a biting cold that crept up her leg and around her hips. Eliza rolled until she struck something. Whether it was another control station or a wall, she wouldn't know until she sat up. Her left leg was covered in a light frost, now melting away in the heat of the room. Above her was a statue of Parker, his pearl white face literally frozen in a scream that never came out of him as she had not heard it. The pistol must have been pointed upwards when it went off as his arm—at least the top half of it—was angled upwards. She looked down to find the gun, still in the grasp of a hand that had not been caught in the blast radius of Jack Frost's shattered capsule. The recoil from his single shot had snapped the man's arm at the elbow, but no blood fell.

It was a storm of mayhem she scrambled into with Bill wrestling a pistol from his captor, Pearson closing on Wellington, and Edison pushing Gantry into the Maestro.

The Maestro brought his massive Gatling arm upwards, swatting Gantry away from him as if he were an annoying housefly. The cannon connected with the man's jaw, and struck with such force that the Usher man's neck snapped. The Gatling arm now came around to bear on Bill.

Eliza reached under her coat for the holster at the small of her back, pointing at the Maestro the only gun she had handy.

The Brouhaha was set for "Pub Brawl," which felt more than appropriate for the current scuffle. She fought to keep the gun steady, and when it fired, Parker exploded into a multitude of white and red shards while the Maestro toppled out of his grand wheelchair. Edison was lifted off his feet and tossed against the wall of the control room, his body landing hard and limp across the floor.

Pearson, caught in the peripheral of the blast, shook his head as if to clear it, then returned his attention to Wellington, also stunned by the exciter.

"Nowhere to go to, I'm afraid, sir," the valet said, flipping from his sleeve the *facón* he had used earlier.

Eliza saw the shadow move in the corner of her eyes, and she dove, screaming, *"Get down!"*

The Gatling's first round tore away at the glass window and wall behind where they once stood. There was a break in the gunfire, and that was when Bill took his three shots on the Maestro, all three deflected as he used his massive metal arm as a shield.

When the madman lowered his Gatling to turn and face Bill, Eliza saw that her sonic attack had done more than just stun him. The blast had also partially removed his mask. She got a good look at his profile, and blinked hard to make sure that good look was better than good.

The fine-chiselled jaw.

The intimidating hawk-like nose.

The cold gaze of a man she had met once before in the office of the Ministry.

"Lord Sussex?" she heard Wellington call behind her.

The one eye that was exposed went wide in a fury and madness that made Eliza think of Harrison Thorne when she had seen him at Bedlam. The scream tearing from his throat, however, was something from a nightmare. It was so loud, so powerful, that she could still hear it over the Gatling gun.

Eliza crawled over to Wellington, who said, "Saw him speak at Parliament. Quite a charismatic individual."

"A recommendation, love," Eliza said. "Don't call the Maestro by his proper name. It seems to rather annoy him."

Before Wellington could reply, Bill appeared around the control panels, shouting, "All right, explain to me why we're still here exactly?"

Above them, chunks of the wall tore apart as the Maestro's Gatling opened fire.

"Oh yeah, that," Bill said with a nod.

The Maestro—Peter Lawson, the Duke of Sussex—was now gasping for breath, his voice vacillating between a whimper and a scream. Eliza, Wellington, and Bill peered out from their hiding places to see Pearson pull himself up and grab the Duke of Sussex's face in his hands to force his eyes on the valet's own.

"Sir, look at me!" he snapped. "You are ill! You need your doctor!"

"Yes," Sussex, the Maestro, whispered drily. "Fetch my doctor."

"Shall we?" Wellington asked.

"Let's," Eliza and Bill returned.

The three leapt from their hiding place, and passed by Eliza's pistols which she quickly snatched up and laid down suppressing fire as the three of them ran for the access door. They had almost made it out of the control room when she bumped into Wellington. He was staring at one of the control panels.

Eliza followed his stare to the control panel where the Jack Frost had dealt its gruesome death to the guard, Parker. She noticed two vertical rows of six lights switching from green to yellow. In a third row were another six lights. They were red, and the top two were blinking.

"We have to go, Welly." And on catching Pearson's gaze, she shouted, *"Now!"*

They didn't dare to look over their shoulder to see if Pearson were on their trail. It was eyes ahead in a mad dash for the cargo bay.

They had reached the landing featuring the "train simulation" when Klaxons sounded all around them.

"Eyes peeled, everyone," Bill shouted as they opened the door to engineering. "We're going to have varmints making things real uncomfortable."

"Halt!" the voice rang out.

"Told you," Bill said to Eliza, turning to the sound of feet pounding against metal.

Two guards appeared from an adjoining stairwell under them. Bill grabbed both railings and kicked, sending them both back down to the platform below. With a quick glance around them, they continued their sprint through engineering.

On reaching the hatch, Eliza unlocked the door, pulled hard, and was about to step through . . .

. . . when she felt a hand yank her back into engineering. A moment later, a heavy pipe cut through the air.

"Felicity, it's us!" Bill shouted over the alarm.

The librarian, wide-eyed and trembling, appeared in the open hatchway, a long, heavy pipe now held aloft in her grasp as if it were the very sword of Joan of Arc herself.

"Alarms are going off!" she shouted. "They're loud! Especially in this cargo bay!"

"Not as loud as a tank firing at you," Eliza offered.

"Now, Eliza, don't tease her," Wellington scolded gently in her ear.

"Why not?" she muttered back. "I like it."

"Can we go now?" the librarian implored.

"Are the boilers at full?" Wellington asked.

"Yes," she said as they entered the cargo bay. "I even took the liberty of starting the car and letting it idle so the boilers would be at full pressure."

"*Bon!*" Wellington exclaimed as he locked the access door and sprinted for his motorcar. He yanked open the car door and began checking gauges by his steering wheel. "Eliza," he shouted over his shoulder, "reset the tumble seat, if you please."

As she rotated the back passenger seat to its original position, Eliza could see Wellington now checking pressure indicators and various lights. Whatever they told him, it appeared to be good news. "Ready to go?" he asked everyone.

Eliza did not get a chance to ask what he meant by that, because Felicity was asking what she was thinking. "Go? Go where? We're in an airship." Her arms spread wide. "In the air!"

Bill guffawed. "And they call me crazy?"

The motorcar revved and rumbled to life as Bill and Felicity settled in the tumble seat while Eliza settled into her own. Wellington launched them forwards, turned the car around, and paused on arriving at where the ramp would begin.

"Eliza," he began, lowering his goggles, "follow my sequence to the letter."

"Sequence?"

"Yes, sequence!" He flipped a switch on his dash, and from a panel in front of her appeared a new series of buttons and switches, ones she had never seen before since riding in this motorcar of his. "Just follow my commands."

"Left to right?" she asked, her breath catching in her throat.

"And timing." He unfurled a belt before slipping out of the motorcar. "You all should find these belts between your cushions," he announced to everyone. "If you want to stay in the car, strap in. Firmly."

As Eliza tightened her own belt to the tightest notch, Wellington took a deep breath and professed, "Know this—just in case we blow up—I love you, Eliza."

Hardly the most opportune of settings she expected to hear his heart; but at this point, Eliza understood that Wellington would never stop catching her off guard. Somehow, this suited her.

"I love you too," she returned.

He took a quick kiss from her before crossing over to the ramp release switch, and threw it down. Quick as a flash, he sprinted back to the motorcar as the airship's aft ramp unlocked and started to lower . . .

. . . into open space.

She lowered her goggles and set her eyes forwards. Eliza was in love with a madman, and she trusted him implicitly. "On your word, Welly."

"All set?" Wellington asked over his shoulder.

Felicity and Bill, their eyes much like wide saucers at present, silently nodded.

Once his own belt was secured tight across his lap, he wrung his hands against the steering wheel and looked over to Eliza. He held his gaze with hers, then turned his eyes back to the now-open bay door.

The motorcar rumbled forwards, and in Eliza's field of vision, the turbulent Pacific Ocean grew wider, and then drew closer as they began to fall. Just over the howling wind, Eliza could hear a single scream. It was hard to ascertain if it was Felicity or Bill.

"Red buttons, together," he called to her, his voice just audible over the rush of air.

She pressed the two red buttons before her. Each side of the car's hood retracted, and both Gatlings ejected, launched free of the car to tumble uselessly to either side of them. She felt the urge to watch them plummet into the ocean but she waited for the next command.

"Yellow," Wellington shouted.

Eliza pressed the yellow button. She felt, with a slight lurch, something launch from behind the car.

"Switches." Wellington glanced at the three sets of lights under each gauge in his own dash. Eliza could see one of the lights turn green. "Blue switch. Now."

She hooked her finger underneath it and saw a puff of thick smoke rise from underneath them. She could hear a whine emitting over the engine, but their speed remained constant.

From Wellington's dash, another light went green.

"Yellow switches! Not together!" he insisted over the building whine from the engine. "Five seconds apart."

Eliza nodded, flipped the first switch, waited, and then flipped the second yellow switch. A moment later, she felt herself thrown back in her seat, as the whine now became a banshee's wail.

"The red button?" she called, the distance between them and the ocean rapidly disappearing.

Wellington shook his head. The indicators—all but one—were green.

Eliza could see whitecaps and ripples of the sea in detail. They had to be only several hundred feet in the air now.

"Wellington!"

The final light turned green.

"Now, Eli—"

He never got the opportunity to finish her name or give the command a second time. She threw herself forwards and pressed the red button with two fingers. The banshee's wail now roared as if it were every typhoon from her childhood in New Zealand, and this time Eliza felt as if she were being thrown back from her front passenger seat into the tumble seat. The last time she felt this sort of acceleration, it was in her mad escape from the pirate airship off the Carolinas. Something moved off to her right. She looked over her side of the car and saw fabric extending across the fixed, taut metal skeleton of a wing. Her stomach lurched as the car's hood slowly lifted upwards. The roar increased as Wellington pulled the steering wheel towards him, and the turbulent blue ocean before her disappeared. Now her stomach slipped into her throat as she felt *rapid* ascension. She wanted to call out to Wellington but fought to keep her mouth shut, in case anything were to come out of it against her—or her stomach's—will.

Then the horizon levelled out before her. They were in the air, and they were now flying high over the Northern California shoreline.

Eliza took a deep breath and then looked over at him. "You could have told me, you know?"

"What? That I had built a flying car in my spare time?" Wellington gave a hearty laugh. "You would have thought me daft."

"No, you twit!" she snapped. "You could have told me that you loved me. Back in England."

Wellington looked at her sideways. "Some of us have to work ourselves up to spilling our feelings into the world. I'm not quite as used to it as you are."

She opened her mouth, thought better of it, and shrugged. "Fair point, Welly! Fair point!"

Eliza looked over her shoulder to Bill and Felicity. The two of them were holding on to their respective hats with one hand. Their other hand grasped the back of the driver and passenger seats. They were catatonic.

"Hang on," Wellington shouted over to her, pointing to the compass. "Hopefully, I can get us in some kind of northerly direction, but first we need to get over the coast, over land."

Whatever he was about to do, Eliza knew better than to interrupt him. Instead, she looked straight down at the blue expanse of the Pacific Ocean.

"Just give me a tick," he said cheerily, flipping a small red switch on his dash. Eliza felt something kick in the stern of their car and they approached the coastline. They still had altitude, but Eliza could feel a sinking feeling of descent.

"Not yet," Wellington growled through clenched teeth. "Not yet."

The sensation of thrust ceased, and one of the green lights on Wellington's dash switched to red.

"Bugger!" Wellington spat. "That is not good."

The car swooped downwards again, but Wellington countered the sudden drop easier this time and guided their car closer and closer to the California cliffside. Eliza could no longer feel her stomach summersaulting, only the tightness in her chest as she was holding her breath. They caught another gust, then another, and Wellington was chuckling happily as if he were on a delightful ride across the country.

Finally, Eliza took a breath as their car passed over the coastline and underneath them was solid ground.

"Now comes the tricky bit," Wellington said, angling the car in a descent.

The motorcar seemed to enjoy losing altitude as it did so quickly and deftly. Wellington on their controlled descent did bank, following the compass heading to a northerly heading. He continued to dip then climb, slowing his descent with each action until their motorcar reached what Eliza guessed would be fifty feet above terra firma.

"Red switch, Eliza!" he called to her.

Eliza flipped the red switch, and the sensation of thrust ceased. Wellington yanked at a handle by his right foot, and a series of parachutes unfurled.

Twenty feet . . . ten feet . . .

Wellington pushed the accelerator forwards, and their motorcar hopped forwards a few feet, hopped a second time, and then they were rolling forwards as the chutes broke free from the retracting wings and stabilizers. The car finally came to a stop.

"Congratulations, Welly," Eliza said.

The flash came from behind them.

She had nearly forgotten about the death ray, and when the four of them turned in the direction of the burst, a brilliant silver beam stretched northerly, stretching through the dusk sky to reach out into the Pacific Ocean. The blast struck the ocean so hard that seconds later they heard a sharp crack followed by a great plume of steam and vapour reaching into the night. Eliza scrambled out of the motorcar and ran across the earth, the earth that was vibrating and rippling underneath her until she could see the impact point. She would not dare the cliff's edge as the tremours were growing in intensity while the steam, flame, and vapour billowed into the growing night.

Her eyes now looked everywhere in the sky above them. The titanic airship was nowhere to be found.

Perhaps San Francisco was saved from destruction; but now she sprinted back for the motorcar. She knew this kind of earthquake, knew the force they could hold; but they had been acts of God and nature. Even the way the ground shook and trembled underneath didn't feel right. This was something unknown, something terrifying. Eliza knew nothing would stop the earthquake that would follow in the wake of Thomas Edison's latest scientific breakthrough.

INTERLUDE

❦

In Which Sophia del Morte Peers into the Tortured Souls of Men

After her dance lesson with Miss Harris, Sophia del Morte knew that she would have to be more careful. She hated being proven wrong in her assessment of the American agent, but it did happen from time to time. On those occasions, when one plan did not work, it simply meant that there had to be another way.

Miss Harris' increase in security was evident to Sophia. There were eyes on the doors and windows, both inside and outside the Palace Hotel, and she was more than certain the prince had earned a few extra shadows as well. All this, Sophia had observed with keen interest earlier that day from a delightful coffee house across from the hotel.

Patience was the discipline of her craft, and that patience had proven its worth with the arrival of a brightly painted caravan with a bold promise emblazoned on its side:

MADAME ZAMORA
PEERS INTO YOUR FUTURE

As she watched the caravan disappear in the alleyway leading to the service entrance, Sophia began preparations for her return to the Palace.

When the sun had reached high noon, Sophia returned to the streets, a simple cloak keeping the unseasonal chill at bay. Her outward fashion attracted no attention, but the one she wore underneath would have. Under the cowl, she began weighing breaching options for the hotel. Guards would still be at the doors and at events that piqued the prince's interest, but the second floor ballroom, where McTighe had crushed her feet for a number of days, had, she observed, a narrow marble lip running along just under the window.

Sophia ducked into the alleyway behind the Palace; and when certain she was out of plain view of San Francisco's afternoon pedestrians, she removed the cloak. Dressed in her preferred fashion for infiltration, her dark hair up and tucked under a knitted cap, Sophia gave a quick cursory glance at the bandolier that fit across her shoulders and down her torso buckled about herself. Each pouch held darts of various potency for the small pistol attached at the waist belt. Considering Agent Harris' abilities, it was not wrong to plan for the worst.

Just beyond the service entrance stood the carriage of Madame Zamora. Sophia pulled herself up into the driver's seat, and began sifting through the papers covering half of the long seat. These documents appeared essential for the fortune-teller's travels. There were flyers for upcoming summer fairs, many of them noted with names, performance rates, and individual notes pertaining to special guests at these events.

Then she spied one for the Palace's current exposition. It had a contact's name, a rather impressive rate, and the number twenty-two.

Sophia returned to the alleyway and slipped her hands inside a gift from the Maestro. With the stealth and swiftness of a cat, she clambered up the side of the caravan, and then clambered up the side of the building, her fingers digging deep into the hotel masonry. The speed and nature of her climb, she knew, would have appeared superhuman, and indeed it was thanks to the "ascent claws" and rubberised footwear.

The second storey did not offer a lot of extra purchase; but that narrow marble decoration was all she needed, her specialised shoes providing excellent grip. She only had to drop and crawl beneath the windows of two other rooms before she was in the right place.

Crouching, Sophia peered into the window. The suite was dim, but for the light from two gas fixtures on the wall. The woman—apparently an actress of some degree as she was checking her makeup in the mirror—slipped over her raven hair a fine salt-and-pepper wig of fantastic curls. Decorated with beads and bangles that Sophia could hear clinking against each other through the window, "Zamora" now flitted over a small table covered by a red-patterned cloth, a crystal ball as the centrepiece, and a deck of large cards. Looking about the room, the performer suddenly caught her breath and then fished out of a pouch hanging from her waist a box of matches. With a quick flick of her wrist, she went from candle to candle, bathing the room in a deep amber glow. Details and atmosphere were always important in the art of the confidence game.

Sophia removed from her belt sheath a thin stiletto, slipped it between the windowpanes, and flipped the latch. Once inside, she removed one of the darts from her bandolier and waited.

When Zamora went to her window to shut the curtains, Sophia jabbed her dart into the woman's wrist. It was not a deadly poison—since some part of her own heritage was Romani—but the confidence woman would remain asleep until morning, and wake with a pounding headache only. Sophia dragged her back into a bedroom, and then opened up the closet to survey the fortune-teller's limited wardrobe.

"Variations on a theme," Sophia said to the slumbering woman. "You should try it sometime."

The outfit Sophia pieced together was similar to the original, but instead of the elderly wig and exaggerated makeup, Sophia wore a scarf decorated with coins and beads on her head. The skirt and puffy blouse, all decorated with the jingling baubles, transformed the assassin into a mystical medium, perhaps with a little more finesse than the other. Now her visitors would find a fetching gypsy rather than a haggard old one. She didn't believe tonight's clients would mind terribly.

It truly was a clever notion, featuring a fortune-teller at a science exposition. There was a notion that clankertons, many

notorious for being sceptical of the supernatural, enjoyed daring
one another to consult supposed psychics and seers, perhaps to
test the boundaries of probability. Others, however, were true
believers, and even based their future projects on premonitions.
Whether a doubter or a believer, Sophia's "Zamora" would have
a most lucrative run here at the exposition.

With the suite's clock chiming thrice, she could hear the
exposition outside begin anew: music, voices, the clattering of
silverware, and the sound of footsteps. Sophia waited patiently,
sitting behind the table, with her hands folded and eyes on the
door.

When her first client came through the door, she was disappointed. He was not the heir to the English throne, although
he was old enough to perhaps be heir to the throne of Caesar.
Sophia sent the crooked old gentleman on his way with an
admonishment to stay away from ladies of easy virtue. Hearing the dreadful wheeze from him when he stood to leave, she
knew she had done him a great kindness.

Another clankerton entered, and soon Sophia began to
warm to her role. It was rather fun to speak in the outrageous
accent most people expected from a gypsy, wave her hand
over the milky depths of the crystal ball she operated through
a pneumatic pedal system. It was a clever contraption this
confidence trickster had employed, as with each pedal under
her right foot, the currents in the sphere changed colour,
direction, and the viscousness of what flowed inside.

Into the evening, Sophia continued to pronounce what the
future held for the Palace patrons through the crystal's parlour tricks or tarot readings. While she knew nothing behind
the meanings of the artful cards, her visitors knew even less.
This made for very active storytelling. Some of her customers
she warned of imminent death; others she told they would
find love. Everything she had learned about judging a character and manipulating a person, translated very well to this
particular con. After only two hours, she had made quite a
tidy sum at it.

When Prince Albert appeared at the door, Sophia felt a
sudden jolt. Of course, she needed to corner the prince, inter-
rogate him; but this was not the jovial prince she had met
under the guise of the contessa. He looked very ill at ease,

shifting from one foot to the other, and glancing through the gap in the door he had left open. He had shadows underneath his eyes, and he looked like he had not slept well since her botched abduction. Perhaps he had been attached to the valet she had murdered. That would not surprise her.

Sophia's suspicions were confirmed when he spoke; his voice was full of genuine grief. "I am sorry, madam, I think I am wasting your time. My colleagues rather shoved me into this, and I really don't believe any of this mumbo jumbo."

Sophia sat up a little taller in her chair. "Well, something has brought you here. Perhaps it is the spirits, perhaps it is fate, or it could simply be a heavy conscience? Whatever it is, you are here. At the very least, I can offer you some insight." She tilted her head, making sure to keep her features in shadow. "What exactly do you not believe?"

Albert stepped in a little, and she understood she had taken the right tack. He was a man that enjoyed a good debate—even with a woman. "I cannot believe in what I cannot see. My mother . . ." His voice trailed off. He leaned back and pushed the door the rest of the way closed. "Well . . . my mother became quite obsessed with the occult after my father was killed. She kept claiming he could talk to her, but that was just grief. I always thought it foolish . . . but over events of the last few days . . ." He paused and adjusted his ascot. "Well, let's just say they have made me think about my own mortality."

Sophia looked at him carefully, judging. He probably didn't notice it, but he had sidled closer to her.

The assassin gestured with one open hand to the chair. "Grief is one thing that can be assuaged by reaching into the darkness. Would you not like to speak to your father also?"

Albert jerked a little, and she realised she had stepped on dangerous ground. "My father was a man of science. The only spirits he believed in were scotch, brandy, and cognac."

The prince was close to banging out of the room, and Sophia could not have that. "Yet as a man of science," she said smoothly, "he would always repeat an experiment before declaring it a failure . . . is that not so?"

They looked hard at each other. Sophia slipped a solitary

hand to her lap where her dart gun resided, just in case the prince saw through her disguise.

With a sharp sigh, the prince sat down in the chair opposite her, and rested his hands on the velvet of the tablecloth. "If you can summon my father, and he answers questions only a family member would know, then I will believe you."

He really did not sound as though he believed her at all. That was perfectly fine; she had no plan to conjure the dead up for him. Instead, Sophia leaned forwards and took his hand.

Prince Albert had no chance to escape. Her fingers wrapped around his, and the tiny spike on the inside of her ring punctured the prince's flesh just enough for her agent to begin its work. By the time he had jerked his hands away it was already too late.

"I say," the prince slurred, his eyes glassy, "what was that?"

The paralytic effect hit him fast, so when Sophia placed her dart gun next to the crystal ball, rose from her chair, and opened the backpack she'd brought with her, there would be no worry that he would escape her. By the time she had turned around, Albert had sagged back in his chair, his gaze fixed on the ceiling, while his arms hung limp on each side of the chair.

Swinging her leg over him, Sophia sat across his lap, face-to-face. It was a position that he would have undoubtedly enjoyed if he were truly conscious.

Over his head she slipped the brass cage with all its screws and struts. Albert's head lolled backwards and forwards in a final act of defiance of trying to escape it, but she held him easily in place before sliding out the brace portion. She hummed under her breath as her fingers flickered over the screws, tightening what needed to be done. The whole device ended up holding his shoulders, neck, and head completely still, facing her. A guttural groan escaped the prince, but that was pretty much all that could get away from her.

Now the tricky part. Sophia's tongue slipped between her teeth as she set about adjusting the cage's lid hooks around the prince's eyes. Each of the reed-thin spindles locked around the flesh of his eyelids with tiny hooks, then pulled them back, keeping his eyes open. It was imperative that the prince did not blink as she worked on him. The information that she needed had to be accurate or the Maestro would be most displeased.

She then used the eyedropper to deliver a clear liquid she didn't know the name of to each eyeball. The prince jerked a little under her, but both the paralytic and the cage held him in place. There must be some chemical in the solution that might burn a little.

With all these devices in place, all that was needed were the goggles, larger and chunkier than any airship pirate or Arctic explorer would have known. These bulky monstrosities were specialised lenses that, even after adjusting them over her own eyes, felt heavy on her. Layers of colours stood between her and the heir's own eyeballs. It was a confusing mess—or at least would have been to one not trained in their use.

The neuro-ocular was not the Maestro's making, but the obsession of a strange Swiss gentleman who had lived twenty years in isolation within the Black Forest. Karl had amused her for a couple of weeks, but then turned rather angry when she'd tried to leave with several of his creations, the neuro-ocular being one of them.

Sophia had left Karl bleeding quietly to death on his own Persian rug.

Still, his devices lived on while Prince Albert remained limp in the chair, his head, shoulders, and eyes held still; and she looked into the royal's brain.

She adjusted the left lens until she could—by squinting—observe the rush of blood through his head. Through the right lens, portions of his brain lit up from thought and sensation. So far everything was still and quiescent.

Now she just had to ask the right questions.

"Who are you?" she whispered, her voice dripping with erotic overtones, as if they were both naked and in bed. The paralytic had made any movement in his privates impossible, but Sophia wriggled slightly, enjoying a tingle of her own. Stripping a man's mind was perhaps the most erotic thing she'd ever done.

"Prince Albert Edward," he replied, his voice flat and lost.

It was a simple question that she used to discern if the equipment was working and to mark the correct rush of fluids, and the twitching of his eyes. However, even in this he had revealed something. He had not mentioned his mother.

It was a little aside that the Maestro might find of interest—once she had told him what she'd discovered lay deeper.

"Do you know the Director of the Ministry of Peculiar Occurrences, Doctor Basil Sound?"

"Yes."

"Have you ever been to the headquarters of that Ministry?" Sophia shifted slightly, wondering at the marvels the prince might have observed there. It was one of the few places that the assassin had not dared. At least not yet.

"Yes." The prince swallowed, and his eyes darted left to right for a minute. There would be, sadly for the prince, no escaping the effects of her device. "I went with my father when I was young, to see it built."

The neuro-ocular was working better than she had hoped. Sophia glanced up at the door, pleased to hear the uninterrupted sounds of the exposition's social gatherings continuing. For a moment she imagined her device released on so many of those amazing minds at the convention. The things she might learn from them!

Perhaps, another time. Sophia would have played this gypsy game once more; but the Maestro had been specific. She had to return to his side immediately, and she must not be caught.

Leaning forwards, she whispered into the prince's ear, allowing her lips to brush the sensitive skin there. "You must have seen many things, Albert. Tell me, did you ever see the Archives?"

A shudder of repressed muscle activity ran through the man. If he'd been capable, she knew he would have lurched upright and thrown her against the far wall. He could not—would not—resist her, and that set her skin aflame. The fact that he was held prisoner thus, made the assassin twitch in her own, much deeper, way.

His brain was alight now, flickering scarlet with flashes of yellow and orange, those flashes showing he was attempting to keep his tongue silent. The movement of blood there told her he still was incapable of lying to her, still well under her control.

"Tell me, Albert," she implored.

"I've been to the Archives many times. Such treasures. Such power." The flashes were nearly blinding Sophia in her right eye, but they dimmed as Albert added, "I've seen the Restricted Area."

This. This was what the Maestro wanted. "What is the Restricted Area?"

Though his jaw was locked tight, he let out a low growl, before choking out, "The beginning and end of all things. Alpha and Omega."

He was not lying to her, but more like he was avoiding the truth. Albert's allegory was difficult for the neuro-ocular to process, the red now punctuated by growing masses of deep blues and black. His stamina and resistance were impressive.

"I need to know more," Sophia demanded, pushing down on him, now gyrating slowly against him, attempting perhaps to ride the truth out of him. "What is in the Restricted Section of the Ministry of Peculiar Occurrences?"

A long drawn out breath was forced from the prince's lips, while through the lense of the neuro-ocular his brain flashed with oranges and golds. He was so close, and she too, that Sophia wanted to scream. "So many things," he finally ground out. "All things. All in joy. All in sorrow."

"What do you mean?" she said with a hiss, her legs quivering around his waist while her fingers wrapped around his arms. "What does Doctor Sound have down there? Tell me now, Albert!"

Albert's trapped eyes flicked this way and that trying to avoid looking at hers. "It is Genesis. It is Revelations. He has . . ." Bertie was gnashing his teeth together, his chin feeling the cool touch of his own spittle as he tried to resist her. "He has . . . all the . . ."

The door to the party flew off its hinges with a resounding *snap.* The ebony-skinned, imperious-looking female agent of OSM stood there, her elegant evening wear billowing with her every move, capped with her dark eyes hidden behind a pair of iridescent glasses. A long device such as a road worker might have, was balanced in her hand, while behind an outraged clankerton was yelling at her a string of obscenities and slurs.

Sophia smiled slightly. She appreciated a woman capable of

making a situation work to her advantage. What she did not appreciate was the terrible timing of this creature's interruption.

"I could see through the door when you got on top of him—but you weren't moving much," she said, yanking down the goggles to let them hang across her neck. "That just didn't seem right."

Glasses that allowed the agent to read heat signatures— quite an advantage, Sophia mused. "So you like to watch?" Sophia clicked her tongue as she slipped away from the prince, her hand reaching behind her for the dart gun. "Naughty girl."

Agent Harris hefted the steam lever in her hands and swung at Sophia, the small boiler travelling on the woman's back puffing and chugging as she did so. The assassin leapt backwards, feeling the heat of Harris' makeshift weapon brush past her. Sophia landed on her feet just as the steam lever shattered the table and crystal ball, sending a light vibration through the floor . . .

. . . which Sophia could still feel through her shoes even after Harris removed the lever from it.

When the chandelier above them and light fixtures began to tremble, Sophia chuckled. "It appears you do not know your own strength, Agent Harris."

The mild tremble was now rumbling and reverberating in their ears. The irate engineer and comrades initially alerted to the skirmish in Zamora's suite now scattered like snowflakes in a wind gust, screams of *"Earthquake!"* flitting into the room and down the hallway. Sophia kept the agent in her sights as lamps and small statues in the room toppled over. A light fixture behind Martha's head exploded, sending out a small plume of fire.

The second exploded, and a hunk of flaming debris landed in the remains of the crystal ball. Sophia recoiled at the sudden explosion of light and heat, and she pressed herself against the closest wall, in an effort to catch her breath and keep her balance as the world continued to shake around her.

When she lowered her arm, she could see Harris struggling to free Prince Albert from the hold of her interrogation device. Looking around at the fire and bits of plaster crumbling from the ceiling, Sophia smiled brightly. Chaos was always the best cover for escape.

Sophia sprinted for the window, grabbing her backpack on the way and thrusting her hands into the form-fitting leather. She pushed open the window and kicked her legs over the sill, allowing momentum to carry her into open space. Her fingers reached forwards, digging once again into the stone. It was now gravity's office, pulling her down, the descent leaving deep grooves in her wake. She gave a push and landed hard in the alleyway, rolling up to her feet on impact and disappearing into the dusk of San Francisco.

That was all that made sense now: run. Find open ground. Or perhaps, better still, run to the harbour, take a boat, get away from shore. Sophia knew she had to get away from the towering structures, which swayed as the earth angrily shook underfoot. She was not certain how far she had run, but she would not stop until she felt safe.

When Sophia looked up, she saw it—a brilliant white light on the horizon. It was not the sun, but a pure white beam of energy. Solid in form, piercing through the blue purple of an oncoming night. It was low on the horizon, and it appeared to be travelling out towards the sea. Whatever this strange anomaly was, it would serve as her beacon to safety.

Something moved to her left. The building a block ahead began to falter, its façade sagging to one side then toppling, tearing down the rest of the building with it. Sophia turned and ran, back in the direction of the Palace, back into the madness, the screams for help that would not come, or at least not come until all was done.

Dare she risk an alleyway? It could provide a shortcut around the way now blocked.

Underneath her, the ground bucked and knocked her forwards. Sophia picked herself up and found her stride again. The open street, she feared, was no longer safe.

Then she heard the building beside her explode, the windows along the third floor cracking in sequence as the shock rippled throughout it. Another grinding pop of stone, and the building leaned towards Sophia, as if it were a giant looking down, eager to consume her.

The ground kicked again, and this time, sent her sprawling. She knew she wouldn't clear the block in time.

So this will be my end, Sophia lamented silently as more

windows shattered, and pieces of architecture freed themselves to rain down from on high.

Sophia dared to look up at the structure teetering over her. This was never the death she envisioned for herself, but she would not allow herself to die as a shrinking violet. She would face it. She would defy the fear it desired from her. As her stomach quivered with a strange tingle, Sophia pulled herself up on her knees and faced her fate.

The world flashed before her. All was light, and then . . .

Sophia's eyes were still struggling from the momentary blinding, but when the white and the black and greys came in focus, and the recognition of colour returned, the assassin found herself in an electroporter chamber.

She swallowed back the grit, dirt, and ash in her mouth, her throat painfully dry and demanding water. She turned to face her saviour . . .

. . . and longed to be back in the earthquake.

The Maestro, flanked by a paler-than-usual Pearson, was looking at her from his mechanical throne, but the state in which she found her lord and master at present filled her with emotions and instincts she had never known. Certainly, Sophia knew fear. She knew it intimately, from both perspectives. She also grew to know the differences, subtle but still prevalent, between fear and terror.

This was something entirely and savagely new.

His goggles struggled to remain on his head, but as they had been knocked askew they shuddered with each laboured breath he drew. His hat and hair—both attached to one another, as was the fashion of this elaborate masquerade, were tousled, as were his fine robes. What made ice tingle within her veins was the expression in his eyes, or at least the one eye that was visible. It was darting around the Electroporter Room, trying to take in the fantastic technology and its frightening power. His gaze was of paralysing helplessness, as if he were trapped in an Edgar Allan Poe story of a man falling asleep in the comforts of home and awakening in a surgery theatre surrounded by surgeons ready to begin their work. He did not know those around him. He was lost, confounded, and smothering in his own madness.

The other eye, the one still covered by the goggle lense,

flared angrily with its crimson glow, a glow that only occurred when he was angry. It was a way for her to gauge how upset he was, and from the deepness of its colour and the glare it shone, the Maestro was incensed. Deaths were inevitable.

Both of these emotions warred within this creature before Sophia, and she did not know what to do.

"The Maestro insisted on seeing you upon your return, signora," Pearson spoke drily. He too looked uncertain. That did not put Sophia at ease. At all.

What had happened on board the *Titan* while she was away?

"Signora," the Maestro, his voice now switching intermittently between the mechanical box designed for him and his usual baritone, wheezed in greeting. "Tell me. How was your stay in San Francisco?"

TWENTY-FIVE

❦

Wherein a Prince Is Found and
Then Promptly Lost Again

Wellington Thornhill Books stood at the window over-looking San Francisco Bay and felt a heavy lethargy stealing over him. It had barely been twenty-four hours since their harrowing adventure over the Pacific Ocean. Shortly after the firing of the Tesla-Edison Death Ray, the massive airship had disappeared in the same spectacular fashion as it had appeared, and the taste of that loss cast a grimy pall over an already heartbreaking calamity.

"I've been told the fires are under control now," Eliza murmured coming up and standing next to him, "and the military have already begun ferrying supplies."

Their view was from a military outpost located on the Oakland Long Wharf. Alongside Army and Navy operations, the town also served as mooring stations for airships. Tonight Oakland skies were filled with traffic, offering resources to tend to San Francisco.

Everything had been reduced to something of a dizzying blur once they had reached the nearest wire station. Wellington silently sorted through all the details of both the encounter in Montara, as well as the events beginning in Norfolk,

Virginia. He knew this was going to be the topic of discussion when Felicity and Bill received communiqués with their new orders:

> *All agents to gather at Oakland. Doctor Sound and Director Highfield to be present.*

It was a very stark room, without any particular decorations except for a portrait of the American president, Grover Cleveland. Only rows of tables laid out parallel to a large blackboard showed the room was meant for humans at all.

Wellington turned and cast a sideways glimpse at the room's only other occupants. Nikola Tesla sat in the far corner, scribbling notes on a pad of paper he had commandeered from one of the airmen. He was entirely ignoring them, and that was quite all right by the archivist. Bill and Felicity also sat at the long table, either taking stock of their transcontinental exploits, or silently mourning the tragedy unfolding in the Bay.

"Did you see him," Wellington asked Eliza in a low tone, "when we picked him up in the airship?"

She frowned. "Of course I saw him, Welly. He might be a mad genius, but he's not invisible."

"No," he went on, "did you see if he was crying . . . or laughing?"

She shot him an odd look. "Why on earth would he be laughing?"

Why indeed. As much as he admired Tesla, Wellington knew he had his weaknesses. What he had seen in the control room of the Duke of Sus— of the Maestro's massive battleship was no illusion, no mistake. Yes, they had been hurried and the standoff was quite the heady rush . . .

. . . but he knew what he had seen.

"It is all so horrible," Eliza said, pressing one hand against the window.

"But there is cold comfort to be taken," he offered, even as he watched plumes of smoke rise into the evening air. "San Francisco, had they received the full brunt of the death ray, would have been levelled to the ground."

"Terrible thought," Eliza murmured.

Everyone, save for Tesla still engrossed in his own notations, turned as the door to the room opened. Doctor Sound, carrying a covered placard of some kind, entered, immediately followed by a dark-skinned man of stunning carriage and confidence. The newcomer was about Sound's age, Wellington observed, with a neatly trimmed beard and lacking the air of joviality that surrounded the Ministry director. In fact, Wellington could feel an intensity exuding from the man. It was as if he was taking the disaster in San Francisco personally.

Sound gestured to the seats before the chalkboard. "If you'll all have a seat." As Wellington and Eliza took seats opposite their counterparts and Tesla, Sound gestured to the black man sitting next to him. "This fine gentleman, Agents Books and Braun, is Mr. Luther Highfield, Chief of the Office of the Supernatural and Metaphysical—my American equal. As this mission is under OSM jurisdiction, I turn the floor over to him."

"Thank you, Director." Highfield stepped forwards, tucked his thumbs into his pockets, and ran his eye over the line of people before him, his gaze lingering on Tesla who still had not acknowledged their entrance. Wellington had been sure he'd never meet someone as imposing as Sound. Highfield lifted that bar higher. He towered over everyone, and his brown eyes were flinty, stern.

"A man of his . . . heritage . . ." Wellington whispered to Eliza, as the chief's attention was currently on Felicity, ". . . in such a high position? I'm impressed."

"Actually," he began, his voice soft but still carrying a tenor that demanded respect, and Highfield turned his attention on Wellington, "no one else wanted this job." His hands on the desk between them, OSM's chief was now giving the archivist his full attention, and that made Wellington feel two inches tall. At best. "Let's just say OSM is not the most prestigious branch of the United States government." He stood up and strode back to the chalkboard. "After yesterday, it is hard to say if that is likely to change."

He unveiled the placard that covered most of the chalkboard. It was a detailed map of the San Francisco Bay Area, and part of the Pacific Ocean. Reaching into his coat pocket, Highfield pulled out a green star slightly bigger than his palm.

It magnetically attached to where Montara was. "You all were there." He attached a red star in an area of the Pacific. "This is the impact point of the death ray, some ten to fifteen miles off the coastline."

Wellington glanced at Tesla. The scientist was paying attention now, and looked as if he were about to correct the chief; but closed his mouth, remaining quiet.

Another red star snapped on to the placard between the impact point and Montara. "Disappearance of the airship. And this," he said, attaching a red circle that covered the western half of San Francisco. "This is the scope of the event Edison caused yesterday. The names of the dead and missing are still coming in." He turned his dark gaze on Tesla who, Wellington would have gathered, would have felt slightly intimidated by the man, had Tesla not returned to his notebook. "Mr. Tesla?"

Covering his open notebook with his hands, Tesla looked up at Chief Highfield, wide-eyed and ready, it appeared, for debriefing.

"Please repeat the events that happened at Montara, leading to the firing of a death ray you were supposed to deactivate."

"I was given the task of taking control of the death ray from the auxiliary control room which, Agent Books here correctly deduced, was located by the lighthouse itself. I would have done so had Edison not engineered what I have heard called a 'fail-safe.' The auxiliary was designed to take primary control if control was lost at the main control point, the airship.

"The fail-safe, however, was also designed to follow an auto-firing protocol if auxiliary was employed without a failure from main. This was a safeguard to prevent the shutdown I was attempting. Once I gained access, the auto-fire sequence initiated. I had few options remaining, so I set all power to maximum in order to burn out the device and repositioned the beam to fire out into the ocean."

"How fortunate you were Edison's fail-safe was so rudimentary," Wellington said. He could see Eliza start at his sudden contribution. "Had it been otherwise, Edison's auto-fire protocol could have locked out would-be sabateours from changing targeting coordinates and overloading circuits." He gave Tesla a slow nod. "Excellent work, Nikola."

He opened his mouth to reply, but then another thought came to him, and he merely returned a tight smile.

"Nikola?" Eliza whispered. "You two are on first name basis?"

Wellington never took his eyes off the scientist. "We are now."

Highfield considered Tesla for a moment, then turned his gaze out the window. "In order to maintain an illusion that we know what is going on, we are *not* correcting the general population who currently believe it was an earthquake."

Suddenly Tesla erupted, making everyone jump. "You are not revealing Edison's part in this?"

"Mr. Edison is very well-known, and his inventions are in widespread use across the nation. If it became known what really happened, there would be widespread panic." Highfield shared a look with Sound. "The director and I have come to an agreement that both British and American agents will abide by this decision."

All of them took this silently, except for Tesla who kicked his chair as he sat down. Wellington imagined the Serbian would need persuading on this front, but then who would believe Tesla if he began ranting about electric death rays?

The chief stepped back, and Doctor Sound now took the floor. "There is one other matter that needs our attention." He turned and called out, "Albert!"

Eliza and Wellington scrambled to their feet when the Prince of Wales opened the door and walked over to stand with the director. Even Felicity let out a little squeak at Albert's entrance. Only Bill and Tesla, neither of them even slightly impressed, remained in their seats.

At his side was a younger woman, dark-skinned, and quite breathtaking. The matter that the Prince of Wales was in the company of an attractive, young woman was no shock. What was shocking was just how well armed this lady was. She had a pistol strapped to her waist, and a throwing knife sheathed in a leather wrist gauntlet.

"Evening, Bill," she said. "You look good, all things considered."

"Likewise, Martha," he replied.

The prince looked tired and downcast, but a slight smile

tugged at the corner of his mouth. "Oh please, don't stand on ceremony . . . besides, I am the *former* Prince of Wales . . ." He trailed off.

Wellington began to feel that they were tumbling further down the rabbit hole. First, Edison in league with the House of Usher. Then the appearance of the Maestro who was, in fact, the Queen's Privy Council. And now, the Prince of Wales? Here? In the States?

Sound cleared his throat, looking almost embarrassed. "Bertie and I are suspicious that the Queen, after so long not taking an interest in him at all, was insistent he come to San Francisco. His attendance at this conference was her idea, and then this Maestro chap shows up—"

"Who just so happens to be one of her Privy Counsellors," Wellington interjected.

"Indeed," Sound intoned solemnly. "When I read that in your report, it confirmed our suspicion that she intended him to be killed."

"Bugger me," Eliza blurted out.

The prince smiled, but it had an edge of despair to it. "Yes, quite. As you can imagine, a shock for me as well, but based on a few close calls I managed to avoid, thanks to the admirable skills of Miss Harris here," the prince said, motioning to the woman at his side, "Basil and I have decided that for the time being, Mother should continue to think that I died in the 'earthquake' along with my valet," and his voice tightened as he uttered the name, "Morton."

"I will be using the æthergate to find a pleasant spot to hide Bertie." Sound afforded a wry grin. "He and his admirable virago, Miss Martha Harris, if you have no objections, Luther?"

"Agent Harris?" he asked her.

Harris gave the prince a slightly hesitant look before saying, "We're used to one another by now. As we know how each other operates, we will be good for each other."

"Where will you send them, Doctor Sound?" Felicity asked.

"A place only I will be privy to," he replied.

Those were the words that sent a chill down Wellington's spine. Sending the Crown Prince of Britain off to who knows where with an American agent in tow, suggested that the director could not trust his own agents.

This rabbit hole was descending deeper and deeper into madness.

"And what of the Maestro or, as he is commonly know, the Duke of Sussex?" Eliza asked. "He's got Edison."

"Yes," the director said, "we shall have to deal with him back home, I am certain, but for now we must be on our way."

The chief and he exchanged a glance, one full of professional courtesy. "We'll leave you to it, Director. We have to debrief Mr. Tesla fully on what he understands of Edison's device."

After salutations and pleasantries were exchanged, Bill and Felicity lingered.

"It's been good working with you," Bill said, slapping Wellington a little too soundly on the shoulder. "Hope we'll meet again." Eliza however got a far more enthusiastic good-bye. The embrace lingered rather too long for the archivist's liking and he appeared to be whispering something in the agent's ear—Wellington distinctly heard "Lizzie" in the exchange— but his chance to protest disappeared when Felicity wrapped him in her arms.

"It was a joy having you here, Mr. Books," she said cheerfully. Perhaps she had come to terms with Eliza's and his reconciliation. "If you are ever in the United States"—and she paused, shooting a look at Eliza—"alone and available, do call on me," she whispered, slipping into his hand her personal card.

Eliza cleared her throat. Felicity, it appeared, still had a dreadful amount of work ahead of her in spycraft.

"Felicity," Eliza said with a far too civil smile.

"Eliza," Felicity returned with a similar smile.

"I would say it has been a pleasure—" Eliza began.

"—but we would both know that would be an utter lie," Felicity completed.

"Take care."

"Bon voyage."

And both ladies giggled at one another in a fashion that made Wellington and Bill share a nervous glance.

Once Bill and Felicity left the room, Sound's veneer of

cheeriness immediately fell away. His eyes now were icy. "I think we all know the waters ahead will be deep and dangerous. So far we do not know the monsters that lurk beneath us, only that they are there."

Albert sat on the edge of the desk. "Something happened before the earthquake, something I am not sure OSM understands the significance of." He glanced over his shoulder. "As Martha here can attest, I was visited not once, but twice, by a very beautiful Italian lady, who went to a great deal of trouble to question me on the secrets of the Ministry and the archives."

Beautiful Italian woman? *Dear Lord, she was the agent the Maestro was referring to,* Wellington thought as he sat back down on a chair with a *thump.* Dimly he heard Eliza exclaim, "That tart Sophia del Morte!"

"She didn't find out much," Albert assured them, "but I thought you should all know about it."

"And considering Sussex recruiting former Agent Campbell, and knowing of Sussex's duality," Sound said, each word dropping on the agents from a great height, "we must exercise caution at the Ministry, and elsewhere. What lies ahead with you, Bertie, will be between those present."

Wellington looked up at his director. "Yes, sir. What else do you require of us?"

"Take an airship immediately from the Oakland aeroport," was not the answer Wellington had been expecting.

"But what about using the æthergate?" Eliza asked in typical fashion, though the archivist understood her desire to get home quickly.

"Æthergate travel is not without its risk, and we need to keep up appearances, so having you all arrive home via standard travel channels would be best," Sound replied. "I also want to keep the details of Bertie and Martha to as few people as possible. This is less about trust and more on the amount of risk I'm subjecting upon my allies, you understand, yes?" Eliza pinched her lips together and sank back into her chair. Doctor Sound folded his arms. "Besides, you would have to leave behind Agent Books' wonderful automobile."

"We will leave immediately," Wellington replied. "Shall we arrange to have our luggage sent there, sir?"

"Already taken care of," Sound stated.

Wellington held out his hand to the prince. "It was an honour to meet you, Your Highness. I hope your exile will be a short one."

Eliza barely had time to say her good-byes before Wellington hustled her out of the room, his mind racing almost as fast as his heart.

"What was that all about, Welly?" she asked once they were outside. The wind blew her dark red hair about her face, and he wanted to kiss her then and there so badly . . .

Instead, he took her hands into his. "Eliza, the Prince of Wales has been threatened by his mother, the man plotting against the Ministry is the same man running a conspiracy against the Empire, and the head of the Ministry has given us a standing order to trust no one. We need to catch the first airship home." He was making wide strides down the street towards their car. "And during the flight, we should share thoughts on preparations."

Eliza scooted in front of him, her patience waning. "Preparations for what exactly?"

"War."

Her eyes grew wide, but she pressed her lips together in a hard line. "I imagine you're right, Wellington. Who knows exactly what we shall find when we return."

Taking her hand in his, he squeezed it tightly, and together they walked off to begin the journey back home.

CODA

❧

Wherein Doctor Sound Plays a Hunch and Offers "Bon Voyage" to an Old Friend

Doctor Basil Sound was siphoned quickly through the layers of security and in short order found himself standing outside the doors of the royal privy chamber. His eyes darted from corner to corner of the lavish receiving room as he paced, tapping the royal summons in his hand. It had been waiting for him when he returned from California via æthergate. He was unsure if this was simply serendipity or something far more sinister.

Finally, the footmen opened the doors, and he walked into the presence of Her Majesty the Queen of England for the second time in nearly as many weeks. He had gone for years without the chance to give his monarch counsel, so to have a second audience within a month was, quite simply, unprecedented.

The room was just as empty of people and just as full of shadows as the last time he'd been there. He could make out the Queen seated at the far end of the room, but the curtains were pulled, the lights dim, and the small shape veiled.

"Director," she began, her voice steady and light, "I believe you have news for me from the Americas?"

"Your Majesty," he said, clearing his throat before continuing, "your son is safe." Bertie was tucked away in distant Fiji, cold comfort in light of what he suspected his monarch of. "The stability of the Empire, however, is in peril."

The Queen shifted slightly. "And what, pray tell, makes you think that?"

This was the difficult part. Considering her outburst and erratic behavior during their last visit, how much could he safely tell her? How would she react to knowing her Lord of the Privy Council was a madman?

"Intelligence," he said. "Ministry intelligence that dark forces are bent on the fall of the Empire. We have a name—the Maestro. He is the spider at the centre of this dastardly web."

"My, my, my," the Queen murmured, rising to her feet. "So very dramatic and sinister—like something from a penny dreadful."

She really didn't seem to be taking him seriously, and considering the history they shared, that was a most alarming thing. Sound tried desperately to make her understand. "We are still gathering information; but this Maestro, we know for certain, nearly destroyed San Francisco, where your son was attending that scientific conference."

"Nearly destroyed?" Victoria clicked her tongue. "What a shame."

Sound stood flabbergasted, unable for a moment to find the words. A chill swept through him as he thought, *What did she mean by that?*

In the silence, Sound summoned up his courage, enough to power his legs as if he were one of the Phoenix Society's Mechamen. He dared to stride up to the Queen, almost to within touching distance of his old friend. It was a severe breach of protocol, but he had to try everything.

"There is more," he said quietly. "This Maestro has abducted Thomas Edison. It is my fear that with their combined resources, the two could come up with something even more terrifying than the death ray unleashed on San Francisco."

The Queen stood silently for a moment but then stepped away from the director, crossing over to a nearby window. Her gloved hand pulled aside the curtain just a fraction, allowing the dying rays of the sun to spill into the gloomy chamber ever so slightly. With her back still turned to Sound, she spoke in a contemplative fashion. "Ever since our first meeting, Director, you have entertained me with your tales of the *très fantastique* and supernatural. You amused and delighted me with the possibility of something greater than what my eyes could tell me." Her head dropped slightly. "In the dark days after my beloved husband's death, it was much needed."

She pulled the curtain a little wider and peered out into the sunset. "However, while we share a colourful history, and you have prospered under my support for the Ministry for many a year, you are not privy to everything that goes on in my Empire. While you have sought out these so-called dark forces that plot against me, I have aligned myself with others possessing a better understanding than you."

Of all the things that had happened to him in his life, this was one of the cruellest blows. The agents of the Ministry would have been quite surprised to see him so visibly shaken.

"Victoria," he pleaded, his voice cracking with emotion, "please remember I have remained loyal to you above all others, and I have always taken the utmost care with your safety . . ."

"Indeed you have," the Queen replied, ignoring his most improper use of her given name, "but that is the problem. You think of me and not the Empire. We are one and the same. Why, this very spring I shall be the longest-reigning monarch ever to sit on the throne, and next year will be my Diamond Jubilee. You claim that the Empire is in danger of toppling, as if it were a house of cards."

She turned to face Sound, and the light coming in through the window filtered through her thick veil in bright golden motes. Her hands went to the lace, pulling it up and over her head. "I say the Empire has never been more stable."

The director's words died in his throat. He'd seen Alexandrina Victoria crowned. Eighteen was young to sit upon the throne, but she had been dazzling with creamy pale skin, a sweet smile. He had never seen such a beautiful, charming girl, but he had come to accept that that girl was long lost, except in paintings.

Yet here was Victoria before him, in the flesh, her youth and vigour restored. It was like looking back in time. However, there was no mirth or joy in the Queen's smile now. Instead, it contained a challenge.

She tilted her head and looked up at him with lovely, gleaming eyes. "The Empire is destined for a long and fruitful life—as am I. I will lead it into another renaissance."

Sound was chilled to the core. Knowing what he now knew, he would be grateful if he made it back to the office alive.

"Your Majesty," he said, bowing low, swallowing his horror, "may you reign forever more."

The smile she gave him was predatory. "Then you have our leave," she said brightly, dismissing him.

He was overjoyed that he managed to take it without running.

Once outside Buckingham Palace, Doctor Sound climbed into the royal hansom and in his mind ran down a list of what he needed to enact straightaway. The Queen had brought him into an inner sanctum of sorts, revealing her terrible secret. The question now was, did this revelation indicate she trusted Sound, or was it meant to instill in him a false sense of security . . . ?

Sound jerked, looking around him. He was in a royal hansom, driven by the Queen's servant.

He rapped his knuckles on the roof of his compartment, but the carriage continued onwards. This time, he put all of his might into it, nearly cracking the rooftop hatch with his fist. The horses gave a whinny of protest as the reins went taut, and the cab lurched to a stop.

"Beg a pardon, sir," the royal coachman called, "but I was asked to return you to Miggins Antiquities."

"I am aware of that," Doctor Sound replied, paying the driver a goodly sum, "and you may report when you last saw me I was of a fit mind and body. I simply decided to take a walk."

"At this time of night, sir?"

"Indeed," he said, tipping his hat to the driver before continuing his way down Buckingham Palace Road on foot.

Night had fallen on London, and there were only a few people out and about in the city. He tipped his hat low to avoid notice and walked as fast as he could without drawing attention, all the while running through the Phantom Protocol procedures, because there was no rescinding the order once given. Signals would be sent, commands issued, and agents would disappear.

It was as he neared the street corner that Sound noticed the horse slowly clopping along *behind* him. He took a moment to give his suit a once-over in a sweetshop window. The ghost of his portly frame inspecting his waistcoat flickered over the glass.

Sound's gaze shifted to another part of the faint reflection. He could see the shadow of a hansom cab drawing to a stop. Even with night closing in around the city as quickly as it was, he could make out the distinct colours of a royal servant's uniform.

Perhaps an indulgence was in order.

Sound straightened his bowler and entered the sweetshop, the bell overhead announcing his entrance to the three people bustling about within the shop.

"I'm sorry, sir," began the gentleman behind the counter. It struck Doctor Sound that, for someone who specialized in sweets, the shopkeeper seemed rather skinny. "We are closing for the night."

"As I would expect at this hour," Sound returned as he approached the counter, his eyes surveying the stock.

"Sir," the shopkeeper said, his tone hardening ever so slightly, "I beg that you kindly—"

"My good man, listen to me and listen very carefully as time is of the essence." Sound spoke quickly, sliding two guineas towards him. "Firstly, I want you to smile brightly and nod. Pretend I am about to commission a rather large order for a celebration. Another two guineas if you make this look convincing."

The shopkeeper paused for only a moment before his stern look dissipated, surrendering to the brightest of smiles. "Why, of course I can accommodate such an order. How can Percy's Sweetshop be of service?"

"Very good," Doctor Sound said, sliding the promised coins over to him. "Now while we are talking, I would very much like you to draw the curtain of your storefront window and lock the door, if you would be so kind."

"Yes, I believe we can whip together some Turkish delight. If you would like to sample what we have here," he said, motioning to a corner of the candy shop. "Danielle, be a dear and draw the blinds, and as this gent is our final customer for the evening, lock the door."

The youngest of the other two workers in the shop gave a quick curtsey before walking to the door. Once it was locked, she grabbed a long pole, caught the latch for each blind, and drew them slowly across the glass. Doctor Sound was holding a small chunk of Turkish delight as the final blind came down.

Sound did not change demeanour or tenor, even as he sampled the chewy treat. Ye gods, how he *hated* this stuff. Fighting back a grimace, he brushed his fingers clean as he asked, "You have a back entrance?"

"Yes, governor."

"Five guineas for your discretion then?"

The shopkeeper's eyes went wide. "Right you are, sir."

Sound followed the man through a small passage behind the counter. The hallway ended at a door that accessed an alleyway.

Coins rang lightly against one another in the shopkeeper's hand.

"I was never here," Sound pressed as he slipped into the alleyway.

While he was a man of learned years and carried with him not only the weight of knowledge but a rather more literal weight from his indulgences, this did not mean that Doctor Sound couldn't run when the situation called for it. This was one of those times. It was hard to say how long Sound had before the driver returned and reported his escape to the Queen.

An empty hansom slowly clopped by him, but it had not gotten far before Sound caught up with it. The driver nearly leapt out of his perch when he felt him grab the cuff of his trousers. The director pulled out the card he always carried in his coat pocket—the one he had hoped never to use—and ordered the cab driver, "Take me to this address." He gave the driver five pounds. This was turning into a most expensive night. "With haste."

"Right you are, sir."

"An extra crown," Sound began as he climbed into the cab, "if you can get me there within the next ten minutes."

There was a crack of a whip and Sound felt himself pushed

back in his seat as they lurched forwards and gained a healthy amount of speed in a matter of moments. The man did not disappoint; Sound had hoped to arrive at the address within ten minutes. They came to a stop in front in just over five.

"Wait here," Sound told the driver. "I shan't be long."

"Very good, sir."

He was at the door, reaching for the knocker, when he paused. He was about to neither tumble down the rabbit hole nor step through the looking glass; this was more akin to shattering a mirror with a Gatling gun.

With a clenching of his jaw, Sound gave the knocker several sharp raps.

When the maid opened the door, she gave a little scream. He ignored her reaction. "Is your master at home?"

"Yes, Doctor Sound, but you are not—" she began.

He waved his hand impatiently, pushing his way into the modest home. "I will be in the parlour. No need to see me there. I know the way."

He heard several locks engage behind him as he removed his hat and hung it on a stand just to his right. Sound wrung his hands as his eyes flitted over to the various decanters on display. A scotch would soothe the nerves, that was certain, but considering his future activation of Phantom Protocol, he would need all his wits about him.

His thoughts scattered when he heard from upstairs a muffled voice exclaim, *"He's here?!"* This was immediately followed by a quick exchange between master and maid. Sound steeled himself as the footsteps thundered down the staircase. Noting he was still clasping his hands tightly, Doctor Sound shook his hands free and took in a long, deep breath.

Yes, this meeting was most unorthodox and highly unusual, but necessary.

The young man entered the parlour, stopping abruptly at the wide archway. He swallowed as he adjusted his spectacles, taking in the sight of the Ministry director. All colour seemed to drain from him the longer he stood there. The master of the house seemed to take on the semblance of a ghost.

I know, lad. I know, Sound lamented silently. *Hardly what you expected.*

"Good evening, Basil," his host finally managed. "Would you care for a scotch?"

"I was about to suggest the same for you."

The man nodded, moving quickly to the decanters. "I would say yes, most assuredly, I need a drink."

Doctor Sound gave his host a wide berth as he fumbled with the decanter and glass. The glass was well over four fingers deep. He could hardly blame him.

"My recommendation, Herbert," Sound began, "is that you enjoy two of those four fingers and then stop there or plan to take the rest of that drink on the road."

Herbert took a deep swig of the amber drink and then gave a long exhale, his back still turned to Doctor Sound. "Am I going on holiday?"

"In about—" Sound pulled out his pocket watch and then glanced out the window. His hired cab still waited for him. Passersby gave the hansom no notice or concern. "Ten minutes, yes."

Herbert took another drink. Perhaps it was a trick of gaslight, but when he turned back around, resigned, colour seemed to be returning to his skin. "It's happening, isn't it?"

"Yes, it is."

"Is it as serious as you believed it would be?"

That scotch was becoming more and more tempting. "It would seem to be far worse than I had anticipated."

"Than you anticipated?" Herbert gave a hard, dry laugh. "We know each other far too well, Basil, to believe this is guesswork on your part."

"But it is, Herbert. How many times do I need to stress that?" Sound retorted. "I have access to limited intelligence, and while I suspected there was a conspiracy afoot, I had no idea how high it reached."

Herbert set down the snifter and stroked his moustache. "So I am to leave the city?"

"The country."

Herbert nodded. "How far up does this go?"

"You must leave England. Tonight." Sound walked over to the hatstand and retrieved his bowler. "I will arrange for you an invitation to a zoological expedition in Belize. The last airship should be departing in a matter of hours. The tickets will be waiting under your name."

Herbert chuckled. "A shame this could not have happened a year or two earlier. My latest book would have fitted this ruse quite well."

"I have no doubt." Sound placed his bowler on his head and gave his waistcoat a slight tug. "Leave tonight. No exceptions."

"I will."

"Excellent."

Sound turned to see the maid frantically unlocking the door, but it was Herbert's words that stopped him. "What about you, Basil? What will you do?"

He turned back to the handsome Renaissance man and gave him a rakish wink. "Best you not ask too many questions."

"You know my nature, Basil," he said with an impish smile.

"All too well." With a tip of his hat, Sound made for the now-open door. "Safe travels to you, Herbert."

Night had now claimed London completely. By now, he was certain Her Majesty either was about to receive or had received word that he had disappeared into a sweetshop mere blocks away from Buckingham Palace. The time for action was now upon him in full.

"Miggins Antiquities, Industry Row," he said to the driver.